THE MALL

S.L. Grey started life as an ordinary upsider, reading too much horror to ward off the nightmares, then got into a cycle of casual jobbing which led to a transfer node. S.L. currently holds a position as propagandist for various ministries, but is in imminent danger of termination.

slgrey.book.co.za

THE MALL

S.L. GREY

CORVUS

Grey,
S.L.

First published in trade paperback in Great Britain
in 2011 by Corvus, an imprint of Atlantic Books Ltd.

This paperback edition published in Great Britain
in 2012 by Corvus, an imprint of Atlantic Books.

9 8 7 6 5 4 3 2 1

A CIP catalogue record for this book is available
from the British Library.

Paperback ISBN: 978-1-84887-887-7
E-book ISBN: 978-0-85789-271-3

Printed and bound by CPI Group (UK) Ltd, Croydon, CR0 4YY

Corvus
An imprint of Atlantic Books Ltd
Ormond House
26-27 Boswell Street
London WC1N 3JZ

www.corvus-books.co.uk

THE MALL

PART 1 >>

chapter 1

RHODA

My first instinct is to grab his hand, snap back his index finger, and floor the fucker. Instead I keep absolutely immobile, sucking in deep jags of oxygen to try and still my heart. It's jack-hammering like it does when I've taken too much MDMA, but it's vital I get my shit together and calm the fuck down. I shrug my shoulder out of his grasp.

'Sir?' he barks, voice nasal and commanding. 'Why were you running?'

'I'm not a sir,' I say, turning my head so that he can get a good look at my face. He flinches as I knew he would, but doesn't bother trying to mask his distaste. Most people at least attempt to hide their shock, but not this guy, although I'm not yet sure if this is because he doesn't give a shit, or because he's too dense to know better. He's swollen-faced, moustachioed, looks like he does his talking with his fists. He's wearing a curry-stained, beige security guard uniform and his belly flops over his trousers like a sack of dead puppies. A whorl of grey Brillo-pad hair and a finger of fish-belly white skin poke through the gap where his trousers are missing their top button.

'Ma'am? Why were you in such a rush, hey?'

The last thing I want to do is ask this Neanderthal for help. But I've run out of options. 'I'm looking for a kid.'

'What do you mean, ma'am?'

'I've lost a child.'

'What do you mean, you've lost a child?'

'I was here at the mall with him and he's disappeared. Clear enough for you?'

The guy stands up straighter, places a hand on the gun holster at his hip and pulls out a walkie-talkie. He stares at me suspiciously, clearly trying to figure out what someone like me is doing out with a child at this time of night. Across the aisle, two shop girls with identical fake hair and smudged eyeliner are goggling at me as they lock up a shop selling cheap accessories. I look directly at them and mouth 'fuck off'. They shrug their glittery bags onto their shoulders and hurry away, heads down, heels echoing on the mall's tiles. They disappear around the end of the corridor, the trace of a nervous giggle floating back my way.

'Your accent,' he says. 'You a tourist? You don't look like a tourist.'

'What do you mean by that?'

He takes stock of my army surplus clothes.

'I'm not a tourist,' I say.

'This child you say is missing, boy or girl?'

'Boy.'

'Where did you last see him, ma'am?'

'At the bookshop.'

'Which one?'

'The big one – Only Books or whatever it's called.'

I wait for him to take a step back before I get to my feet. My knees are bruised and crack sickeningly as I stand up straight. The bastard hasn't tried to help me up or ask if I'm okay. My palms are numb from where I tried to catch my fall, and I shake them vigorously to try and get some life back into them. I make a fist, and the thumb on my right hand feels stiff, the joint popping when I swivel it. I shove my hands in my pockets, fingers finding the envelope and curling over it protectively.

If he calls the cops I'm fucked. I have to appear normal. Under control.

'Can you describe this child for me, ma'am?'

I have to clear my throat a couple of times to force the words out calmly. 'About eight years old, Sponge Bob T-shirt, black hair, bit overweight.' I take a deep breath, which helps. 'He's probably just wandered off.'

The guy holds up a hand. 'I'll be the judge of that, ma'am.' He growls self-importantly into his walkie-talkie: 'Simon, come in, Simon.'

There's the crackle of static, then: 'Ja, boss, Simon here, over.'

'Simon, we have an issue here. Small child lost his mother. Keep an eye out for a small black boy—'

'He's white!'

He glares at me again. His eyes have a yellowish, jaundiced look about them. The flaccid skin on his face is pitted with ancient acne.

'Excuse me, ma'am?'

'He's not my kid. I'm just looking after him.'

'What is the name of this child, ma'am?'

I open my mouth to answer, but nothing comes out.

Fuck.

I can't remember.

'What were you doing while you left him at the bookshop, ma'am?' Yellow Eyes asks again.

'I told you. I had to go to the toilet. I thought he'd be cool there.'

I glance up at the wall clock. Nine fifteen. Zinzi said she'd be home at ten thirty or so. She's going to freak the fuck out when she gets back and finds that the kid and her car are AWOL. But she'll be fired for sure if the parents find out she's let someone like me babysit their son. Mind you, they can't be that fussy if they've employed Zinzi. Supernanny she's not.

Sweat dribbles down my back, and I'm adding my own stench of nervous perspiration to the foul odours in the windowless security office. It already reeks of old cigarettes, dirty carpet and pizza topping.

Next to me, the man I've dubbed Fingerling is checking the security camera footage. He's the only one in here who didn't flinch at the sight of my face, probably because he's also a freak. There are two shiny stumps on his right hand where his index and middle fingers once were.

'Let's go through this again, ma'am,' Yellow Eyes says, clearly enjoying this. 'You say that a friend of yours asked you to watch the child while she went out?'

'How many more times? She's not a friend. She's my cousin.'

'She also a Brit?'

'No.'

'And what is your business in South Africa, ma'am?'

'What does it matter?'

'We're just trying to get the facts straight, ma'am.'

'Yeah? Oh well, in that case I thought I'd come out here, do a bit of big game hunting, you know the usual shit you do in Africa. Look, what's with all the questions? Can't you just go and find the kid?'

My phone beeps and vibrates in my pocket. I pull it out and check the screen. It's a message from Zinzi:

<Hey babes. Will b home @ 11.30. That cool?>

I breathe out with relief. I've got an extra hour.

'You think it's a good idea to leave a child alone in a mall, ma'am?' Yellow Eyes says.

6

'Don't tell me,' I say. 'They chucked you out of the police force, right?'

His face reddens. I turn to Fingerling.

'Please. You must find him,' I say. 'Please.' Right now I'll do anything. Beg, scream, plead. Right now I'm willing to make any kind of deal.

Something nasty is squirming in my belly. Something that's telling me the shit's about to hit the fan.

I know I shouldn't have left him. But I only thought I'd be gone for five minutes. I wasn't really worried when I legged it back to the bookshop, maybe slightly anxious about how I was going to convince the kid to keep his mouth shut about our spur-of-the-moment outing to Highgate Mall. I pushed past the skinny chick restocking the New Arrivals shelf and headed to the kids' section where I'd left him absorbed in the *Where's Wally* books. I was already fingering the car keys in my pocket, mentally already back at the house, opening the precious little package I'd just bought.

But the floor of the children's area was empty except for a pile of pink and green scatter cushions. I darted through the aisles: past Cookery, Self Help, World Religions, increasing my pace as I passed the bright shiny blur of Science Fiction and Fantasy, the glossy magazine aisle, the titles blurring in front of me. When I reached African Literature I was actually jogging, pulse quickening, feeling the first tendrils of panic.

The blonde behind the counter was flicking lazily through *Heat* magazine, licking a finger as she turned each page.

'Hi,' I said, struggling to keep my voice steady. 'I'm looking for a kid.'

She looked up, mouth puckering into a moue of revulsion as she took in the left side of my face. 'Sorry?'

'A kid. Wearing a Sponge Bob T-shirt. He was here. I left him here.'

'You're not supposed to do that.'

Now wasn't the time to lose my temper. 'Did you see where he went?' I said.

'Sorry,' she said, turning back to the magazine.

I slapped the counter, palm stinging with the force of it, feeling a burst of satisfaction when the bitch jumped. A sandy-haired guy, who was methodically bundling credit card slips behind her, glanced up.

'Problem?' he said to the blonde.

'This person says they've lost a child, Bradley,' the blonde said.

'Small kid, about eight?' I said. 'He was in the children's section. You seen him?'

The guy shook his head. 'Would you like us to call security?' he asked, voice slightly concerned, but it was clear he didn't really want to get involved.

'I'm sure he's around somewhere,' I said. 'I'll let you know.'

I checked the aisles again, knowing it was pointless, knowing that he wasn't there. I saw a quick flash of pale white skin disappearing around a corner opposite the magazine display and I followed, feet thudding on the rough carpeting, heart skipping with relief.

The aisle was empty.

If I didn't find the kid, I would be fucked in so many ways. Just starting to think of it made me feel sick.

My phone beeped. I ignored it, stashed it in the pocket of my combats. It wouldn't be him; he's the only kid in Joburg without a phone. I couldn't talk to anyone until I found him. But *where the fuck was he?*

Then I had it – the computer store. He wanted to check out the games when we'd first arrived, kept babbling about *Grand Theft Auto* or some shit. I hadn't really been listening, too busy worrying about the meeting with Jacob, too busy thinking about what I was going to say to convince him to give me what I needed.

I raced blindly out of the bookshop, bumping into an obese woman laden down with late-night groceries. We danced around each other, pirouetting ridiculously as we kept blocking each other's paths. I shrugged past her, sending a bag of hair dye and tampons skittering across the floor. I didn't stop to apologise, too intent on trying to remember which floor the fucking store was on. Increasing my pace, I pulled my hood over my head, shielding my face from the stares of the passing meanderthals. I dodged bins, skipped past blank-faced cleaners pushing brooms, and thudded onto the escalator. I shoved my way between two teenage girls standing side by side, ignoring their yelps, and almost fell over my feet at the top. My All Stars squeaked and slapped over the tiles as I raced past darkened shop windows, and then I saw it.

A Lara Croft cut-out stared back at me seductively, no sign of life behind her. The shop was shut. I rattled the doors anyway; I had to do something.

I had to think logically about this. What the hell did small kids get up to in malls? Then I looked up and saw the stick figure signs for the toilets. That was it! He'd wanted to go just after we'd arrived.

The door to the men's screamed as I pushed my way inside, ignoring the stench of piss and the guy shaking himself off in front of a urinal. He looked me up and down then exited hurriedly as I started booting open the stalls, one after the other. Nothing but stainless steel bowls, sodden discarded toilet paper squares and cracked tiles. One of the floors was wet with Christ knows what.

Could he have gone back to the car? Would he remember where the hell it was parked? I backtracked, searching for the parking-lot exit, mind blank, but with the vague idea that it was next to a store selling fake Persian carpets and hubbly-bubblies.

I flew down the escalator again, and that's when I skidded as my wet shoes hit the tiles. I landed hard, next to a marbled pot plant, and right into Yellow Eyes' grip and a world of shit.

Fingerling manoeuvres the mouse with his good hand, and the screen wobbles, comes to life. It takes me a few seconds to realise that the too-skinny, hooded figure racing blindly down shiny anonymous corridors, leaping up the escalator and pushing past two miniskirted teenage girls, is actually me. My mad rush through the mall hadn't gone unnoticed – strangers' faces stare after me, they shake their heads, look disapproving.

'It was before this! Look in the bookshop. About an hour ago.'

Fingerling looks up and shrugs. 'Can't. Power went out. Lost most of the footage.'

'No it didn't.'

I'd remember if it had, wouldn't I? I don't recall the lights flickering, dimming, and then surging as they do when the backup generators kick in. I would have been at the Vida e Caffè in the food court, stomach squirming, waiting for Jacob, toying with my latte, jumping every time I caught sight of a tall rangy guy that could be him. I'd give anything to be back there now.

'Just try! Please! Don't you have backups?'

At the back of the room a lanky guy with cruel eyes, over-grown eyebrows and a name tag reading 'Simon' enters. He catches my eye and shakes his head. I can't read his expression.

The screen wobbles and rights itself again. I immediately recognise the guy on screen. He's standing behind the counter of the bookshop, serving a customer who's buying a pile of meaty novels with shiny covers. The clerk had blatantly stared at me when I'd first entered the bookshop with the kid. He was ruder than most. Eyes flicked from my left cheek to my chest, couldn't tear his gaze away. I'd told him to fuck off. Who was he to stare, anyway? Dyed black hair and My Chemical Romance T-shirt. May as well have had 'emo' tattooed on his forehead. Thinking about it, he hadn't been there when I'd returned to find the kid gone.

Simon walks over to me. He stands too close, deliberately invading my space. I catch a whiff of cheap deodorant and the tang of a breath mint that doesn't hide the booze on his breath.

'Ma'am, we might have a problem here.'

'Of course we've got a fucking problem!'

'No need for that sort of language,' Yellow Eyes barks. 'What do you mean, Simon?'

'Ma'am, we've spoken to the people who work in the book-shop. They say they don't remember any child.'

My stomach plummets again. 'What the fuck do you mean?'

'No one remembers seeing you with a child. They remember you, though. Very clearly.'

'You need to talk to that guy!' I say, not liking the way my voice sounds. I point to the screen, at the black-and-white image of the emo guy. 'That black-haired guy! He saw us! He definitely saw us!'

'He says he saw nothing,' says Simon.

Fingerling shakes his shaggy head, pauses the screen and reaches for the phone.

I'm limp with relief. 'Yeah, that's it,' I say, encouraging him. 'Call him again. He's talking shite.'

'I'm calling the cops, ma'am.'

'No!' I say too quickly. 'The kid will turn up. I know he will.'

'Madam,' Fingerling says warily, 'we have to.'

I check out the distance to the door. Five metres. If I don't think too hard about it, if I just get up and run, if I do it imme-diately, I can just about make it.

Chapter 2
DANIEL

I'm sitting in my alcove in the service corridor behind Only Books, eating a packet of Niknaks. I watch Josie and Katrien as they lean against the wall under an emergency strip light, smoking. They can't see me where I sit and I get the chance to see Josie acting relaxed.

'It was hectic,' Katrien is saying. 'Five minutes till the end of the shift and there's a fucking lockdown.'

'Shame, man,' Josie empathises. She takes a drag on her cigarette and shifts her foot on the wall behind her. Her knee juts out a little higher and her short skirt rides further up her thigh. She scratches at her hip. She's wearing a tight purple shirt with a white design of a phoenix, and her green velvet skirt sits above the knee. The way the light's falling, I can see the soft fluff on her upper leg, the part blondes don't have to shave. I like the way Josie acts when she's alone, or with someone like Katrien, someone she obviously trusts. With the customers watching, or even with the rest of the bookshop's night staff, Josie feels like she has to be on show. She's that beautiful. Seriously. It must be hard for her.

'I had to meet Bobby at ten and the bloody lockdown lasted till after eleven,' Katrien says.

'Ja, and I heard it wasn't anything serious. Just, like, three guys with one gun, and they only hit McDonald's. Complete overreaction.' Josie takes a deep drag, the smoke seeps out of her nose as she exhales, trickling out of the corner of her mouth. She pinches the bridge of her nose and closes her eyes and I wonder what she's thinking.

'I think I heard there was a politician here for dinner, so I suppose...'

Josie drops her stub and mashes it out with her sandal. 'It's ridiculous, I swear.'

She's about to light another one when we all hear the sound of footsteps along the corridor.

'Bradley, sweetie,' Josie performs as he comes along, jangling his keys in his trouser pockets. I can't understand how anyone could flirt with Bradley. He's so insipid, yet they fall over to laugh at his unfunny jokes. That's what you get if you're the boss, I suppose. Big boss that he is. Floor manager of a bookshop. Whoopee.

'Stalker,' laughs Katrien. 'I'm going to report you to the authorities.'

'I am the authorities,' Bradley says. 'And it's time to get back on counter. Movies are over and the zombies have descended.'

'Another Dan Brown flick and everyone's suddenly a reader,' mumbles Katrien.

'I need to buy a drink first, okay?' says Josie.

'Sure, I'll come with you,' Bradley says. 'For the walk.'

They turn and notice me sitting there. Katrien smiles at me. Josie grimaces like the dog just shat on the carpet. Bradley blushes up his scrawny neck. 'What are you doing here?'

I feel my face burning in response. 'Uh, dinner break?'

'Well, it's getting busy. You're supposed to be merchandising with Khosi.'

'Ja, I'm coming.'

Stupid fucker. He always sends Khosi and me to merchandise at the end of a shift so that he can hang over the counter making inane small talk with the girls. Of course, Khosi's a girl, but she's not Bradley's type, I guess. So it's always her and me, doing the invisible duties. As if Bradley's got a chance with any of the late-staff girls anyway. And he's mainly got the horn for Josie. Katrien always hangs out with Josie but I don't think they've got much in common. She's not bad herself, I suppose; she's like Josie's supporting actress, but she dresses in these shapeless out-dated hippie clothes.

The three of them walk away and I can hear Bradley saying something in his monotone and Josie replying with a peal of gig-gles, looking back at me, then giggling again.

I crumple up the Niknaks bag, chuck it in one of the janitor's buckets and start on the Nosh bar. The minute hand on my watch nudges up to the nine. No fucking way I'm going back on shift early. In fact, I'm taking an extra few minutes; call it my smoke break.

I hear someone whistling, the echoing slap of rubber footfalls. A butcher from Woolworths, bald head covered in a plastic cap and stained white overalls tucked into blue wellingtons, ambles by, picking his nose as he goes. He stands for a while outside the coldroom door, its triple-glazed port window spider-webbed from an old robbery, finishes his nostrilful and keys in the entrance code: 1-2-3-4. I've watched them dial that code in countless times. Woolworths install this hi-tech security system and then don't trust their staff to remember the code.

I count down four seconds and the blast of cold meat-air whooshes up the corridor like the wind in front of a subway train. If I were someone else, the stench of frozen blood might put me off steak for life. But I'm not.

I'd better get back on shift now. As I'm walking toward the mall exit, the neon lights flicker off and the emergency lights come on. The air-con grinds to a halt, like someone switching off the sea. At first I think it's another lockdown like last night's. But this is not just a brief brown-out; the emergency lights stay on. Great, a power cut. They were amusing the first few times. I'd get to go home early, maybe get a drink first. But now they happen every week, and Only Books has installed minimal battery backups. Which means we have to carry on working, writing everything down and then spend ages after our shift when the power comes back on entering all the sales and manual credit card transactions. Management has its way of spoiling my fun.

My heart sinks a little at the sight of the corridor's double exit doors, lined with their thick and scuffed black rubber fold, sealing Highgate Mall's workers and deliverymen away from the shoppers. Out of my safe place and back into the world of retail slavery. I'm just about to open them and step back onto the stage when a kid slams in and runs down the corridor. I almost shit myself. He's a fat little dark-haired guy in a red T-shirt and jeans, and goes sprinting past me. But he's making no sound. Maybe he's barefoot, I don't know. I think about following him to see where he's going, to see if he's okay, but then the lights come up with a suck of power and I decide to head back. It's not as if there's anywhere for him to go.

Khosi is on a ladder in the Only Books display window, filling it with the crap that people who proudly say 'I don't read' read. Only Books. Yeah right, make that Only Books, Coffee, Chocolates, Chips, Gift wrap, Stationery, Even Fucking Cellphones. Corporate bullshit.

When I walk in there's a sour old bitch haranguing Katrien at the counter. Bradley, who a minute ago was probably regaling her with stories of his weekend Dungeons and Dragons blowout or some such shit, is nowhere to be seen.

'I haven't driven all the way over here to waste my time. You people said the book was here and I expect it to be here!'

Katrien's saying, 'Ma'am, can you just tell me who—'

'I don't care!' screams the woman, glancing at the three customers waiting behind her, assuming they'll support her. 'My God. The service here is pathetic, isn't it?' They shift on their feet, trying not to be part of the scene.

Katrien's tapping away at the computer, mumbling, '*The Leonardo Code*... we don't seem to have a record of that one.' Baiting the woman, seeing whether she can score a star on the Crack Chart we hide in the back office.

'Listen, darling,' the woman drawls in the tone she obviously reserves for retarded waitresses. 'Just call your manager, okay?'

Eventually Katrien's forced to call Bradley. Po-faced, he finds the right book on the Evergreen Backlist display heap and sends the woman on her way with the standard ingratiations. Katrien and the next customer stifle their smiles as the woman huffs out of the shop.

'Where've you been?' Bradley asks me, tapping his watch.

'Uh, tidying poetry.'

'Mm,' he says, already forgetting me and taking up his place against the counter. I load a trolley with books for shelving.

A few minutes later Simon, the mall security guy, comes into the shop trailed by Sipho, our store security guard. At this hour it must be serious to get Simon out of the security office and away from their special coffee and porn.

I watch him talking to Katrien and Bradley, then Bradley beckons me over to the counter. Katrien mutters, 'Something about a missing kid.'

'What sort of kid? Did they—'

Simon stands across the counter from me. He reeks of high-proof, low-quality alcohol and halitosis.

'What's your name?' Simon asks me.

'Daniel.'

'You see a small kid anywhere? Uh, eight, nine. Black. We've got this… uh… lady… in the office who says you saw her with him here.'

'When?'

'An hour ago, she says.' Behind him Sipho shifts uneasily, not sure what he should be doing. Intimidating me, tearing up books, strip-searching the customers, whatever they teach you in security guard school. So he starts fiddling with the products on the counter.

'I don't know. Lots of people come into the shop.'

'You'll remember this… lady,' Simon lowers his voice a fraction, glancing at Khosi loading the window. '*Blerrie boemelaar.* Bald and scars and everything.'

'Oh, ja. I did see her. But I don't remember any child with her.'

'Okay,' says Simon. 'Nobody saw anything here.' I can see this investigation is exhausting him and he just wants to go back to his office and have another drink. 'Thanks, Chief,' he says to Sipho, who jerks around to escort him out and knocks over a stand of Nelson Mandela commemorative fridge magnets on his way out.

I can't help but remember that weird-looking woman. She was in the store about an hour ago. There are certain customers who just make me want to run the moment I see them, and they are the ones who always, without fail, end up at my till. This one was a youngish black woman with an unconvincing English accent she was obviously putting on to make her sound posher than she was. Because she had a shaved head and dressed like a bum. On the side of her face was this huge scar, the sort of scar you don't know how to look at. She was hanging edgily around the counter, smelling of smoke and sweat, but I could see she wasn't going to buy anything. I didn't want to help her, but I wanted her to go away and stop lurking around where I could see her. That scar was making me uncomfortable.

So I said, 'Can I help you?'

She took a long look at me, appraising me up and down like I'm some sort of freak show, her lips curling in disgust. Then she said, 'Fuck you', and walked a few paces away, jittering, her eyes twitching from door to shelf to floor to counter.

Now I wonder if the missing child could be the boy I saw in the service corridor. It can't have been the same one. Hers is a black kid, right? The boy I saw was white, Greek or Portuguese or something. Although it's quite a complex route from the back of the bookshop, there's no way out except back into the mall. That kid would never have got lost back there. It's not worth worrying about. He's probably sleeping in his parents' car on the way home by now.

I start picking up the Mandela magnets and tidying the other junk that's mixed up on the counter. Nine twenty-five; five minutes to closing. Jesus, what a long day. I need a drink.

I go into the orders cupboard and flick the lights to signal the time to the remaining customers and Bradley follows me in.

'Hey, Daniel, buddy.'

'Yes?'

'You mind locking up for me tonight?' he says, handing me his shop keys.

What the fuck, arsehole? I'd rather you do the hour's extra work you're paid triple to do and leave me the fuck alone. 'Ja, sure, no problem.'

'You are working tomorrow morning, right? So you'll have to get here first to open up. Seven thirty?'

'Okay.' I know I'm being a bloody pushover, but what am I supposed to do? If I cash up regularly and always keep the keys safely, maybe Bradley will make me supervisor. I could really do with the extra money.

Bradley skips over to where Josie is waiting and says, 'We're on.' She smiles and they go to the back office to collect their stuff.

The safe key isn't on Bradley's bunch so I follow them. I tap in the code and open the back office door.

'I knew he'd—' Josie's saying and then she stops and blushes.

Bradley's laughing, then turns his back when he realises I'm there.

I smile at Josie. 'Oh, hi.' Then tell Bradley that I don't have the safe key.

'Oh, sure. Here.' Bradley fishes the key out of his pocket.

I try to stay calm as I walk back to close the front door, but I have visions of ramming Bradley's long safe key up his fucking nostril.

chapter 3
RHODA

There are fewer places to hide in malls than you'd think. I squash myself in between an abandoned cleaner's trolley and one of those giant, pointless plant pots, scrunching my knees up to my chest. The stench of dirty rags and bleach makes my eyes water, and the damp stinking tendrils of a mop brush against my cheek. I pull out my phone, click it onto silent, hold my breath and wait.

The clip-clop of Fingerling's boots echo past me, then, just as I'm sure I'm safe, he hesitates. Fuck. He's so close I could reach around the pot and grab his trouser cuffs. The mall's muzak cuts out abruptly, and his walkie-talkie erupts into a hissing buzz of static, making me jump. Yellow Eyes' voice cuts through the crackle, saying something in guttural Afrikaans that I can't understand. Fingerling responds with a sigh and the words: 'Nee, boss.'

My lungs are aching from the frantic chase earlier, and the shallow breaths I'm sucking in through my nose aren't helping. Christ. I should've got the fuck out of here when I had the chance. I'd easily lost Yellow Eyes after I'd dodged into the parking garage (fat bastard), and I'm pretty sure Simon the Sadist must still be curled into a ball on the filthy carpet in the office, clutching his bollocks.

There's no sign of the cops yet, but even if the South African police are as hopelessly crap as I've heard, I probably only have five minutes at the most.

Fingerling's heavy tread backtracks towards the escalators, and I breathe out in relief and shift my position to ease the cramp in my thighs.

Should I? Why the hell not? I reach into my pocket, pull out the envelope and pick open one of the wraps. I dip my finger into the powder and rub it over my gums. It's heavily cut with baby-powder, but weak shit or not, it's as if a breeze of cool oxygen has blasted into my brain, instantly clearing my head. It tastes bitter and familiar, and I start to breathe easier, the stitch in my side fading.

I peer out from behind the pot, and shuck forward on my knees to get a better view of the bookshop's entrance. The doors are closed, the windows darkened and blank. A couple stalks past, the guy pressing his hand into the small of the woman's back, pushing her onwards. They don't glance in my direction, too intent on getting the hell out of here. I don't blame them. Maybe it's the blow messing with my head, but the mall seems to have taken on a seriously creepy atmosphere. I hate malls at the best of times, but now that I'm surrounded by lifeless shop windows, deserted aisles and empty moving escalators I can see why *Dawn of the Dead* was such a mind-fuck.

The bookshop's glass doors finally crack open, and the blonde bitch emerges, laughing at something the guy next to her is saying. Even from here I can tell that she's not really listening to him, too busy thinking about the next thing she's going to say. She flicks her hair over a shoulder, runs her hand through it and adjusts her shoulder bag. They push through the blue door opposite the shop, the guy checking out her arse as she walks through in front of him.

But where the hell is the lying bastard? If he's left already, I'm fucked. My last chance. If I don't find the kid there's no way I can go back to Zinzi's place. Would Jacob help me out? Not much hope of that. If I clear out my account I'll have enough cash for a couple of tanks of petrol, but that's it. Nowhere near enough to get me to Cape Town. And forget buying a ticket home. Even if I had the cash there's no way I'm going back there.

But I don't have a choice. I can't hang around here any longer.

I stand up carefully, stretching my feet one at a time to shake out the pins and needles. Slipping behind a pillar, I check both directions. No sign of Fingerling or Yellow Eyes. Taking another pinch of blow to fuel my escape I prepare myself to leg it.

There's a rattle of keys and the bookshop's door screeches open again. I crouch back down.

Thank fuck. It's him.

He peers up and down the corridor as if he's looking for some-one (as if that blonde bitch would give a twat like him the time of day), his shoulders slump and he mutters something under his breath. He pulls out an iPod, sticks the earphones in his ears and slouches across the aisle to the door opposite. I count to ten and race across the aisle, slipping into the stairwell behind him. I take the stairs two at a time, making sure that I keep one level below him at all times, but it looks as if he's going all the way to the top. I hang back when I hear the exit door banging open, then leg it up to the top of the stairs and push my way out into the night.

The roof is deserted, the empty parking spaces illuminated by yellow lights, and after being inside the stuffy mall I'm momen-tarily disoriented. The bunker shapes of the various mall entrances cast deep shadows around the flat concrete roof, and the neighbouring buildings loom uninvitingly in the distance.

But where the fuck has he gone? It's not as if there's anywhere to disappear to. I jog a few metres away from the exit, and then I see him. He's trudging towards the far end of the lot, back hunched, muttering to himself again. He doesn't even glance around as I close the distance between us, ears probably full of Nickelback or whatever toss wankers like him listen to. He's heading towards the only car – a crappy red Fox with rusting hubcaps and bald tyres – which is half-concealed behind a pay station. While he fiddles with the door lock I race up behind him, grab his left arm and shove it up behind his back.

'What? No!'

'Shut up!' I say, pushing his arm higher and using my weight to slam him into the side of the car. He bellows in pain.

'Keep quiet and I won't hurt you,' I hiss.

'No, man, please! You can take it. Whatever. You can...' His voice is way too loud. I yank his earphones out and they dangle out of his pocket. A faint tinny trace of music pulses out.

'Shut the fuck up,' I say. 'Shut the fuck up.'

'Let me go!' He wriggles again, and I'm forced to yank his arm up even higher. Air hisses out of his mouth as he gasps in agony, and his knees buckle and smash against the car door. He's way taller than me, has a good few kilos on me as well, but the flesh on his arm feels flabby beneath the fabric of his shirt.

'What do you want? I haven't got any money!' His voice is panicked, almost tearful. 'Please don't hurt me. You can take the car.'

'I don't want your piece of shit car,' I say to him. I lean my body into his. He reeks of some sort of cologne – the sort you get free in magazines.

'What do you want?' His voice escapes in a squeak, which would be comical if I felt like fucking laughing right now.

'I've got a few questions for you,' I say.

'I'll do what you want. Just let go of me.'

I release my grip on his arm, and he falls forward against the car. He swivels his shoulder and rubs his arm. I wait for him to turn around to face me.

'You!' he says, eyes wide with recognition. 'It's you!' His face is paler than before, and his cheeks are trembling with fear or shock or both. For a second I almost feel sorry for him. He's a good head taller than me, and from the way he suddenly clenches his jaw and tenses his body it's clear that he's realised this. But I don't wait for him to react. Lashing out with my right foot I slam it into his crotch. He drops instantly, writhing on the ground, rolling in the tarmac, the edge of his T-shirt trailing in a pool of oil.

He gasps desperately for air, face scrunched up in pain, tears streaming blackly down his cheeks as his eyeliner smudges. He gags and a thin stream of white puke dribbles out of his mouth. I pull out my cigarettes and light up while I wait for him to stop moaning, puking and coughing. My hands are trembling, but I can't let him see any sign of weakness.

'What did you do that for?' he says when he can speak. He struggles up onto his hands and knees, then sinks back down again, clutching his balls. 'Fucking psycho!'

'Why did *you* do it, eh?' I say, blasting smoke in his face.

'What do you mean? Do what?' he whines.

'Tell them you didn't see the kid.'

'What? I don't under—'

I boot him in the stomach, slightly harder than I'd actually meant to. He makes a 'whoof' sound and whips his head around desperately, clearly searching for someone to come to his aid. Not much chance of that. There's the roar of an engine below us, the screech of sirens in the distance and steam billows out from one of the air-conditioner vents. But the parking lot remains desolate.

I drop to my haunches and look down into his eyes. 'Let's try this again,' I say.

'Ugh – please, what do you want?'

'Why did you lie?'

'I didn't... I don't know wh—' I place my foot over his hand and press down gently, letting him know I could stomp on it at anytime.

He puts his free hand up in surrender. 'Okay, okay.'

'Did you see where the kid went?'

'What kid?'

For fuck's sake. 'The kid I was with when I came into the store. You saw me. Don't pretend you didn't.'

Something stirs in his eyes. 'White kid, right?'

'Now we're getting somewhere.'

'He was really with you? But he looked so...' He wisely leaves the word 'respectable' unspoken.

'Did you see him?'

'Yeah.'

Thank Christ. 'Where?'

'In the corridor behind the shop.'

'Was he with anyone?' He doesn't answer immediately and I press my foot down with more force.

'Hurts!'

'Was he with anyone!'

'No. I thought he was just playing around.'

'Why didn't you stop him?'

'I told you. I thought he was just messing around.' Now there's a flash of impatience in his voice that surprises me. I'd better take charge again, take a different tack.

'Get up!'

'Huh?'

'Get up!'

'Okay! Okay!' His eyes shift again, and his fingers skitter towards the bunch of keys that have fallen under the car. I know exactly what he's thinking.

'Don't even think about it.'

'Think about what?' he hedges as he stands slowly and leans back against the car.

'What's your name?'

'What's that got to do—' I grip his collar and snarl in his face.

'Daniel, Dan.'

'Well, Dan. Nice to meet you. I'm Rhoda. So tell me something, you want me to tell your boss you fucking lied? Maybe have a word with that blonde you want to fuck?' He blushes and I press home my advantage. 'You want to be known as the prick who let a child get lost and did nothing about it?'

'I didn't know. I fucking told you.'

'You lied for a reason, Dan,' I say, dropping the cigarette butt next to his hand and stomping it out. He flinches. 'I know the security guards questioned you, and you lied.'

'They said the missing kid was black.'

'What?'

'That's what they said, I swear.'

Fuck. Morons.

'What were you doing with the kid, anyway?' he says. Shit. It could be that he's not as stupid as I'd assumed.

'I was babysitting. Kid ran off.'

He wipes his puke-snot with his sleeves, shakes his head and smooths his hair. 'So it's you who fucked up,' he says. 'Not me.'

'I need to find the kid,' I say. 'And you're going to help me.'

A sneaky expression flicks into his eyes. 'You can't make me,' he says.

I really didn't want to have to do this. I reach into the inside pocket of my hoodie and retrieve Zinzi's knife. I actually have no clue how I'm supposed to use it, but Dan doesn't know that. Far as he knows I'm some high-strung junkie arsehole. I do my best, trying to recall scenes from Guy Ritchie movies. I press the button on the side and it clicks open smoothly.

'I'll ask you again,' I say, making my voice sound almost bored. 'Will you help me?'

He doesn't speak for a few seconds, eyes not leaving the knife. He grimaces and wipes his mouth again.

'Well?' I say, almost cheerfully.

He nods.

I've pulled up my hood as a precaution, but we don't meet anyone as we head down towards the mall's delivery entrance. We wander past an empty truck, a few wooden crates, cardboard boxes and an abandoned forklift, a crumpled box of Rothmans on the seat. Dan walks slightly bow-legged in front of me, dawdling almost. I think about elbowing him in the spine so that he'll get a move on, but decide against it. I don't want to push my luck.

He stops and points towards a pair of thick metal doors cut into the side of the windowless building.

'Through there,' he says.

'After you.'

'What? Why do I have to come?'

'Just go.'

He pushes against the doors. 'Locked,' he says. 'It's after hours. See, we can't get in.'

Fuck. There's no way I want to go back through the mall again, but there's a keypad next to the door, and Dan is avoiding looking at it.

'Why do I think you know the combination?' I say.

'I don't!' he whinges.

'Dan, Dan, Dan,' I say, now almost enjoying myself. 'What am I going to do with you?' I pull out the knife again and click it open.

'Okay, okay!' His fingers tremble as he keys in the number. I file it away for future reference. 1-2-3-4. Always the same. 'You

27

need help,' he says as we push through the doors and into a narrow brick-lined corridor. 'Psychiatric help.'

He trudges ahead, and I reach into my pocket for another pinch of blow.

'Where now?' I say. The corridor snakes off in opposite ways. I've lost all sense of direction, so I can only hope he isn't going to do anything stupid, like lead us straight to the security office.

'This way.'

He takes the left-hand fork and we head deeper into the gloom. The corridor reeks of oil, concrete dust and a faint trace of rotten meat. Clearly this is the part of Highgate Mall that the customers never get to see, and it's as basic and stripped down as it gets. There's not even a ceiling to mask the workings of the air-conditioning system; massive silver pipes and insulated wires loop from the ceiling like spilled metal innards. We push through another set of those heavy black doors, and he strides on confidently.

'What happened to your face?' he says without turning around.

'Fuck you.'

He shrugs. 'Just trying to be friendly. You're not from here, are you?'

'What's it to you?'

'What's with the accent?'

'What's with the questions? Let's just find the kid, get out of here. You'll never have to see me again.'

'Okay.'

The ceiling is even lower here, and I have to shrug off the beginnings of claustrophobia, which isn't helped by the effects of the blow.

I open my mouth to speak 'You sure you—'

He whirls around, and before I have a chance to block him, his elbow rams into the side of my face. Pain explodes in my cheekbone, and I reel back and slam into the brick wall.

Fuck!

He's haring back the way we came, and the bastard's quicker than I would have expected. Blocking out the bright bloom of agony and the taste of blood in my throat, I race after him. I round the corner, then slow to a jog.

He's slamming his body into the heavy black doors, punching and kicking at them like a toddler. He's practically howling in frustration.

'Hey!' he shouts at the top of his lungs. 'Hey! Help! Let me out!'

He pushes against the doors again, but it's clear that they're not going to give.

Slowly, eyes wide with panic, he turns to face me.

I am going to fucking kill him.

chapter 4

DANIEL

It's near eleven and we're in Woolworths. It closed at nine; the display windows are quarter-lit and only a few downlighters around the periphery of the shop are kept on. The perfume counters are lit up from inside, and the spotlights under the mannequins shine up their skirts. The mirrors at the perfume counters reflect them jaggedly and the mannequins look on, watching their own humiliation from a thousand angles.

I never liked mannequins. Their dead eyes, their peeling skin, their pert little nipples, hard as the rest of them to the touch.

Scarface is hurrying me on. 'Come on, come on,' she keeps saying.

'You think I want to hang around here? In fact, this isn't my idea of—'

'I said come the fuck *on!*' she screams and shoves me in the back. 'Shut *up!*'

'Okay,' I say.

I'm going to show her that the child is gone and then I'm going home. This is how this evening is going to go. And you know what they say when you're getting held up or hijacked or whatever. Just co-operate and it will be over.

We navigate our way along a line of light-impaled mannequins into the food section. Scarface looks around nervously, as if she's being followed. In an empty shop. Here was proof of what I'd heard about drugs: delusions and paranoia. She hasn't stopped sticking her powdery fingers in her mouth since she found me in the parking lot.

I knew the scary bitch was on drugs. Cocaine, heroin, tik, whatever it is. But while I'm bigger than her, she's faster than me, and vicious. I can still taste puke in my mouth, and my stomach fucking hurts. It's the first time I've been beaten up since high school, and never so seriously. I thought she was going to kill me when I tried to run, but I think she realises that she needs me to get her through the mall. I don't know what she expects to see once we get there. That kid's long gone.

She's forced me to bring her through the Woolworths delivery entrance instead of back through the mall, so now I have to take her the long route through the store. But with any luck the silent alarm was triggered as soon as we came in, and the cops are on their way right now.

You know, if she wasn't so aggressive I might actually want to help her. All she wants, after all, is to find that boy she's lost. I'm just glad she's put away the knife.

'What the fuck are you waiting for? You're not going to try—'

'Give me a break, okay. I'm trying to figure out where the back exit is.'

'Try there,' she orders, pointing out a door with a small window and an electronic keypad.

'Nah, cash office. We're looking for the coldroom. That's the door that opens out to our corridor.'

She pulls her hoodie further over her head so that I can barely see her face any more.

'What are—' I start, then notice the red-spotted security camera over the cash-office door. *Fuck.* Do I act like a criminal and rip a coat and a cap off the nearest hanger or do I act innocent? Wait a minute. I *am* innocent. I've been kidnapped by this drug-addled crazy woman. When they see the tapes, they'll know exactly what happened. I look straight at the security camera and make a fearful face in Scarface's direction. I wonder if anyone is monitoring the cameras now.

Again she smashes me in the back, right in my kidneys. 'Good try, Danny. Your Oscar's in the mail. Now let's fucking *go*.'

'Christ,' I shout. 'Stop hitting me, okay? I'm helping you out here. You could try and be nicer.' She starts laughing, an empty cackle that sounds like a lifetime of desperation. 'I know you're in trouble. I'm trying to help you.'

The laughter dries up. 'Yeah. A prat like you would willingly help someone like me. I know what you think of me.'

'Ja? What do I think of you?' I challenge, rubbing the small of my back.

'Ugly unladylike darkie freak with a drug and anger problem. Typical of these black bitches who think they're above their station.'

Well, at least she isn't deluded. Aggressive. Paranoid. Fucked up on drugs. But, to her credit, she is not deluded. 'You're wrong. You don't know me.' I stop short before I say, 'Nobody knows me.' That would be pathetic, and at least we're talking, and for now she's stopped hitting me.

She seems unconcerned that this whole show is going on right on Woolworths' television screens. I gesture to the camera.

'You think I care? That's the least of my worries.'

'Anyway, it's probably a false camera,' I say, hoping to sound streetwise. 'You wouldn't know where they hid the real cameras.' At Only Books they put hidden cameras right over the tillpoints. Bastards are far more interested in catching their staff red-handed than busting a customer stealing a book.

'I guess the coldroom door will be behind there,' she says,

pointing out the fish and butchery counters. The slabs of meat lie in dark rows, wrapped in plastic, and the fish seem almost fluorescent in the gloom, their shocked and sunken eyes reflecting a glow from somewhere.

'You're probably right,' I say and lead the way behind the counter. We navigate by the light of a few low-wattage strip lights and their reflection off the stainless steel industrial fridges. The floor and the walls are tiled with the same plain white tiles and I try not to think of the knife in the junkie's pocket and the slicing and hacking that goes on back here. My heart is beating too fast and too high. I have to concentrate to push back the wooziness that's threatening to cloud me. The air stinks; an intense concentration of that frozen blood smell that I know from down the corridor, mixed with ammonia and fish. The massive fridges, no doubt full of hanging carcasses, wheeze and crack as we pass.

I hear a crumpling thump behind me and Scarface curses under her breath. I turn around and see her picking herself up from the floor, swearing in that joke accent of hers. She wipes at the knees of her jeans and her hands come away dark.

'Jesus H. Christ. It's fucking fish blood or something. I need to wash my fucking hands.'

She finds a sink and some stainless steel counters ahead of us. I look down at the pool of blood, unconvincing in this light, and then up, half-expecting to see a massive fish hanging from a hook in the ceiling, but there's nothing. The darkness and the smell are getting to me. This has to be the goods receiving area and the delivery door has to be somewhere near. It has to be. I want to show this freak where I saw the boy and I want to go home.

Now Scarface has finished washing her hands – surprisingly fussily – and is shaking them dry. I walk past her around a bend to the right and, thank God, see the delivery door that leads into my corridor. I recognise the web of cracks where the bulletproof glass in the little window was shot. I type the access code into the keypad and the door hisses open.

The air in the familiar corridor rushes into my lungs like the breeze from a Highveld storm. I have never felt so happy to see full-strength neon lighting, cheap face brick and slick concrete in my life. I'm on home ground again. Fifty metres away is the scuff mark where Josie and countless other smokers lean against the wall. Just past that is my alcove, my safe place. It's been two hours; it seems like weeks.

The door behind me slams with a clank. I whirl around to see Scarface behind me, pushing at it.

'Shit. It slipped. I was trying to wedge it open.'

'Don't stress. We can unlock it with the keypad if we come back. But it's really easier to go back through the mall.'

'We're not going back through the mall.'

'What did you do?'

'I told you to stop asking questions. Show me where you saw... him.' The way she says this makes me think she doesn't even know his name.

'It was right here. I was... standing... there.' I indicate the far end of the corridor. 'And he ran past me down here. There's nowhere he could have gone but back out to the mall. All the doors stay locked.'

'Okay, show me.'

'The way out? But it was hours ago. You'll never fi—'

She grabs my T-shirt and tries to push me against the wall. I smell her dangerous chemical sweat. I wince; she's grabbing my chest hair along with the shirt.

'Do I look like I'm asking you, Dan?'

She looks exhausted. She hasn't had a nostrilful of coke for at least five minutes. I'm thinking about that knife, but she doesn't seem so threatening any more; she just seems desperate.

'Yes, yes. Just relax,' I say.

I lead her along the corridor to the mall exit, past the grey doors to the music shop and the hairdresser and Crazy Toys, the familiar delivery door of Only Books, past the alcove. The doors to the mall are locked. I didn't even know they could lock. But I can't budge them. I can't even seem to find the seam between the two doors. I kick half-heartedly at them. They respond with a heavy, muffled thunk and I know I'm wasting my time.

'What the hell are you playing at?' Scarface complains. 'You trying to fuck with me?'

'Honestly. I don't know wh—'

She's already running back the way we came. 'I'm running out of fucking time!' she rages as she goes.

She's taken the wrong fork, because when we turn left and left again, we're in a part of the service corridor I've never seen. The dark face-brick walls and scuffed concrete floors are all the same, the conduits and ducts and wiring, the gunmetal doors, but we're not behind Only Books any more.

'Hang on,' I say. 'We've gone wrong somewhere.' I lead us right and right again, but we come out in a different stretch. The numbers stencilled on the back doors are in the M80s. Mezzanine level; that must be a mistake. We're still on the upper level; we haven't gone down any stairs.

'Christ, Dan, what the fuck?'

I'm utterly lost now, and it doesn't help having this crazy woman behind me. I can't think straight if I'm in fear of being nailed in the kidneys every time I make a wrong turn. My best hope is just to go straight, to follow one stretch of corridor until we reach another exit.

But there isn't a straight span of passage anywhere in this godforsaken maze. Now I'm running, watching the numbers on the doors flick by: M87, M89, M91, M65, M63, M1, round a corner then M121, M123, M43, M41, M39. Dead end. Turn back. Take the first right. M14, M12, M10, M8. Oh, thank Christ, there's an exit door. M6, M4. Just a fucking fire door. We push our way through. L92, L76, L84, L22, L20, L18. What the hell?

We haven't gone down any stairs, but it feels like we're lower down: that subtle lift feeling in my ears. The air is warmer, heavier.

On this side of the fire doors it's darker, maybe every third neon light is on. The air-con is off, the air stale and still. As the fire door slams behind us, the comforting grinding noise of the fans immediately recedes. For the first time, I can hear myself panting for breath. Scarface's shoes screech against the floor; she snorts back some phlegm, she looks around.

'Okay. Where are we?'

'I have no idea.'

'I thought...' She doesn't bother finishing her sentence. Talking to me is a waste of her time. She reaches into her pocket and for another moment I think she's going to kill me. This would be a good place to do it. She takes out her phone.

'Have you got reception?' she asks.

I take my phone out of my pocket. Battery full; reception zero. I go through the motions of raising it up and waving it around. Nothing.

'Me neither.'

Our phones beep at the same time. I've got a message. How did that happen with no reception?

<work's hell, danny, you should know – come joinus, doit yourself>

Scarface is reading her message. We swap phones without a word. Hers reads: <welcome princess here's the game – shoptil-youdrop – dead ofcos.lol> The two of us are trapped deep in this concrete box, all alone. But someone knows we're here. The hair on the back of my neck stands up.

'Does it mean anything to you?' I ask.

'Uh-uh.'

I'm starting to feel claustrophobic, a feeling I've never had before. The urge to get out of here is stronger than ever. I start jogging again, following the line of back doors wherever it takes us. It *has* to take us out some time.

Left. Left. L74. L72. L70. L34. L36. B22. B20. B18.

'There are no fucking shops in the basement,' I scream at the walls. I'm answered by an echo, the sound of our footfalls and Scarface's snorting and puffing.

Another left and I lose my feet in a pool of oily liquid. I crack my hip and my knee against the hard concrete and slide to a stop in a recess in the wall. Scarface curses to a halt behind me.

Christ. This is *my alcove*. There are the crumpled Niknaks bags I ate tonight, the Iron Brew can I drank. But this is *not* my corridor.

The pain from the fall kicks in, taking all the space in my brain. My leg feels shattered from hip to ankle.

'What is this stuff?' Scarface asks, squatting down to inspect the ooze I slipped in. It smells and looks like black oil, an iridescent sheen playing in the low lighting, but it's chunky, the consistency of lumpy custard.

Then we hear it. The sound an elephant might make when in heat, but muffled, liquid, encased in wet concrete. It reverberates more than it is loud. But we know it's near.

'Holy Christ.'

I writhe to get up, but can't move. Fear and pain and bewilderment overload my body. The far end of this stretch of corridor is dark, but I hear a familiar hiss. Something – someone – is ducking inside that same old bullet-shot door. Instinctively, I count down, waiting for the slap of meat-blood. 4-3-2-1, and we are assaulted by a hot reek of putrid air, shit-eating breath licking us. While she gags above me, I try to bury my nose near the tar ooze. As near as I can without breathing it in.

The dying elephant roar again. Louder this time.

I'm sliding along the floor. Scarface has my wrist and is dragging me down the passage. I'm sliding along a snail trail of the black gloop. Then the scrape of my carcass along the cement as she heaves and we are into the centre of the shit stink. My ears are buzzing. She kicks me aside across the soft, filthy floor, slams the door shut and slumps down beside me in the wavering darkness.

The screaming elephant roar on the other side of the door. I take a gulp of viscous brown air and something violent and thick lodges in my nose. The air is solid with flies, the floor carpeted with maggots. Now I recognise what's causing the acid itch on my flesh.

She jumps up screaming, batting at herself, running away to where there might be anything but this.

I have to get up. I have to follow.

chapter 5
RHODA

My Nokia's clock icon has somehow erased itself off the LCD screen, so I have absolutely no fucking idea how long we've been holed up in this cramped, stinking room. I've never been great in confined spaces, and it doesn't help that the air's so dank it's like breathing through putrid syrup. But it could be worse. Apart from a rusty can of Vim and the scrunched-up corpse of a spider, the room's empty. As it is there's barely enough space for the two of us, but beggars can't be choosers – this door was the only one that wasn't locked.

Dan's positioned himself as far away from the entrance as he can get, his gangly praying-mantis legs pulled up to his chest. His breath escapes in shallow bursts and his eyes are screwed shut. There's a writhing maggot stuck in a clump of hair just above his ear. I reach over to pluck it out and he jumps and slaps at my hand.

'Don't touch me!'

'Fine.' I flick the maggot back to him. It lands on his shoulder and he frantically brushes it away.

'Fuck you,' he says, closing his eyes again.

The stench that's roiling off our clothes is immense: one part rotten meat, one part engine oil. What sort of dead animal reeks like that? There was way too much gloop for it to have been a rat. A dog, maybe? I pull out my cigarettes. Hopefully the smoke will mask the stink. Dan's eyes flick open the second I click my lighter.

'You can't smoke in here. There's no ventilation.'

'You have got to be fucking kidding me.'

'Seriously. Put it out. I get asthma.'

'Liar. You are a complete fucking fuckwit, Dan. Anyone ever tell you that?'

He does his best to shoot daggers at me, but his eyeliner is smudged into panda rings around his eyes and the result is more comical than anything else. I blow a thick cloud of smoke towards him, and he coughs. But fun as it is toying with the fuckwit, my mouth's too dry to smoke and I kill the cigarette. I pull off my hoodie and tie it around my waist. At least the T-shirt underneath is fairly free of that foul liquid stuff.

I press my ear against the door. I can't hear anything except for a muffled mechanical hum.

'Let's go,' I say, getting to my feet.

'No way,' he says. 'There's no way I'm going back out there.'

'So what do you suggest?'

'Let's wait it out. Someone will come for us.'

'Christ, you're a retard. No one's been down here for months, years probably.' I kick the ancient can of Vim towards him. Judging by the rust and its retro logo, it was last used some time in the 1950s.

'But that thing…' he says, his voice wavering. 'What if it's still out there?'

'Chill the fuck out. It was just some freak. Some hobo or bergie or whatever you call them here. Probably gone off to find his next hit of meths.'

'But that sound it was making…'

'Look, this is Joburg, isn't it? Far as I can tell, it's full of fucked-up people. Probably just some guy escaped from a mental home, found his way down here.'

'Yeah,' he says, nodding too quickly as if he's desperate to believe me. 'But I don't understand,' he says, barely able to get the words out, 'I don't understand how... the corridors, they...'

'How they what?'

'How they changed.'

'Jesus, Dan. Get a grip. We just took a wrong turn, freaked ourselves out.' As I say the words I almost start to believe them myself. 'Look, if you want to stay in here for the rest of your life, that's your fucking problem. I'm out of here.'

'What about the kid?'

'What about him?'

'What if that *thing* got him?'

'Don't say that!'

'And those SMSes. You think someone's deliberately trying to mess with us?'

'You know anyone who'd want to do that to you?' I ask.

'You're the one who should be answering that question.'

'What the fuck do you mean by that? I know hardly anyone in Joburg.'

'What about your dealer?'

'My what?'

'I know you're on drugs.'

He's more observant than I thought. 'It's just coke, Dan. I'm not a smack-head or anything.' Not any more, anyway. 'Besides. Who the hell would have both our cell numbers?'

His eyes flick to the scar on my face and then his gaze lingers on my forearms again. It's clear he's thinking that no one he knows would be seen dead with a freak like me. 'Must be spam, then.'

'Yeah. That's all it is. We got spammed. Big fucking deal. Now hurry the fuck *up*.'

I yank the door open before I lose my nerve. The passageway is gloomier than I remember it being on our mad dash down here. The walls are damp and criss-crossed with fingers of pale green moss, and under the flickering fluorescent light the brick-work seems to shimmer as if we're actually underwater.

'Okay, Dan, which way?'

He shrugs. Typical. Looks like it's up to me.

To our right, the passageway curves towards an unknown but apparently well-lit destination. To our left, the corridor seems to drift away into a cloying blackness that instantly gives me the creeps.

No contest.

'Come on,' I say. Without checking to see if he's going to follow, I set off.

There's no doubt about it, the floor's definitely sloping down-wards now, and rivulets of water snake down the walls. Christ, I'm thirsty. My mouth's gummy and tastes like I've been snog-ging a drain or something. Probably best not to take another hit of blow, although I could do with the energy boost. Now the adrenaline and coke have worn off, my leg muscles are scream-ing and the back of my head is throbbing. I had fuck-all sleep last night, and God knows when I last ate anything.

I stumble towards the end of the passage, which splits and curves in both directions.

'Left or right?' I say. No answer. 'Dan! Which fucking way should we go?'

'Right,' he mumbles.

'*Thank* you. Fuck.'

The ceiling in this corridor is lower than the others, and I quicken my pace. The strip lighting hisses and pops worryingly – especially considering the sodden walls. Please God, let this one lead somewhere. The soles of my feet are starting to ache now. We must have woven our way through a good kilometre and a half of connecting passageways and they have to end up somewhere at some point.

'How the hell can there be so many tunnels? You think we're still underneath the mall?' I say.

Dan shrugs.

'Can you at least answer me? For fuck's sake, we could be anywhere!'

'You're the one that wanted to leave the room,' he mumbles.

'That's helpful.'

'We should have stayed put.'

I can't take it any more. I grab the front of his shirt and shove him into the wall. It takes all of my control not to punch him in the face. 'Dan, I swear to fucking God I have never met such a fucking pussy!'

'Fuck you!' he yells, and pushes me away so roughly that I stumble back and bash my tailbone on the opposite wall. Before I can grab his arm, he's stalking off around the corner.

'Bastard!' I haul myself up and sprint after him, not bothering to dodge around a puddle of dirty water. I skid around the sharp right-angled turn, wet feet sliding on the concrete, and whack straight into Dan's back with such force that both of us are almost thrown onto the ground.

'What the fuck do you—'

'Look,' he says, voice flat.

Fuck me.

We've stumbled upon some kind of hideous, bloodless massacre. Naked female bodies are piled across the narrow passageway in front of us. There are so many limbs and torsos and hairless heads that it's difficult to tell where one ends and the other begins. Several severed body parts are scattered carelessly around the heap: there's a leg just half a metre away from us, and a hand seems to be pointing back the way we came, warning us to come no further. The bodies are stacked so randomly that they could have been vomited out of the ceiling, but this corridor's roof is sealed with water-stained ceiling board, and there are no doors or apertures in its walls.

'What the hell are they doing here?' I say.

Dan doesn't answer, but he must be thinking the same thing as me. *Someone brought them here deliberately.*

Far as I know we could be miles away from the mall. Not that I can imagine these particular mannequins being used by Truworths or any of the other chain fashion shops. There's something just... *wrong* about them.

It's the heads that are the most disturbing. The majority seem to be attached to some sort of body, although there are a few severed ones in among the limbs. But disembodied or not, the eyes all seem to be staring directly at us, like those portraits where the subject's gaze follows you around the room. All of them have flat black irises and too-long eyelashes like wolf spiders' legs. And unlike the pouty blank expressions you see on the dolls displaying overpriced tat in the stores, none of them are smiling. With their too-wide eyes and slightly down-turned lips, they seem to be gazing at us in despair, or (some part of my brain insists) pity. The grisly scene isn't helped by the fact that the usual fluorescents have been exchanged for two naked bulbs that hang from the ceiling, lazily swinging in opposite directions. One moment the tableau is lit almost too brightly, and has the look of an over-the-top art student project; the next it's a shadowy nightmare of twisted limbs and pseudo-suffering.

'Fuck,' Dan breathes. 'I nearly had a heart attack. I thought they were real.'

I spot something at the end of the corridor – a familiar flash of green neon. The light bulb sweeps in its direction again.

Thank. Fucking. God.

'Come on!' I say, heading towards the body pile.

'What are you doing?'

'Climbing over them. What does it look like?'

'No ways! Let's just go back.'

'Try and look past the plastic tits, Dan,' I say. 'We're home and fucking dry.'

'What are you...?' His voice trails away as he catches sight of the exit sign.

The pile can't be higher than a metre at the most, but the mannequins' skin is ultra slippery, and as I climb up, their fingers snag on my clothing, almost as if they're deliberately slowing my progress. There's also something awful about the way their skin feels; it's warmer and clammier than I was expecting. I'm nearly at the top when one of the dolls beneath me starts sliding backwards and my left hand reaches up reflexively to steady myself and lands on a small breast with a pert nipple. Next to me Dan's having the same trouble. He slips and grabs hold of a sculpted crotch. We glance at each other.

'Shouldn't you buy her a drink first?' I say.

'Nah,' he fires back. 'She's a good Christian girl.'

Before I can stop myself, I'm giggling, and after a second or two, Dan joins in. I try to control the laughter, but it seems to be erupting from deep inside me, and tears are now streaming down my cheeks.

Finally I manage to get myself under control. I take a deep breath, propel my body upwards and swing my legs over the pile. I slide down, narrowly avoiding being blinded by a curled finger.

My brief shriek escapes before I can stop it.

'What is it?' Dan calls, twisting his body and sliding down feet-first.

'See for yourself.'

'Fuck! Ugh!'

This is seriously sick. There are a couple of mannequins

propped up against the wall next to the pile, but these aren't as innocently naked as the others. One of them is strapped to a wheelchair-like contraption, which has toppled over onto its side. Its handles are wrapped in barbed wire, and it's only when I squeeze past it that I realise that the doll strapped into it has no mouth, just a shiny blank nothingness. The other one is partially hidden in the shadows, but they're not deep enough to conceal the chain looping around its neck, the rusted handcuffs around its wrists, or the fact that its eyes have been gouged out, leaving gaping holes.

My phone beeps, and I scramble in my pocket.

'You got a signal?' he says hopefully.

I check my LCD screen, but the reception bars are still flat.

'No,' I say. 'Just a message.'

'So if there's no reception, how did you receive it?'

'How the fuck would I know?'

I click through and read it. <Congratulations, Rhoda Hlophe! As you're our veryspecial millionest shopper you've won the grand prize of a curatorial secretary head! Claim your prize and don't forget to mention your free gift the gift of life oh yes LOL>

What the fuck? I pass my phone to him. He scans the message and then his own phone beeps. He pulls out his phone and stares at the screen, his eyes wide.

'Well?' I say.

He hands me his phone.

<Congratulations, DanielStevenJacobson! As you're our veryspecial millionest fuckwit rundanrunnowrundananddon't-lookback!>

'Huh?'

There's the sound of cracking plastic, and I glance behind me. The doll pile is shifting; the bodies on the top starting to roll forwards as if someone (something?) on the other side is trying to scramble upwards.

'Go!' Dan screams in my ear, shoving me forward so hard that I almost trip over my feet.

Before I'm really aware of what I'm doing, I'm sprinting towards the exit sign, vaguely aware that Dan is shrieking, 'Nononononono!' behind me. I slam my shoulder into the door, but it's too heavy to budge. Dan throws his body into mine and his added weight provides enough momentum for us to slip through. I have to grab onto a rusty banister to stop myself from tumbling down the steep stairwell that stretches into the gloom in front of us. The door slams behind us, and both of us descend, taking the stairs two at a time.

We only start to falter as the light gradually fades. The stairwell bends to the right and leads down into inky darkness. Grasping the banister as tightly as I can, I start edging down the stairs, one at a time. They're getting narrower and steeper as we go, and several feel crumbly and shift beneath my feet. Both of us are breathing so heavily that it's impossible to tell if anything's following us or not, but we haven't heard the door banging again, which has to be a good sign.

The light has now faded completely and I wait for my eyes to adjust to the gloom. They don't. The darkness around us is impenetrable.

'I really don't like this,' Dan says.

I save my breath and don't bother answering him. I creep further forward, now clutching the banister with both hands and moving down sideways like a crab. The air feels colder the deeper we get, and reeks of urine and something else – a smoky, familiar odour.

Then I hear something echoing towards us through the walls.

I'm almost sure it's the sound of voices.

I listen again, but this time there's nothing but a faint mechanical whirring.

'Come on,' I say to him. 'There's someone down here.' But

how much further can we descend? There's not much chance of us exiting into a street somewhere, we're way too low for that. Christ. Would the kid have come this way? We've been choosing our direction almost at random.

I increase my pace slightly, but then my foot hits empty air, and I have to cling to the banister to stop myself from plummeting forwards.

'Dan! Stop!' He bumps into me, and I struggle to regain my balance. 'Just wait, you fuckwit!'

'What's going on?' he whispers.

'We've come to the end of the steps. There's nothing in front of me.'

'Huh? How come? It's a concrete stairway.'

'I don't know! I'm just telling you how it is.'

Holding onto the edge of the banister I drop my leg down as far as I can and swing it around experimentally. Nothing.

'Shit. Can you see the floor from there?' he says.

'Of course not. Hand me your phone.'

'What?'

'So I can use the light. Mine's useless.'

His clothes rustle as he fumbles around, and then I feel the phone pressing into my palm. I shine the screen towards the darkness below me, but it's way too dense for the light to have any effect other than to illuminate the edge of the steps.

'Keep as quiet as you can.' I drop the knife down and hear it clank onto a solid surface less than a second later. 'It's not too far. Wait for me to get clear before you drop.'

I sit on the last step and let my legs dangle over the edge. Counting to three, I jump forward into the gloom, praying that I won't impale myself on anything sharp or break a limb. But I land on both feet, stumbling forward with the momentum. My shoe knocks against something that skids away with a metallic clatter. Must be the knife. I reach down and feel across the floor's dusty, rough surface. My fingers close over the handle and something skitters over my hand. Something with too many legs.

'Ugh!'

Dan lands heavily behind me. 'What?'

'Christ! I don't know. Probably a spider or something.'

'Ugh! I hate spiders.'

'Look, shine your cellphone around again.'

He sighs as if I'm asking him to do something unreasonable, but finally does as he's told. He flinches and knocks against me as several pairs of pinprick eyes glow back at us half a metre from where we're standing. The light snaps off.

'Relax, Dan. Just rats.'

'I hate rats!'

'Listen.' True enough there's the sound of scuttling feet on concrete and something brushes over my shoe. 'See? There had to be some somewhere.'

'What now?' he says.

'I'm going to start moving forward.' I reach across to my right and my fingers graze a brick wall. 'Give me your hand.' His palm feels clammy and hot and I hold it as loosely as I can as we shuffle forward, using the wall as a guide. It starts to curve to the left, and then, bit by bit, I start to make out the details of our surroundings. It's clear that we're in a low-ceilinged tunnel, and the more it curves, the lighter it becomes.

'Light at the end of the tunnel,' Dan says, burping out a giggle.

I drop his hand and start jogging towards the exit, ignoring the stitch in my side and the fact that my lungs feel like they've been napalmed. Dan shuffles up behind me.

It's only a matter of metres before we reach the end of it.

'Oh God,' Dan says as we both stare out at the scene in front of us. 'I can't take much more of this.'

We've ended up in a vast area the size of an airplane hangar. The soot-caked brick walls instantly remind me of old disused

London Underground stations – although there's no sign of a train. The ceiling is scored with ancient fluorescent lights, mostly broken or dim.

'Hello?' I call out. 'Hello?'

'What are you doing?' Dan hisses. 'We don't know what kind of people are down here.'

'At least we know there are people here,' I say, pointing towards the fires flickering in the dented oil drums around us. The floor is covered with debris, old bundles of rags, cardboard boxes and the occasional blackened mannequin and overturned shopping trolley. A couple of bloated, albino rats totter sluggishly away to our right and disappear behind a rusted structure that might once have been a car. Although the ceiling is high and a faint cool breeze seems to be wafting in from somewhere, the stench of piss is thick in the air.

Dan stares up at the ceiling. 'I think I know where we are,' he says. But he's not looking where he's going. He stumbles over one of the rag bundles and, before I can react, a scabby, filthy hand darts out from its depths and clasps his ankle.

chapter 6
DANIEL

Surely this isn't real. You can't feel this way for so long and still be living. It can't be real. It's a dream. I'll wake up.

Wake up. Please wake up.

Once again I'm cowering in a dark place, in fear for my life. Peering over the incomplete counter I've ducked behind, I make out a half-finished parking garage, rusted girders sticking out of concrete columns, warped and battered scaffolding jacks holding up the ceiling. A wide sweeping arc of shopfronts funnelling into a food court. I'm holed up in what would have been a restaurant with a romantic view over the parking lot.

Rhoda scoots next to me. For about ten seconds, I'd forgotten about her. It was a relief. I don't want to be doing this with her. I want her out of my nightmare. I want to go home. But she's trailing me like a rabid dog. As long as she's here it's impossible to fool myself.

'What the fuck are you doing running like that?' she pants.

'They were going to get me.'

'Get you?' she snorts. 'I don't think a posse of blind hobos is likely to "get" you.'

'What? They're not bli—'

51

But they are. The two men anyway. One of them yells out in our direction, but not exactly at us. His words are incomprehensible. I can feel his anger, though. A recognisable rage, in some bizarre way more frightening than the terror of being chased by that screaming elephant thing.

The trio of rag-people mill around at the kerb of the parking lot, grumbling. They have a grey, mouldy sheen over their skin, like potatoes forgotten in the cupboard under the sink. The rags that used to be their clothes have the same coating, so when they move, they look like parts of the concrete walls and floors shifting in chaotic patterns. They have grey eyes, too, mole-eyes atrophying in the barely lit cavern. They must have lived here for years.

After all this running, I don't know if I'm relieved or depressed or terrified to know that we're still in Highgate bloody Mall. We must have been running around in circles for hours. A few years ago there was talk about opening a new wing of the shopping centre. Working at the bookshop, we heard the subterranean thumping of jackhammers and mallets for a couple of months, then the financial crisis hit and everything went quiet. Talk of the new wing just petered out as if it had never really happened.

Here we are. The new wing. I'm amazed they got this far and then just left it. But what's weird is that this place should only be one level underground. We're way lower than that. There's no hint of sunlight, or moonlight, or anything outside. I have no idea what time it is. My watch is broken and the cellphone seems to be fucked. Currently its time reads: <27:79>.

'Come on,' Rhoda says.

I hesitate.

'They're not doing anything, Dan,' she says. 'They're staying where they are.'

'What if they try and grab us again?'

'They got a fright, that's all. You stood on one of them.'

I feel like a complete fucking moron. Middle-class white boy runs away from poor people. I follow her into the food court from where we'll have a better lookout. The tables and chairs bolted into the centre of the food court, never used by diners, are dusty and slashed in some places with dark stains, a sticky substance long-since dried. We sit down at a table facing the parking lot. Twenty metres away, the three grey people stand at the kerb, discussing us in low tones.

'Now what?' I say, out of habit.

'Jesus!' Rhoda pokes her dirty finger at my face. 'Can't you make a decision for yourself? Just once?'

'Fuck you,' I say wearily. I didn't really expect an answer. This is my dream. I have to decide what to do next. 'You dragged me down here,' I remind her. 'I've got nothing to do with any of this.'

'You're supposed to know where we're going.'

I get up and stalk back into the restaurant. I need to piss, and right now if I have a choice between sitting next to that putrid freak and a hand-to-hand battle with the fucking elephant thing with my dick hanging out, I'll choose the latter.

When I get back, the table's empty. Rhoda's at the edge of the parking garage, her dirty clothes blending in with the bums'. I suppose I don't look any better. She's standing about two metres away from them and I can't make out what's going on. I hear raised voices but I don't know whose. I almost follow the impulse to go and help her out, but I think twice. She's probably the sort of feminist who objects to chivalry, and I'm not going to risk being embarrassed or sworn at or smacked by her again. She's made her own fucking bed.

The middle figure of the three comes forward, raising herself taller than the men, who stand around staring at nothing. She's just as grey and dusty as they are, but her clothes are not quite as ragged; she's fashioned herself some sort of robe and a headcloth.

She takes a step up onto the kerb and Rhoda shifts a couple of steps backwards. The grey woman swoops along to the table where I'm sitting. I try to stand up, catch my foot on the leg of the table and sprawl backwards, knocking the back of my head on concrete. I lie there trying to get up but my foot is still caught as she comes to stand right over me.

'What do you want here?' she says in a ravaged croak.

'I, I. Uh, she...' I try to point out Rhoda, who is standing a little way back from us.

'Why are you here?' the woman insists, letting out a barking fit of lung-scouring coughing. A gob of phlegm spatters just past my head, and I crick my neck trying to avoid it.

Finally I pick myself up off the floor, rubbing my throbbing head. It's so fucking sore I want to cry or scream or both.

'We're looking for a kid,' says Rhoda. 'A small boy who came down here. He—'

'There are no children here. Get out. It will follow you.' The woman raises her voice, and I can hear the fear around its edges, underneath the wetness.

'Can you help us?' Rhoda presses. 'We can help you.' She disgorges her pockets onto the table: a few coins, keys, tissues, two half-smoked cigarettes, her cellphone. She doesn't empty her jacket pockets, where I know she keeps the other cigarettes and her stash.

'You must get away,' the grey woman repeats, her eyes darting between the far side of the food court and the booty on the table.

'We'll leave you alone as soon as you tell us where the kid is,' says Rhoda.

The grey woman looks at the pockets of my jeans. The outlines of my phone, my wallet and my keys bulge out blatantly.

'Come on,' hisses Rhoda.

'Fuck, I need this stuff,' I complain as I dump everything on the table.

'For this, food.' She picks up Rhoda's phone. The woman rifles her grimy fingers through the wallet Mom gave me for my birthday. I've only got fifty bucks and a few coins. She takes it all, leaving a dusty smear in its place.

'We don't want food,' Rhoda says. 'Just tell us about the kid and we'll be on our way.'

The woman ignores her and walks back towards two braziers across the lot, trailed by the men. We just stand there, Rhoda cursing under her breath.

'Hey,' I say, too late to make any difference, 'that's my stuff.'

'You want food?' the woman calls back at us. 'Something fresh today.' She lets out a dry cackle that sounds as if it hasn't been exercised for centuries. The men chuckle to themselves, their laughter ricocheting hollowly through the silent space.

'So. You want food?' Rhoda says to me, doing a pretty good impression of the old hag.

My stomach grumbles. I'm fucking starving. I wonder if she's got any chips. I'm really hungry for chips.

'I'd think there's more important things to worry about tonight, but come on,' she shrugs.

We follow.

The woman leads us into a stinking alcove, walls scuffed with person-filth up to waist height, flattened cardboard boxes and plastic sheeting layered into a nest. The men feel their way to the fire, shuffling with tiny steps as if it's pitch dark. The grey woman digs behind a wall of cardboard for a plastic bag, barks a phlegmy series of coughs into her hand then rummages in the bag.

I hope to God that the seeping wax-wrapped package she pulls out isn't the meal we've just bought. But no gods are listening: it is. In addition, she finds a bottle of water and an un-wrapped half-loaf of white bread, which she wipes on her top before handing it to us.

'Eat there,' she says, indicating the tables at the food court where we spoke. 'Then you go.'

'There's no way I'm eating—' I start, but Rhoda nudges me.

'Thanks,' says Rhoda. I thought at least she'd argue.

We walk back across the parking lot to our table.

'This shit is not a meal. Come on. You're prepared to fight about everything else. Why couldn't you...' But I know I'm wast-ing my breath.

'I didn't hear you complaining.'

'Well, you're the one with the street experience, aren't you? You should know what's normal in this sort of situation.'

Rhoda spits out a laugh. I can't tell if it's sarcastic or gen-uinely amused. 'Normal? Okay, tell me. We're lost underneath a mall that keeps on changing direction, buying food from a grey woman in a ghost parking lot, being chased by a screaming mon-ster and getting texted by the marketers from hell. What "sort of situation" do you call that? Sounds more like a normal day in your neck of the woods, shop boy. What's normal in my life is having a hit and chilling the fuck out.'

'Well, I'm not eating that crap. Look, this bread is covered with mould,' I say as we sit down.

'Bit of penicillin never hurt anyone. Fact, it's good for you,' she says as she unwraps the greasy brown whatever-it-is, folds the sides of the wrapper up so that it doesn't ooze all over the table, and dunks the bread in it. 'Yum yum,' she says.

I'd better follow suit or lose all credibility and I smear a hunk of bread into the sauce. I raise it to my lips.

'I can't believe you were going to fucking eat that!' Rhoda peals as she flips her bread onto the floor.

She leans back and lights up one of her prize cigarettes, then another, and passes it to me. I take it without saying anything. I don't smoke, but, Christ, if ever there's a moment... The first drag makes me gag, and Rhoda smirks at me. The nicotine coats my tongue, the taste acrid and unfamiliar. I take another tentative pull, cough, and try again. This time I hold it in, dragging it deep into my lungs far more easily than I thought it would be.

'Glad to see the asthma's cured, Dan,' she says.

'Whatever,' I mumble.

'You're quite a sick puppy,' she chortles to herself.

'Fuck you,' I say.

Rhoda sits quietly, puffing, watching the three hobos lurking by their fire as if she hasn't a care in the world. I want the illusion that I'm on some seaside holiday to last, but the silence, broken only by the occasional snap of the fire, is freaking me out.

'I can't believe she took your phone instead of mine,' I say. 'It's a piece of shit.'

She smirks, but doesn't say anything. She takes another long drag and the smoke seeps out of her nose. I try that myself.

'So, Rhoda Hlophe, huh?' I venture, remembering the surname on her last phone message.

'What's it to you, *Dan*?' Her tone is light.

'That's not a British name.'

'No.'

I wait. She offers nothing more. 'Where are you from?' This is officially the longest conversation I've ever had with a strange woman. I try not to concentrate on my smoking style.

'Jesus. Quizzy boy, aren't you?'

I look at her arms, the array of scars ranged along them. I don't know what to say, but I want to carry on talking. 'I'm confused, that's all.'

'How a black woman with a South African name gets such a whack accent?'

'Ja.'

'Ever heard of exile in your lily-white suburbs?'

'No way you're an exile. All the real exiles are old. Dead or dying.'

'True. But shit has a way of filtering down through generations. Anyway, I need to take a piss.'

She walks off to the shell I pissed in earlier. I watch her go, then I start fretting again. Of all the things to obsess about, the thing that's bothering me most of all is how I managed to take a wrong turn outside Only Books. I've walked that way a thousand times. If I had just got us out of there then, none of this would be happening.

Jesus. My mom will be really worried by now. Maybe she'll call the police. Maybe they'll come looking for me. Rhoda comes back, wiping her hands on her jeans.

'What now?' I ask.

'I need to get my phone back.'

'How?' But she's off already, striding across the parking lot. I trail behind her.

The three hobos are standing around the brazier, holding sticks into it, mumbling in low tones. The woman looks up from the fire as we approach, and the men shift their heads with their shoulders, following their ears. Up close, their eyes are scarred pits, and by the way they murmur, I realise they're probably half-mute too. Jesus, what would a blind mute do upstairs in Joburg? Stand by a traffic light, get pulled around to car windows by some con artist who'll take all their money at the end of the day? They're probably better off down here.

'I need my phone,' says Rhoda, mincing no words. The woman watches her cautiously, keeping one eye on the skewer hidden in the brazier.

'I'll give you, uh,' Rhoda says, casting around for something of value to exchange for her phone, 'his watch.'

'*What?*' I say.

'Dan,' Rhoda hisses. 'We *need* our phones in here. We don't *need* your watch. I'm asking nicely now. But I'm not fucking around.'

'You're crazy, you know that?' I give up the watch. Truth is, it's a piece of shit and doesn't keep time, but the woman takes the deal. She obviously knows that a phone with a disabled SIM card and a flat battery is of no use to anybody.

She rests her skewer on the makeshift crate-table next to the fire and digs through her plastic tote bag while Rhoda and I try not to look at the two skinned and charred rats steaming in the dank air.

As Rhoda takes her phone she spots something red at the neck of the woman's shopping bag.

'What the fuck?' She lunges at it. A little red toy robot. 'Where did you get this?' But the woman is scurrying back into their shelter. Rhoda runs to catch up and grabs the woman by the throat. 'Where did you get this? Tell me!'

Rhoda's about to hit the woman, but she hesitates. The woman musters enough strength to stop gibbering and talk. The quicker she speaks, the quicker we'll be gone, and right now that's all that is important to her.

'People leave things. Here. Or there. I gather things. That people leave.'

'Where?' shouts Rhoda. 'Where did you find it?' The grey woman points to the far end of the food court, the same area she was eyeing when she first spoke to us. 'It will follow you.'

Rhoda and I look at each other. She pockets her phone and the toy and goes off in the direction the woman pointed.

'She says she found the toy here, so the kid must have come through here. If he didn't come back the way he came – which is highly fucking unlikely – he must have gone through here. There's got to be a door here somewhere. Where would the fire stairs have been built?'

We trace our way past all the empty shop-shells and find a narrow opening partially covered by a stack of scaffolding planks. The door leads to a pitch-dark stairwell.

Rhoda feels her way into the darkness. I wait for a worrying moment then hear a crumple and a meaty, cursing thump. 'Jesus motherfucking Christ! Who puts a fucking brick wall at the top of the fucking stairs?' Rhoda comes limping out, rubbing her forehead. I bite my tongue not to laugh, and she goes hobbling around the food court, searching for another exit.

My phone beeps. What now?

<Danny! Today is market day. Get down here to runaway-fromyourlife. The faster you run the faster you go. Special offers on darksoulkillthemall. You'll be lost without it!>

I put my phone back in my pocket as Rhoda comes back, 'Nada,' she reports. 'There's definitely no way through here. The kid couldn't have come this way.'

Just then, her phone beeps. She shows her message to me.

<Rhoda! Get a new life. Get a new face. Today is market day. Carcrashing sale now special offers on posies from Jewboys miss out and urout!>

chapter 7

RHODA

Fuck.

Only four cigarettes left.

I know I should really ration them, but I sit at a food court table, light up and take a deep drag. My lungs ache from breathing in this foul smoky air, and my throat's itchy and sore. I nip the fag and slide it back into the box. Checking that Dan isn't about to emerge from the rancid hole of the 'men's', I pull out the envelope and snort a pinch of blow, which should help sort out the headache that's been festering. Nothing like a healthy diet to keep the system in check.

'What are you doing?' Dan says from behind me. I jump guiltily and fumble to hide the envelope. His eyes drift to my pocket and it's obvious that he knows exactly what I've been doing.

'What's it to you?' I say.

'Chill. I'm just asking. I thought we'd decided to call a truce.'

For a second I feel slightly guilty. But 'being nice' isn't one of my strong points. 'Dan, don't take this the wrong way, but you look like utter fucking shite.'

He runs his hand self-consciously through his hair, which is almost entirely matted and grey with dust, like those freaky hobos back there. His pores are clogged with pinpricks of black dirt, as if his face is teeming with blackheads, and his clothes are rumpled and stained. I've done my fair share of sleeping rough, but I can't remember the last time I felt this disgusting. Even though we've only been in this maze for probably a few hours – I can't tell exactly because that hobo witch seems to have fucked the time on my phone – the dust and dirt have eked their way deep under my nails, my eyes feel as if they've been sand-blasted and my teeth are furry and gritty. I would do almost anything for a shower right now.

'You're not exactly Angelina Jolie yourself,' he says.

'Yeah, well, I'm not going to win a beauty pageant any time soon, am I?' I snap.

'I didn't mean—'

'Forget it.' I hold out my hand. 'Give me your phone.'

'Can't you at least say "please?"'

'Oh, I'm sorry, Dan. I didn't mean to offend your delicate sensibilities.' I put on a girly-girl voice and flutter my eyelashes. 'May I please, *pretty* please, borrow your phone if it isn't too much of an inconvenience to you?'

Good Christ, is he blushing? Without looking me in the eye, he hands me the phone. I scroll down to the messages and read them again. 'What's this shit about a market? What kind of market?'

'Fuck knows.'

'I tell you something, this is not spam, Dan.'

'You're a poet and you don't know it.' He lets out a giggle that verges on hysteria. Not good.

'Are you okay?' I say. 'You're not going to lose it, are you?' Although I wouldn't blame him if he did.

He rubs his face with the palm of his hand, looking about twelve years old. 'I just can't get my head around all this.'

'You and me both.'

'I mean, what the *fuck* is going on?'

'It's like we've both taken some really bad acid or something,' I say. He shoots me a loaded look. 'Don't worry, shithead. I haven't slipped you anything. I wouldn't waste my stash on you.'

He holds my gaze for several seconds and then nods as if he believes me. 'I did have one idea,' he says.

'Go on.'

'The kid.'

'What about the kid?'

'What if... you know... he was snatched and the people who are fucking with us are trying to put us off the scent?' he says. 'You know, like people-smugglers – paedophiles or something.'

'But you said you didn't see him with anyone.'

'Ja. But I'm just saying. It's possible.'

'We're not in a Bruce Willis movie, Dan. Don't be so fucking stupid.' I wait for him to fire back at me, but he remains silent. 'Look,' I say, softening my voice, 'if they were badass human traffickers they'd just kill us, wouldn't they? Besides, that doesn't explain how they know our names.'

'So what is this, then? Blind homeless psychos, tunnels and corridors that don't seem to lead anywhere, mannequins in bondage and text messages from someone who not only knows our names but sounds like the spammer from hell. Seriously, Rhoda. I'm beginning to think we're in the twilight zone here.'

'I've seen worse.'

'You have?'

I haven't – not even close. And I've been in some pretty fucking hairy situations in the past. But I'm not going to tell him that. 'We've just slipped through the cracks of society, Dan. Plenty of people opt out of working for the Man and paying their taxes.' But most of them don't eat rodents and live under malls.

'You really believe that?'

'Sure,' I say. Fortunately lying *is* one of my strong points.

'And the text messages?'

'Some psycho hacker. Probably works at Vodacom. Has access to customer accounts. Must be.'

'I'm not with Vodacom.'

'Whatever. Something like that. I'm just saying.' It's clear that he doesn't believe me, but what other explanation is there? None that either of us wants to dwell on right now.

'So, what's the plan?' he says, trying to sound game.

'If the kid's here we need to find him. That's top priority. He could be in serious shit if he bumps into a nut-job like that freak of a woman back there. There's only one other way he could have gone.' I point to the far end of the lot. It stretches back into the gloom, and it's impossible to make out any details at that end, thanks to that same disturbing pitch-blackness we met in the dead-end stairwell. 'And for that we need a proper light. Any ideas?'

'Hey! That old woman's got a paraffin lamp in her stuff. I saw it when she was getting out the food.'

'She's never going to give it to us, and we won't be able to nick it without her noticing.'

'Then we'll have to trade.'

'With what? Apart from my phone and your crappy watch she didn't want any of our stuff.'

'Yeah. But what about the other stuff?'

'What other stuff?'

'You know.'

'Oh fuck off, Dan.'

But there's no other option.

'That thing stinks!'

'Trust me,' Dan sighs, 'if the old witch had a torch I'd much rather have taken that.'

Oily black smoke billows out of the top of the lamp, which looks like one of those old-school oil lanterns you see in BBC adaptations of Jane Austen or whatever. It clearly hasn't been cleaned for a while and the fuel smells more like petrol than paraffin. Still, at least it's providing enough of a glow so that we can walk without braining ourselves on the jagged pipes and concrete pillars that loom out of the darkness every so often. And I guess it was cheap at the price. I'd given the hag the ketamine in exchange, and I was only going to sell that on anyway. It'll probably do her and her cronies some good.

We're making slow progress, but even so, the parking lot seems to be stretching on further than it has any right to. But at least there's no debris scattered around, just the occasional loose wall panel spilling the severed worms of thick conduit wires. A rat scuttles past my foot, and it sounds like it's dragging something fairly heavy behind it. Thankfully Dan doesn't wave the light its way. Neither of us really wants to know the details of that particular scenario.

'We'll have to find an exit or something soon,' Dan says. 'This thing's getting almost too hot to hold.'

I unwrap my hoodie from around my waist and hand it to him, and he balls it around his hand. 'Thanks,' he says.

We shuffle along for a few more metres and then Dan stops abruptly.

'What?'

'Look!'

To our left, I can make out the shadowy edges of a wide concrete ramp, which presumably leads down into the deep darkness of the floor below.

'Oh great,' I say. 'Down another level. What the fuck were they thinking going down this deep?'

Dan doesn't answer.

As we get closer, a large laminated sign that's stuck onto the wall in front of us emerges. Dan holds the lamp up to it, and the red plastic letters shine in the lamp's glow. He reads it aloud: "'Level X. Authorised personnel only past this point. Danger; Gevaar; Ingozi.'"

'Level X? That's like ten or something in Roman numerals, isn't it?'

'Hang on, there's something else written below.'

He waves the light along the edge of the sign, but the print is too small for me to make out the words.

'Well?' I say. 'What does it say?'

'You don't want to know.'

'Of course I bloody well want to know! What does it say?'

'It doesn't make sense. It reads: "Do not attempt to enter under any circumstances. All trespassers will be corrected."'

'What the fuck do they mean by "corrected"?' I ask.

There's a long pause before Dan answers. 'It makes me think of getting caned at school. Or corrective surgery.'

I don't really want to consider either of these options, but now Dan has put some seriously gothic imagery in my mind. I try to shake it out. 'Oh for fuck's sake. This is totally mental.'

'So what now?'

I pull out the stompie and light up. I take a couple of drags and watch the thin grey smoke melding and dancing with the black emissions from the paraffin lamp. 'We don't have a choice,' I say. 'Trousers down it is.' Dan smiles at me for the first time, and even though the yellowish light makes his too-white skin seem ghoulish, he actually looks like a different person. 'I mean,' I say, nipping the butt and leaving one last drag for later, 'after what we've already been through, how bad can it really get?'

This floor seems to extend even further along than the one above. Enough parking for all the cars in Joburg. The ceiling is lower down here and I'm starting to feel the walls pressing in. And the cigarette and blow aren't helping to calm my heart or soothe my stomach, which is bunched into a tight knot of nausea.

Dan pauses and holds the lamp out to me. 'Can you hold it for a while? It's burning my fingers.'

He passes the lamp to me, and even through the hoodie's layers I almost drop it when I feel the heat. He must have really struggled to hold it for so long. 'Fucking hell, Dan! You should have said something earlier!'

He shrugs. 'Ja. It wasn't—'

'Shhh!' I say. 'Hear that?'

'What?'

'Listen!'

The sound drifts back towards us.

'Is that... music?' Dan says.

Both of us keep absolutely still. It comes again. It's a jaunty folksy tune that for some reason reminds me of the Mos Eisley Cantina riff in *Star Wars*.

We quicken our pace, and I almost forget about the uncomfortable heat of the lamp. A stark white door with a reassuringly normal metal handle appears out of the gloom to greet us, the only feature in an otherwise solid concrete barrier ahead.

'You think it's locked?' Dan asks.

'Only one way to find out.'

He pulls open the door and both of us have to shield our faces against the sudden glare of light that blasts back at us. We've been in the dark for so long that my eyes tear up, and it takes me a second to realise what I'm seeing. It's another one of those narrow stairwells, this one at least heading upwards. The stairs, walls and ceiling are tiled in a seamless white mosaic, giving it the antiseptic look of an institutional corridor. With the door open the sound of the music floats down towards us with more clarity. And there's something else – a familiar low rumbling sound.

'Shit,' Dan breathes. 'Voices! There are people up there!'

'You think this leads back into the mall?' I say. 'Like a back entrance or something?'

Dan shrugs. 'Fuck knows, Rhoda. We're way underground now.' His eyes are beyond tired. He's wearing the same expression you see on disaster victims on CNN, one of weary acceptance.

'You want to take a break?'

'No,' he says. 'I want to get this over with.'

I place the lamp carefully on the ground, and, without speaking, we both start heading up.

I'd expected the stairwell to lead upwards for ever, like everything in this fucking place. But after navigating just a few flights, we've reached a white melamine door and neither of us is rushing to pull it open. From the sounds we can make out from here, it's already clear that whatever we're about to encounter it's not going to be the bland muzak and polished shopfronts of the mall. The music actually sounds creepily similar to old-school funfair calliope music – the kind that scores low-budget horror films. Every so often there's a sudden burst of deep, humourless laughter and the rumbling murmur of what has to be a large crowd of people. But it's not just the eerie music and voices that are holding us back. There's another one of those fucked-up laminated signs stuck on the door:

Patrons are advised to enter the market at their own risk.
Management will not be responsible for injuries resulting
from choking on small parts, exsanguinations, unlicensed
amputations, theft, transplants, broken pointy bits of glass
or death.

'Okay,' I say. 'Dan. We have a choice here. We can try and go back the way we came and run into that… creature, or we can go through this door. But I'm telling you, I really don't have a good feeling about this.'

Dan rubs both hands over his face, and holds my gaze for a long second. 'The message said something about market day. This is the place...' I'm pretty sure that the fear in his eyes is mirrored perfectly in mine. 'Christ, Rhoda,' he says. 'Let's just do it.'

He holds out his hand, and, without hesitating, I take it.

He opens the door and we step through.

chapter 8
DANIEL

Everything's white. Rhoda closes the door behind us and we lean back against it, waiting for our eyes to acclimatise. Gradually details start to emerge from the snowsheer glare. Powder-white floor, powder-white walls, a hall the size of, say, your average church or Pep store, but featureless, just a square box with glaring white floors and walls. Bright spotlights set into the powder-white ceiling like polka dots pierce down at us. We can hear the same crazed hurdy-gurdy music as we did outside, but now more distant, smothered and forced, like a live band is playing from inside the walls, its members suffocating in the concrete as they play. Its volume shifts in waves, coming up and then receding as if we've imagined it, before fading in again. There are markings stripped out in silver duct tape on the floor, mapped-out boundaries in two dimensions tracing a convoluted design. Labels chalked out on the floor – illuminator, apothecary, tavern, weaver – make it clear that this is the layout of the market. But there's nothing here.

'Is this it?' I ask. 'Are we supposed to pretend, or what?'

Rhoda stalks around the hall, leaving dusty shoe prints on the floor as she goes. She tries the door.

'Fuck. It's stuck.' She pulls the handle as hard as she can. 'We're stuck.'

She checks the walls, inspects the floor. 'Fuck,' she says from the other side of the hall. Her voice echoes in the blank space. When the music ebbs, it's dead quiet in here. I can hear my own breathing.

My phone beeps.

<Dan, you lazy smalldickmommiesboy. Sleeping when you should promotion. And we invited so nicely, brainsplatmeatpuppet. Are you still with us? Do you still want to play?>

Holy shit. These people are really watching us. Right now. This isn't some random spam. These people are genuinely toying with us. Who are they and what the fuck do they want? A vivid picture of my mom at home comes into my head, panicking about where I am. I see her on the phone, crying to my uncle down in Cape Town. I see my bedroom. I want to go home. I want to hug my mom, tell her I'm okay. I want to be okay. I want to wake up now.

I drop the phone, put my hands over my face and let out an incoherent sob. It has to be forceful enough to wake me up. You know, just like when you're about to die in a dream, you wake yourself up.

Rhoda joins me, picks up the phone and reads the message. 'Christ. Evidently this is not it. We're late.'

Beep beep. Beep beep.

Rhoda fishes out her phone, looks at it. 'It's yours again.'

I open the message.

<Well? We're asking youaquestion. In or out?>

'Just tell us how to get out of here!' I scream at the ceiling. There must be a camera or something. 'We just want to go. I don't give a fuck what you're doing down here! Just let us *out*!'

Beep beep. Beep beep.

<You like bloodpainschoolslaughtercrushedballs dont you? Last chance. INOROUT?>

'Holy fuck,' says Rhoda. 'You better type something back, and it had better not be "out".'

I key <reply> and write back: <Plse let us go. We dont care what ur doing down here. We wont tell anyone. Let us go>

'Wait! I'm not sure if—' Rhoda starts. But I've already hit <send>.

'Ohhh fuck,' she says. '"We won't tell anyone"? "We won't tell anyone"? When have you heard that before? Just before the fucking annoying little extra has his fucking brains blown out. *That's* when!'

Then it's black. All the lights switch off with a whine of capacitors. The music in the walls dies just as quickly. I grab at Rhoda's arm as she grabs at mine. Just our breathing, my heart beating, the seep of my piss draining into my sock. Then a grinding in the walls, like they're walking towards us in the darkness. The sound buildings make in an earthquake.

Then there's nothing. I can't see or hear anything. Until

Beep beep. Beep beep.

It's Rhoda's.

<Your boyfriend likes the hard way. Pass the test and you're still in. In or out?>

<in> she keys back.

A few seconds later. <59:59>. The numbers on Rhoda's phone are counting down <59.57> <59.56> <59.55>.

A whoosh of power. Powder-white glaring brightness. The singe of a thousand spotlights on our heads. And now mirrors. Mirrors lining the two long side walls, so that looking in that direction we can see nothing but white receding, and two dirty creatures huddled to infinity.

'What the *fuck* is going on here?' Rhoda explodes as we scuttle like kicked dogs to the front end of the room so that we can see as little of ourselves as possible. The ricocheting reflections have me too bewildered to speak.

'Now what?' she says. She's picking up my speech habits. 'What is this "test"? God, I feel like a fucking lab rat.'

I look back across the white floor, just silver tape and white and our dirty trail wherever we've walked. Where we sit, our trousers leave smudgy haloes of oily dust. I've never felt so filthy.

'It's got to be the mirrors. That's the only thing here.'

'But what's the question?'

'These guys are bullies. They talk exactly like the cunts who used to terrorise the juniors at my high school.'

'Boy's school, huh?'

'How did you guess?' I was beginning to find something to like in this woman. 'This whole thing reminds me of a hazing ritual.'

'So what's the point?'

'That's the problem. There's no fucking point. It's just to show how strong the bullies are. There's no way the new kid can win.'

'This has to be different, then,' she says. 'If this is a test, there has to be some way of passing it.'

'What makes you think they're playing by some sort of rules?'

'I don't know. Just a feeling. Like this is some existing game we've stumbled into.'

'Fuck!' She springs up, unable to contain her agitation any longer. 'We're wasting our fucking time. We've got to *do* something.' She shows me her phone. <56.45>. She paces away and starts examining the mirror on one wall.

I just sit.

'Come on, Dan. Get up! You go that side and search the mirror for a seam, some opening. Maybe it's as simple as that. Just find a way out.'

'I don't think so. I'm telling you. There's no answer. This is designed to be a no-win situation. Besides, I don't do mirrors.'

'Christ. Don't be such a pussy. We were getting along just fine. Let's try and keep it that way.'

And despite myself, the threat of a woman's disapproval works its charm, as it always has. I want her to like me, despite myself. I stand up and start searching the opposite mirror.

I really don't like mirrors. I'm getting to a place in my life where I'm starting to feel halfway decent about myself, as long as I can just forget what I look like. My giant freak nose, my black-bagged skull eyes, my scrawny neck, zits. I thought that shit was supposed to end when you stop being a teenager. Inside, when I'm feeling good, I think I'm a nice guy, someone a girl would talk to, someone who might one day be loved. Sometimes a girl even smiles at me as if they see that grown-up inside me.

Then a fucking mirror comes along and reminds me I never had a chance. That ghastly vision brands itself on me, and I carry that freak inside me wherever I go. And whether I try to hide it with kohl or T-shirts or dye or tattoos or whatever the fuck, it's still me. This leering, skinny, ugly, pimply freak.

And I have to work in a mall. Fucking malls, with their mirrors on every available surface; beautiful girls beautifully dressed telling me with every sexy spike-heeled step that I have no chance; mannequins and magazines and money; everything just grinding home the fact that I am there to serve, and that I will never, ever be one of them.

Keep in your place, boy. You are worth nothing.

This is what those SMS fuckers are doing. I know that tone. The pricks at high school, bullying all the little kids just because for some utterly mysterious reason they were in the right group. For some utterly mysterious reason they were in a position of power. They were butt-ugly and stupid, but for some reason they had the confidence to believe otherwise.

Real power, they should know, is not having to use it. Motherfuckers.

I look at myself again, repressing that urge to avert my eyes. I really look. At least now I have some reason to look awful. At least I look like I've been through something. My face is greasy with dirt, the pores clogged up with sweat and dust. If I had a cigarette in my lips it would complete the look. I'd look like a bum who didn't give a fuck. I really want not to give a fuck.

I glance across at Rhoda and wonder how she manages. I wonder how she got the scar on her face, what made her want to cut herself on her arms. Now she's cocky and strong, scary as shit. Where did she get that?

'Nothing here,' I call across. 'Can I bum another cigarette?'

'Jesus,' she says. 'I've created a fucking monster. I've only got a couple left. But since you asked so nicely.' She meets me halfway across the floor and lights one up for me before lighting a pinched half for herself. I sit down right there and inhale with a sigh.

'Maybe don't sit here, Dan,' says Rhoda. 'Shift up a bit.' She points out the word 'butchery' taped onto the floor.

'Ja, probably right.' I move across to 'cheese' and Rhoda sits facing me, staring past me to the opposite bank of mirrors. <47.21>.

'I feel like the turd floating in the punchbowl.'

'At a wedding.'

'At Princess fucking Di's wedding.'

I smoke. Then I know what I have to do. I grind out the stub on the white floor, smudging the ashes as far as they'll go, then I stand up and run and scream, scream as much of this godawful place out of my lungs, scream until the hall rings with overlapping waves, until my lungs become part of my throat, my whole body resonating the sound.

Running. And SMASH. Body block straight into the mirrored wall.

A squeaking shear as the first crack shoots up the length of the mirror, then the sound of hell's window breaking as the silvered panes plummet into vicious, jagged dust at my feet, nothing but blank wall behind it. I curl my head under my arms and stand there as the brief apocalypse comes down. I must be a bit demented, the glass chips spattering all over my boots and into my clothes, but I don't feel a thing, and while the echoes are still ringing around the hall I plough into the next shard of mirror and then the next.

At some stage, I notice that Rhoda is doing the same on her side, screaming like a banshee and kicking wild karate kicks at the mirrors. I'm laughing till it hurts.

Fuck your test, motherfuckers. I've passed my own.

When it's finished, I crunch over the debris back to cheese and stand there. I'm shaking. I look at my hands. They're covered with blood; back and front, hundreds of pinpricks and slivers. I pick up a palm-sized mirror shard and look at my face. A few shallow cuts. Not too bad. I pick out what glass bits I can and rub the blood off my brow.

Now I look like I've been through something. Something in my pathetic little life. Though what it means, who knows? Nothing, probably. Nothing, of course. The high dissipates as quickly as it arrives.

'Good going, Dan,' says Rhoda. 'Knew there was a psycho somewhere inside there. You want me to…' She reaches out and takes some shards out of my hair.

I walk across to my wall and smear my blood along its surface. I consider writing some words, but I don't think I'll have enough blood. It doesn't go very far, but it looks great against the white. Then I come back and sit picking glass out of my skin for the next few minutes.

'Now what?' I say. <32.55>

'I'm going to have another look. There must be some way out.'

Then blindness again. Pitch dark. Whining down. Silence except for Rhoda's footsteps on the broken glass. Then a heavy crunching from the other side of the hall.

'Rhoda?'

'Dan!'

'Rhoda?'

'Take out your phone, Dan. See if you can get some light. Do you see me?' Her phone flickers alight, reflecting off thousands of mirror shards. I can't make out the original, but I know which direction she's in. I thumb my phone on and make for her light. My shoes crunching on glass. Crackling ahead where Rhoda is. And another heavy clink behind me.

'Rhoda. Jesus. Do you hear that?'

'Ignore it! Get here.'

I make it across to where Rhoda is squatting, sweeping her phone's light across the floor. The silver duct tape reflects dully back to us.

'I saw a glimpse of something here. Something different. Use your phone.' The crunching is coming closer. I can hear a snoring sort of breath.

'What're we looking for? Jesus, that thing.'

'Here! Here!' I shine my light where Rhoda's just was. One word is taped in strips of weak luminous green. 'Downstairs', it says.

The steps behind slow, the stumping turning to a padding.

'But it's the floor,' I say. 'What—'

'Come on, Dan. Please. Help me find it. It's a trapdoor. It's got to be.'

The breathing is loud now, I can hear the wetness of the throat, the snoring, but high above me. I scrabble my hands across the floor. Fuck, yes, a ridge.

'Got it! Here.'

We find the latch together. A gob of spit spatters on the back of my neck as I crouch. Pull. Pull. It's too heavy to move.

The breathing stops.

chapter 9

RHODA

I can barely feel my fingers.

The metal rungs are icy and flecked with rust, and my hands are starting to cramp up.

It's been ten minutes or so since I last looked down, but I'm not going to make the same mistake again. That resulted in a vicious wave of nausea and crushing claustrophobia, and I really don't want to know how far down we've still got to climb. The stiffness in my fingers isn't helped by the fact that the air is now lung-achingly cold.

The only light comes from the occasional caged bulb stuck into the wall, but the lower we go, the weaker they get, and we're in danger of ending up in the dark. We've climbed down so far that the top of the narrow shaft is nothing but a faint pinprick above us. At least the rungs feel secure; they're bolted tightly onto the wall, but the rust is worrying.

I pause and scrape my knuckles against the rough brick wall, trying to force some feeling back into my fingers. My shoulders and forearms still throb from the exertion of hefting open the fucking trapdoor. Good old adrenaline; under normal circumstances I don't think I could have budged it an inch.

Above me I can hear Dan's laboured breathing. There's a good ten metres between me and his shadowy shape, but it looks like he's slowing down.

'Dan?' I say.

'What?' he sounds understandably exhausted, but I really don't like the defeated edge in his voice.

'You doing okay?'

He doesn't answer.

'Dan?'

Silence.

Shit. If he loses his grip or misses his footing, he's going to land directly on top of me. I've got to get him talking.

'Listen, Dan, okay?' My voice reverberates around the confined space as I climb downwards. 'There's this TV show we had in the UK when I was a kid, it was like this freaky fantasy game started by that guy... fuck, what's his face... Who's the guy who wrote *The Rocky Horror Picture Show*?'

'Tim Curry,' Dan says.

Thank God. His voice is faint, but at least he's answered me, at least he's moving again. 'No. He played Doctor Frankenfurter in the movie, he didn't write it. The guy I'm talking about... *shit*... it's Richard somebody.'

'Get to the point, Rhoda,' Dan snipes, sounding almost like his usual self.

'Anyway, this Richard bloke, he created this game where contestants had to pass this series of random tasks and tests, like mazes and stuff, and it was set in this alien space world or something. It was called...' Christ, it's as if my brain's as numb as my fingers. It's on the tip of my tongue. Then I have it. '*The Crystal Maze*!'

'Ja? So?'

'So what I'm saying is, that show is kind of like this shite we've got ourselves into.'

'Right. Except that was filmed in a fucking studio and this is real fucking life.'

'That's my point. Because I've been thinking. What if we're in some sick reality show? What if we *are* being filmed?'

'Jesus, Rhoda.'

'Well, why not? Stranger things have happened. You ever seen that movie *The Cube*? Or that one with the guy who tortures people and shit—'

'*The Silence of the Lambs*?'

'No, dumbass. *Saw*.'

'No. I'm not really into torture porn or stuff like—'

A blast of ice shoots up my right leg and I can't stop the scream that explodes out of my throat.

'What?' Dan yells.

What the fuck? I yank my leg upwards so quickly my knee bangs painfully on a rung, and my fingers almost lose their grip. I gingerly reach down and touch my calf. My combats are soaking wet.

'Fuck! We've just hit water.'

'How can there be...? You sure?'

'Course I'm fucking sure!'

'Okaaay, how deep is it?'

I spread my legs as far as they'll go on the narrow rung and peer down between my feet. The water almost touches my shoes and glints blackly up at me. I can make out three more rungs below its surface, and then, just darkness.

'Have we hit the bottom?' Dan calls.

'I don't think so, just wait.'

I edge down further, wincing as the water seeps over my calves, and then clings icily to my thighs. It fucking stinks like a railway station toilet. I stop before it reaches my pockets and soaks my phone and the remains of the blow.

'This is getting ridiculous,' I snap.

'It's getting ridiculous *now*?'

'You want to go back up?'

He knows this is not an option. 'So how deep is the water?'

'I can't tell.'

'Shit. Well, we've got no choice. We'll have to go down.'

'Dan,' I say, keeping my voice level. 'Can you swim?'

'Ja. Of course.'

'Thing is... I can't.'

'Oh fuck. You're not serious?'

'As a heart attack.' As serious as someone who's fucked up her life for five hundred rands' worth of blow can get. 'I really can't swim.'

I wait for him to snark or laugh at me. He doesn't.

'How am I going to get past you?' he says instead.

'Wait.'

I squash my body as far over to the side of the shaft as possible and cling on with my left arm curled around the rungs, my spine crushed uncomfortably against the brickwork.

It takes him ages to creep down towards me, and he narrowly avoids clonking me on the head with his boots. He manoeuvres his body alongside mine, and for a second we're face to face, lips almost touching. I can feel his breath on my cheeks. He's clearly scared shitless, but there's no way, right now, that he can be anywhere near as terrified as I am.

'You sure you want to do this?' I say.

'Someone's got to check it out,' he says.

True. And there's no fucking way it's going to be me.

He hands me his phone. He moves carefully down past me, and in seconds I'm looking down at the top of his head.

'Any last words?' I say, doing my best to smile.

'Ja,' he says. But he doesn't tell me what they are. I watch as he climbs, hand over hand, down into the depths, not even wincing as the cold water tops his shoulders. Looking straight up at me he takes several deep breaths, and without another word, pulls himself under. The water laps over his head, feathering his hair out in long wispy fingers, and then he's gone, leaving behind nothing but a lonely air bubble that pops to the surface.

My fucking hero.

How long can someone hold their breath for? Thirty seconds? A minute? Two minutes? Fuck it. Didn't that stupid magician prick hold his breath for like ten minutes or something? But he nearly died, didn't he? Shit.

I try not to count, but I can't help it:

One white horse.

Two white horses.

Three white horses…

It's not as if I can go and rescue him if he gets into trouble.

This was a stupid idea. I peer upwards, trying to figure out how long it would take me to climb up if I had to.

I can't even see the trapdoor any more. Not even a pinprick. And I'm not sure I'd have the energy to make it. Not to mention the rabid hobo or monster or salivating mutant that's waiting for us at the top.

It must be at least forty white horses now. For a second I have an eerily clear picture of forty white horses galloping across Hampstead Heath. Then fifty.

Fifty white horses. Imagine.

Sixty.

Jesus Christ, oh please, Dan, come up now. I pull out my phone, remembering that creepy countdown thing. It now reads: <24:10>.

Fuck.

I watch the seconds slip away.

Nine, eight, seven, six.

I look away for what feels like a moment and the numbers now read: <22:50>.

Dan's been gone for over three minutes. My teeth are beginning to chatter now, and I'm pretty sure the freezing water isn't the cause. To take my mind off it, I pull out his phone and scroll through his inbox. I skip past the freakazoid messages from the psycho fuckwits, but there aren't many others. There are a few from 'MOM', most along the lines of: <Don't forget the milk>; and a couple from someone called KARL: <dan my man, howzit got the new true blood will trade for psychoville :O>; and one that's quite interesting. <howzit dan howz blondie? Done the deed yet? lets have a brewski> Who's blondie? The bitch from the store? Has naughty Dan been telling porkies to his mates? His 'sent message' box doesn't tell me much. Either he empties it out religiously, or he's not much of a communicator. There are no stored photos.

The clock now reads: <21:02>. I slip the phone back into my pocket and then, suddenly, the water below froths and his head appears, his hair slicked back and shiny.

'Oh thank fuck!'

He takes in deep lungfuls of air in shuddering breaths, and shakes his head, spattering droplets everywhere.

'Well?' I say. 'Is there a way out?'

He nods, gasping, still unable to speak. He clings to the rungs of the ladder, and finally seems to get his breathing under control.

'How bad is it?' I say.

'You ever see that movie? The one about the boat?'

'*The Perfect Storm*?'

'No. The one about the ocean liner that goes down.'

Oh fuck. '*The Poseidon Adventure*?'

'Ja.'

'Oh, fuck you, Dan.' Talk about sensitive. The original one gave me nightmares for weeks.

'Sorry.' He doesn't sound that sorry. 'Rhoda, can you really not swim at all?'

'Almost drowned when I was a kid. At the Tipton Leisure Centre. Haven't tried since. Not much call for swimming in Birmingham.'

'Is that where you're from?'

I nod. My heart's rat-a-tat-tatting in my chest, and I can't seem to get enough oxygen into my lungs. 'Not at first. We moved around a bit. My dad, you know, he's an academic and so we kind of moved around a lot when I was a kid, although most of the time we stayed in Orpington and then we moved to Ipswich and then Birmingham and then when my dad got tenure we...' I'm really babbling now, and I allow my voice to trail away. I'd rather hang here on a rung and shoot the shit all day than get any closer to that fucking three-minute water. There's a lump in my throat the size of a sewer rat.

'It's going to be okay,' he says.

'But our phones... they'll get wet and...'

'Fuck it. Do we really want another message from whoever's doing this?'

I shake my head. I have never been this scared. 'I can't do this, Dan.'

'Listen. I'm going to go down first. It's not too far, and you can use the rungs to pull yourself down – and don't swallow any of the water. Trust me. It's fucking awful.'

'Okay.'

'When your feet hit the bottom, drop to your knees, there's an opening to your right that leads into some sort of outlet pipe, we need to swim through that to get to the other side.'

'How far is it?'

He shakes his head again, but avoids my eyes.

'How far?'

'Not far.' He's really crap at lying.

'Seriously, Dan. How far?'

'Ten metres – but I'm going to help you.'

'Fuuuuck.'

'It's not that bad, really. Easy peasy.'

'Is that why you were so long? You came out the other side?'
He nods.

'Okay,' I say. 'Dan... you know how you said you hated mirrors?'

'Ja.'

'Well, I really, *really* hate water.'

'You think they know that? The arseholes who are fucking with us?'

'What do you think?'

From above us there's the sound of the trapdoor clanging. I swear I can make out that thing's snotty panting. We've run out of time.

'Take a deep breath,' Dan says.

'Wait,' I say. 'I can do better than that.'

I pull out the envelope, and not caring what he thinks of me, I snort the last of the blow. It's a massive hit, and as most of it's still clogged together, a chunk gets stuck in my nose. I snort it back, and wince as it catches in my throat. 'I'm ready.'

I wait for him to duck back down below the surface, and then, trying to push away the image of that fat woman in *The Poseidon Adventure* stuck lifelessly in the flooded cargo hold, I suck as much air into my lungs as I can and allow myself to sink under the surface.

Nothing more can come up. It's impossible.

Dan waits for me to finish retching before he speaks. He's holding me up under the arms, and I'm really battling to pull enough air into my lungs. I heave again and foul water gushes up into my mouth. It tastes of old ponds and reminds me of dead rotting things forgotten on grass verges, and I realise that I'm babbling again, and crying all at once and no one has ever seen me this vulnerable. Except for once, and that was under-standable.

'You okay?' he says.

I try and nod, but my eyes are streaming and my throat feels like it's been sandpapered. But that's nothing compared to the blow-torch burning in my lungs.

'You did really well,' he lies.

I'd started to panic way before my feet had hit the bottom of the shaft, and if Dan hadn't dragged me backwards and through the underground tunnel I would probably have sucked in enough water to fill a swimming pool.

My lungs finally allow me to breathe. As my head clears, and my breathing steadies, I'm aware of other sensations: my back's also on fire where I scraped it against the floor of the tunnel, and my elbow throbs where I must have whacked it on the low-est rung.

I realise that Dan's still holding me, and I shrug out of his grasp.

'You going to be okay?' he asks.

'Yeah,' I say.

There's a couple of seconds of supreme awkwardness, and I heave myself up onto my hands and knees. I allow myself another hefty coughing fit, and finally take stock of our sur-roundings. We're on a ledge next to a filthy underground canal which flows through a domed brick tunnel. There's a solid wall behind us, and weak light is filtering through from the far end, but even from here I can tell it isn't daylight, just a sickly yellow glow. Still, I allow myself to hope that we've ended up in a sewage outlet and will wash out somewhere in the real world. Now my senses are back on track, the disgusting stench of the water fills my nostrils. The top of the water shines greasily as if it's coated with a thin layer of cooking oil. There's something floating and knocking gently against the side. It's instantly recognisable as a severed mannequin hand, the fingers curled into a fist, a metal bone protruding from the wrist.

'We made it, Rhoda,' Dan says.

'Yeah,' I say, trying to smile and ending up coughing again.

'And look! We're in another tunnel.'

'Thank fuck for that,' I say. 'I was beginning to miss them.'

Dan laughs, but it's a broken, relieved sound, devoid of any humour.

'I tell you something, Dan. There's no way the kid came down here.'

'Ja. But remember what the message said. "You'll be lost without it." We missed out on the market.'

'Why am I not too disappointed about that?'

'I'm sure they meant that if we missed the market we'd get lost. So I'm saying that if the kid did come down here, he more than likely took a different route through the market.'

One that I really don't want to think about. 'And that thing? Think it followed us down here?'

'I fucking hope not.'

'Which way now?'

'Haven't got much of a choice,' Dan says. He's right. We can follow the path next to the canal and see where it leads, or return. And right now I'd rather die down here than retrace those particular steps. 'You okay to get moving?'

He holds out his hand to help me up.

'I feel like an old lady,' I say, wincing as I stretch out my limbs.

'Yeah, I know how you—'

We both jump as the water next to us starts to bubble and froth. A spurt of adrenaline hits me so hard that I can taste it, and then we're running flat out along the side of the canal, feet slapping on the raw brick, splashing through shallow puddles.

My elbow is suddenly yanked from behind, and I spin around

and bash straight into Dan's chest.

'What you do that for?' I yell, trying to wriggle free from his grip. From behind us there's another churning splash.

He points to the left. There's an archway built into the brick and beyond it a brightly lit area tiled in white. I would have run right past it. He pulls me along, and our wet feet immediately start sliding on the slick tiled floor. Dan slips and now it's my turn to grab his elbow and pull him up. We skid along as we both try and get a grip on the floor, like a scene in a stupid slapstick comedy. The corridor curves to the right and then both of us stop dead as if we've hit an invisible brick wall.

'You have got to be kidding me,' Dan says.

It looks so unbelievably, reassuringly, banally *normal*.

In front of us is a grey metal lift door, the kind you see in low-end strip malls. There are two buttons either side of it, pointing up and down, and a row of back-lit numbers, ranging from 0 to 10 along the top of it. I look around for a stairwell door, but the rest of the wall is blank.

Looks like it's the lift or nothing.

My phone beeps, making both of us jump.

'Impossible,' Dan says. 'The battery must be soaked through.'

I scrabble in my pocket, hands fumbling and shaking, and pull out the last remains of the sodden envelope, my lighter, a tampon that's blown up to the size of a swollen thumb (which Dan looks away from in embarrassment), and finally grab my phone. The digital clock on the screen reads: <00:36>. There's no message, but both of us watch as the numbers count backwards: <00.32>, <00.31>, <00.30>.

'What the hell do you think happens at zero?' Dan says.

'I really don't want to know,' I say.

From the end of the corridor there's the sound of an enormous slap, as if a bloody side of beef has been splatted from a great height onto a metal table.

In unison we both press the buttons. The number 10 glows red, then 9, 8, 7...

I look around the area for some sort of weapon, but there's nothing – just plain walls and porcelain tiles. I fumble in my pockets again, trying to locate the knife, but I can't seem to find it. Fuck! What if I lost it in the water?

We smell it before we hear it, that same rotten-meat, engine-oil stench, followed by a low inhuman howl.

'Come on!' Dan screams at the door, lashing out at it with his foot.

<00.05>, <00.04>.

Ping!

The door hisses open and we throw ourselves inside.

'Press the close button!' I scream.

Dan whacks the control panel with his fist, and the door slides shut with infuriating slowness. There's a brief pause and then something slams into the door. The entire lift rocks, and I throw myself over to Dan's side and whack my palm on the buttons, hitting them at random.

With a screech of grinding machinery the lift begins to move, shuddering and creaking. We cling to the greasy metal rail stuck onto the side of the walls.

'Are we going up or down?' Dan says, his voice sounding remarkably normal, although his eyes are glassy with shock.

'I don't know.' I don't. The motion is disorienting; one second I'm certain we're travelling upwards, the next I'm convinced we're headed downwards.

'Fuck. That was close,' I say.

Dan starts to shake violently, and it's only when I run my hand over my face that I realise that I'm shaking too. I tell myself it's just the cold water.

The lift's gears screech again, and it judders and seems to slow down.

My phone beeps again and both of us jump. It's another message. I click it open.

<heitaRhoda san! Youever seen that moviedanisgoingtofuckingdie? It's awesomeman, the best!>

Oh fuck.

Dan's staring straight at me. I look down. 'What?'

'Nothing. Can't understand it. Just gibberish.' I press delete, praying that it disappears off the screen.

Dan opens his mouth to insist, and then his phone vibrates and beeps.

'Shit,' he says, reading the message. He passes it to me.

<hola dan-my-man. Youever been stuck inna elevator with someone you hate, like forever man? name that tunemuthafucka>

'What the fuck does that mean?' I say.

Then the lights go out and the lift drops sickeningly two or three floors before slamming to a rocking halt.

'Oh fuck,' Dan says, in the dark. 'What now?'

There's the sound of gears screaming again, and then, bizarrely, piped music starts wafting out of the roof.

chapter 10

DANIEL

The only lights are the lift's buttons, three rows of ten. 1 to 25, B for basement, G for ground, door open, door close and the emergency bell. I know it's a waste of my time to try that one, even as I thumb it. Dead. Of course.

Nothing to show which level we're on.

Rhoda is pacing around the lift, oddly keeping time with the muzak piping out from somewhere. 'I've got to get out of here, Dan, I'm serious. I'm going to suffocate. Give me a foot up.'

'Where?'

'*Do it!*' she hisses.

'Fine.' I offer her my cupped hands to who-knows-where she wants to climb. She scrabbles at the ceiling. She's jerking around, almost falling off the platform I'm making for her, punching at the ceiling. For the second time today, I notice just how light she is. She shouldn't be this light. It's like if she relaxed all those tight sinews she'd break into pieces.

I don't want to think too much about that now, so I try and break the ice. 'Jesus, Rhoda, you're quite hardcore for an academic's daughter.'

'Fuck off.'

'I can't believe you're, like, wealthy and shit. I could have sworn you were—'

'What? What? Some blacks have money, you know, Daniel.'

'Jeez. You don't have to tell me... I wasn't—' She's got this fucking unsettling way of turning everything I say around.

She's still squirming and wriggling in my grip. Her filthy gritty shoes are hurting my hands; sewer water is dripping off the hem of her trousers. I'm scared I'm about to drop her. 'Hurry up, Rhoda. What are you trying to do?'

'I'm just tryna...' comes the muffled response.

'It's pointless. You'll come out onto the top of a lift in a shaft that's fuck knows how deep. Just as dark, just as airless.'

'Shut up!'

'If this lift shaft is anything like that bottomless pit we climbed down... And it has a bottom. A bottom we can smash on like melons from the fucking tower of Pisa.' Now I'm just babbling, and I should just shut up, but I can't. The fucking pan-pipes are driving me insane.

'I said shut the fuck up,' she bellows as she jumps out of my braced hands. I shake them out. Rhoda punches the wall again. She's breathing too fast, and it dawns on me that her panic is for real.

'Hey, Rhoda,' I say, intent on calming her down. 'Listen to the music. I know this tune.'

The panpipe muzak piping out of the roof was designed to be calming, and to my surprise it's working. On me, if not Rhoda.

'It reminds me of a holiday we took to Durban when we visited my cousin,' I continue talking her down. 'He was three months older than me, had much cooler toys, much cooler stuff. He put on this soppy CD and showed me a poem a girl at school had written for him. She'd copied the lyrics word for word.'

Rhoda's breathing is starting to slow. 'God, I'm going to puke,' she says, but at least she's starting to calm down to normal. If you can call her usual condition normal. It hasn't escaped me that she's probably about to start going into some sort of drug withdrawal now that her stash has been washed down the sewer. 'Lionel motherfucking Richie. They're cruel bastards. We know that much.'

'I was fucking jealous of my cousin,' I continue, trying to keep it boring. 'Girlfriends writing him poems. He became a rabbi. Never married. Wonder how much his Lionel-Richie-toting primary-school sweetheart had to do with that.'

She manages a smile. 'Yeah. Probably had a lot to do with it. "Hello",' she croons half-heartedly, strangling the words as if she hates them. '"Is it me you're looking for? Cos I wonder what you are and I wonder blah blah blah".' She peters out.

Okay. She's back. Thank God. 'Just carry on thinking of open spaces, okay. Listen to the music. Imagine you're in the desert, on the open sea, in a meadow. Anything fresh and clean. Okay?' She doesn't ask how I know so much about claustrophobia.

'Yeah, okay. Thanks, Dr Phil. I got it now. Breathe and think about fairies and unicorns,' she says. 'It would be easier if we weren't *stuck in a fucking falling lift*! What the fuck do we do, Dan?'

'Well, we know the name of the song... What do we do with it?' I ask, more to myself than her. 'The message said "name that tune". Who do we tell? How?' If there's one thing I know a lot about, it's games. And I know this is too easy. This is Level One. And I know Rhoda isn't ready to hear that just yet.

'I guess we just text the name back.' Rhoda pulls out her phone.

'No, wait. I don't think so. Nobody's going to design a game based on cellphones. The coverage and the relay time are just too unreliable. Maybe in the future. The control has to be something internal.'

She looks at me like I'm talking in Vulcan. 'What are you on about? That sounds fucking complicated. We need to keep things simple, all right?'

'Rhoda, listen. This is a game. It runs on its own internal logic. I doubt these fucks are sitting around waiting for us to SMS anyway. They just set the game in motion and they're probably sitting at home listening to Britney Spears and jerking off.'

'You don't know—'

'You may have lived twenty lives on the streets and know all sorts of shit about all sorts of shit. But I've lived twenty thousand lives in front of consoles. I know games. This is just a game.'

'In games players don't really die, though.'

'To play a game well you have to feel like you're going to die. You get into the zone and nothing outside matters. This is just a game without a manual. I've played hundreds of pirated games before. We have to figure it out, that's all.'

'We've got no time, for fuck's sake, Dan. What the hell do you—'

'Let me think.' And I block out her noise, just like I've blocked out my mother's nagging so often in the past.

The only control panel here is the lift's buttons. That must be the input device. If we have to input a word, we need an alphabet. So it's either one to nine like a cellphone, or... the buttons – it has to be the buttons. Thirty buttons, twenty-six letters in the alphabet. Which four do we leave out? Door open, door close, alarm – gone. One left. Space bar? Which one?

The song's nearly finished, arsehole! my mind screams at me. But the dominant part of me stays calm. I'm in the zone. I'm breathing deeply. You stay calm, you breathe deeply, your time remaining stretches out. You panic, it's over. You go blank. Not today. Breathe.

Probably B, but I wouldn't know. Is it a simple substitution cipher? Ground=A, 1=B, 2=C. Or 1=A, 2=B, 3=C. That's very easy. Too easy. But maybe that's part of the trick. Maybe the input is not supposed to be the hard part; the guessing game is.

How many chances do you think we have, dumbfuck? We can't start again in this *game.* Shut the fuck up. Make a choice. Trust your intuition. You know how you get that feeling when you're really in the sweet spot, you can almost foresee the future, you're so in synch with the machine. Listen to the best voice. Trust yourself. I know her soft and sexy voice; she sounds like an angel.

Okay. 1=A. Here we go.

8 – 5 – 12 – 12 – 15.

A lurch and my stomach's in my throat. Instinctively I push myself into the corner of the lift, my knees bent like I'm sitting on an invisible chair, my arms pushing against the two walls as hard as they can. I've seen it on TV somewhere. They showed what happens when you're in a falling lift. First your legs shatter, then you bounce up and smash your skull against the ceiling. So what you want to do is become a shock absorber, keep your legs flexible to buffer the force, then hold on so you don't bounce.

'Brace!' I scream at Rhoda. 'Brace like me!' She squeezes into her corner as we plummet. We're going so fast, I'm feeling light; any faster we'll be in zero-G.

The lift slows, then jerks to a halt.

'Fuck! Nice going, gameboy. Let's do it my way now, okay?' She thumbs at her phone.

'No!' But it's too late. She's hit <send>. Nothing happens for a while. We look at each other. Then the lift descends with a whine. Just a floor or two. No plummeting.

'Is that good or bad?' I ask, but my gut tells me down is bad. I see the endless tunnel again. If we are anywhere in the middle of a shaft that deep, we have plenty of space still to fall.

Now Rhoda's working on prising the doors open. Even if she manages to open the door, I'm sure we'd see nothing but blank concrete. I just watch her. I'm so tired.

The closing bars of the music snap us out of our fugues.

'Christ, Dan. It's ending. I don't think we'll get another chance.'

My angel whispers in my ear.

It's a fucking QWERTY keyboard.

Which end does it start? Do we exclude caps lock or colons on the middle row? No time. The last words are sung; the final notes are kicking in. And what the hell was the order of the letters?

Breathe, my angel tells me. *You know how to touch-type. You've IMed for years. Write me a message. Say hello. Don't think. Trust yourself.*

I'm in the sweet spot. I can't hear the music any more. It's just me, the perfume of my angel, her feathers drifting in the white air.

$12 - 2 - 21 - 21 - 20$

'You cut that a bit fine,' Rhoda's saying when I open my eyes. But she's smiling thinly. We're going up. Slowly.

The Lionel Richie song dies; the lift stops. Another panpipe rendition comes on.

'Here it goes again,' I say. 'I knew that wasn't all.' I don't recognise the tune. Jazzy easy listening, but without any particular harmony standing out.

Rhoda's checking her phone. Nothing. Nothing on mine either. 'Bastards, what the fu—' She pauses. 'I know this,' she says. But instead of looking pleased, her face pales and glistens with a fresh sheen of sweat.

'What's the matter?'

'There's no way they could...' she's muttering to herself.

'Come on, Rhoda. You need to talk to me. If you know the song give me the fucking title.'

'"Nonhlanhla",' she says.

'Huh? I didn't—'

'"Non-hlan-hla",' she reiterates like I'm a moron. 'It's a common name, jerkoff, not some weird alien shit. There's probably more Nonhlanhlas in South Africa than there are Dans.'

'Okay. Whatever. Just give me the spelling. We can do the PC bullshit later, okay. Have you forgotten where we are?'

'Christ, you're a dick—'

'How. The fuck. Do you spell it. *Rhoda*.'

'N–O–N–H—'

13–20–13. 'Hang on, hang on. I can't think where the keys are. You need to go slower. I can't…'

'H. H, man! Write it down or something.'

12–12–

And we're falling so fast I'm thrown against the side of the lift. I try to get into my brace position and Rhoda's screaming at me: 'Try again!'

'There's no way to clear this thing. I don't know. How am I…' This is too much for me. My fucking angel has left the building and all the knowledge I have left is how this game has worked up to now. That's all I can trust. I have to believe that we're going to stop and get another chance. I've been acting so macho and like I know what I'm doing. But I'm going to kill us both. I don't want that as my last action. I don't want that as my last thought. I want to go home. I want to wake up. I think about screaming, but then the lift judders to a stop.

'Okay, let's try that again,' Rhoda says, her voice softer. 'I'll go slowly.'

I nod. 'Any idea how long this song is?'

All she says is 'N'. I press 13.

'O' 20

'N' 13

'H' 12

'L' 21

'A' Door open? Fuck, I've got it wrong. This can't be right. But we're halfway and I can't reset. There's no fucking undo in this game. I press the button, Rhoda's eyes widen, doubting me as much as I doubt myself. The doors don't open. I can't tell if that was good or bad. We just have to finish this entry.

'N' 13

'H' 12

'L' 21

'A' Door open. A shudder and I think oh God this is it, we're dead, but then the lift is hoisting us up gently.

'How did you know that?' I ask as we ascend.

'My dad used to play it when we were first in… in the UK. It was his favourite song. "Nonhlanhla" by Chubby Khoabane. It's goddamn sacrilege to change Chubby's trumpet into fucking pan-pipes. Dad would be…' She stops.

'Well done,' I say when I realise she's not going to tell me any more. 'Good for your dad.'

'He named me after this song.'

'What? Rhoda?'

'Nonhlanhla's my real name. Rhoda's my slave name, if you like.'

'Better than Lastchance or Nomore, I suppose.'

She gives me a fuck-off look. 'What I don't know is how these fuckers knew. Nobody knows my name. Nobody.'

If that's her name, I have an idea what's coming next. Sure enough, soon as the lift stops again, another perfect muzak tune follows. Barely into the first bar I start pressing the buttons: 3 – door open – 13 – 17 – 2 – 21, and we're on our way up again.

'Clever,' says Rhoda. 'We've got HELLO NONHLANHLA DANIEL. I can't wait to hear what they're going to say next.'

But I'm thinking of home again. How my mother would put on that Elton John song to soothe me after Dad died. I think soothed her too, to sing along to it softly, combing her fingers through my hair. We had the same hair, Dad and me, thin and straight, got knotted a bit, could respond to the gentle tug of Mom's fingers. This has to be some fucked-up dream. My dad's ghost coming back to me in the middle of a long and terrifying night to shit on me for not mourning him properly. What the fuck was I supposed to do? I was thirteen. You don't know how to grieve at thirteen. When are you supposed to learn how to grieve?

I wipe at my eyes. It's sore as if it was yesterday. I wonder if Rhoda's noticed I'm crying, but she's standing at the other side of our box, just staring into nothing, a blank look on her face.

'Hey, Rhoda. You okay?' She looks at me dully, as if she's just woken up.

She slurs, 'No. I don't think so.'

I rifle through her jacket pockets, still damp and stinking from the sewer. They have to be ruined, surely. But in the lower inside pocket I find a crumpled box of Stuyvesant, the plastic wrapping protecting the lone cigarette from too much damage. It's bent and damp, but it will do. I rummage for the lighter, and have to click it several times before it catches. I take a deep drag and put it between her lips.

'Here.'

She pulls the smoke deep into her lungs, coughs, and shakes herself straight.

'Thanks. That's better.' Resuscitating someone with cigarettes. Ironic. My life has changed a bit.

She takes another drag, hands me the cigarette and then there's screaming and grinding machines and the lift is imploding and people are chainsawing things and smashing cars and I realise we've stopped and music has come on again but these are no panpipes this is war and a guy or an army is screaming from the pit of their stomachs and then holy shit I recognise the noise somewhere in the noise a pattern not of music nothing so regular but I see a scene of blood and carnage headslayer five level eight with all weapons unlocked that is the racket that accompanied the full-on slaughter and now I remember Karl has the game soundtrack video and my head is so tuned into the noise that I can read the caption on his screen as we play I am blowing his monsters to blood clots band is called Sons of Tombspawn and the track number seventeen level eight unlocked was called

READY TO DIE

5 – 2 – door open – 3 – 11

Shit. Space? I look to Rhoda, but she's just standing there, covering her mouth, eyes wide and this noise is killing me, I can't think straight. Which one did I say was the fucking space?

I try 25 and we start to plummet again, the familiar buffeting and I don't even bother to brace because honestly having my brains knocked out would be better than this noise, this trying, this up and down and this TINY FUCKING BOX MY BRAIN'S GOING TO EXPLODE I'm going to stop breathing. Then it will be quiet. Then I can go and walk out on my meadow, wash in the cool stream, lie in the sun. Die in peace.

Then my angel speaks to me in a calm, clear voice. *You can do it.* I want to believe it.

5 – 2 – door open – 3 – 11 – 8 – 20 – 3 – 17 – 2

Ding.

The lift opens. We're in the mall.

chapter 11

RHODA

'So we're seriously locked in, then?'

'Looks like it,' Dan says.

'After all that? We get back here and we can't even leave?'

He shrugs. He doesn't seem too outwardly bothered by this setback; no doubt he's still overwhelmed with relief that we're not a pile of shattered limbs at the bottom of the lift shaft. But Christ, it's a killer not being able to get out of this fucking place. From what I could make out after we fled from the lift, the four interlinking aisles that make up this floor don't seem to lead anywhere, and every shop window is concealed behind roll-down metal shutters. Total security overkill. We can't even get up to the next level. Another gate seals the top of a pair of frozen escalators that lead to the floor above.

I sit down on the bottom step of the escalator, wincing as the metal grooves dig into the bones of my bum. 'So the only way out is the lift again,' I say. 'And that's out of the fucking question.'

'No shit,' he mumbles.

'Where in the mall are we, Dan?'

He shrugs. 'I'm not sure.'

'How can you not be sure? I thought you worked here?'

'Ja, but it's a big place, Rhoda.' He sighs. 'This looks like one of the enclosed mezzanines.'

'So where's your bookshop in relation to here, do you think?'

'Probably up.'

'Oh brilliant, Dan. Thanks. You're a great help.'

'What do you want me to do, Rhoda? We're back in the mall, what more do you want?'

'I want to get the fuck out of here, Dan, obviously. We've just been to the fucking twilight zone, and I really, *really* need a shower.'

We both start giggling, although I didn't actually say anything that funny. Besides, it's true – I *am* desperate to get clean. Both of us reek of that putrid water, and my skin feels greasy, damp and itchy.

But I suppose that's the least of my problems. My legs are throbbing with exhaustion; my thigh muscles feel as if they've been beaten with a metal pipe, and the rest of my body aches like one big bruise. And I don't even want to delve into my mind and see how that's holding up. There's no way anyone could go through all that crazy, fucked-up, unbelievable shit without some sort of psychological damage, is there? Images of the nightmare swim in that stinking canal keep bubbling up, but I'm just not ready to go there. I stand up, hobble over to one of the shopfronts, and rattle the metal shutter that masks the window display. It's impossible to tell what the shop sells and the signage doesn't help. The words 'Bite Size!' are printed in jumbo Comic Sans lettering above the window.

'This normal?' I say, kicking the metal shutter for good measure. 'I mean, we're inside a mall, right? Isn't this security a bit OTT?'

'Probably another lockdown,' Dan says.

'A what?'

'It's what they do when there's been an incident in the mall. You know, like an armed robbery, that kind of thing.'

'So they'll open the exits up soon?'

'Maybe. Or if it happened near closing time they'll probably leave them sealed off until the morning.'

'Fuck. And we don't even know what time it is. We could be stuck here for hours.'

He shrugs again. 'It's possible.'

'What do you think they sell in this store?'

'I dunno. Sweets? Teeth? Dental supplies? Who cares?' He slumps down on the escalator. He drops his head and runs his fingers through his wet hair.

Although my legs are screaming for me to sit the fuck down and relax, I'm twitchy and on edge. I should be relieved. I should be on my hands and knees kissing the floor tiles and thanking God that we're alive. But I can't crush the nagging feeling that something's wrong. Could it be because the place is so quiet? Save for the squeak of my sodden trainers on the tiles, it's ominously silent. I can't even hear the background buzz of electricity or air-con. And the lighting is way more subdued than I remember it being. Maybe they're trying to save electricity.

But why bother with lights at all if the place is sealed up tighter than a bank vault?

Then something strikes me. 'But why isn't this place alarmed?'

'Nah, the mall itself isn't. The individual shops are,' Dan says without raising his head. 'Relax, Rhoda. We're safe, okay?'

'You might be.'

'Are you still worried about the security guards? After all that's happened?'

He's got a point. If Fingerling and Yellow Eyes were to pitch up right now, I'd probably hug them. I'd do almost anything to be sitting safely in their stinking office right now.

'We have to tell someone about the kid,' I say. 'Tell them that he got lost down there ASAP. They need to send out a search party.'

'The security guards would have called the cops, Rhoda.' His patronising tone is beginning to grate.

'They need us to tell them where he went, though.' I fumble in my pocket and pull out the phone, my fingers grazing over the knife's handle. 'We'll get a signal here, right?' He slaps his forehead like an old-school comedian parodying forgetfulness, and pulls out his own cell. My Nokia's screen is blank, and it's so out of juice it won't even switch on. Either that or it's finally succumbed to water damage. 'Shit. Dead. You?'

'Also.'

'Fuck.'

'Look, don't worry,' he says. 'There'll be someone here early to open up. Cleaners or whatever. We've just got to wait it out.'

'What about payphones?'

'They're normally next to the toilets.'

I don't remember seeing any after we'd raced out of the lift, but I hadn't really been looking. Too hysterical with relief to think about anything else. And the mention of toilets makes me realise that I need to pee really desperately.

'Come on,' I say.

'Huh? Where you going?'

'See if I can find a phone. And a fucking toilet.'

'I really don't want to go back there, Rhoda,' he says.

'I'm not going near the lift, Dan. Anyway, we jammed the door open, there's no way that psycho can get up here after us.'

'You still think it's a psycho?'

I don't know what to think. I just know I can't think about that right now. Besides, even though my stomach's telling me something's off about this place, my mind's still dizzy with relief at the normality of our surroundings.

'Whatever. Look, you can hang here if you like, but I'm going to check it out.'

I stride off, not waiting to see if he's going to follow. I've barely gone ten metres when I hear the slap of his boots behind me.

We walk past shops sealed with uniform metal security gates; the signs above the battened-down windows are each as brightly coloured as the next, and just as crassly named: Clips 'n' Crap, Curl Up & Die (although shouldn't that be 'Curl Up & Dye'?) and Diabeatties. Dan slows down as we reach the point where the four aisles meet. At the end of the aisle to our left, the lift is still wide open, the empty trolley we'd used to keep the doors open still jammed in place.

'See?' I say. 'We're cool. Like you said, we're safe.'

Dan tries to grin at me, but fails miserably.

The aisle in front of us ends in a locked-down dead end, so I hang a right – the only other option. The shops in this section are similarly shielded, but none have the garish signs above the windows.

Dan grabs the back of my T-shirt. 'Wait, Rhoda!'

'What?'

'Check.'

There's a narrow corridor to our right. It's gloomy and ends in a brick wall. There's no sign of a phone, but there are two doors opposite each other about halfway down. I follow Dan towards them.

'What the hell?' he says.

Both doors are emblazoned with toilet signs, but they're nothing like any I've ever seen before. The men's decal is a silhouette of a man holding a huge stylised penis over a urinal. The ladies' shows a fat woman balancing over a too-small toilet seat. If they weren't so neatly rendered I'd assume they were Banksy-style jokes.

'Fuck it,' I say. 'I bloody hope they're not locked. I really, really have to go.' I push the door of the ladies' tentatively, and it creaks open. 'Thank God. See you in a bit.'

Dan nods and disappears into the men's.

Bloody hell.

Whoever designed the ladies' bathroom won't be winning any awards for subtlety. It's like walking into a tiled womb – everything is pink, right down to the toilet bowls, the double sink and the stall doors. The taps are gold-plated and shaped like the heads of swans, and even the tampon dispenser is spray-painted pink. There are mirrors everywhere, including a full-length one on the far wall that cruelly reflects a gaunt grubby skeleton with too-large eyes and baggy trousers. But now I'm here, my bladder can't hold on a second longer. All of the stall doors, except for one at the far end, are double width, as if for disabled people. I choose a middle stall and the relief is almost overwhelming.

I flush and steel myself for another assault by mirror.

It's worse the second time. The water in that canal must have been way filthier than I realised; my grey T-shirt is a dull brown colour, and there are rust-coloured stains splotched all over my combats. As usual, I avoid looking too closely at my face. But it's clear enough that I'm a human turd in antiseptic Barbieland, and the stench rolling off me is making my stomach churn. I need to clean myself up.

I plug the sink and turn the taps on full. I dunk my head, letting warm water pour over my neck, not caring as it flows into dirty pools on the floor. I fill my hands with squirt after squirt of pink floral-scented liquid soap and work it into my scalp, rinse it off, and repeat the process.

Better. Much better. But not good enough. I pull off my T-shirt, smother it in soap, and scrub it as best I can. The water turns black, but it's doing the trick. Using my T-shirt as a swab, I scrub under my arms and around the back of my neck.

I turn my back to the mirror and peer over my shoulder. The familiar old keloid scar tissue that bleeds down from my neck and over my shoulder leads down into a thick bloom of new bruises, and an ugly scrape spreads across my ribcage. I've seen worse. No permanent damage.

I rinse out the T-shirt and wring out the soap. The water still runs slightly muddy, but fuck it, the shirt no longer stinks of sweat and gore and maggoty water. Is it worth sticking it under the hand-dryer? Probably not. It would take hours to dry.

There's the sound of a flushing toilet behind me, and I jump and drop the shirt. I whirl around. The stalls' doors are all open, except for the one nearest the entrance.

'Hello? Is someone there?'

Nothing.

The dread coils in my stomach again, and my heart goes into a gallop.

I walk over to the closed stall and nudge the door with my foot. It doesn't budge. Whoever was responsible for designing the toilet signs has excelled with this one. I have no clue what it's supposed to represent. It shows a stick-thin figure leaning on crutches, its out-of-proportion, misshapen head cocked spastic- ally to one side, its single leg too thin to hold up the weight of its body. Bizarre. Maybe it's a toilet for one-legged amputees. The signs must be Banksy-style piss-takes after all.

I knock. 'Hello?'

Still nothing.

The toilet flushes again. I put my ear to the door. I can't hear anything but the last traces of water running into the cistern. There's no tell-tale sound of scuffing feet or rustling of clothes.

Fuck it.

I get down onto the floor to peer under the door. There's a good fifteen centimetres of space above the floor, and I wince as my naked stomach and breasts press against the cold pink tiles.

The stall appears to be empty. No feet, no shoes, just a sodden square of toilet paper and a spreading puddle of brown water around the base of the toilet.

A blocked toilet. What could be more normal than that? What the hell's wrong with me? Nothing's going to come after us here. Like Dan says. We're safe.

'Rhoda!'

The scream lodges in my throat and I sit up too quickly, stars dancing in front of my eyes.

Dan's looking down at me, eyes wide. And it's not my face he's staring at.

I get to my feet and cross my arms over my breasts.

'You could have fucking well knocked!'

'Sorry. You were ages. I'll just…' He starts backing away to the door. 'Hang on, what were you doing on the floor?'

'Just fuck off, Dan!'

'Okay. Look, sorry, I'll just go…'

'Yeah. Do that.'

I retrieve the sodden T-shirt from the floor and pull it over my head, shivering slightly. It's warm down here, so the damp clothes shouldn't be too uncomfortable.

Dan's waiting for me outside, and doesn't catch my eye when I join him.

'Look, Rhoda, I'm really sor—'

'Whatever.'

Apart from his acute embarrassment, he's looking better. His hair is also sopping wet and clean, and his face is free from the worst of the dirt.

'Let's head back to the escalators,' I say.

'Okay.' He still won't meet my eyes.

'Dan. It's cool, okay? Chill out. No big deal.'

He nods.

'I mean, it's not as if there was much there to see, right?'

This time he does catch my eye. 'I'm still, you know…' His stomach growls, and we share a smile, breaking the awkwardness.

'Ditto,' I say. 'I'm also fucking starving.'

'How long have we been gone?' he says.

'No idea.' I've totally lost track of time. But it can't be longer than twenty-four hours, surely?

There's one of those mall-style bins pretending to be something else in the centre of the aisle, and I flip open the lid and start rooting through it.

'What are you doing?' Dan says prissily.

'Thought you were hungry?'

'I am, but—'

'Beggars can't be choosers, Dan.'

There's not much in here, just a balled-up newspaper, an empty soda can and a pile of those styrofoam chips people use to pack fragile ornaments. I dig down deeper, and pull out a half-eaten baguette filled with cheese and mayonnaise. Bingo! It's almost as if it was left there for us. I sniff it. 'Seems cool.'

I strip off the plastic covering, break it in half and offer Dan a piece. He may not approve of my shopping methods, but he doesn't hesitate to grab it out of my hand. We eat while we head back to the escalators, and it takes us less than thirty seconds to polish off the food. My stomach begs for more. I'm even hungrier now that I've eaten something.

'Not bad, was it?' I say.

'Nah. First time I've ever eaten... you know...'

'Bin food?'

'Is that the technical term?' he asks.

'Yeah. I'm a regular fucking connoisseur of eating shit.'

He looks as if he's thinking about a snappy comeback, but he's clearly way too knackered for that. We both are.

We head between the escalators and sit down side by side with our backs to the wall in an alcove that's actually pretty snug. It wouldn't be a bad place to hide, and I have to remind myself that this time we actually want to be found. I stretch out my legs and allow myself to relax. The shifting dread in my stomach is lessening somewhat. It's over. We're okay.

Dan yawns. 'What's the first thing you're going to do when you get home?' he says.

'I don't have a home.'

'When you get out of here, then.'

'Have a fucking shower, try not to get arrested, make sure that kid is found.'

'In that order?'

'Sure. You?'

He rests his head on the wall behind him. 'Double Quarter-Pounder with Cheese. Then a trip to a psychologist.'

'Seriously?'

'No. I hate McDonald's.'

It's a lame joke but we both try and smile anyway.

'How are we going to explain to the cops what happened?' he says.

'God knows.'

'Because we *are* going to have to go to the police, you know that, right?'

'What are you trying to say, Dan?'

'I just mean… maybe you don't want to because…'

'Because I'm clearly a criminal?'

'No…' He pauses. 'Well… yeah.'

'Dan, I just bought a bit of blow off a guy, no big deal. Besides, whoever was fucking with us down there needs to be stopped before someone actually gets killed.'

I can imagine the conversation with the cops: Yes, officers, things started going pear-shaped after I dumped the kid to buy some drugs, kidnapped Dan at knifepoint and ran into a maggot-spewing monster. It's not going to go down well. But one thing's for sure. I can't keep on running.

There's nowhere to run *to*.

But I'm not totally without options.

'Dan? Look, I know you don't know me very well, but I couldn't crash at your place for a night, could I?'

He doesn't answer. His head is resting against the wall behind him, hands slack in his lap. I can tell by his measured breathing that he's fast asleep.

chapter 12

DANIEL

I'm paddling in the sea. It's a perfect-weather day, body-temper-ature water, and I'm bobbing there, feeling... feeling nothing. No fear, no expectation, no judgement, no eyes watching me. Invisible. It's pure contentment. I see a distant figure walking toward me across the beach. At first I think it's Josie and I enjoy watching her long legs as she approaches, but then it morphs into Rhoda. As the figure gets closer, though, it becomes bigger and bigger, too big. It's covered in dirty scabs. It isn't human.

Then I hear that strangled, drowning-elephant shriek again, like a thousand wrongful deaths balled up into this blob of hate. It's coming fast. I try to turn and a wave smashes me down, punches all the breath out of my lungs. It rolls over me with a metallic grating like tools being crushed in a house-sized blender. I can't breathe; I'm drowning, but in my last moment I'm grateful to the sea for saving me from the creature.

I wake up suddenly, adrenaline bypassing the normal morning formalities. Where am I? How could I let my guard down? Ready to run, I look around. Rhoda's hunched in a ball next to me, stir-ring from her own sleep. I breathe the dream out with relief.

These bright corridors still seem a bit unreal. As if all of it was a dream. But my shit-and-whatever stained jeans, the bruises and cuts on my body, Rhoda herself rubbing the sleep out of her eyes in the corner of the alcove, tell a different story. Despite myself, my mind lodges on the memory of her topless in the bathroom last night.

'The fuck you looking at?' mutters Rhoda. The closest I'll get to a sweet and cheery 'Good morning' from her.

'Not much else to look at. Either hideous security shutters or you. I got tired of looking at the shutters.'

'Arsehole,' she mutters. Closest I'll get to a laugh, I suppose. 'Hey, Dan. Listen to that. The escalators are working.'

Thank fuck. The roller door that was blocking the top of the escalator has been raised. That means the mall's open and we're going to go home. Rhoda scales the escalator two steps at a time, slings her frame around the corner and bounds up the next flight. When I catch up with her, she's standing on the middle level. My level.

The flight of escalators ends here, forcing shoppers to track through the entire level to get to the next floor. Architects who design malls clearly graduate from the Satan-fucking-with-rats-in-mazes-for-sport academy. It's a relief to know exactly where I'm going now. 'You sure you want to get out of here?' I ask. 'You don't want to do some window shopping? Check out the sales? Brunch?'

'Fucking funny. Ha ha. Now let's go. Jesus, I need to see the sky.'

Rhoda races ahead, following the signs to the main entrance, past shops with their lights on, but their doors closed. I check my cellphone for the time but it's dead, of course. Beads of condensation stipple the screen. The phone rattles when I shake it. I can tell it's about half past eight by the mall's state of almost-readiness.

'Fuck it!' Rhoda swears when we get to the main exit. It's still locked down. She kicks at the metal door and the crash resonates through the marbled halls. I rattle the shutter too. More to prove to Rhoda that I'm trying to do something than expecting any effect.

'Hey!' someone shouts from above. A grotesque man with purple jowls is leering over the mezzanine railing. He's dressed in an elaborate admiral's uniform, gold braiding, medals, cap and the whole bit, but the get-up has this cheap, over-ironed sheen that spells Security Guard. Christ, they pay these poor buggers nothing and then make them dress up like clowns to suit the mall's theme. Except admirals don't belong in a Joburg mall, six hundred kilometres from the nearest sea. And the poor guy looks so unhealthy that there's no way he could chase down a shoplifter. His face blooms as if he's about to suffer a heart attack any minute. More immediately, the way he's leaning over the railing, I worry that he's going to fall over it any second.

Rhoda and I step back out of falling-freak range.

'Don't shake the door!' the man yells, jowls juddering.

'Sorry. Can you help us?' I try. 'Um, what time will the door open?'

'Open?' he says, as if he hasn't heard of the concept.

'Yes. We need to get out.'

'You know you need access. You browns don't have access.'

'What the fuck,' hisses Rhoda.

'You stay there,' the security man orders, medals jangling as he stumps towards the stairs. 'You need to go to control. Wait there. I'm coming down. And you, dark brown, don't kick the door.'

'Do you think the lockdown's because of me?' said Rhoda. 'What are they going to—'

'Relax. They only do a shutdown if there's something really serious. They wouldn't want to restrict shopping hours. Something else might have happened. Probably a bank robbery. There's like two a week. There's no way they would do all this just for you. You didn't even steal anything.'

'Yeah, but Fingerling and Yellow Eyes really had it in for me. And I did kick that Simon bastard in the balls.'

'Don't stress. It's not about you. We'll just clear everything up with security.'

'I've got a bad feeling about this, Dan.'

'Okay. Come. Let's go to Only Books. Someone there will tell us what the lockdown's for and then we'll go to security.'

We head off before Admiral Security can reach us. When we get to the shop, I notice that someone has painted an 'L' in front of the ONLY on the shop's big sign: LONLY BOOKS. It's brilliantly done; the font and colour are excellently matched. It was probably Matt, the art student who worked here for a few months before being canned by Bradley for chewing gum at the counter or calling a customer a bitch or Christ knows what.

The shop's still closed, though, the glass doors locked. The lights are on but I can't see anyone inside.

'Jesus. Nice job, evil bookseller,' Rhoda says, pointing towards the business books display in the main shop window. Bradley's idea, no doubt. *Fuck the Poor*, *Neurolinguistic Brainwashing for Lazy Arseholes* in the familiar yellow and black branding, *Jesus Wants You to be Pimp-Rich* and so on.

'I've never heard of any of these,' I say. 'Plenty like them, but not these exact ones.'

But Rhoda's moved on and is jiggling the door, nervously looking over her shoulder. The Admiral is stumping towards us from the far side of the main thoroughfare. I knock on the door. Nothing. I knock louder. Surely it's nearly opening time. Someone has to be inside. I knock three times, and eventually a staffer stands up from behind the counter. He's nobody I know. He's wearing a fucking suit and tie. Jesus, this must be one of Bradley's new recruits. He looks like a Jehovah's Witness, and, short of being a miniskirted beauty queen, is Bradley's wet dream of a proper employee. He stands there ramrod straight, stares piously at us but doesn't budge.

I gesticulate for him to let us in, but he doesn't move. Wanker.

'Fuck it, Dan,' says Rhoda. The Admiral is getting closer. 'We can't stand here the whole day. Let's just go.' I dart after her down a side corridor.

'In here,' Rhoda says, pointing towards the only open shop we've come across. I hesitate and check out the signage. It's the same blue logo as Vodacom's but the name is Last Call. What the fuck? Whichever marketing twat passed that should be fired.

We duck inside, staying out of sight of anyone who might be passing, and pretend to look at the phones. What I see in the cabinets clears my head of any other thought. 'Jeez. Look at this tech, Rhoda.'

'What about it?'

None of the equipment on display looks familiar. Most of the handsets – if that's what they are – are made of palm-sized blocks of multicoloured jelly. Wobbly, sticky-looking. Nice bright colours, but no evident buttons or screens. This must be the new biotech comms I read about in *Wired* – but I thought it was still in prototype. 'It's beautiful, that's what.'

Rhoda just makes a sound in her throat and glances out of the door.

We only notice the girl behind the counter now. She's pulling a gel earplug out of her ear and puts the phone on the counter. It sits there, morphing around its basic shape, shimmering green and blue; a constant play of clean, bright curves.

'Jesus, that is the coolest phone I've ever fucking seen,' I mutter.

'Hi. How can I help you?' The girl flicks her long black hair back over her ear. Her smile makes me warm inside. She reminds me so much of Lexy who used to work down at the music shop.

She was this goth girl I was scared of, but once I built up the courage to chat to her, she laughed at my stupid jokes as if she was nervous of talking to *me*. This girl has the same smile, and the same pale skin, almost blue-white. Her eyes are ice blue too and I can tell she isn't trying to make herself up like a goth. She just is. Even though she's wearing a shapeless blue Last Call T-shirt, she manages to look good.

'Yeah, can we borrow a charger?' Rhoda's voice breaks the spell. She holds out her phone, and I fish my own out. It will be a fucking miracle if it's just our phones' batteries that are at fault.

'Wow,' the shop girl says, turning Rhoda's phone over in her hand. 'This is great. It's so… heavy. Hard. How do you dock it?'

'Um,' I say, 'I think it works differently from the new ones.' I seriously want one of her jelly things.

'You know, I've seen a couple of these actually.' She shuffles through a drawer behind the counter. 'Other brown people brought them with them.'

'Other *what*?' barks Rhoda.

'Brown people,' the girl repeats, her face sweet and innocent. 'Like you two? I must admit, though, I haven't seen that many brown people in my life, and you are the darkest one I've seen,' she says to Rhoda.

'Fuck you, bitch. I don't need—'

'Wait, Rhoda. Chill. I'm sure she—'

The girl's face falls in what looks like genuine confusion and remorse. 'I seem to have caused you offence, ma'am. I didn't mean to. I sincerely apologise on behalf of my representative and of the Last Call group of companies.'

'Crazy fucking cow,' Rhoda mutters under her breath. The girl carries on scratching through the drawer.

'Here!' She lifts up a regular Nokia charger. 'I knew it was here somewhere. It was left behind by a brow…' she glances at

Rhoda who's still seething, but keeping herself under control '... uh, by a visitor. Will it work?'

'Thanks, it looks like it will,' I say. The girl takes another lump of jelly from a drawer and bends down behind the counter to plug in the charger. I connect Rhoda's phone to it. A few seconds later Rhoda's phone display lights up and the charging icon appears.

'Great, it's still working,' I say to Rhoda, but she's pacing around, poking her head out the shop door, scanning for the security guard.

'Do you know anything about this shutdown?' I ask the shop girl.

'What do you mean?'

'When do you think it will be lifted? When will the mall open?'

'Open?'

'Christ,' Rhoda mutters from the doorway, loud enough for me to hear. 'The only fucking shop that's open and there's a dumb bimbo working in it. What can't you fucking understand?' The shop girl either doesn't hear or doesn't appear to take offence. Her face remains angelic. Then Rhoda says louder, 'Dan, we need to go. I'm not staying here any longer than necessary.'

'We should charge our phones first. Besides, I don't think the mall's open yet.'

'The mall's always open,' the girl says. Okay, she's probably not the crunchiest cookie in the jar, but she's cute and friendly. Frankly, her attitude makes a nice change from Rhoda's.

'I need a cigarette,' Rhoda says as she stalks out. As she strides edgily up and down outside the shop window, I switch her phone on. The display must have got a bit screwed in the water. The time reads: <08:69>. But at least there's no countdown on the screen. I'm never going to use a stopwatch again, ever in my fucking li—

Beep beep.

The girl looks at the phone with interest. 'What does that do?'

'Rhoda, you've got a message,' I call.

She comes in and picks up the phone. 'Probably Zinzi. Wondering where the fuck I am.'

'You think they found the kid?'

No response. Rhoda's staring at the message.

'What is it?'

She holds out the phone to me.

<You can run but you can't hide>

'Oh shit.'

Beep beep.

Rhoda grabs the phone back from me and reads the message.

'Motherfucker!' Rhoda shoves the phone back to me.

<Unless you buy AllSports rainproof running gear. On special this month only!>

'What? Is it…'

'Spam. I once entered a competition for some bling gold sneakers at that poxy shop and they've been sending me spam ever since. First thing I do when I get out of here is go to the nearest AllSports and kick the fucking manager's arse. There's not an AllSports in here, is there?' she asks me.

'All what?' asks the girl, thinking Rhoda's asking her. 'I don't think I—'

Rhoda rolls her eyes. 'Give me a fucking break. I wasn't talking to you, dimbo.'

'Come on, Rhoda, she's just trying to help.' I turn to the girl. 'Sorry, I—'

Rhoda unplugs her phone and snatches it off the counter. 'That's enough for a top-up. I'm gone. I haven't got time to fuck around. You can fucking stay here and swap geek bullshit with your new girlfriend for all I care. While you're at it, you can tell her how you spent the last couple of days crying and pissing in your pants.'

She gives me the finger and storms out of the shop.

What the fuck? 'Rhoda, wait. Come on. Wait!'

She slows down at the end of the corridor.

'I don't know what just happened, but can't you just wait another few minutes? I'll plug my phone in and we can check what's—'

'No, Dan. It's done now. You're back where you belong. I've still got a whole lot of shit to deal with. I need to call Zinzi and find out about the kid. I need to... sort some other things out, okay. I don't belong here. I really, really need to go.'

'But I need to... I want to find out about the boy too. And I also want to know that you're... okay. Give me your number at least.'

She rolls her eyes and sighs as if she's doing me a favour. 'All right.'

She stands there as I run back to the Last Call shop to borrow a piece of paper and a pen. We swap numbers.

'Call me, okay? Before tonight. You don't need to sleep somewhere dodgy. I live close by.' I'll deal with that one if it happens. *Hi, Mom, sorry I've been gone for however many days, but here's Rhoda, my druggie runaway friend, and she needs to crash.* I'm such a fucking loser not to have my own place.

'Thanks,' she says, and disappears around the corner. I feel really weird.

When I get back to the phone shop, the girl's arranging gelphones in a cabinet. She catches me looking at her and smiles that stomach-warming smile again. Now that she's away from the counter I can tell she has a nice body, slim, but curvy under the black skinny jeans she's wearing. She bends down to remove the adaptor.

She's chained to the counter by her left ankle.

chapter 13

RHODA

Fuck Dan.

And fuck this shit.

If he wants to stay and get it on with that freaky racist white-trash goth, then let him. After all we've been through, if he wants to act like an arsehole and drop me like I'm a piece of bog roll he picked up on his shoe, that's his loss.

So good luck, Dan. And good fucking riddance.

Christ. I can't *wait* to get out of this hellhole and get as far away from here as possible. See the sky, for a start. Breathe some fresh air, maybe bum a ciggy (or two) off someone outside. But first things first. I need to get hold of Zinzi. She may be a fuck-up, but she's all I've got. And she's my cousin, so she'll have to help me. Mind you, God knows what she's thinking right now. I bloody hope she doesn't think I've kidnapped the kid or something. But I'll explain things to her. Let her scream in my ear for a bit first, get it out of her system. And anyway, I've covered for her before; call it payback. I was doing her a favour looking after the kid in the first place.

Still, my stomach squirms as I scroll down to her number and press <call>. The phone makes a beep-beep-beep sound and then a breathy woman's voice warbles in my ear: 'We're sorry, but the number you have requested is not viable, please try again later.'

I try the number again. This time there's nothing but static. Third time lucky: there's a second of dead air, then... something that sounds like breathing. Nasty, congested breathing, like a kid trying to breathe really quickly through a lungful of phlegm. I hang up and try once more. This time the screen goes dead, followed by:

<Network not found>

Bollocks.

I try the emergency number.

<Network not found>

Now what?

Should I try and get hold of Yellow Eyes and crew? Get them to start the ball rolling looking for the kid in the tunnels? Would they listen to me? What if they don't? What if that bastard Simon tries to get me arrested for grievous bodily harm?

Crap. I really don't know what to do.

But there's something niggling at me. As if I've forgotten or lost something.

Your mind! a maniacal voice screams in my head.

'Shut up!' I've spoken out loud, but the mall is empty, most of the windows on this level still shuttered, and there's no one to hear me.

Think, stupid!

Then I have it.

Zinzi's car!

Talk about being a complete retard. I rummage in my pockets, fingers fumbling over my lighter, a soggy packet of cherry Halls, the handle of the knife, but Zinzi's beaded chilli-pepper keyring isn't here. Come to think of it, I haven't seen it since all this shit started. Since I tripped and bumped into Yellow Eyes a million years ago.

But maybe Zinzi has a spare? Fat chance, knowing her, but it's worth a shot. So. Here's the plan. Find the car, hope against hope that she's hidden a spare key somewhere, and then worry about how the hell to get out of the parking lot without paying for the ticket, which seems to have gone the way of the keys.

Piece of cake.

There's just one small problem. Which level did I park on? And where the fuck's the car park entrance?

Shit. It's as if a cloud of fog has seeped into my memory banks.

Think back. Be logical about this.

What was the first thing the kid and I did when we arrived here? Christ. I can't even picture his face. He wasn't a bad kid, though. He'd asked me about my scar straight away when Zinzi introduced us. I liked that. Most people either stare and say nothing, or pretend it doesn't exist. And he'd seemed quite excited at the prospect of a late-night trip to the mall. Now I wish I'd let him look in the computer games store… which was one of the first shops we saw when we left the parking lot! And the door to the parking garage was one floor up from Bastard Dan's Only Books, wasn't it?

Easy.

I head back, pausing as I reach the phone shop. Should I go in? Tell Dan what I think about him? Why bother? I've got his cell number if I need him to back me up when the cops start asking questions. The door's shut, and I can't see any movement within. Dan's probably made his way out. Probably already heading home to his mum's sofa and a plate of beans on toast. Probably already convincing himself that everything that happened to us was just an interesting side effect of his fucking antidepressants.

I back away from the window, and bash into something squishy but unyielding. I spin around and

Fuck me.

I'm face to face with the fattest woman I've ever seen. She's draped in a huge floral dress but the giant rolls of blubber wobble noticeably beneath it, and lardy layers smother her feet, swallowing her shoes. Her eyes are almost entirely hidden beneath the pudding of flesh that coats her face. Her skin is so white and translucent I can see every blue vein that's fighting to breathe underneath the fatty covering.

It isn't *normal*. At that size she shouldn't be able to stand up, let alone walk.

I open my mouth to apologise for backing into her, but the words get stuck in my throat. She stinks. Probably even worse than I do. I still reek of that vile floral soap, but there are waves of fishy BO just blasting off her body. She smiles at me. Bad dental hygiene. Really bad. Her teeth are just black nubs in her mouth. But she's looking at me like I'm her new best friend or something.

If she speaks to me I think I might scream.

Heart thudding, legs feeling watery and insubstantial, I back away from her, and hare towards the escalators, taking the steps two at a time. I look around for the creepy guy in the admiral's costume, but he's nowhere around. The exit door at the far end is still tightly shuttered. Does that mean the door to the parking lot will also be locked? And what if I've got it wrong? What if the computer store isn't where I think it is?

I head down the left-hand aisle, praying that I'm heading in the right direction. I'm starting to panic again, and the air suddenly feels too thin to breathe.

Calm the fuck down.

Then I see it.

Thank fuck!

It's definitely the same store the kid had wanted to check out, although I don't remember it being called Time Suckers. Whoever came up with that name needs to be fired and quickly. The shutters are up, and as I get closer I can make out the outline of the Lara Croft cut-out in the window. But there's something... different about her. Lara Croft's knowing pout is gone in favour of a traumatised, shell-shocked expression, there's a bruise blooming over her left eye, and her long hair looks to be matted with blood. Her thighs in those too-short shorts are pitted with cellulite; her braless breasts sag noticeably. I can't imagine many schoolboys wanking over this version. Could it be some sort of clever in-joke?

What do you think?

The floor seems to tip as I'm hit with a wave of dizziness. I sink down onto my haunches and take a deep, shuddering breath. Count to ten.

What's happening to me? Am I finally losing it?

Just low blood sugar. Chill out.

There's the harsh scrape of metal as the shutters of the shop opposite start rising. They crank up by themselves, some invisible piece of machinery whirring into action. I can't see the window display yet, but it must be a chemist, some sort of Boots-style store: the sign above the window says Medi-Sin. Crap pun. The shutters roll up higher and it takes me a good few seconds to get my head around the bizarre tableau in the window. There's a mannequin on a hospital gurney bed, IV needles jammed into its arms, a bedpan resting on its knees. But it's anything but clinical. The sheet covering the body – I'm sure it's meant to be a body and not a patient, the thing's face is slack and empty and it appears to be missing one of its legs – is stained with yellow and rusty brown splotches. The bed is surrounded by spindly wheelchairs, filled with slumped mannequins, most of whom have their heads cocked at impossible angles. There's a sign painted in cheery script at the bottom of the window: 'You'll *die* for our schedule 5 and 6 specials!'

No. Fucking. Way.

The giggle bubbles up and explodes, but it's actually the sound you'd expect to hear in the padded rooms of a nuthouse.

Where you're headed, my internal voice says.

'No I'm not.'

Get yourself under control.

'I can't.'

You'd better, bitch.

'I have to get to the parking lot. Get out of here.'

So do it. The door's at the end of the aisle, retard.

'Fuck you.' But the voice is right. Can't be more than ten metres away.

I haul myself to my feet and trudge towards it, making a conscious effort not to look into the windows of any of the stores I pass.

Here's the deal. If it opens and the car is still there I'll bite the bullet, phone the folks, get out of this fucking country and get my life in order.

If it's shut…

Don't even go there.

I hesitate. I know it won't open. It won't be that easy.

I push it. It gives. And I'm through.

It's cold in here – I don't recall it being so chilly, and without the mall's piped muzak it's graveyard quiet. The ceiling is lower than I remember and there's the plop-plop-plop sound of water dripping from the roof. But where did I park Zinzi's Honda? Somewhere in the middle, wasn't it? The parking spaces closest to me are all empty, but there is a cluster of vehicles in the shadowy middle of the lot. The place is lit with piss-yellow lights, and there doesn't seem to be any natural light floating in from anywhere. I'm only partly reassured by the usual car park smell of petrol fumes, uriney concrete and rubber.

More worryingly, I can't see an exit ramp, or even any signs for one.

I don't like this.

I try and picture driving here, in a desperate attempt to get my bearings. But I'm fucked if I can remember that. All I could think about was topping up my stash, keeping the kid quiet, then getting home and flumming on the couch with a DVD.

There's probably an exit ramp at the other side of the lot, hidden behind the cars.

Something's not right, Rhoda.

'Shut up.'

I've got a baaaaaaaaaad feeling about this.

'Fuck you.'

I'm the only person in here, but that's probably because it's still really early, right? And I'm almost sure the Honda must be hidden among the other cars, most of which look to be huge American-style gas-guzzlers, although I can't tell the makes from here.

Why's it so quiet?

'It's early.'

It's not that early.

Ignoring the voice, I walk on. My legs seem to move by their own volition, and it's almost as if I'm watching what's happening from a huge distance away.

Rhoda: The Movie.

I pass a 4x4 with blacked-out windows. It's massive. Bigger than any gas-guzzler I've ever seen. It looks to be twice the size of a Hummer, and it doesn't seem to have any door handles, windscreen wipers or side mirrors. It's jammed between two concrete pillars, so tightly boxed in that it would be impossible to open the doors.

What the hell is this?

Still think everything's kosher?

I skirt around it and the sight of the car behind it makes me stop dead in my tracks. It's a three-wheel contraption with a silver glass roof, like one of those old-fashioned bubble cars. I can't make out a steering wheel in the cramped interior. Maybe there's some kind of designer car show on or something.

At least the rest of the vehicles around it look relatively normal. Square boxy cars, all reassuringly equipped with door handles, windscreen wipers and the usual shit you see on cars. I try and peer past them to spot the white shape of the Honda, but the cars in the rows behind are all dark, and the thick concrete pillars block my view.

Feet clopping over the concrete, the sound of my breathing loud in the silence, I head into the next row. Still no sign of the Honda. I edge past a low blood-red sports car and stop dead.

A limo is parked sideways, practically filling up the entire row. The windows are tinted, and it's got to be ten metres from bonnet to trunk. How could it have got in here? It doesn't make any sense. It's hemmed in by two pillars, and its tyres are just smooth rubber spheres with no hubcaps, like the kind of wheels a child would draw. I trace my fingers over the bodywork as I walk towards the front of it. The bonnet feels warm.

I can't do this any more. The strength leaves my legs instantly and I sink down so fast on my bum that I knock my spine painfully against the limo's bonnet and jar my tailbone. I rest my back against the smooth front of the limo, wrap my arms around my knees and bury my head into them. I close my eyes; I have never been this tired.

Get up.

'Can't.'

Get. Up. Now.

'Leave me alone.' I look up at the pillar directly in front of me. Someone's spray-painted 'Life's better with butter' in blood-red swooping letters.

You're not alone.

'Yes I am.'

Think, retard.

Maybe Schizo Voice has a point? I pull out my phone and scrabble in my pocket for the piece of paper with Dan's number on it. It's hidden between the folds of my wallet. I tap in the number.

Beep beep beep, then, <Network not found>

'Fuck!'

Try texting him.

Fingers shaking, I type in: <help plese rhoda> and press <send>.

I have to tell him what I've known deep down ever since we left the lifts. We haven't left the game at all. In fact—

It's only just started.

My phone beeps. Thank God! I click on the message.

<Sawuboner Rhoda mySweet. This is going to be so much remembertoshoptilyoudrop FUN!!!!! LOL NSFW!!!>

Oh fuck.

Told you!

Behind me, the limo starts rocking.

Get. Up. Now.

I can't move. Part of me just wants to sit here, on the damp concrete and let whatever's going to happen to me just happen.

There's a click and a clunk as one of the limo's doors opens behind me.

Get up! You have to get up now!

I heave myself to my hands and knees, using the bonnet for leverage. The door is open, all right, but no one has emerged.

Look!

There's an emergency-exit sign on the wall almost directly in front of me. The door below it is blocked by a triple row of cars, but it's way closer than the entrance I came through. I don't have any choice. I edge past the end of the limo's bonnet, trying to resist looking at the open door. But I can't help it.

A black pointed man's shoe emerges. It has a high stacked heel and the toe of it is filed to a sharp point. A sharp metal point, like a thick syringe.

Run!

And this time, I listen.

chapter 14

DANIEL

I stare at the chain around the shop girl's ankle, and back at her face. She's looking at me with a generic smile, like *Yeees*? I think of asking her outright, *Why are you chained to your counter?* but that would just sound stupid. I must be missing something.

Then I finally get it. Of course! She's into S&M and the whole slave thing. I've heard about this. They sometimes get so far into their act that it becomes their everyday behaviour. Come to think of it, it's like gaming in that way. I'm surprised her managers let her do this chain thing in the shop, though. It isn't very professional. But I suppose in a quiet shop like this, the manager probably shows his face once a week.

'Uh,' I say, playing along. 'Do you ever eat? Go out for a drink?' It'll make my shifts a bit less boring if I have someone cool to hang out with. Someone who doesn't work at that fucking shop.

'Yes. I get a moist break between shifts three and four, and a victual break between shifts seven and eight.'

Okaaay. 'Okay. Well. Are you working tomorrow?'

'What do you mean, sir?' She smooths her hair behind her ear again.

I smile, laugh, pretend I'm hip to her scene. Either she's seriously fucking with me, or she's flirting in some coy way I don't really understand.

I grab my phone and pocket it. 'Well,' I say, because I don't really know what the next move is, 'I hope to see you soon.'

'Please call again, sir,' she says. 'I'd love to assist you again.'

'Um. Sure. Thanks.'

I head towards Exit 9, thinking about what she said. Usually in the movies, the leading lady says something like that with a seductive arch of the eyebrow. Nothing from S&M phone girl. Deadpan. But I suppose that's her game. Fascinating.

The entrance is still closed. For fuck's sake, man. What the fuck's going on today? Was the Pope hijacked on his way to Only Books to buy Bibles? The President and his wives held hostage during a shopping spree? I look at the time on my phone. <09:92>. I should have asked the girl if they do repairs. That way I'll have an excuse to visit her again.

I wander past Charles Pratt jewellers to look at the watches. That's no help either; they're all set to different times. In the last window along an advertising poster catches my eye. What the fuck? At first I think it's just typical wish-fulfilment advertising: a white yacht lit with fairy lights, glamorous Mediterranean dusk scene in the background. But sprawled out on the deck in the foreground there's a skeletal woman in a bikini modelling Pratt's jewellery, her diamond-encrusted watch displayed on a stump instead of a wrist. The model has to be some famous fucking Paralympian or something, but still, fuck. Actually, the more I stare at the picture, the more nauseated I become, against-the-odds fucking sports hero or not. The woman is so thin her bikini bottoms don't even clamp around her skin-and-bone pelvis and I can see wispy pubic hair sticking out. This is another example of a marketing campaign missing the boat.

A waft of raw sewage passes me and I gag. What the... then I realise it's me. Though I washed my shirt when we got back here, I still reek. There's a stash of old promotional T-shirts at Only Books, so I head that way. More shops have opened their doors and I notice a few customers wandering about, trapped by the shutdown. They must be from the Highgate Mall apartments.

Typical of early-morning shoppers, most of them are freaks and losers. Fat, ugly, skinny, crippled, amputees or just plain weird. The type that don't go to parties. I know their type well from my shifts at the bookshop. Especially on weekends. While the casual staff are nursing their hangovers inside the shop at five to nine, trying to get ready for opening, there are always these early-morning zombies with nothing better to do with their lives than scratch on the doors to get in, mouthing: *I see you inside, come on, just open up, I need my newspaper or my porno mag or my computer manual or whatever the fuck else I need at this time of a Sunday morning.* Fucking freaks.

When I reach Only Books – Lonly Books, ha ha – the door's still closed and that dick in the suit is still standing like a corporate android at the counter. I knock and the guy revolves his head towards me then points to the sign on the door.

Monday–Thursday 8:88–8:88. Friday 8:88–8:88. Saturday, Sunday and Feast Days 8:88–8:88.

Ja, right. Helpful. Always a fucking clever graphic designer on every night shift.

I rattle the door again. *Come on, arsehole, I work here. I've worked here for three years and you've worked here for one minute so OPEN THE FUCKING DOOR.*

Nothing.

I kick the door and a siren starts up somewhere inside the shop. Good. Maybe Bradley the Fuckwit or whoever's the shift supervisor today will come out and open for me.

A few seconds later the door buzzes and springs open a crack. I stride past the android without acknowledging him and he greets my back with a chirpy, 'Good morning, sir! How may I help you?'

Christ, I'm surprised they haven't made this arsecreep Bradley's deputy instead of putting him on counter duty. I hurry through the shop and punch the code into the chromed numerical buttons of the poky lock on the back office door. Fuck. They must have changed the stupid combination again. I knock on the door and wait.

I knock again. Nothing. On a hunch, I push 1-2-3-4 and turn the knob. The door opens. One of these days, I swear, I'm going to 'borrow' Bradley's ATM card.

The back office is empty. Who the fuck buzzed me in, then? It's too quiet in here. Normally at opening time the computer servers are whirring away and I'll hear the music playing in the front, staffers chatting over their nicotine or caffeine pick-me-ups, guys slamming piles of new books for shelving onto trolleys. There's nobody here and nothing's happening. Maybe all the staff are stuck outside the mall waiting for the lockdown to lift. But then where did android boy come from? Did he sleep here?

I find the box of promo shirts under the tea sink and scratch through it for a large black T-shirt. I take out one with a cool-enough design on the front. Whatever, as long as it's clean and fits fine. I check to see that nobody's coming in, unlace my boots, strip off my jeans and after another quick glance, throw my underpants into the bin. The hot water flows russet brown for ages as I rinse the jeans; then finally they're clean. Ish. I wring them as dry as I can, then stroll across the office, arse out, to Bradley's desk. I feel kind of like when nobody was at home and my friend Karl and I went through his sister's underwear drawer.

Across from me, at Gilda's worktop, her chair lists tiredly to one side. The cushion has a permanent arse imprint the size of an elephant's on it. Gilda isn't svelte by any means, but the chair looks really badly injured. I hang my jeans over it, pressing them into the chair's exhausted sponge to blot the remaining water out.

There's a pile of coffee-table books on Bradley's desk. I sit down, the fabric rough against the bare skin of my butt. On top of the pile is a copy of the Taschen *Torture Book*. The cover shows a trussed woman with an iron snare cutting into her head; a man in a mask poking something into her thigh. I page through the book thinking about Rhoda. What the hell happened down there? Was it just a drug trip or something? Now, fresh-arsed and back at home, the fear and the filth of the last couple of days are disappearing like a bad dream. Paging past pictures of women being staked and people getting suspended over crocodile pits wrapped in meat, Chinese soldiers with bamboo plants growing under their fingernails, Arabs being waterboarded, I try to remember what I saw down there but I can't visualise it as clearly as these pictures. I can almost believe it was just a bad dream, my overactive imagination. Almost. But I look again at the lurid bruises on my thighs, feel the lingering nausea in my gut, smell the faint remnants of that shitty water on my skin.

I set the book aside. It's still dead quiet in the back office. I worry for a moment that the suit-geek will come in and see me, but somehow I don't really care. Josie, Bradley, Katrien, that'd be blind, but they aren't here. I fart deep into the meat of Bradley's chair and carry on reading.

The next design book is called *Fashion Today*. On the cover is a parody of a Calvin Klein underwear ad. Three women and two men. Two of the women are skeletal girls with hairy legs and saggy tits and pointy nipples, the other is enormous and sort of green; both men have massive, erect bulges in their pants, bloodshot eyes, flabby stomachs and hairy chests. One of the men is coronary purple like the admiral guard, the other pale white under the hairy tufts. The purple man is grabbing the woman in front of him by the crotch. It must be some sort of advertising or fine-art joke. I think of the stump-skeleton in the jeweller's shop.

By now my jeans have dried a bit and as I squeeze them some more I notice a flash of yellow movement in my peripheral vision. There again. It's Josie! God, I'll be relieved to see a familiar face. I whirl around before remembering I'm wearing nothing other than an Only Books T-shirt and my socks. I duck down behind the desk and struggle to pull my damp jeans on. But when I get up and scan the office, there's nobody here. Josie probably just ducked in to drop off her bag and went back out to the counter.

I lace up my boots and head out to the shop floor. There's still only the android guy at the front counter.

'Good morning, sir. How can I help you?' he spouts cultishly as I get within range.

'Hi, sorry, have you seen Josie? I need to ask her something.'

'Excuse me, sir?'

'Josie? Have. You. Seen. *Josie?*'

He turns to the screen in front of him. 'Let me look it up,' he says.

'Never mind. Any idea when the lockdown will be over?'

'Lockdown?'

'When the fucking mall will be open?' I know I should keep my temper in check, but *come on*. Is this guy a fucking retard?

'Open? The mall is always open, sir.'

'Then where… Oh, never mind.' I bite my tongue and leave the shop.

'You! Brown! Stop there!'

My fuck! Admiral Security has caught up with me. For a moment I think he can't be serious. I haven't done anything. But then he pulls a pistol out of a holster. My stunned mind takes a second to register the fucking gun is styled like an old pirate's flintlock pistol. I don't hang around to see if it works.

chapter 15

RHODA

It's the smell that brings me to my senses.

It's a familiar, comforting aroma that for some reason reminds me of childhood. For a second I struggle to place it – then it hits.

It's popcorn!

My stomach growls. I may be traumatised and definitely on the verge of cracking, but I'm also famished, and my empty stomach isn't going to let me forget it. My shins are throbbing from where I bashed them against the cars as I fled from the parking lot. Otherwise, far as I can tell, I'm pretty much intact.

Apart from your mind, that is.

Great. So I'm still schizo. Just what I need right now.

Look on the bright side, two minds are better than one.

'Fuck off.'

Temper, temper.

A windowless corridor painted a shiny industrial green stretches in front of me; the tiled floor littered with popcorn kernels, scrunched-up tissue paper and discarded soft-drink containers. It leads to a pair of double doors clad in some sort of padded velvety material, round windows at the top of each one.

Apart from the parking lot door behind me, it's the only way out of here.

Your choice.

'Not much of a choice.'

Seriously, right?

But there's no way I want to find out what kind of fucked-up freak those syringe shoes belong to.

I sprint towards the padded doors, feet crunching over stale popcorn. I slam my shoulder into the middle of the doors and slip through.

It's instantly clear where I am. I should have figured it out as soon as I smelled the popcorn. Because what goes with pop-corn?

The movies, of course!

I'm in a large carpeted lobby area, one side dominated by a big semi-circular ticket-and-refreshment counter. The place is deserted; the only sound the rapid-fire pop-pop-pop coming from the huge glass popcorn machine on the counter. My stom-ach growls again as I'm hit with the aroma of melted butter, flavoured salt and burnt sugar.

First things first. Find the exit and get the fuck out of Dodge.

'Easier said than done.'

To my left, a red Hollywood-style rope is strung between two large marble pillars. Behind them, a red carpet stretches towards double doors leading into the various cinemas. Enormous movie posters line the walls around the doors, but none of the films look familiar. One shows a lazily rendered cartoon tug boat, a maniacal grin splashed across its bow, and the title, *Boats That Talk!*, in bubble writing above it. The next one along shows Nicolas Cage and John Cusak posing in front of a massive explo-sion. They don't look like their usual action-hero selves. Nicolas Cage looks to have aged a good decade, a few wisps of hair combed over his otherwise bald pate, a paunch hanging over the top of his too-tight trousers. John Cusak's face is a mass of wrinkles and sun spots, and he's also sporting a beer belly. Both are grinning humourlessly, and their teeth look chipped and nicotine-stained. There's no title, but the strapline reads: 'This time... the world really *does* end.'

There are no obvious exits or even an entrance that I can see. The only doors seem to be the ones I came through and the pair leading to the theatres. So how the fuck do people get here? Not just through the parking lot, surely?

Your guess is as good as mine.

I head towards the refreshment counter, skirting a cardboard cut-out display in the centre of the room. A giant-sized Disney-esque prince and princess stand back to back, arms folded and scowling over their shoulders at each other, the title, *Cinderella 2: The Divorce*, written in colourful script above their heads.

Oh God. This place is fucked.

Like you don't even know, right?

The counter is deserted, and I'm tempted to climb across and grab a handful of the chocolate and sweets displayed behind it. Why not? Who's going to stop me? And maybe there's a phone – a landline – behind the counter.

And who you gonna call? Ghostbusters?

'Shut up!' I say out loud before I can stop myself.

A woman suddenly springs up from behind the counter, and I jump back, unable to stop the scream. 'Fuck!'

She grins at me brightly, but there's something forced and ric-tus-like about her smile. 'Hi!' she says. 'May I offer you a carton of GM puffs?'

Heart still thudding, I shake my head.

'How about a cup of Ice-o-Toxin or a SugarGas or you can get one of our combos, Ice-o-Toxin-and-GM-Puffs-plus-MSG-Drops-and—'

'*No!* I mean... no thanks.'

Confusion flits across her face. 'No GM puffs?'

'No thanks. Look, I—'

'No? Okay, then!' she says chirpily.

She vanishes behind the counter again, so swiftly that it takes me a couple of seconds to realise she's actually gone. I lean over and stare down at her back. She's curled into a foetal ball, her head between her knees.

'Hey!' I call.

She jumps up again, fixed grin back on her face. It's surreal – almost comical – like a ridiculous slapstick skit.

Maybe you should ask her if this is a cheese shop.

Not funny. Not even remotely.

What's wrong, Rhoda? Lost your sense of tumour?

Could I be imagining all this from inside an insane asylum somewhere? The real Rhoda locked in a padded cell? Listening to her mind unravel? Holding conversations with herself (maybe occasionally referring to herself in the third person) and babbling away like one of the nutters in *One Flew Over the Cuckoo's Nest*?

You'd be so lucky. Girl, Interrupted *is more your style.*

'GM puffs now?' The woman is still grinning at me brightly but the smile doesn't reach her eyes. They're focused on me, but there's something odd about them; they're as flat and lifeless as a doll's. Is she stoned? Pissed, maybe? She's giving me the hee-bies whatever the reason. The veins stand out in her arms and neck like thick worms and her skin is so white it's almost blue.

Morgue skin.

But there's no one else here and Christ knows I need help. I do my best to slap on a friendly smile. 'Hi!'

'Hi to you! Can I get you some GM puffs and an ultra-GI drink?'

'No. Look—'

'If you're not that peckish can I suggest one of our thinning options like maybe mini GM puffs and teeny SugarGas with—'

'No, you're not getting it—'

She clicks her fingers. 'How about some nachos?'

'No!' *Christ.* 'Look, have you got a phone I can use?'

She smiles at me brightly again, eyes still sinisterly vacant. 'A phone?'

'Yes. I need to call the police. There's been—'

'I can Oversize your order if you like!'

This is insane. I take a deep breath. 'Can you *please* just tell me where the exit is?'

She starts scratching at her head, and the paper cap she's wearing slips drunkenly over one eye. Her hair is shaved over her ear and a thick, barely healed scar snakes up from the back of her neck and around the top of her ear. Car accident?

Believe that if you want to.

'Sorry ma'am, could you repeat the request?' she says.

'The exit. How do I get the fu... how do I get out of here?'

'Out?'

It takes all my strength to resist punching her in the face.

Calm down. Try again.

'What time does this place open?'

'It is open, ma'am.'

'How do customers get here from the mall?'

'Can you repeat your request, ma'am?'

I slam my palm on the counter, and she jumps slightly. 'For fuck's sake! Where's the fucking exit?'

'Exit?'

'What are you, a fucking echo?'

The girl taps the name badge attached to her shirt. There's a bloody fingerprint on it. 'I'm Tracy.'

But the name badge reads: 'Doug'.

'Forget it.'

'Okay!'

She grins blankly and disappears behind the counter again.

Fuck.

Now what?

Back to the parking lot.

'No way,' I mutter under my breath.

You'd easily make it to the other side.

There's no way I'm doing that. Then something strikes me. Maybe there's an exit in one of the cinemas? Of course! A fire exit. There must be, surely?

Don't be so sure.

Ignoring the voice of doom, I head back towards the pillars. But as I approach, the double doors leading into the theatres start to edge open. I slip in behind the *Cinderella* display. There's a small cut-out space between the figures, and I have a perfect view.

Someone's emerging. It's a guy, way too skinny, dressed in filthy rags and with matted, ropy blonde dreadlocks that fall halfway down his back. He looks nervously around him, and creeps towards the large rubbish bin just outside the doors. He rummages in it, pulls out a cardboard container and a giant-sized slush cup, and shoves them into the plastic bag he's carrying. He's mumbling to himself and keeps darting his head around like an animal continually checking for predators. Unlike the robotic retard behind the refreshment counter he looks... alive. And judging from his wide eyes and trembling hands he's scared. The expression on his face mirrors exactly how I'm feeling. Bizarrely, this is reassuring.

I step out from behind the display.

'Hi!' I say, not knowing what else to start with. 'Can you help me?'

He looks up and our eyes lock. His mouth falls open, and I'm treated to the sight of mossy teeth. Tucking the plastic bag's handles into his belt, he slips back through the doors. They close behind him with a crump.

Should I follow?

No!

Ignoring the voice, I stalk towards the rope. Something clamps around my wrist, and swallowing the scream, I jump, whirl round and try and pull myself free. There's an old woman on her hands and knees next to me, gnarled fingers digging into my wrist.

'What the fuck? Let go!'

She looks up at me and grins, showing off a set of wooden teeth. 'Ticket please, dear!'

Fuck me. 'What?'

'Ticket please, dear!'

I try and pull out of her grip, but she's strong. Using my free hand, I grab her index finger and yank it back sharply, and she finally loosens her grasp. I must have hurt her quite badly, but she doesn't show any signs of pain. And holy shit... there's a metal cuff attached to her ankle, a chain leading from it to one of the pillars. How come I didn't see her before?

Probably curled up like the popcorn girl. Waiting for a customer.

The woman absentmindedly shakes her injured hand.

'Are you okay?' I ask.

'Me? I'm fine dear. Just perfect.' Her eyes are as vacant as the popcorn girl's. Maybe more so. Like the eyes on those mannequins that Dan and I had to climb over in the tunnels. 'Can I please see your ticket?'

'I don't have a ticket.'

'You can't go past the red ropes without a ticket, dear,' she says. 'Unless you are a Shopper, of course. Are you?'

What the fuck is she talking about? 'Please! I have to—'

'The ticket seller will happily sell you a ticket, dear.'

'I don't have any money.'

143

'Ticket, please!'

'I don't have a fucking ticket!'

Something flickers in her eyes – some sign of life – then, almost immediately, it dwindles again.

'What's going on here? Why are you chained up?'

'Chained, dear?'

Now I'm sure her expression just shifted. 'Help me!' I say to her. 'Please! I have to get out of here.'

'Ticket, please!'

Rhoda, let's just go. Let's go back to the car park. Take our chances. Get back to the phone shop. This situation is fucked.

I try pleading with the woman again. 'I really need some help.'

'May I see your ticket?'

That's it. I've had enough. The anger is starting to build and I welcome it. I've been scared for so long now that any other emotion is a relief. I step forward, and she scuttles in front of me, moving alarmingly quickly on her hands and knees.

Rhoda! Don't do anything stupid!

I stare straight at her. 'Okay. Now listen to me very closely, you fucked-up bitch. Are you going to let me pass, or am I going to have to fight my way through you?'

There's a part of me, a nasty cold part, that would relish this. I dig my hands in my pocket, fingers curling over the knife's handle.

Beating up old ladies, very nice.

The woman looks at me blankly, and then suddenly her mouth twists into a vicious snarl. I back away – I can't help it – but she doesn't approach.

That's it. Come on. Back to the parking lot. She's mad. Don't take any chances.

My phone beeps. Keeping the old woman in my sights, I quickly scan the message.

<Hiya Rhoda! Miss me I know u did LOL; / BTW you can

catch a flik if you think it will help (hint it wont) but don't forget you've got shoppingtodo stufftobuy peopletokill>

What is this shit? I step forward again.

'Are you going to let me pass? Last chance.'

The animal grimace is now gone from her face. She glances at the phone and nods. 'Of course. Go ahead, dear. Enjoy your movie.'

Holding my breath, I walk past her and climb over the red rope.

No! Go back!

'You won't like what you find,' the old woman says from behind me, her voice as flat and dead as her eyes.

'That'll make a fucking change, then.' I spit the words out.

If you do this, you're on your own.

'Good.'

I head towards the black doors, and, without looking back, push my way through and into a darkened corridor, lined with double doors.

I wait for the voice in my head to protest.

It doesn't. It's gone.

I'm not sure if I'm relieved or disappointed.

I head down the corridor, pushing against each door as I go. Each one is flanked by more of those warped movie posters. I pass an insanely grinning Sandra Bullock in *Schmaltz*, a smug Morgan Freeman in *Token Black President* and an ashen-faced Robert Pattinson in *Borderline Stalker*, but all of the doors seem to be locked. I can make out the faint traces of various movie soundtracks floating out from behind them: a scream here, an explosion there, a burst of canned laughter from behind another. There's only one left to try at the end of the corridor. Last chance. I push it tentatively, and it gives.

Thank Christ.

I'm hit with a blast of jaunty old-fashioned cartoon music,

and it takes several seconds for my eyes to adjust to the darkness. I'm in a small, intimate cinema, and I can make out the shadowy shapes of several rows of seats, but not much else. Doing my best to navigate by the light of the screen, I creep down the aisle along the wall, peering into the rows of empty chairs. There's no sign of the dreadlocked guy anywhere, and there's definitely no reassuring green glint of an emergency-exit sign. There are several metres of carpeted space in front of the screen, but no side doors, or even a middle aisle. Fuck. The voice was right.

I head to the front row. Where could Dreads have gone, though? Could he be hiding on the floor? I get down on my hands and knees and peer under the seats. I can't see much in the darkness, just the blackened shapes of empty popcorn cartons, spilled soft drinks and balled-up tissues, but there's definitely no sign of a person.

'Hello?' I have to shout over the soundtrack.

Nothing.

'Hello! Anyone here?'

I'm alone.

Fuck it. I slump down on one of the seats in the front row, and stare at the screen.

The film's familiar. A baby deer scampers into shot, gambolling through autumn leaves with a rabbit. *Bambi*. I remember going to see it years ago with Dad, and I'm suddenly hit with homesickness so acute that it makes me gasp out loud. My chest hitches, and my eyes start filling with tears. If I snap now, I'm not sure I'll be able to pull myself together, and I concentrate on the animals on screen in an attempt to get myself under control. I don't remember them being quite so realistically rendered. The rabbit – Thumper – doesn't seem to have that cheeky glint in his eye, and his fur looks matted and covered in burrs and dirt. And none of the cartoon characters are talking. They don't seem to be doing much of anything at all: basically just foraging around in the cartoon forest, nibbling at leaves. It's actually quite relaxing watching them. Soothing, almost.

My eyes are getting heavy. I know I shouldn't. Stupid to fall asleep. Insane to put myself at such a disadvantage. But fuck it. What's the worst that can happen?

I mean, how could things possibly get any worse?

The screams jolt me awake.

I leap up out of the chair, heart thudding, and almost trip over my feet in my haste to get away. Then it dawns that the screams are blasting out of the speakers – part of the movie's soundtrack. And the scream isn't human. It's the sound of an animal in terrible pain.

On screen, Bambi's mother is in the process of being gutted, faceless hunters with gruff voices slicing into her side with curved hunting knives, unpeeling her skin and pulling out her intestines. The fact that the scene is animated somehow makes the gore and horror even more visceral and revolting. Christ. I sink back in my chair. On screen the little fawn limps away and collapses under a bush. There's a shot of autumnal leaves blowing from branches, signifying the passing of the seasons, and snowflakes drift down, falling onto Bambi's body. He stares glassily into shot. His ribs stick out and it's pretty clear that he's in the process of freezing to death.

I can't watch this any more. This place, this world, this reality – whatever the fuck it is – is twisted. Seriously twisted. Sick. I'll have to do what the schizoid voice suggested, head back into the parking lot, and make a run for it to the other door. Find Dan; warn him that we're in some serious shit here.

Oh, fuck.

The soundtrack's way too loud, the orchestra blaring out sad Bambi's-about-to-die-music, but I'm pretty sure I just heard the sound of popcorn crunching behind me.

I keep as still as I can, barely daring to breathe.

Then I hear it again. The unmistakeable crackle as someone chomps down on a mouthful of popcorn.

I really, really don't want to turn around.

But I have no choice.

I get to my feet and slowly turn to face the back of the cinema. There's the silhouetted shape of someone (some*thing*) three rows away from me. I can't make out its facial features, but there's something wrong with its head. It looks too large for its body: a bulbous, inhuman shape, stuck onto a too-thin neck. The thing's silhouette looks horribly like the sign on that toilet door in the Barbie-pink bathroom.

Without taking my eyes from it I back away, stumbling as the floor slopes downwards, until my back's against the screen. I catch a blur of movement to my right. The carpet is shifting upwards, and a square panel cut into the floor lifts up and drops down with a clunk, revealing a dark fathomless hole. A hand appears, followed by a head. In the flickering light of the screen I can make out a shock of filthy dreadlocks. Our eyes meet, and he frantically waves at me to approach.

Fuck! What to do?

My phone beeps. Numbly, automatically, I fumble in my pocket and pull it out.

The message reads: <hey! Rhoda me old mate. No time for a brown study when there's shopping todo. Come oooon you know you want to check out those specials!!! LOL!!!!!!!>

The thing with the bulbous, misshapen head gets to its feet and starts edging along the row towards the aisle. The sound-track swells to a crescendo. The hobo guy extends his hand towards me.

Fuck it.

I reach down and take it.

chapter 16

DANIEL

There's a limp bang like a wet firework behind me and the window of the travel shop next to me shears into a spider web. Holy shit, this guy isn't fucking around.

I sprint to Entrance 1, turning a corner at every opportunity so that the Admiral can't get a straight shot at me. Motherfucker. I'm being *shot* at!

Come on! Entrance 1 is still blocked. They must have forgotten to lift the security gate because all the shops are open and the lockdown's plainly over. Shit. I'd better try Entrance 7. I look over my shoulder, and the Admiral's just rounding the last corner. Though he looks like he's about to keel over any minute, he's managing to keep up. He stops to tamp and load his pistol with another ball and that gives me time to race down another side-aisle.

I'm nowhere near Entrance 7 and somehow the Admiral has managed to gain on me. I may not make it in time, and what if it's locked? I duck into an ATM cubby, shielding myself behind the bank machine's smoked-glass barrier, and look around to orient myself.

I'm just across the aisle from the phone shop. Will I make it?

I have to try. I count to three and dart out into the open. I skid in and shelter in a corner of the shop, my ragged breathing breaking the peaceful quiet.

'Good morning, sir. How can I help you?' says the shop girl, completely unfazed by my panicked entrance.

'Hi. Um.' Fuck. What do I say?

I don't have long to think because now the Admiral's filling the shop's doorway, gasping hard to get his breath back. He raises the flintlock at me again, lowers it, then strides into the shop heady with power. Oh God. This is it.

'I don't know what I've done,' I blabber, appealing to the girl for help. 'I don't know what he wants. But he's trying to kill me.'

'Don't worry, I'll speak to him,' she tells me. 'Ensign. I know this is an unregistered brown, but he is interviewing today and I am his sponsor.'

The Admiral looks at me with a florid glare. 'Well, why didn't you say so, brown? Are you karking retarded? I've been up and down this karking...' He tails off as if he realises he's wasting his time talking to an idiot. 'Customer Care Officer,' he says to the girl, 'you're its sponsor. Ensure it's registered by tomorrow.'

'Yes, Ensign.'

'This brown has caused me enough trouble for one day. I'm warning you. If it isn't registered by the end of shifts, I will hold you responsible.'

'Yes, Ensign.'

With that the Admiral – the Ensign, actually – stumps out of the shop.

'Oh, thank you. God. I thought...' I say.

'If I might ask, sir, what were you doing loitering unregistered? Surely you know—'

'I know nothing. I don't know what the fuck's going on here!'

'I have a victual break coming up in' ...she looks at her gelphone '...three moments. Would you like to devour with me?'

Huh? 'Um, okay, that sounds good. That'll be nice.'

'Good, sir. I'll try to assist you.'

I gesture towards the door. 'Should I just, uh…?'

'Yes, please, sir.'

I move to the doorway and stand awkwardly as she smiles a blank smile through me, ready to welcome any other customer who might come through the door. She poses there like a mannequin, just like the smarmy android guy at the bookshop, I realise, only hotter.

The gelphone in the shop girl's hand glows a cycle of teal and aqua, throbs and bulges for a moment. 'Here it is, the breaktime code from Management,' she says. She taps the code onto her chain's anklet and it slides open. She steps out of it and bundles the chain and the anklet neatly behind the counter. Simultaneously a dorky-looking, skinny guy in an oversized blue Last Call T-shirt stands up like a meerkat behind the counter. My fuck, surely this guy hasn't been crouching behind there the whole time? If his shift is just beginning, when and where did he come in?

His *shift*? His fucking *shift*? Here's a girl who chains herself to the shop counter by the ankle and a guy who hides behind the counter all morning and I'm standing here worrying about when their *shifts* start.

'God,' starts the girl as she guides me in her direction then falls into step beside me. I follow numbly. 'It's been a shift. Nobody in at all and then suddenly there's five at a time, and there's only one CCO per shift because it's Slaughterday and the Management doesn't expect it to be busy. But they always do this, crowd in in groups, and Management sits in its vaycay tower without realising what actually goes on during Dead Shifts.' The talk flows like water out of a bath, until it empties and slows. After hours of hyperpoliteness, her relief is palpable. All that 'How can I help you?', 'The mall's open, sir' must be exhausting.

'Anyway, sorry, I'm Colt,' she says, and stops and turns to face me. She smooths her jet hair over her neck. Her knuckles come back with a smear of blood that she absentmindedly rubs on the hip of her jeans.

Wait a minute... *what*?

Not quite concealed under the hair is a vicious gash on her white neck, a gaping slash from her ear to her jawline. She's tried to cover it with powder, but the thing is still moist with fresh blood, and all the powder does is gather in dark clumps along the edge of the wound.

My God, I can't drag my eyes away from it but then she smooths the hair over the wound again and carries on walking. 'I've got plenty of tokens for McColon's if you don't mind going there,' she starts up again. 'They've got a promotion going with Last Call and they wanted us to devour there for a whole month and by the second week, I would rather go without victuals. But now it's okay. You know, you can do McColon's a few times a week, but not every day, don't you think?'

She grabs my arm and pulls me out of the way of an oncoming man. Another shopper who looks like he should be in hospital, his hands and face swathed in putrid, raggy bandages. 'You don't want to have bodily contact with Mr Boils, rich or not. Tomas did, and he went to Wards and he never came back.' Her touch is icy on the surface of my skin. On her fingers I feel the remnant of sticky blood from her neck.

'Here we are.' The sign says 'McColon's' but it's written in the same familiar swooping yellow font as McDonald's.

'Clog your intestines with crap so that you don't get hungry,' declares a poster at the door. 'Just 10.99.' The kind-of-familiar clown looks fat and complacent; peaceful, not as threatening as the usual one. The Thieving Kid in the corner of the picture is emaciated and wears street-kid rags and his usual eye-mask. 'I'm hungry, that's why I do crime,' he says in a small speech bubble.

'Micro burgers, just 0.99.' Another sign advertises 'Open 38/8'.

My phone beeps. It's probably Rhoda and the thrill of relief at the thought surprises me. I thumb open the message.

<homesick dannyboy? gotityet, retard? this is not your home, motherfucker. sooner you realise youre never going home again sooner you can killthemall>

Nausea. Disappointment.

Holy. Fuck.

Where the fuck am I?

Then it hits.

Fuck.

Of course.

I'm playing a game. I'm still playing the game! Just like in the lift. Just like in the corridors. I've just reached the next level.

An assortment of freaks crowds around the counter. Missing limbs, extra limbs; scabies, scabs and scurvy; pungent breath and malicious body odour; a medieval collection of mechanical aids: archaic leg braces, corrective shoes, hearing aids, slings, crutches, unwieldy wheelchairs ferrying obese corpses, bandages on arms and feet that needed changing last month; everyone jostling impatiently, in no semblance of order. One or two of the freaks look at me and give me a pitying smile. I huddle in the sanctuary of space to the side of the entrance, praying nobody will touch me.

Colt looks back over her shoulder. 'What do you want?' she calls. The menu above the counter has the familiar lettering, but the names are different. Big Number Two, Cheeselike, Oil and Salt Starchsticks.

Come on. Snap out of it. You have to say something. You're playing a game. They're waiting for input. 'You choose,' I call back.

Colt comes back in a minute with a tray laden with enormous cups and packages. She finds us a table and we sit. 'I didn't know if you wanted Supersized or Oversized so I got you Over. Hope that's okay? I'm so sick of fattening, so I got Super today. And plus my teeth are sore. I haven't had all my replacements yet.' She sucks at her massive fizzy drink. 'Ouch. There's a rumour going around that SugarGas drinks make your birth-teeth sore.'

I heft my two-litre cup off the tray and take a sip. It's like pure Coke syrup, as if they have forgotten to add any water, but put in too much gas. It bubbles stickily down my throat. I watch as a heavy drip slicks thickly down the side of Colt's slightly smaller cup.

She's making conversation. She's my ally. I'm going to need help. I'm going to need information. I've got to say something. 'From what I understand, that's true.'

'Oh well, it's my fault really. I should have got my replacements by now but I've just been lazy.'

Mindful of my strategy of keeping Colt on my side, I mirror her as we unwrap our burgers. She has what looks like a double Big Mac, while mine is about twice as wide and twice as high. It's stacked in four layers. The bun looks okay, but the four plate-sized burger patties are bleeding. Not just seeping red juice, they're bleeding. The thick, warm blood spurts out in a rhythm like it has a beating heart. The patties are dolloped with ladlefuls of mayonnaise that smells rotten, the reek of sulphurous eggs mixed with the fizz of off milk. I lean closer to the thing and lift the top portion of bun and a jet of blood shoots into my eye.

'Ha ha,' trills Colt. 'Watch out! Eating disorder!' as if this is an everyday mishap like spraying a shook-up can of Coke up your nose. 'I got the Fat Big Number Two for you. I hope you don't mind. I don't know if you're fattening or not. It's always awkward to assume, isn't it?'

Info bite number one: What the fuck is 'fattening'? 'Do, are a lot of people fattening here?' I ask, putting the burger down and wiping my hands on my jeans. I'm hungry. I don't know when I last ate. But I can't imagine putting that flesh in my mouth. I go for a chip. It's okay, a bit salty; I grab a handful more.

'Kark, everyone. Either that or Starving-and-Amputating. When you look like me, there's so much pressure to look like the magazines and things. If you don't get admitted to Wards at least once a month, it's like there's something wrong with you. I try, really, but sometimes I just stop caring. And I've got used to Management too.' She stops and takes a huge bite from her burger; blood dribbles out of her mouth and stains the translucent skin on her neck.

Management. Key protagonist. I need to gather as much intel about them as possible. 'What do you mean?'

She chews for a while, then answers with her mouth half full. 'They can be nasty. You must know by now. Let me see…' She takes her gelphone out of her pocket and scrolls through some messages. 'Read these signals.' She hands me the phone.

I take the lump of gel from her hand, and her icy fingers brush mine, then she sits back and tucks into her meal. I have a moment alone with her phone. I can see a phone like this is going to be essential inventory; I'd better learn how to use it. As she passes it over, the thing moulds itself to my hand. It's dry to the touch and settles with a matt finish into my hand, like a taut mass of muscle suddenly relaxing to my touch. Like I'm holding a living heart. The teals and blues shimmer across it, counterpointed by more ice colours in the depths of the gel. Projected a micron above the surface is a text message in slashing red and orange.

<Colt, you skinnybitch. Time to fatten. You salarysiphon look ugly and spoil our decor. Honestly, do something about it. You could look better>

<Do you hear that laughter, Colt? It's your Colleagues behind-your back. It's your karking mother, bitch. And your daddy's crying because you wont fatten. Want aloneforever?>

155

I don't want to read more. I hand the phone back to Colt and open my mouth to say something sympathetic but my phone beeps. I open it under the table, ashamed of my plastic piece of shit. A few of the cuts on my hands are bleeding again. I think of Rhoda, who seems so far, so long away. It would be nice if the message was from her, but I know it's not.

<Dan-i-el! Think we forgot you? Gettajob gettalife brown. There's only one way>

'Management can be bungholes, can't they?' says Colt. I ignore the fact that she seems to know who my message – my 'signal' in her terms – is from and what it says. Maybe one of her skills is prescience or telepathy. I'll find out later in the game. I must just be on the lookout for more clues.

'How would I get a job here?' I ask instead. That seems to be the next stage. Even if it's a dead end, I'm sure I'll learn more about the setup here if I just follow the obvious clues for now. And stick with Colt.

'Where would you want to work?'

'The bookshop would be okay, I suppose.'

'They only take people who read books. Do you read books?'

'Yes.'

'Do you have retail experience?' I nod. 'Then all you need to do is interview with Management. I'm sure you'd get the job. Not so many people around here have much experience. Management likes hiring browns. I think they – uh, you – are harder workers.'

I'm figuring this out, I think. 'We work hard because there's no other choice. We only come... here if we're desperate.' Wherever 'here' is. That's what I can't figure out yet. How I got dumped here. Or why. It will probably become clearer as the game progresses.

She smiles, and some colour appears in her icy skin. 'Something like that.' She thinks for a moment while she sucks her syrup and rifles through the shoebox of starchsticks. 'I wish I could work at the bookshop. I'm sure they're more tolerant there. I bet the Management Reps wouldn't go on about my weight all the time. I bet they worry more about ideas and character than what people look like.' She averts her eyes as she sucks more out of her cup.

'Well, I think you look great.'

'You would say that,' she snorts. 'I look like a karking brown.' She's not smiling. Fuck, I'm going to lose her. We sit in uneasy silence for a moment while members of a grotesque family heave themselves into a booth with heavy trays.

'No offence,' she follows up. 'I need to go now. My shift starts in three moments.'

'Thanks for the lunch.' I stay sitting. I'm not sure how to play it next. I can't tell if she's brushing me off, or if she wants me to walk with her. If I play it wrong, I'm going to lose the only ally I have.

Colt notices my indecision. 'Please walk back with me. I get a shuddering spasm from hearing fresh browns talk. When they stay, they start talking normally so quickly.' She grabs my hand and leads me through the stifling, malodorous crowd. When we're outside McColon's she notices that the blood from my cuts has spread over her translucent skin. She wipes it calmly onto her jeans.

'I didn't want to pry, but how did you get these cuts?'

'Oh, I broke a mirror.' How long ago was that? It feels like a dream. I think of Rhoda. I have no idea when now is. 'Do you mind if I ask about your neck?'

'What about… Oh,' Colt smiles. 'You browns are so funny. You're like you were born in Dispatch.' She walks on, then realises I'm waiting for an answer. 'This is my hole, of course. We have penetration every second Moneyday, so it doesn't really ever have time to heal. But at Last Call, the Management Reps supply us with sterile wipes after penetration, so it doesn't hurt so much. Of course, a lot of CCOs were lost in Wards before Last Call felt moved to change policy.'

'I've got to go now,' she says as I follow her into the shop. 'Come back after Glut Shift and I'll help you prepare for your interview.' Her colleague is gooddaying me from behind the counter but I ignore him. Colt's already behind the counter with the dorky guy, uncoiling her chain, about to click the manacle around her ankle. 'Oh,' she says, and detaches a piece of gel from her phone. 'Here are some tokens for apparel. You want to look catalogue for your interview.'

'Oh, thanks.' I take the gel, having no idea what to do with it. 'Where can I use it?'

Colt laughs. 'You're acting brown again. You do it really well. I can't tell if you're just karking with me or not.' Then she says slowly, as if to an idiot child, 'They're apparel tokens. They're. For. Apparel.' That smile again, then she bends over and clicks in.

'Thank you for calling, sir. Please come again soon,' she says to me.

She's fucking with me, surely.

chapter 17

RHODA

Oh fucking hell.

This was a really, *really* stupid idea.

I'm following Hobo Dreadlock Guy through some sort of stinking crawlspace and there's not even enough headroom in here to stand upright. We're forced to creep along on our hands and knees and the torch he's using to light our way is doing bugger-all to penetrate the darkness. My back is slick with sweat and rivulets of perspiration are trickling down from my scalp and stinging my eyes. And Christ, the smell! The air in the narrow concrete space is thick with the stench of sweat, diesel oil and shit, and although I'm doing my best to breathe through my mouth, it still keeps making me gag. I'd have turned back ages ago if it wasn't for the thought of that thing with the bulbous head waiting for me back in the cinema. I'm a hair's breadth away from a full-on claustrophobic meltdown, and let's face it, absolutely no one knows I'm down here. This guy could easily be some deranged rapist lunatic and it's quite possible that I could disappear down here and no one would ever find out.

He stops suddenly and I almost bash into his back. He's

scrabbling at the wall in front of him, but I can't see exactly what he's doing.

'Where are we?' I ask again, trying to keep the panic out of my voice.

He hasn't spoken since we set off. He reverses a couple of paces and I have to scramble backwards to avoid getting a mouthful of boot. He's removing a metal grate covering a square hole in front of him, and he stashes it to one side. Anaemic light floats towards me from the opening, and a phenomenally power-ful stench hits me like a fist. Fuck me; it's horrendous. It's a mixture of shit, the ammonia reek of urine and something else: a feral animal smell that makes my stomach plummet.

Without looking back to see if I'm going to follow him, he pulls his body head-first through the opening, his feet finally disappearing into the space beyond.

I really, really don't want to go down there.

But if he was going to attack me, he would have done so already, wouldn't he? Fuck it. I've come this far, I may as well go the whole hog.

Doing my best to swallow the burning ball of bile in my throat, I twist my body around in the tight space. There's no way I'm going head-first and risk adding a concussion to the list of how unbelievably fucked up my life is right now. Wriggling on my belly, I squeeze myself through feet first. There's only a drop of one and a half metres or so, and when I land I have to blink sev-eral times for my eyes to adjust to the light. Bloody hell. The smell is now almost overpowering. I pull the edge of my T-shirt up over my mouth and nose, but it doesn't really help. I'm in an area that looks to be ten metres square or so; it's hard to tell exactly, as it's strewn with junk. There are several smoky oil lamps dotted around the space, and the ceiling is low, extending just half a metre above my head. In the background I can make out a mechanical hum coming from somewhere beyond the room's walls, but there's also a disturbing mewling sound that I'm almost certain is coming from in here. Rats?

Thank fuck for the knife. I slip my hand in my pocket and grip the handle, keeping my finger poised over the switchblade button.

The guy waves me forward. I almost stumble over a covered bucket that sloshes when I bash into it, but thankfully doesn't tip over (I'm pretty sure this accounts for the stink of shit), and in the dim light I make out a broken glittery high-heel shoe, a mannequin's headless torso, a square packing crate draped with a flowery sheet, and in the corner of the room, a mouldy mattress covered with a lumpen pile of rags.

Oh Christ. As far as I can tell there's no other exit apart from the way we came in, and Dreadlock Hobo Guy is between me and my only way out. I tense my body just in case he decides to try anything. But it doesn't look as if violence is on his mind. He pulls a three-legged wooden chair out from under a pile of coat hangers, wipes the dust off the seat with his hand and motions for me to sit down. Worst-case scenario, I can always use it as a weapon if anything happens to the knife.

Dreadlock Guy scuttles past me and crouches down on the mattress. I start to relax a little now that he's not between me and the entrance. For a second we just stare at each other. It's impossible to tell how old he is. His face is unlined, but when he yawns I can see that several of his mossy teeth are missing, causing his cheeks to cave in and no doubt adding a good twenty years to his age.

Now what?

I clear my throat. 'Hi,' I say. 'My name's *oh shit*!'

The bundle of rags next to him is moving – and I almost topple off my chair as I jump back in shock. The bundle sits up and stretches. There's someone else in here. The stench of dried shit rolls off its body and grubby hands push hanks of matted hair away from its face. I lean closer to get a better look. It appears to be a woman. Hard to tell as her face is filthy, but the bone structure was probably once delicate. She stares at me glassily, then, covering her mouth in a peculiarly ladylike gesture, she yawns.

Dreadlock Hobo Guy hands the plastic bag to the woman and she snatches it and greedily roots through it. She grabs a handful of popcorn and stuffs it into her mouth, then takes a slurp of bright green melted slush to wash it down. It dribbles over her chin.

Both of them are acting as if they've forgotten I'm here. I bloody hope they're capable of holding a conversation.

'Hi,' I try again. 'I'm Rhoda.'

The man looks up at me, tucks his dreads behind his ears, and clears his throat. 'I'm Ben,' he says. 'And this is Palesa.' Whoa! I wasn't expecting that. His voice is posh, English South African. The kind of voice you'd expect to hear from a rich businessman or professor, not from a hobo who clearly hasn't had a bath in a hundred years or whatever. Still, I'm relieved he sounds relatively... normal. Or what goes for normal in this place at any rate.

'Nice to meet you,' I say. Surreal thing to say in the circumstances, but I've got so many questions I don't know where to start. 'You're not like the other people I've seen here.' Images of the Elephant Man thing and the grossly fat woman pop into my head and I shudder.

'No,' he says matter-of-factly.

'Where are you from?' I ask.

He waves his hand vaguely in the air.

'Seriously, where are you from? Here? Joburg?'

He glances at the woman as if to ask her opinion on whether or not to answer. She shrugs. 'Bryanston,' he says.

Wherever the fuck that is. 'Right,' I say. 'Can you tell me... what is this place?'

The woman – Palesa – barks out a short, sharp laugh. 'Sisi, that is not a question you want to ask.' Her voice is deep and rich – a singer's voice.

'Maybe so. But either I'm locked up in a madhouse somewhere and I'm imagining all of this, or I'm dead, and this is hell – no offence – or I've somehow ended up in another dimension like in the *X-Files* or some shit.'

Palesa drops her head and continues to munch through the bag of popcorn. 'You must believe what you want.'

'But what do you believe?'

She shrugs. My stomach groans, and Palesa looks up at me. 'You hungry?' she says.

'Yes.'

'Make a bowl with your hands.'

I lean forward and cup my palms together and she pours a handful of popcorn into them. It smells delicious. I shove as much as I can into my mouth. It's stale, but salty, and I munch through it so fast I almost choke.

'How did you get here?' I ask when I've swallowed my last mouthful. 'Through the back corridors?'

'The back corridors?' Palesa repeats.

'You know... from the...' what to call it? 'The other mall?'

Ben laughs humourlessly. 'I like that! The other mall. Yes. I suppose you could say that.'

'How long have you been here?' I ask.

He shrugs. 'We don't like to count. Palesa's been here longer than I have.'

The woman nods. He smiles at her and takes her hand. Her fingers loop through his. Then, the front of her raggedy shirt starts rippling, and a tiny hairy face peeks out of the collar. It's a baby rat. She picks it up and cradles it, bringing its face to her mouth and kissing its nose. Ugh. I try to keep my expression neutral. She coos at it and Ben looks on fondly like a proud parent. I'm pretty sure I'm not in danger here, but fuck, they're giving me the creeps.

The woman suddenly jabs her head forward and peers straight at the left-hand side of my face. She furrows her brow as if she's confused about something. 'What is that on your face?'

'It's a scar.'

'Oh. You know,' she says, wrapping the rat's tail tightly around her finger. It squeaks in distress. 'You might fit in here quite nicely.'

'What do you mean by that?'

'She doesn't mean anything,' Ben says, too quickly.

'Are you saying that I'm as freaky as those people out there?'

Palesa shrugs. But she's one to talk. I may be dirty, scarred and barely holding onto my sanity, but at least I don't live in a toilet. 'And what are they?' I say to Ben. 'The people out there? You know, the woman working at the popcorn stand… she was…'

'Empty?' Palesa finishes for me.

'Exactly. Well? Who or what are they?'

'We don't know,' Ben says, but there's something about the way his eyes slide away from mine when he says this that makes me not believe him. I decide not to push it. Just yet.

'Are there others like you?' I ask.

'Other browns?' he says.

'What's with this fucking "browns" shit?'

Palesa tuts. 'Please, Rhoda, we do not like bad language here.'

Bizarre in the circumstances, but what can I say to that? Fuck you? I'm tempted, but I need them far more than they need me. 'Sorry. Are there others?' I swallow my disgust. 'Other… browns?'

'There were.'

'And?'

'We don't like to talk about them.'

'Why not? Are they dead?'

'You can say that.'

Just great. 'So. How do I get out of here? How can I get back?'

Palesa shakes her head. 'You can't.'

'What do you mean?'

'You have three choices. You can live like us. Underground. Or you can conform, and apply for a position…'

'Huh? A position as what?'

They both look at me as if I've said something monumentally stupid.

'You mean work in this place?'

'Where else?' Palesa says.

'What's outside it?'

'There's nothing outside.'

'There must be *something* outside.'

'How can there be?' Ben smiles, showing off his appalling gums again. 'There are no exits.'

This conversation isn't exactly going the way I was hoping. 'You said there were three choices. What's the other one?'

Palesa shrugs. 'You can become a Shopper. If you are chosen.'

I sit back, thinking about the phone messages. 'And what does a Shopper do?'

Ben chuckles. 'Shops.'

'Yes!' Palesa says. 'Till you drop!'

Oh fucking hell. I've had enough of this pseudo-cryptic bull-shit. 'Who's running this place?' I snap.

Palesa looks straight at me. 'Why, God of course.'

'Right.' She's clearly insane. I turn to Ben. 'Listen. You have to help me. There's someone else with me.' They look at each other, but I can't read their expressions. 'A… friend. We came here together. I need to warn him. He doesn't know he's in danger.'

'If he conforms he won't be in danger,' Palesa says, smiling for the first time. Her teeth don't look too bad. It's possible that under the grime she's maybe mid-twenties – not much older than I am.

My phone beeps and vibrates in my pocket, but Ben and Palesa don't seem to be bothered by it. I haul it out of my pocket and click onto the message. It's from 'Your Service Provider'. Yeah, right. I scan the message: <konnichiwa sisi help me, obi-rhoda-kenobi you're my only hope. Cum check out the three-for-one-deal at lonly books asap okay? xxxxx>

Fuck. I wave the phone in Ben and Palesa's direction. 'I keep getting these crazy messages. Like I'm in some sort of a game. Is that what it is?'

Palesa shrugs. 'Or a job interview.'

Is that a crazy attempt at humour? 'Who's doing this?' I say to Ben, who I suspect is the saner of the two. 'Who's fu— messing with us? Do you know?'

'The Management, of course,' he says.

Christ. Maybe he's as crazy as she is, after all. 'And can I go and see them? This Management?'

Palesa shakes her head.

'If you've made it this far, you're doing well,' Ben says. 'But you'll have to make a decision soon. Work, shop or hide.'

'I'm not going to apply for any fucking job in this madhouse,' I say, ignoring Palesa's wince at the swear word. 'I'm getting out of here.'

Palesa suddenly throws her heads back and laughs. 'Good luck doing that, sisi.'

'What do you mean?'

'No one can leave.'

'What? No one at all. Ever?'

'There is someone,' Ben says quietly.

'Who?'

Palesa sighs, kisses the baby rat once more and tucks it inside her shirt. Her grimy hands are covered in tiny pinprick cuts. Rat bites?

'There's one woman – Napumla. She got out,' Ben says.

I sit forward so far in my chair I almost tumble off. 'She got out? How?'

Ben shrugs. 'I don't know. But you can ask her.'

Palesa laughs her creepy laugh. 'You can *try* asking her.'

'Hang on. You mean this woman – this Napumla – is here? In the mall?'

'Yes.'

'How can she be here if she got out?'

'She came back,' Ben says.

'What the fu— why did she do that?'

'They always do,' Palesa says. 'Always.'

'And you're saying that she's working here?'

Ben nods. 'Working or Shopping. It's hard to know.'

'Where? Which shop?'

'I'm not sure,' Ben says. He's lying.

'And what about you? How did you end up like this? Did you fail the interview or something?'

Palesa stiffens. 'Like we said. We made the choice. Just like *you* will have to choose.'

Christ almighty. That's it. Time to split.

'Is there another way into the mall from here?'

Ben shakes his head. 'No.'

Shit. I really don't want to go back out through the cinema.

'Will you come with me?' I say to Ben. 'To find my friend?'

'But why would you want to leave?' Palesa says softly. 'You can stay with us.'

I can't stop the snort of disgust, and with it I get another nose-ful of shit smell. 'Thanks, but no thanks.'

I look straight at Ben. 'Will you help me?'

He drops his eyes, but doesn't respond.

'Rhoda?' Palesa says. 'Can I show you something?'

She stands up alarmingly quickly and this time the chair does topple over as I try to move away from her, dumping me on the floor. I jar my elbow on the severed leg of a mannequin, but I jump to my feet as fast as possible.

'Are you hurt?' Ben asks, but he doesn't sound too concerned.

'No. Look, I think I should—'

'Wait,' Palesa says. 'I want to show you something. Something... beautiful.'

She leans closer to me, and underneath the grime on the skin around her mouth I can make out several large circular sores that look barely healed. And there's something in her eyes – something shining and dangerous – that I really don't like. I pull out the knife, keeping it close to my thigh where she can't see it.

'Okay,' I say. Probably best to humour her. There are two of them, one of me.

She moves over towards the large packing crate and beckons me forward. Ben stays seated on the mattress, but if it looks like he's about to move then I'll have to make a run for it. Fight my way out if I have to.

'Come,' Palesa says. 'Come and see.'

'What is it?'

'It's my art,' she says.

'Our hobby,' Ben says proudly.

I edge nearer to the box. Despite myself, I'm curious. Smiling at me, she slowly pulls the sheet off it. Whatever's inside it stinks even worse than the toilet bucket – I'm hit with a blast of that feral, animal odour – and I have to cover my mouth with my hand again to stop myself from gagging. I look down into the box. I can't tell what it is at first. It's just a writhing mass of fur, about the size of a small dog. It's making a mewling sound, and gradually I start to make out more features of the thing – several beady eyes, and a knot of hairless, clumped-together tails.

Oh God.

'I start when they're babies,' Palesa says. 'With their tails. That way they become one. One organism. In His family. Do you see?'

Oh fucking hell. I suddenly realise what I'm looking at. Bile floods into my mouth before I can stop it and I bend over and throw up the undigested popcorn.

The thing in the cage is a knitted-together mass of rat bodies.

I wipe my mouth, gag again and start backing away from her, clicking the button on the flick-knife and holding it in front of me.

'You're sick,' I say. 'Fucking sick.'

'Where are you going, Rhoda?' Ben says.

'Stay away from me!'

I start backing towards the opening that leads to the crawl-space. Ben stays seated on the mattress, but Palesa takes a step towards me.

'Stay away! I'm warning you!'

'We're not going to hurt you, Rhoda,' Palesa says in that disturbingly soft voice.

I retch again, but there's nothing left to come up.

'We want to help you. Make it easier for you,' Ben says.

'Make what easier?'

'Your decision to take up our path, of course,' Palesa says.

I'm nearly at the opening, but I'm going to have to turn my back on them to pull myself into the crawlspace.

'Stay the *fuck* away from me!' I say, my voice wobbling.

'You'll be back,' Palesa says. 'We'll see you soon.'

'In your fucking dreams, bitch!' I say. I make a running jump for the opening in the wall, chucking the knife ahead of me, and kicking back with my legs as I pull my way up and into the crawlspace, just in case Palesa tries to grab at them.

'Good luck, Rhoda!' Ben calls. 'Come and see us again soon!'

'We love you!' Palesa's voice echoes behind me.

I scramble for the knife and shove it back into my pocket. Without Ben's torch, the crawlspace is pitch black and I grope my way along blindly, knocking my knees and elbows on the rough side of the concrete walls, fuelled by panic. How far did it extend? I can't remember, but I concentrate on putting as much distance between me and those sick fucks as I can.

When I estimate that I must be nearing the end of the crawl-space I slow down, holding my hand out in front of me, not wanting to bash my head on the wall. Finally my fingers touch the rungs of the makeshift rope ladder that leads up towards the panel in the cinema's floor. I carefully pull myself up into a standing position and try to catch my breath.

Now for the fun part.

My imagination runs overtime as I steel myself for the worst: a circle of freaks with sharp gnashing teeth waiting to grab me; the Elephant Man thing leaning down to pull me up by my face. But let's be honest. How can whatever's waiting for me be more horrific than what I've just seen?

Before I lose my nerve, I scramble up the rope ladder and heave open the trapdoor. I pull myself up and out, wincing as I'm hit with a blast of light. The cinema is fully lit, the screen blank and dead. I look around frantically, but the seats are all empty. In the bright light the place looks shoddy and neglected: the chairs are threadbare and the carpet is scuffed, filthy and covered in dark brown stains. Taking a second to breathe clean(ish) air, I heave myself up, stalk up the aisle and push through into the corridor.

I'm sprinting as I reach the lobby, and I don't even pause to see if the old woman is at her post by the pillar. I leap over the red rope and hare towards the padded doors. It's eerily quiet in here now, and even the popcorn machine is silent. The place has the aura of an abandoned movie set and the desperation to get out of here as fast as possible is turning into barely controlled panic again. The padded doors swing open easily and my feet crunch over the discarded popcorn as I head towards the door that leads into the parking lot. I reach for the handle. My phone beeps. I ignore it.

It beeps again.

Fuck it. If I don't go now I could lose my nerve. But still. I rip the phone out of my pocket and thumb through to the messages. My hands are shaking like crazy and I almost drop the phone.

Both are from 'Your Service Provider'.

<hey babes! CAN'T WAIT to finally meet u LOL XXXXX >

I click onto the next.

<sum advice: Shoptillyoudrop. Who needs electroshocks when you've got retail therapy? Congrats rhoda you made the cut mybrumybrewskimyspecialchina>

'Fuck you,' I say under my breath. Then I turn the handle and, without looking back, walk through into the parking lot.

chapter 18
DANIEL

At first, Sweat Shop looks like any other Edgars department store but as I drift down the aisles looking for some clothes – some 'apparel' – for the interview, I notice what looks like a funfair mirror on a column. It somehow contorts my body double and gives me giant hyperbaric eyes. I stare at the mirror, trying to figure out how the hunchback illusion works, when my reflection gasps at me wetly, 'Can I help you?'

Fuck. Not a reflection. A fucking customer. Move on, Dan. 'Sorry,' I mumble as I scuttle off. Remember what you're here for. You need to progress to the next level. Don't get caught up in the distracting detail.

A signboard dangling above me indicates directions to Fattened, Amputees, Abnormal and, painted in gold script, Shoppers. Judging by what Colt said about her own body shape, I guess I should start at Abnormal. I should have asked her what I would be expected to wear at the interview. But if I go back now she'll probably just give me the 'How can I help you, sir?' routine again. I always wear jeans and a T-shirt to work but that android at the bookshop was wearing a suit.

And I know now it's not my bookshop. It's not my mall.

I'm not at home. This place – whatever it is – is so much like Highgate Mall, but then again so different. The people are the weirdest part. Most of them are really freakish, but they walk around buying clothes, having coffee, trying on shoes and hats as if they're normal. I'm struggling to get my head around it, but I can't think about that now.

At last I find the Abnormal clothes in the dingiest corner of the shop, just near the emergency escape door and the workers' tea room. They're shoved on the shelves and in display crates in no particular order and I have to scuffle through the piles before I eventually find something in my size. A suit will look too desperate, I guess, but jeans too casual, so I opt for a pair of blue chinos and a blue-striped shirt with a grey tie. That has to be neat enough. The idea of wearing these fucking Bradley-clothes makes me sick. My skin crawls at the thought of starchy trousers and choking button shirts. But I'll never get through the interview test if I don't play properly. I head to the changing room. I usually never try clothes on – my jeans are 32/32 and my shirts are L – but I make an exception here.

As I walk in to the over-bright booth, a fan of rebounding reflections spreads before me. A rush of nausea hits me without warning and I have to crouch down and hide my face in my hands. My body remembers the massive mirrored hall Rhoda and I were in. Most of all I remember our own stink and filth in that room; we were shit-smeared and piss-drenched, covered with the effluence of that elephant creature and the sewage we swam through. Every detail of the reek comes back to me now, making me feel as disgusting as I did then. I can't look at myself; I turn to face the changing-room door. As I strip off my trousers and shirt, the bruises and smears all over my body seem to hover over my skin under the buzzing neon light.

When I put on the new clothes, the panic attack is gone as quickly as it came. Now I can look at myself again. The clothes are fine. Ish. The trousers are a little loose, too much space in the hips, too thin at the ankle. The shirt is baggy and has a large flap sewn into the back, which I have to crumple down to get the shirt to fit half-decently. They're fine; I don't want to spend any more time in here than necessary. I have to keep cool. I can't allow myself to be blindsided by emotional reactions again. I need to stay in the zone if I'm going to make it out of here. Just hurry up and pay and get to the interview. I strip the new clothes off and put on my jeans and T-shirt.

As I bend over to tie my laces I glimpse a flicker of movement in the mirror. A flash of blonde hair, of pink skin. I spin around instinctively, despite knowing in my mind that I won't see anything. The shape moves across the mirror like a pendulum swinging, but if I look at it directly it isn't there. Catching it just right, in my peripheral vision, it looks like a lifesize doll of Josie. The same blonde haircut. Swing. Nothing. Swing. Those long legs. Swing. Gone. Swing. A red mess in the middle. Swing. Nothing. The neon flashes off. Darkness. Flash. Swing. The red streaming under and over her skirt, down her legs. Darkness. A heavy thump. Lights on. Nothing but my face. Wide eyes, pupils contracting.

Josie.

It's just a game. It's just a game. They're just fucking with me. They just want to distract me. But my mind is shuddering with horror. I have to keep it in.

Repressing the urge to vomit, I take the clothes to the counter. The skinny girl behind it regards me with a complex look of disgust and pity – a look I'm quickly becoming used to. I dig the gel token out of my pocket and place it on the counter. She picks it up with a claw made of a long thumb and forefinger. The other three fingers on her right hand have been neatly amputated below the second knuckle, their stumps painted decoratively with lacquer stars and moons. The little stumps wiggle as she picks up the token.

She swipes the gel in front of her terminal and gives me a sad look. 'I apologise, sir,' she says. 'This is a Customer Care Officer's token. You need to select CCO apparel from the CCO office.' She points across the shop to a door marked Customer Care Officers.

'Thank you,' I say.

'It's only a pleasure, sir,' she says with a missionary smile, smoothing her stringy brown hair with her claw. 'It's always a pleasure to assist… visitors… to make the right choice.'

The door to the back office is made of heavy steel painted a matt white. I push at it and it swings open onto a long stretch of unadorned concrete lined with blue and red pipes and electrical conduits. Galvanised doors are set into the wall every dozen paces or so. I walk down the corridor, trying each door, but they are all locked. Further down the corridor, the neon strip lighting seems to get higher and duller until at the end of the corridor there is just a nauseating yellow wash. That must be it.

I make it down to the last door. I try the handle. It seems stuck. I knock.

This corridor reminds me of fear, of running from that snot-rasping, screaming-elephant thing. I remember its breathing, its dripping saliva.

I knock again.

'Yes? Come in.'

I wrench the handle again and it gives.

The woman behind the desk in the Customer Care Officers' office looks at me indifferently. The room is lined with rails of clothes, and the shop's muzak pipes from the ceiling. 'I'm Going Through Changes'? I try to slow my breathing as the woman watches, her wooden foot tap-tap-tapping impatiently at the modesty board of the desk. I hold up my gel token and she points me across the room to a couple of bins marked Returns beside an old-fashioned changing screen.

'You'll find plenty of Abnormals there,' she calls after me.

The only clothes I can dig out that look anywhere near my size are a satiny suit jacket in silver and black candy stripes and a pair of matching trousers with a complex Velcro fly. A ruffled canary-yellow shirt completes the outfit. I try it on behind the screen, worrying that the woman at the desk can see me, or worse, smell me from there. I can see her, but she's reading a magazine, her wooden foot going tap tap tap. There's only a small shaving mirror hanging on a hook behind the screen and I take it down and scan myself.

I look like a fucking clown. Or someone from a New Romantic boy band. I try losing the yellow shirt and just keeping the T-shirt on under the jacket, but that looks even worse. All I would need is a pork pie hat and I'm some naff fucker straight from VH1 Classic. I put the shirt back on. Oh well.

I keep the ensemble on and present the woman with my token. She swipes it at the machine.

'Interviewing today?' she asks. I nod. 'Good luck.' She looks pointedly at my dirty boots.

'Thanks.'

I swear I can feel something slick in the crotch of the trousers, but I try to shove the thought out of my head. I didn't have the stomach to try on any underpants from the returns bin, and I regret throwing mine away at Lonly Books. I try not to think of who returned these clothes; and the more I try not to, the larger the parade of suppurating freaks passing through my mind grows. Maybe a leper, someone with seeping sores. I feel an itch in my crotch, spreading over my thighs. I swear there's a sticky patch.

'Are you all right, sir?' asks the desk-woman.

I'm just imagining it. I'm just imagining it.

'Uh, yes. Thanks.'

Don't scratch your penis, Daniel, it's a filthy habit.

I have to get out of here. I have to get to the interview.

I'm just imagining it.

chapter 19
RHODA

I made it.

I lean against the parking lot's door and wait for the stitch in my side to fade. My panicked sprint through the car park has used up my last reserves of energy (and probably sanity), and my chest aches from drawing in jagged, hungry breaths. I try to concentrate on the plinkety-plonk of the mall's muzak to ground myself. The limousine was still in its impossible parking bay, and although it had rocked on its suspension springs as I passed it, there was no sign of that creepy syringe guy.

Maybe I *did* just imagine him.

Yeah right. Just like I imagined Elephant Head in the movie theatre and Horrible Rat Woman and the twisted text messages and the rest of the fucked-up shit that's been happening.

So now what?

First priority: find Dan, and then try and track down that woman Ben the Freak said had escaped this nightmare.

Should be a piece of cake.

NOT.

Brilliant. The schizo voice is back. Just what I need right now.

From down the corridor there's a burst of laughter, followed by the clip-clop of approaching footsteps. A couple is heading along the aisle towards me. It looks like they've just exited a shop that – judging from the bright pink signage painted on the windows (Get Nailed!) and the giant plastic hand display – sells nothing but fingernails. The guy must be over two metres tall; his head looks too square for his body, as if it's actually a breeze-block balancing on top of his head, and the woman clinging to his arm is staggering on towering translucent stripper heels. Her sequined dress barely covers her bum and the shoes are so high that her calf muscles stand out like lumpy knots of wood. Both of them are spray-tanned a vibrant orange, and even from here, a good ten metres away, I can make out the extraordinary amount of make-up on the woman's face: lipstick smeared over the edges of her mouth like a clown's smile; drag-queen eyelashes stuck onto her lids. Both are clutching giant plastic bags bulging with goods.

My exhausted brain refuses to react to their outlandish appearance. It's as if my consciousness has decided, 'Fuck, it, Rhoda, let's just go with the flow'. I actually don't care any more. I really don't. I'm becoming detached from all this bullshit; as if I'm just waiting for my mind to snap once and for all. And anyway, let's face it, I've seen a lot worse than this display of outrageous bad taste. In fact, compared to Horrible Rat Woman and the other freaks around here, they're pretty tame.

'Howzit!' The woman smiles at me as they pass, batting her eyelashes. Close up it's obvious that her cheekbones aren't the ones she was born with. Plastic surgery overload. And I can tell by the taut shiny skin in between her cleavage that her giant tits are as fake as her skin colour.

'Hi,' I say.

She pauses. 'You know, you should really check out the lounge furniture in Flammable City. It's simply to *die* for!'

The guy grunts in agreement. He's also wearing make-up. His

pores are clogged with foundation, and the thick black kohl smeared around his eyes gives him the look of Uncle Fester from the Addams Family. He grins at me, showing off toothless black gums.

'Right,' I say. 'Cheers.' My instinct is to step back a couple of paces, but they seem friendly enough, which is a major improvement on everyone else I've encountered.

'Oh,' the woman says, using the neon pink talons on her remaining hand to dig under the dry blonde tresses of her hair. 'And I heard a rumour that Scrape has new stock. We're on our way there now. Would you like to join us?'

'Thanks,' I say, trying not to think about what the fuck a shop called Scrape could possibly sell. 'That's nice of you, but I –' *have to get the fuck out of this madhouse* '– have to meet a friend.'

'Another time, then. Have a primo shopping day!' the woman says, and they both head off.

What the hell was that all about?

Do I really care?

Just more crazy shit.

Okay. Back to the plan. First warn Dan that we're no longer in Kansas (although he must have figured this out himself by now), somehow track down the woman who managed to get out of this hellhole and pump her for information, then leave.

Like it's going to be that simple.

Buy cigarettes, tell the cops about the missing kid, beg or borrow enough cash to buy a plane ticket home, and then get on with my life.

What life?

'Shut *up*!'

I'm not sure how I feel about schizo voice's re-emergence. Isn't talking to yourself the first sign of madness? And if so, what's the second sign?

Arguing with yourself, of course!

'Oh, ha ha. Fucking hysterical.'

I start heading in the direction of the escalators. I pass an enormous high-end clothes shop, the mannequins in the window a mix of the surreal and the sickening.

'Greetings, ma'am!' I jump as a salesman pokes his head out of the shop's door. 'I see you're admiring our display,' he says in an over-the-top camp voice. His hair is gelled into a ridiculous spike on the top of his head, his eyebrows are shaven and drawn back on with what looks like thick felt-tip, and there's a fuchsia silk scarf draped around his neck, but otherwise he looks almost normal.

'Hi,' I say warily. Why's everyone suddenly being over-friendly?

'Please,' he says, grinning at me and stepping backwards as if to usher me into the store.

'Huh?'

'Now, I hope you don't mind me being forward, but I took one look at you and I just knew you were the perfect size starvation. Am I right?'

'You taking the piss?'

'I'm sorry?' he says looking genuinely confused. 'Have I offended you, ma'am?'

'Fuck you,' I say.

The guy throws back his head and laughs. 'Ma'am! A figure to die for and a sense of humour!'

He pauses as a skinny woman dressed in tiny cycling shorts approaches. Christ. Her obviously fake breasts are way too large for her tiny frame and under her strapless Lycra top it's clear that they're misshapen and lumpy, the skin around them stretched almost to splitting point. There's a stained bandage covering one of her ears, and giant-sized false eyelashes are glued to her lids, one of which is peeling off. She smiles nervously at the shop assistant and hesitates as if she's about to enter the store, but he glares at her and curls his lip. She drops her head and scuttles past. What the hell was that all about?

'Don't you just hate them?' he says to me in a conspiratorial whisper.

'Hate who?'

He gestures towards the woman. 'Wannabes. As if I would be fooled. I mean, did you see the work? Substandard beyond belief.'

He smiles again and gestures towards the open door.

I hesitate. Maybe I can get some information out of him. It's worth a shot.

'Please,' he says, this time sounding almost desperate. 'Please come in, ma'am.'

Don't do it, Rhoda. Remember the plan.

I suppose the schizo voice does have a point, but I have to start somewhere.

Fuck it.

I follow him into the boutique. A fine golden chain is attached to his ankle, snaking its way out from behind the polished wooden counter at the far end of the room, and he gathers it up discreetly as he ushers me forward.

Uh-oh. Not good.

I tune out the voice and check out my surroundings. The shop is clearly one of those exclusive stores that only sells designer goods. It looks like the lounge of a country house. Beige leather couches are dotted around the vast space, and silk dresses, tailored suits and the kind of clothes you only see on celebrities are sparsely displayed on the headless torsos that line the room. It's the kind of sneering exclusive store that under normal circumstances I wouldn't even dream of entering.

But what's normal about these circumstances, eh, Rhoda?

Camp Assistant claps his hands. 'Patrice! Quickly! We have a fresh Shopper!'

A guy pops up from behind the counter with the speed of a jack-in-the-box. 'Oh!' he says. 'How absolutely marvellous! Welcome, ma'am. And congratulations.' One of the arms of his suit jacket ends in a jagged tear just above the elbow, and a seeping, bandaged stump peeks out of the bottom of it. I realise that I don't actually feel any surprise or disgust at the sight of this. It's like I'm watching all of this from the ceiling, or on a monitor somewhere.

'Thank you so much for shopping with us today,' Camp Assistant says. 'May I offer you some refreshments? Champagne? Maybe an espresso?'

'Huh?'

He waves me towards one of the leather couches. 'Please, have a seat!'

He nods at his companion and the one-armed assistant scurries out from behind the counter and sprints across the shop floor to a curtained-off area at the back of the room. His ankle is also shackled to the desk, but again, my detached brain refuses to give a shit about this. It's just much more comfortable not to worry.

I sink into the couch, and my leg muscles sigh with relief.

Camp Assistant smiles at me ingratiatingly. 'May I just thank you again for shopping with us, ma'am?'

Would he know the woman – (what was her name? Nthombi? Nyameka? Napumla – that's it) – who'd managed to escape this place? Only one way to find out. 'Look,' I say, 'I wonder if you can help me?'

'Help you? But of course I can help you! Just wait here.'

He minces off and disappears towards the rear of the shop.

What now?

What now? WHAT NOW? Get out of here and find Dan!

Ignoring the voice, I lean back in the couch, letting myself relax fully. Every inch of me aches, and it's utterly delicious to be sitting somewhere comfortable for once. I put my filthy sneakers up on the coffee table in front of me. It's strewn with fashion magazines, but the models on the front covers all look like they've literally been starving themselves; most have the sickly pallor and over-accentuated cheekbones of hunger-strikers. I can feel my eyelids getting heavy – it would be so easy to close my eyes and drift away.

Don't you fucking dare!

The voice is right. I sit up and stretch my arms above my head, gazing around at the rest of the store. There are several black-and-white framed photographs behind the counter that I haven't noticed before. They're the kind of posed headshots of celebrities you see in restaurants, and several have thick black crosses scored across their faces.

One-Arm returns balancing a tray loaded with a cafetière and, oh God, a plate of what looks to be smoked salmon sandwiches, with the crusts cut off.

'I see you're admiring our gallery,' he says. I can't take my eyes off the food on the tray. My stomach growls.

'Gallery?' I say.

He nods towards the photos. 'Our beautiful gallery of Shoppers past.'

Now what the hell did he mean by that?

Duh. Shop till you drop, Rhoda, literally.

'Now, you make yourself comfortable,' he says. 'I'm going to help Clive find the perfect outfit for you!'

'Wait! I have to—'

'Relax!' he says, and there's something desperate about the way he says this. 'Please!' He stares at me anxiously, but he needn't worry. I'm already salivating.

He scuttles off as I fall on the sandwiches, stuffing them into my mouth. I pour out a cup of coffee, and glug back a mouthful, scalding my tongue. I have never tasted anything so delicious. I can't cram the sandwiches in quickly enough, and almost choke trying to swallow.

'Here we are!'

Both assistants are standing in front of me, clothes draped over their arms. 'Now, I hope you don't think I'm too forward,' Camp Assistant says, 'but with your colouring, I was thinking olive green. What do you think?'

He holds up a silk dress that even I have to admit is beautiful.

'Would you like to try it on?'

'Sure,' I say with a shrug.

No. No you don't. It's not even your colour!

One-Arm ushers me towards a changing booth, and Camp Assistant hurries over and hands me a leather jacket and a pair of silk stockings. Both of them are acting as if they're assisting the Queen of England and not some down-and-out ex-druggie who smells like death on toast. But who am I to fucking well argue? Worst-case scenario, I can always grab the clothes and do a runner.

It wouldn't be the first time.

The booth is surrounded by mirrors, but for some reason they make me look taller, less skinny and shapeless, and for once I don't actually mind looking at my reflection. Even the scar looks less disfiguring. A trick?

Of course! It's all bullshit. The shop assistants are fucking chained up! How can this be a good thing?

I'm suddenly aware of how much I loathe the clothes I'm wearing and I pull them off as fast as I can. I hold the olive green dress up to my naked body. I haven't worn a dress since I was seven or so, but it's got to be better than the damp T-shirt and the combats that still hold the stink of Horrible Rat Woman's shit-infested lair. I slide the dress over my head. It fits perfectly, skimming over my non-existent hips, the hem finishing a good twelve centimetres above my knees. I pull on the tights, snagging them on my toes, and pick up the leather jacket. It feels impossibly soft and buttery, and not like any leather I've ever felt before.

I check out my reflection. Fuck me. A stranger stares back. I really don't look like me at all. I look…

Elegant? Yeah right. Come on, you're not that deluded.

'Yoo-hoo!' Camp Assistant calls. 'Don't leave us in suspense!'

I open the changing-room curtain and step out.

'Oh my! You look beautiful! Simply stunning!' Camp Assistant claps his hands. 'Patrice! Come and see!'

One-Arm pops up from his perch behind the counter and checks me out, looking as if he's about to burst into tears of rapture. 'Oh! How *divine*!' he says. 'You must have the lot!'

'Oh, you must!' Camp Assistant says. 'Really!'

'Yeah right,' I say. 'Like I can afford to pay for them.'

'Pay?' They both look at each other as if I've said something totally outlandish. 'But you're a Shopper!'

'What do you mean?'

'You're a Shopper,' Camp Assistant repeats as if saying it twice will make it clearer.

'You just said that…' Both of them are looking at me with that concerned expression people use when patronising the temporarily deranged.

'Okay,' I say. 'What the hell. I'll take the lot.'

'Wonderful!' Camp Assistant says, clearly relieved.

'Clive!' One-Arm says. 'Haven't we forgotten something?'

Here we go… don't say I didn't warn you…

Fuck. Maybe I should have listened to schizo voice. And Christ, my knife is still in the pocket of my combats that are pooled on the changing-room floor. I should have known it was too good to be true. I wait for Camp Assistant to say something horrible: perhaps that the leather jacket is made out of human skin, or maybe he's about to point out that all the mannequins are actually cadavers or something.

There's no such thing as a free lunch, Rhoda. They'll want some kind of payment. Here's the part where they ask you to lop off one of your fingers. Maybe dig out an eyeball.

Camp Assistant cocks his head to one side and clicks his fingers. 'Of course! Patrice, you're absolutely right.' He turns to me. 'How remiss of me! Ma'am, please, let me show you the handbags, they are to *die* for.'

'Lovely jacket,' a wannabe Shopper with a diamanté eye-patch and a severe case of psoriasis says to me as he passes me on the escalators. I ignore him and concentrate on balancing on the escalator's steps in the unfamiliar high heels. I almost stumble as I reach the top and start clacking my way towards the phone store.

I keep catching glimpses of my reflection in the shop windows and it's really starting to freak me out. The boots I picked up in Toe Jam next to the clothes store are the same chestnut brown leather as my bag and jacket, and the scarf I found in Splurge complements the dress underneath perfectly, but my hair just doesn't go.

Haven't you got more important things to worry about, Rhoda? Like finding Dan, like staying alive?

'Shut up!'

'Ma'am, were you talking to me?' A woman with a white afro and a leg that I'm almost sure has been cadged from a mannequin and stapled to the stump of her thigh smiles at me. The chain around her ankle is made of heavy spiked metal and disappears into the depths of the store behind her.

'No,' I say. 'I wasn't talking to anyone.'

'Please!' the woman fawns. 'Come in. I just know I've got the perfect match for you.'

'The perfect what?'

I look past her to try and gauge what shop she's attached to.

It's a plainly furnished store with nothing but photographs of apartments in the windows. An estate agency.

Oh shit.

'You know, I saw you and I thought, now there's a Shopper in the market for a super-deluxe-special-three-sleeproomer-with-a-champagne-bar-and-access-to-the-swimming-pool-heated-of-course-and-don't-forget-the-sauna-and-it's-a-stone's-throw-from-the-modification-Wards.'

She gasps in a deep breath and edges closer, the chain attached to her ankle now almost taut. She cocks her head to one side. 'It's just come on the market, the last owner recycled. Would you like to see it? It's got underfloor eating and a coruscated massage bed comes as an optional extra.'

Snap out of it, Rhoda!

'Um...'

The woman smiles brightly at me again. She's now so close that I can smell the queer medicinal odour that's wafting out of her pores. 'Most Shoppers would give their right leg to live there,' she says, her voice now a honeyed whisper. 'Did I mention it has a Jacuzzi?'

'A Jacuzzi? Really?'

'Oh yes,' she says. 'A big one. There's no harm in looking, is there? What do you say?'

No!

I follow the woman into the agency, tuning out the voice of doom.

'I say it must be fate,' I say.

chapter 20

DANIEL

I get back to the phone shop just as Colt is clicking out. She suppresses a laugh when she catches sight of me at the door. 'Catalogue!' she says. 'Are you ready?'

She leads me to a bank of lifts behind the escalators and presses the up button.

'Can't we take the stairs?'

Colt just laughs and shakes her head in that 'funny brown' sort of way. 'You'd walk a long time to get to Management. They're in the Golden Tower.'

'I don't like lifts.'

'Don't worry. These are fast. And they have music.'

I bite my tongue and force myself to follow her in. It'll be fine, nothing will happen. I'm doing what they want, conforming, playing by the rules. I'm with one of their own. There's no reason for them to fuck with me now.

The muzak in the lift stays in the background as Colt stares at the doors and fiddles idly with the hair falling over the wound on her neck, humming along with the panpipe-and-synth rendition of 'Nine to Five'. There's no display inside the lift to tell us which floor we're on. The lift hums steadily for a minute or two and I breathe out with relief when the doors open. We enter a spacious, marble-floored reception area with a large sign saying Personnel behind the wide counter. My heart thunders. We're in the lion's den. I can almost feel them nearby, I can almost smell the funk of evil seeping out from behind the marble façade.

Bright light shines through a bank of windows to our left. Leaving Colt at the counter, I head over to them, hoping to catch a glimpse of Joburg beyond, hoping to orient myself, get some perspective on where the fuck I am; hoping to discover an escape route. But the windows only look onto a small recess with back-lit advertising posters shining through them. One of them shows the amputated watch model, this time sprawled across the handles of a rusted motorbike. When I get back to the reception desk, Colt is talking to an orange-bewigged person in an expensively tailored suit. 'I'm sponsoring a brown for employment.'

'Its name?'

'Daniel...'

'Jacobson,' I fill in. The woman – I think – doesn't look at me.

'And he's a he,' Colt adds. She says it so neutrally that I can't tell if she's being defiant or simply stating a demographic fact.

'Business unit?' the receptionist asks Colt.

'Retail. Books.'

The receptionist fingers something onto her computer screen, then finally looks at me. I stare into blank, black eyes in a grey face under the absurd orange wig. The receptionist's hard face confirms what I already know about the Management. If you defy them in any way, you'll regret it. They are cruel.

She points a lump of gel at me, pokes at the computer again. 'Yes. All right. This is one of two browns who entered today. We will update his status pending the result of the application. Its companion has been assigned as a Shopper.'

'Wow!' says Colt. 'You didn't tell me, Daniel. She's a Shopper!

Wow!' She's beaming dreamily like a teenager at a poster of a semi-naked movie vampire. 'I'd do anything to be a Shopper. And you actually *know* one.' Orange Hair clears her throat, the sound of cheese graters meeting funny bones, and Colt tails off.

'I lost contact with her,' I say. 'I thought she was trying to leave the mall.'

'Leave?' says Colt, in that confused tone of hers.

The receptionist shoots a look at Colt and pulls a face. Browns. Lying and stupid, all of them.

'Please present at Welcome Room 387 in five moments.' She dismisses us to sit in the waiting area.

Colt whispers to me, 'I would never have thought your... friend... could be a Shopper. No offence, but she was really... rough. But I suppose now that I think of it, she definitely has the look. She's self-starved, and she's even got natural scarification. God, people pay a fortune to get that done. You know, when I wen—'

She's starting to babble so I interrupt her. 'I don't know what that means – a Shopper. Does it mean that she's okay? What will happen to her? Can she leave? Where do you think I could find her?'

'Find her? CCOs don't find Shoppers, Daniel. If we're lucky – and only *if* – Shoppers come to us. My God, Daniel, and *you knew* her. You knew a Shopper. You're *so* lucky.' She pauses, looks away, looks back at me again. 'How well did you know her?'

In a few moments I'm about to come face to face with people who have tried to kill me, I have no idea of where I am or where I'm going, but the tone of Colt's question makes me happy. She's jealous of Rhoda. This hot girl is jealous of Rhoda!

I shrug. 'I don't know...'

Colt looks away from me. 'You knew a Shopper,' she mumbles.

We're ushered into the interview room by an Abnormal with a rudimentary steel shaft for an arm. She has a kind, almost regular face; she's probably a specialist in interviewing browns because of her familiar looks. The round table is set with empty vases and a small sheaf of papers. At one modified seat sits a squat and sweaty man who looks like an octopus in a suit. His down-mouth disappears into his slick jowls and gives him a look of utter disgust.

'Welcome, Darneel,' says the woman. 'I am Welcome Agent Jossiefeen, and this is the Lonly Books Management Representative, Badly.' She speaks the names like misremembered foreign phrases. 'I am so glad you have decided to seek employment with us. We find that brown persons like yourself are an asset to the company and add a range of experience and diversity and empathy to our operations that is demonstrably appreciated by the clientele of the various business units. We find that when brown persons serve our clients, purchases are processed more quickly, and queries handled with more alacrity than the average. Result: more brown persons in our employ, more income for the company. It's a win situation.'

As she shuffles the pages in front of her, the steel arm smacks against the table top and the octopus man judders inside his swiftly moistening suit.

'This is not to say that our own are not highly prized CCOs, of course. Your sponsor, CCO Colt, has excellent numbers, despite her... her... challenges... which we have discussed with her.' Colt looks at the floor. I wonder if they're referring to her body shape. Christ, what a place to bring that up.

'Right. Let's just go through the standard security questions, then. And then if Representative Badly has any further questions for you, Darneel, you may answer them. Remember, CCO Colt, that as Sponsor, you may be held liable for any false declarations on this application. And, of course, for any disregard on behalf of the applicant.' The agent says this in a serious tone and I wonder what exactly will happen to Colt if I fuck it up.

'Yes, Agent,' Colt says, equally gravely, as if she's just sworn some sort of oath to the company. I'd just better not fuck it up, for her sake as much as mine.

'All right. To your knowledge or in your experience has this brown ever belonged to an underground cult or organic terrorist group?' How is Colt supposed to know anything about me? Of course, I'd better keep my mouth shut. Octopus Man glares at me through wet eyes.

'No,' Colt says.

'To your knowledge or in your experience has this brown ever beheaded one of our own?' *Huh?*

'No.'

'To your knowledge or in your experience has this brown ever devoured offspring – his own or that of others?'

'No.'

Jossiefeen is rattling off the questions in a bored tone as if this is a standard immigration questionnaire. The questions are evidently just as stupid. 'To your knowledge or in your experience has this brown ever been sought by the Guardian?' What the fuck is the guardian? I wouldn't even know if I've been—

'No,' Colt answers certainly.

'To your knowledge or in your experience is this brown infected with any pathogens that may affect our own?'

'No.'

'To your knowledge or in your experience has this brown ever purloined?'

'No.'

'Well, then. That's in order,' Jossiefeen says, cheerfully ticking off her list. 'Representative Badly?'

'Uh,' the Representative grunts, clears an oceanful of phlegm from his throat and spits a huge yellow wad into the vase on the table in front of him. 'This associate of yours. The dark brown. If it doesn't start consuming to its quota soon, it will become unassigned. We can't have disregard.'

'Um. I hardly know...' I don't know what to say. Colt rubs my leg in support. It gives me strength. 'We went through a lot together, she and I. Rhoda – uh, the dark brown – helped me make it across here. I wouldn't be applying for this wonderful opportunity if she hadn't helped me. She won't be any problem to you.'

'Uh. You're in no position to vouch for—'

'Representative Badly, I am inclined to believe this young brown. And given our current personnel constr— Given that. I don't think we should judge this young worker on his associates. We know how browns are. This is why we enhanced the penetration system. Disregard is not an issue to the business units any more.'

'Gflk.' The octopus man shrugs his blubbery chest and neck in lieu of shoulders. 'You, Agent...' he looks down at the application form '...Jossiefeen, are the Personnel Agent on the application, and I am the Management Representative. I will leave you to do your job.' He fixes those massive, rheumy eyes on mine. 'But I warn you, Darneel, I *will* do my job. I will be sur-veilling you. Any disregard or any hint of purloining and...' He leaves the threat hanging.

Welcome Agent Jossiefeen smiles at me and shifts her eyes as if to say, *Don't worry about him, he's just a grumpy old octopus and his job is to pretend to be threatening, he's a pussycat, really.* Her subtle, normal eyes are essential to this task. 'Well, I'm pre-pared to accept your application and would be delighted if you could start today, on the Dead Shift. That will give you some time to get some proper apparel and to get a phone and open an account and learn about your tokens. You'll be pleased to know that we've raised the Welcome contribution, so you'll have ample tokens for anything you might need to get started. CCO Colt, could you please help orient CCO Darneel before his shift starts.'

'Yes, Agent.' Colt smiles at me. She's got a really pretty smile.

'Could you wait here for a few moments?' Agent Jossiefeen holds the door open while Representative Badly hefts himself up and grunts his way through it.

'Felicitations,' says Colt when both agents have left the room. 'You made it. We'll be able to devour together every day!'

'Is that it? They didn't even ask about my experience, what I knew about bookselling.'

'It doesn't really matter, does it?'

'I don't know anything about my pay, my shifts, nothing.'

'Don't worry, I'll help you. I'm your sponsor.'

'But… why are you helping me? How could you answer those questions? You know nothing about me.'

'I like you,' Colt says. 'You make me feel… normal.'

Agent Jossiefeen comes in again with a long black case. 'Last thing, of course, is equipping you with the Service Enhancer and performing the induction penetration.' She unpacks a chain and an anklet onto the table, a package of sterile wipes and what looks like a half-sized pneumatic drill.

Holy fuck. What the hell have I gotten myself into? No. No! I thought it was just Colt. Just the phone shop. I didn't think. Oh my God.

Fuck.

How stupid. *How fucking stupid.* The android guy at the bookshop. I didn't think. Oh fuck. I need to vomit. This is not.

Wrong choice. I need a reload.

'Wait,' I say. 'Is there any chance to…' What am I going to say? Change my mind? Start again? I'm here in the Management's nerve centre. They'll never let me get out.

Jossiefeen isn't listening; she's rifling through the black case.

'Oh bother. They keep on taking the adaptor away. I'll just be another moment.'

Colt stands up to stretch her legs. She paces to the wall and idly reads some laminated posters on the wall.

'I didn't know this... this... thing...' I indicate the drill on the desk '...that everyone got it. I thought it was—'

'Don't worry,' she says without turning around, 'it'll be fine. It's sterile, see? There's nothing to worry about.'

Last chance. I flip out my phone and type <rhoda please come am in shit dan>

I pray to everything I know. Colt's tranquillity is making me even more anxious. She's acting like a robot. She's not going to help me.

Thank God, my phone vibrates. Rhoda will get me out of this.

<Fatal error: message terminated>

'Here we go.' Agent Jossiefeen bustles in and plugs in the drill. 'Colt, will you assist, please?'

Colt moves behind me and hugs me around my chest with a surprisingly strong grip. Her touch must stun me a little, because next thing the spike on the drill is whizzing in front of my face with a well-oiled buzz and Jossiefeen is crouching down beside me.

I feel Colt's lips on my ear, her hair tickling my neck. 'Don't worry, Daniel, you get used to it.'

Jossiefeen finds her spot, just under my skull bone below the ear, and the drill goes in, smooth and hard like a screwdriver into a rubber doll.

chapter 21

RHODA

Holy shit. The apartment is twice the size of my parents' house, and no expense was spared with the decor. The floors are marble, the ceilings are high and intricately moulded, and the kitchen's a gleaming expanse of brushed stainless steel. The walls are all painted in shades of tasteful off-white, and I've counted three spare bedrooms, all with state-of-the-art en suite bathrooms (two even have bidets). And there really is a Jacuzzi in the master bedroom, roomy enough to house half of Manchester United.

I wander back through to the open-plan lounge. There's a huge widescreen television on the wall above the mantelpiece, and a conversation pit dominated by a porcelain wood-burning heater. It's the kind of place you see featured in the pages of *Hello!* magazine. It only needs designer furnishings and Nigella Lawson or Victoria Beckham propping themselves up against the polished kitchen counter to complete the picture.

'You like?' The estate agent hovers next to the breakfast bar. I let her sweat for a bit, enjoying the feeling of power. She's been checking her watch almost continually since we arrived, but I don't want to let her know what I really think about the place –

best to pretend to be nonchalant, like someone who's used to swanning around in this type of luxury.

'It's okay,' I say, shrugging.

But there's something strange about the apartment... something I can't quite put my finger on. Then I have it: there are no windows. It's so elegantly lit that I haven't noticed the lack of a view.

I rack my brain to think of the sort of questions you're supposed to ask estate agents without looking too desperate.

'Um. Why is it on the market?'

'The last inhabitant depreciated, of course.'

'Depreciated?'

'Yes, ma'am.' The estate agent clears her throat. 'Have you made a decision? I can really see you in here, ma'am, I really can, oh yes I really think this is the right place for you the place you want to be.' Her estate agent's patter is losing its lustre, and she's now clearly on edge. The attachment on her real leg starts beeping and she eyes it nervously.

'What's that?' I say, pointing to the red flashing light just above her ankle.

'That's the Management letting me know I have to get back to my post soon.'

'How long have you got?'

'We have fifteen minutes to close with a client.'

'And if you don't?'

She smiles at me brightly again. Sweat beads her forehead.

Shit. I'm being cruel. Time to put her out of her misery. 'In that case. I'll take it.'

She sighs with relief. 'Thank you.'

And anyway, it's just for now. Just until I find Dan and we sort ourselves out. We might need a base, after all.

'What about furniture?' I ask.

'Oh, ma'am,' she says, handing over a triangular-shaped keycard. 'That's up to you. I just know you'll have a wonderful time filling it with lovely things. Thank you so much for letting me be your houser.'

She nods, and backs out swiftly, plastic leg clacking over the tiles.

I wander back into the bedroom and check out New Rhoda in the bevelled mirror. Not bad. Not bad at all. I really do look taller, and I'm sure it's not just the new boots. The dress hangs slightly loosely from my shoulders, but there's nothing I can do about that.

Should I treat myself to a quick Jacuzzi before I leave? It would almost be a crime not to.

There's a knock on the door. It's probably just the estate agent again.

But when I open the door I come face to face with a half-naked giant of a man.

'Howzit, neighbour!' he says.

'Um... Hi.'

Christ. He must be at least two metres tall, and his shirtless frame almost fills the doorway. His oiled skin strains over pecs and abs that are too defined and sculpted to be real – they have the look of CGI about them – and I can make out the criss-crossed scars where the implants were inserted. And he's done something bizarre to his chin, it's way too large to be natural and there's a cleft in the end of it large enough to fit several fingers. Ugh. His skin has the same ghostly pallor I've seen on everyone in the mall. Even dark-skinned people look faded somehow. I guess that's what happens when you don't see sunlight for fuck knows how long.

'Just wanted to welcome you to the neighbourhood,' he says.

I struggle to smile back. That chin is really freaking me out. 'Thanks.'

He peers past me and into the kitchen. 'I'm so glad it's no longer vacant.'

'Right. And how long *has* it been vacant?'

He scratches his chin. 'Hours,' he says.

'*Hours?* Seriously?'

He nods. 'I know. Ages. But I wanted to tell you the primo news. Needless Things is having a sale!'

I can't help the thrill of excitement, which is stupid, really. I mean, what's the point of a sale when everything's free?

'Thanks,' I say.

My phone beeps.

Aren't you going to get that?

Oh good. The voice, which has been absent for a while, has decided to show itself again.

'Go away,' I hiss.

The guy looks at me in confusion.

'Sorry,' I say. 'Just talking to myself.'

'Oh. Try the brain-drainer on Ward level G. Worked wonders for me.'

'Thanks.' Maybe that explains the fucked-up work he's had done. I raise my eyebrows in an 'is that it?' fashion, and fortunately he gets the hint.

'Oh,' he says, turning around as I'm about to shut the door on him. 'Sleep when you're dead.'

'What?'

'Level D. Great pillows.'

'Awesome. Thanks.' I slam the door before he has a chance to speak again.

I thumb through to the message. Thinking about it, how could the battery have remained charged for so long? Another mystery. Like the fact that I've just been given a free luxury apartment.

Like I said, there's no such thing as a free lunch.

'Whatever.'

I check out the message. <Well, hello, Rhoda. Sonice to have

youbackwhere youbelong. But that hair. Dahling. It just won't do will it?>

Dan never had a problem with your hair.

'Shut up.' I'm speaking out loud again. Must stop that. And the voice is right. I'm not going to find Dan by hanging around here.

Looking both ways to make sure Cleft Chin isn't anywhere to be seen, I make my way down the corridor towards the mall. The doors to the other apartments stretch into the distance like those in a generic hotel. I pause to listen at a couple of them, but can't hear anything. Their occupants are probably all at the mall. Shopping till they drop.

I think you mean shopping till they die.

As I reach the end of the corridor, an emaciated guy wearing one of those admiral costumes pops up from behind a concierge desk and rushes to open the glass doors that lead into the mall. 'May I wish you a primo shopping experience, ma'am,' he says.

'Cheers,' I say.

'And may I mention that there's a sale on at Corpsicle.'

'Thanks.'

'Better hurry,' he says. 'You don't want to miss out.'

I hesitate. 'You worked here long?' I say.

'Indeed,' he says proudly. 'Since school.'

'Did you know the person who lived in...' Christ, I've forgotten the number of my apartment.

401.

'Right! 401. The shopper who lived there before me – did you know him or her?'

'Shopper De Nooy? Of course I knew him. I know all the Shoppers, ma'am.'

'What happened to him? Was he sick or old or something? Did he move?'

He chuckles. 'Move? Your language is interesting if I may say so, ma'am.' He glances at his watch. 'If I'm not mistaken he was recycled at oh nine seventy. Is there a problem with your new apartment? I can inform Management if so.'

'No problem. None at all.'

I nod at him and hustle away. I don't actually want to know any more.

Coward.

It takes me a while to get my bearings. I hadn't really been looking where I was going as I followed the estate agent to the apartment block. I decide to head towards the escalators, try to figure out where to go from there. A couple of approaching middle-aged women dressed in teenagers' clothes step to the side as I pass. One of them has wrapped cling film around her neck in a poor attempt to smooth her wrinkles, and her friend has done something to her nose – the nostrils look as if they're sealed up. They smile at me admiringly as I pass.

'Hi,' Cling Film says to me, and her friend gasps and nudges her.

'I can't believe you just spoke to a Shopper!' the whisper follows me down the aisle. 'Isn't she beautiful!'

I could get used to this.

I sit back in the booth and take a deep drag on the Turkish cigarette. I picked up a carton from Emfyseema, after I'd checked out the sale in Jean-Pool. The picture on the fag box is almost laughably graphic: a man lying in a hospital bed, his legs gorily amputated, but who cares?

Not me.

My feet are killing me – I'm still battling to get used to the boots' high heels – and my arms are aching from the weight of the bags I've been carrying around. But it's a different sort of ache, almost comforting, as if I've achieved something. Which I suppose I have. Who knew I was such a natural at this shopping thing? I take a sip of champagne and mentally tot up my acqui-sitions. Not a bad haul. Practically a brand new wardrobe, plus there's the water bed, the kid-leather lounge suite and the sheep-skin rug I just had to have the second I saw it. I'll need a table of some sort, but I've got my heart set on that see-through glass one I saw at Four Legs. Should I get it now? What if someone else nabs it in the meantime? My stomach squirms with anxiety at the thought, but I decide to finish my fag first.

'More champagne, madam?'

I nod and the waiter refills my glass. I try not to stare at the huge scab on the back of his neck as he wanders away. It's his choice, though, right? At least that's what Horrible Rat Woman said. The bubbles tickle my nose, and my head buzzes pleas-antly. I'd discovered the oyster and champagne bar next to the lingerie emporium (Slut Bucket), and the waiter had almost fainted with delight as I'd followed him inside.

This is the life.

Of course, it isn't really a life at all, is it?

'Whatever.'

The orange couple I'd seen earlier look over from their place at the bar and raise their champagne glasses to me. I smile back at them, light another cigarette with my brand new Zippo, and wrap a strand of my new hair extensions around my fingers. The hairdresser suggested I get my nails done next, and she might have a point. My bitten nubs don't really go with the look, and a full set of red talons is a tempting proposition. And I should really check out that waxing place next to the Hippie Titus tattoo parlour.

The couple slide from their stools and clack their way over to my booth.

'Can we join you?' the man says in a lispy, oddly high voice.

'Please,' I say. I glance at his feet. The toes of his shoes are filed to a sharp point. Something shifts in my head, but I push it away. I can't stop thinking about that table. It really would go perfectly.

The Shoppers sit down in front of me, squashing their bags around their legs. Now I'm up close to them, I can really see the amount of work they've had done. Tiny white scars nick the corners of the woman's eyes where they've clearly been uplifted, and scar tissue scores the man's forehead as if he's had major surgery. Which I suppose he has. The top of his head bulges. Has he had some kind of bony prosthesis added there? Several expensive-looking watches are looped around the stump of the woman's arm. She catches me looking at them and smiles.

'Charles Pratt,' she says. 'Best in the mall. You *must* shop there.'

The man nods and grins broadly, showing off his black gums that I now realise are tattooed. 'Yes. You must.' He strokes the woman's arm. 'Leletia is their mascot.'

'Their what?'

'We were just saying,' the man says as if I haven't spoken, 'that you would make the perfect mascot for Skin Deep.'

'Your skin,' the woman says, gazing at the scar. 'It's so beautiful.'

'Have you been assigned yet?' the man asks.

'Um. No. Not that I know of.'

'Well, you must go there straight away. You can't be a Shopper without advertising, can you? Not unless you *want* to depreciate.'

They share a chuckle.

'Can I ask you a question?' I say. 'This depreciate thing – what exactly does it mean?'

You already know, Rhoda. Don't be dense.

The woman frowns and glances at her companion in confusion.

'I'm new here,' I say. 'Don't know all the rules yet.'

'Depreciation is a matter for the Management. They decide when, of course.'

'Right. And what actually happens to you?'

'You get sent to the terminal Wards, of course!' the woman says cheerfully.

The man taps the top of his head, tracing a finger around the scar where his hairline would be. 'For recycling.'

Oh. My. Fucking. God.

The woman smiles sympathetically and touches my arm. 'But don't worry, it takes ages to depreciate.'

'How long?'

'That all depends on your purchasing output. And if you get a mascot contract you can extend your Shopping life for much longer.'

'We must fly,' the man says. 'Shopping waits for no man, as they say!'

They get to their feet, struggling with the bulging bags.

'And remember,' the woman says as they head out. 'Skin Deep. You'll be perfect!'

My phone beeps. I scramble though my bags trying to remember which one I'd dumped it into. I finally locate it in the zip-up pocket of my new silk evening purse.

<congrats Rhoda old buddy old mate. You look simply stunning mah deah! But time is tick-tocking so hurry and get mascotting. Or else (LOL!!)>

Will you listen now?

'Listen to what?'

To what I've been telling you. Time to snap the fuck out of it. If you don't leave now you're dead, Rhoda. DEAD.

'You don't know that for sure.'

And what about Dan?

'Dan can look after himself.'

Okay. If you don't care about Dan, what about the kid?

'What kid?'

The waiter is watching me curiously. I've been speaking out loud again.

THE KID! THE FUCKING KID! THE KID WHO'S THE REASON YOU'RE HERE IN THE FIRST PLACE!

Oh fuck. I haven't thought about him in Christ knows how long.

What the hell was I thinking?

And what the fucking hell am I doing?

I stand up, sending my champagne glass flying across the table.

Goth retard girl smiles at me vacantly as I race into the phone shop, stumbling in the unfamiliar boots, no sign of recognition on her stupid face. Mind you, what with the fake hair and bling clothes I must look like a completely different person.

'Hello, ma'am!' she says cheerily. 'How wonderful to see you! May I—'

'Where the fuck is Dan?' I snap.

Her smile slips slightly. 'I'm sorry, ma'am?'

'Cut the crap!' I reach across the counter and grab the front of her T-shirt, pulling my face close to hers. 'Where. The. Fuck. Is. Dan?' I grab her shoulder and shake her roughly, but she continues to stare blankly back at me. 'I know you know where he is. Now tell me!'

Around me there's the beep-beep-beep as every phone flashes into life.

'I think that's for you, ma'am!' the girl says.

My own phone beeps and vibrates in the pocket of my leather jacket. But fuck that, I'm not going to play their game any longer.

I decide to try a different tactic. I slap a smile onto my face. 'I need help. Last time I was here I was with a guy. Tall, longish black hair. Real coffin kid, you know.'

'I do?'

Deep breath. Don't give up.

'He was a... a... brown, like me.'

'But you're a Shopper.'

'Yes,' I say, 'but I wasn't always.'

Now, that *didn't sound totally schizo.*

She clicks her fingers as if she suddenly understands. 'You want to return something?'

That's it. If I stay here a second longer I'm going to punch her in the fucking face. I hare out of the shop.

I skitter down the aisle, ignoring the smiles and admiring glances of the other Shoppers and wannabes, all of whom are lugging bulging plastic bags or pushing trolleys piled high with shit. How can I have taken their various plastic surgeries or injuries for granted for the last few hours?

Duh. Brainwashed, that's what you are.

I can't argue with that.

'Ma'am!' a shop assistant calls from the doorway of a boutique selling complicated and painful-looking bondage gear. 'We're having a sale!'

'Fuck off!' I snap at her as I pass.

'Thank you for your time, ma'am!' she calls after me.

I've got myself into such a state that I race past the bookshop, and have to double back.

Please be there, Dan, *please*!

Might be too little too late. Prepare yourself.

The store looks empty, but I can make out a figure behind the counter – a tall figure with long dark hair. Thank Christ.

'Dan!' I yell.

He looks up.

'Oh thank God!' I say as I race up to him, now completely out of breath.

He stares at me, eyes blank. I'm not sure what's worse – his zombie stare or the fucking awful clown suit he's wearing. But maybe he just doesn't recognise me.

'I know – the hair, right? Look, don't ask. Now, get your arse into gear, we have to get the fuck out of here.'

He stares back at me vacantly, and then a grin spreads across his face. 'Good day, ma'am,' he says. 'How may I help you?'

Oh shit. They've got to him. 'It's me, Rhoda!' I yell into his face. 'You know, scruffy Rhoda who kept telling you to fuck off?'

He pushes a pile of books towards me. Their covers are emblazoned with Day-Glo stickers: Buy one, get three free, publishers clearing house. Wow. That's a good deal. But I'd have to get a bookcase, and I'm sure I—

RHODA!

Christ. I tear my eyes away from the books. 'Come on, Dan, say something!'

For a second I think I can make out the glimmer of recognition in his eyes. I reach over and slap him on the cheek. 'Dan! Come on! Snap out of it!'

He shakes his head, as if he's trying to clear it. There's a filthy bandage taped to the back of his head, and my stomach slips as I take in the dark brown and pus-yellow stains on it.

'Oh fuck,' I breathe. 'What have they done to you?'

'Rhoda?' he says in a small, tired voice.

'Yes! It's me!'

He pauses, drops his head, and then raises it again, the inane grin back on his face. 'Would you like to hear about our latest bestsellers?'

chapter 22

DANIEL

'Would you like to hear about our latest bestsellers?' I'm pleased with myself. I feel like I've chosen the exact right words.

The Shopper gives me an angry glare but her rage only pumps more calm through me. She's saying something else but I can't really understand it because it doesn't seem to have anything to do with our product range. I listen for keywords.

The Shopper grabs my shirt. I can smell the delicious fragrance of her perfume. Touched by a Shopper on my first day! I hope the Representative is watching this! '... you don't frhak dfao jakdgf, I Wilbur you...'

'Wilbur Williams? We have it. We have most of his backlist too. The new one is only due at Creditmas, but we have his latest in paperback.'

'... gadtggg hut the fuck up, Dan fgakst...'

'Oh, yes. We do have it: *Shut the Fuck Up and Earn*. It's currently on our business promotion and you get fifteen per cent off and bonus loyalty points with every purchase.'

She removes her talons from my shirt and smooths it down over my chest. 'Did you say bonus loyalty points?' Now I can hear her.

'Yes, ma'am. Double bonus points.'

'And what can I do with the points?' The Shopper starts to breathe more heavily, the satiny green of her dress rising and falling with each breath. It's almost time to close the deal.

It's Rhoda, you fucking idiot. What have they done to her?

'You get Book Bucks towards the purchase of your next book. Ma'am, our loyal Shoppers are very important clients. I can tell just by looking at you that you would spend your Book Bucks most elegantly.'

The Shopper smiles. 'Do you get a card?'

What have they done to her?

'Oh yes, ma'am. It's a very attractive one.' I pull one of the glittery, violet loyalty cards from under the register. She reaches out for it. I giggle coyly and snatch it away and slip a form and a pen in front of her. 'Just your details and signature, ma'am, and it's all yours.'

What have they done to you? Rhoda?

'Rhoda?'

A contraction jolts down my brain stem. I must have said something wrong but I can't remember what it was. The service enhancer will keep me in check.

The Shopper looks at me and puts down the pen, shakes her head like she's trying to dislodge something out of her ears. Kark, I'm losing her. They would be so proud of me if I sign up a Shopper on my first day. But now I've done something disregardful and I'm losing her.

'Ma'am, has my service disappointed you? I will try harder. Or I may direct your custom to an officer you feel may better serve you.'

'... ffgsak dghjcoo msbudgscx...' The Shopper shakes her head and stalks away. *Rhoda. It's me, Dan. Help me.*

Kark! I've lost her. So close. So karking close.

My phone beeps. The message contains the code for my thirty-moment victual break. I start copying it from my phone to my anklet and *don't just stand there idiot. You're off shift. Go and find Rhoda* I'm not sure whether to click out, because it is rated as highly disregardful to move from behind the register when you are on a register shift. If I work hard enough, if I sign up some Shoppers and make high-percentile sales, then perhaps I will be assigned a merchandising shift. How long will it take before I get a merchandising shift? That's a reward worth working towards! How exciting it will be to *Shut the fuck up for Christ's sake! Move! If you lose Rhoda now, it's your last chance gone.*

Gordon arrives to cover me while I am on victual break.

'You're on break, Darneel.' I admire his suit and his neat hair-style while he speaks.

'Oh. I wasn't sure what to… I didn't want to disregard…'

'You browns are a spasm. It's disregard *not* to go on break. Off you go. You only have twenty-eight moments left.'

'Okay, thanks.' I remember how to walk. I'm so pleased to have such reassuring colleagues. I am really loving my first day on the job.

I enter the rest of the code and click out and suddenly I'm hearing these voices shouting in my head again. They're confusing me. I should get some victuals but I'm not sure what this week's tokens are for. Should I get a *Daniel! Fuck's sake! You're running out of time. Find Rhoda!*

I rub at my penetration wound. This is new. My fingers come back bloody. What the fuck is this on my neck? Where am I? Where's Rhoda?

I'm trying to orient myself in the shop when jags of searing pain brand the back of my neck. I swing around.

'Rhoda?' She's wearing a ridiculous green mini and leather jacket; her overdone make-up amplifies the burn scar on her face. She looks like she should be selling herself on Oxford Road. Not that that's necessarily a bad thing. Her legs are thin and very long, and the mini very short. What a lovely Shopper, and I have had my neck scratched by her. My new colleagues are going to be so—

Whack. Her slap brings me to myself again. 'Christ, Rhoda,' I manage to mumble, 'what have they done to you?' We're standing in the greeting card section. 'Congratulations on your illness', reads one in lavender script lettering. 'You put the amp in amputation', says another.

'Speak for yourself. What the hell have you...' She stops mid-rant. It's unsettling to hear the voice of the Rhoda I know coming out of this disturbingly dressed woman. 'There's no time. We have to get out of here.'

'Out?' I ask. She draws her arm back again but I raise my hands in defence. 'No. No. I'm me. I'm here. Promise. I mean did you find a way out?' I eye her up and down. 'And why are you still here?'

'You can't trust anyone in this place. You can't trust yourself. There are three options and they're all a trap. We have to find the fourth.'

'I don't understand. What three options? Where have you been?' There are too many questions. I feel myself ebbing and flowing, at one moment I'm me, and the next, I'm me. Colt was right. She said it would take a while to get used to clicking in and out.

Rhoda pulls me out of the bookshop, babbling away in my ear. It takes all of my concentration to make sense of what she's saying. Something about rat people under a cinema, shopping, depreci-something, and a person called Napumla. 'So it's vital we find Napumla and ask her how she got the fuck out of here.'

I check my gelphone. 'I've got to get back soon.' This flat-out rushing and loud-talking is anti-productive. A Primo Shopper with double-bone head implants passes us, shaking his head. The commotion Rhoda's causing is creating a jarring environment for the Shoppers. It strikes me as disregard. 'I've only got twenty-five moments left of my break.'

'Minutes, arsehole, not moments. Remember where you're... What will happen if you miss your shift? If you just don't go back?'

'Jesus, Rhoda,' I whisper, as if Management can't hear me. 'Don't ask me questions like that. I don't want to find out, okay?' I don't want to lose my job. It's going well; I have a real aptitude for retail. And I owe Colt my regard.'

I try to pull my arm from Rhoda's grip. I almost free myself, but she shoots me a look that stops me dead. Not of anger, not of threat. It's a look of desperation.

'Okay. I'll skip my victuals. And my pee. Where do we find her? This Napumla?'

Rhoda shakes her head. 'How would I know?'

Her eyes stray to the other side of the aisle. A Shopper with a huge chin and a bare chest is rushing towards the escalators.

'Wait here,' she says to me. 'Do *not* go back to the bookshop.'

I watch as she totters towards the Shopper in her ridiculous boots. He pauses and smiles and then they're gabbing away like two housewives at the school fête. My fingers find my gelphone again. I could just slip back now, while Rhoda is busy. She looks so much... like she belongs. It would be the easiest thing in the—

'Dan!' she yells, racing back towards me, heels sliding over the tiles. 'That Shopper says Kinky Corsets is having a Squeeze Sale for one hour only! Napumla *must* be there, she'd be crazy to miss it. He says everything's on sale. Can you believe it? I mean *everything*. Vollers, Westwood, Lulu and Lush, Nyla, Diva, the whole toot. I swear, you could just—'

'Rhoda!' I bark.

'Right,' she says, shaking her head clear again. I know how she feels. The wound below my ear is itching badly now. I stick my finger under the bandage and dart it into the hole. There's slick blood, a thicker ooze, and at the end of my finger a plug of some sort of gel. I scratch it, pressing deeper because that's where the itch lies and the corridor melts into a shower of sparks. *Holy fuck. What's that? That is so fucking awesome.* I dig around a bit more to see what will happen.

'Dan, please,' begs Rhoda from a small, quiet corner of the fireworks display. 'Don't do that. Let's go.' She must have grabbed my hand because the moment my finger comes out of the hole the walls and floors become solid again. I pat the grubby bandage back over the wound and get my bearings. She steers me onto the escalators, and I can make out Kinky Corsets' garish pink signage on the floor below us. Rhoda manoeuvres off the escalator then teeters to a comical stop on her stiletto boots, almost breaking her ankle. She immediately starts ogling the medieval wares in the window. Now it's my turn to remind her to keep focused, and I nudge her in the ribs. We're acting like Laurel and Hardy. On acid.

I expected hordes of elbowing and shoving freaks rifling through bargain bins, but the shop is all but empty. A discreet sign in the window spells out: 'Squeeze Sale Now On. Shoppers Only'. A little ideogram of an Abnormal woman being thrown out of the shop door illustrates the sign.

A dozen or so absurdly and expensively dressed people saunter around the shop. They're either emaciated, scarred, amputated or huge and dripping with metal and jewels. There are no Abnormals. These Shoppers look like they'd easily feature in a glossy magazine advert. Just like Rhoda. I hesitate at the door. I don't want to go in. I'm ashamed of my body. The sales assistant and some of the customers glance admiringly at Rhoda, their expressions changing instantly when they catch sight of me. *What is that – creature – doing with that lovely Shopper?* their curled lips sneer.

'You go in,' I say to Rhoda. 'I'll just, uh…'

Rhoda opens her mouth to argue, but she also hasn't missed the disgusted looks I've been getting. 'Okay.' She puts her hand on my arm. 'I'll see if Napumla is inside and we can talk to her outside.' I take shelter next to the shop where nobody will notice me. Rhoda flicks a switch in her brain and sashays into the shop. I watch her bum moving as she goes.

I peer through the very edge of the window and watch Rhoda working the room. She feels up some whalebone stays, remembers herself and looks back at me guiltily. She totters on, scanning the other shoppers. She sighs in frustration.

'Napumla!' she calls. I can't believe she just did that. Security's going to... But I remember that Rhoda is a Shopper now. She can behave anyway she pleases. A couple of impressively fattened Shoppers look at her curiously, but no one else reacts.

'Napumla! Are you here?' Rhoda shouts again.

The curtain of the changing room twitches.

'Yes?'

A woman emerges. She has to be Napumla. She's starved and bleached and blue-veined to hell, but under it all, she is recognisably brown. If her face could move, it would show alarm as Rhoda approaches, but it's botoxed to Anchorage and back. She tries to dart away, but her six-inch stilettos are not made for darting. Rhoda speaks to her intensely for a moment then hustles her outside and tries to drag her into the nearest service corridor.

'Kark, darling,' Napumla shrills, 'not in there, please. You of all people should know how dangerous it is in there. That's the Guardian's terrain.' She gestures towards the back corridors; she only has three fingers on her left hand.

'Well, let's make it quick and we won't need to hang around,' Rhoda says, but we stop on the mall side of the service door.

'You're new, aren't you? I see you've made your choices. You'll make a good Shopper,' she tells Rhoda. 'You're beautiful.' She lifts her hand and strokes it over Rhoda's jawline and cheekbones, smooth side and scar side. To my surprise, Rhoda doesn't break her fucking arm. She just stands there, looking like a pampered cat.

'The best you could do,' Napumla turns to me without concealing her distaste, 'is Customer Care. But you know they'll want you to fatten. When I was Customer Care they wanted me to fatten. Can you believe it? Me? I had so much more potential as an S & A. My God, to think that—'

'Shut up!' I snap. 'We know you left. How? We need to know how.'

'That's not really the right question, now is it?' She speaks to Rhoda, as if I'm too low to address. 'The question is *why*.'

Rhoda stands motionless, staring at her amputations, Napumla's ears and nose pinned and stretched and moulded, her lips pouting, the whole thing like a rubber mask. There's something in Rhoda's eyes; fear, excitement, I can't tell. Is she looking into the void, or at an object of lust?

'How much longer do you think you're going to last?' she asks Napumla.

'How dare you?'

'I'm not insulting you, Napumla. I need to know. We're the same.'

'My girl,' Napumla says wearily, 'we are not the same. You're new here. You'll go out with the latest trend. I have been here longer than you can imagine; I've lasted seasons upon seasons.'

My gelphone buzzes briefly. A time reminder. Fifteen moments. I feel an urgent need to get back to work. 'Listen, Rhoda, I've got to get back. I'm hungry and I need to pee before my shift starts.'

Napumla takes my interruption as a signal to head out of the service corridor and back to the shop.

'Wait!' Rhoda calls. 'Wait… Please. We need to know how you got out.'

Napumla glances into the shadowy reaches of the corridor. 'Why?'

'We want to go home.'

'Home? Where do you think that is, my girl?'

'Please, just tell us.'

Napumla sighs, looks at her watch. 'Whatever. You go to the exit. You signal Management to let you out. If they ask you a question, answer honestly. That's all.'

'The exit? What exit?' I ask.

'There are no exits!' Rhoda says at the same time. 'Ben and Palesa said that—'

'They're wrong,' Napumla interrupts. 'There is one, if you know where to look.'

Rhoda sighs and swears under her breath. 'And do you know where to look?'

Napumla allows herself a look of superiority. 'Door seventy-two. Lower basement.'

'How do you know this?' I ask.

'I'd hate to stay and chat, darlings, but this corridor is giving me an itch in my crotch and the Squeeze Sale ends in a few moments.'

'Okay,' says Rhoda. 'Thanks.'

'Wait…' I call after her. 'This isn't good enough. You just walk out the door? *You just walk out the fucking door?* Then what? We need directions. We need to know what's waiting on the other side of the door.'

'I told you the how, but you'll find the why is more important,' Napumla says over her shoulder as she staggers away. Her twig-legs look like they're about to break. 'Why do you think I came back?'

'She's bullshitting us, Rhoda.'

'I don't know. Who knows?' she says. She's in some sort of daze. I feel limp too. All I want to do is get a snack and go back to work. I don't want to run. I don't want to open doors. I don't want to disregard. I don't want to be late for my shift.

'What's your girlfriend's name?' Rhoda says, snapping me out of it.

'Huh?'

'Your girlfriend. The chick at the phone shop.'

'She's not... Colt. Why?'

'We have to ask her how to get to door seventy-two.'

'What? Now?' I need to get back onto my shift. I'm hungry and I need to pee. 'We can do it later. Tomorrow.'

'If we don't do it now, we'll never do it.' Her voice is calm, no trace of emotion on her face, but it's the scariest thing I've ever heard her say.

'Okay.'

We hurry to the phone shop. Colt's behind the counter. I rush inside, leaving Rhoda gazing at the shoe shop across the walk. 'Colt, we need to talk.'

'Good day, sir.'

'Colt, it's me. Daniel.' What am I going to say? That we're going to leave? That, as my sponsor, she's going to have to deal with the consequences? 'I need your help to find a... place.'

'How can I help you, sir?' She flashes me her public smile. She's inside there somewhere, but I can't find her. *Fuck*. I try something different.

'What would happen if you were late for your shift?'

'Why, sir, I am loyal to the Last Call team. I would never disregard their ethos.'

'But, say... something came up. An emergency. An accident.'

'Are you all right, sir?' Is this Colt speaking now?

'What if you didn't report to work?' My gelphone buzzes again like the school bell at the end of break. Five moments.

'Why, sir? What else would you do?'

'What would they do to you? Management.'

'Do? Nothing, sir. I'm not a brown – no offence – I don't have to work. But I need to consume. Without work, I can't consume. Really, sir, what else would I do?' Are her eyes trying to reach me? Is she asking me to throw her a lifeline? To give her another option?

'Colt. Thank you for everything. I just want to say... Thanks.'

'A pleasure to be of assistance, sir. Call again!'

I don't want to leave it like that. Again, I have a powerful urge to go back to work. I can meet up with Colt for victuals. Nothing will happen to her. But I look across at Rhoda standing in front of some sort of poster board, and remember her words, the tiny spark in her dull eyes when she said them.

If we don't do it now, we'll never do it.

I leave the phone shop and join Rhoda.

'It's no good. She's clicked in and can't help us.'

'It doesn't matter,' she says with a laugh in her voice, the first natural Rhodaness I've heard from her since she found me. She's pointing at the poster, but it isn't actually a poster at all – it's a store directory and map. 'Here it is.' Written in cheerful blue script are the words 'Door 72, lower basement', and an arrow helpfully points towards a narrow alcove squeezed between two shops. It can't be that easy, can it? *It's not the how, it's the why.* There are still too many voices in my head.

'You coming?' asks Rhoda. She's already halfway down the corridor. I'm not going to let her get away this time. I trot after her. She smiles – a tired, effortful smile – peels her boots off and leaves them where they lie.

'Jesus, that Napumla was a fuckup,' she says as we jog to the down escalator. 'You would've thought she'd be happy to see some other people from... up there. Other browns. I don't know if she was angry or afraid or just fucking embarrassed.'

'Maybe she just didn't like being reminded of where she came from. You aren't tempted to become like her, are you?'

'I'm already like her,' Rhoda mumbles, and for a second I wonder if I've heard her correctly.

Rhoda stops dead. 'Fuuuuck,' she breathes out.

We've found it. Off the escalator, two lefts, just like the map said. Inset into an alcove, a door marked LB72.

Rhoda is already thumbing a message into her phone. She shows me the screen. She's written: <We want to leave. Open the door>

'Is that cool?' she says. But she hits <send> before I can answer. 'You think I should have said please?'

I'm more worried about what lies beyond the door. The Guardian? Is that what they call that fucking slavering creature? I don't know if I have the will to go through all that again. I can't remember when I last ate or drank, and I'll need all my energy. Make eating and resting a priority. Avoid the creature rather than confront it. Somehow I've been given another life on this level of this game. I'll have to be smarter this time; I'll have to think on my feet.

'You up to this?' I ask Rhoda. My phone buzzes silently. I lift it to the mouth of my pocket and peek at it.

<time up>

I push the phone back down without showing Rhoda the message.

She looks up. 'I don't know.'

'Me neither.'

Rhoda smiles and squeezes my arm. 'We'll make it. We're a good team. Plus I got us some fags.' She shakes the large tote bag that's slung over her shoulder. 'They make them fucking strong here. And look what else I've got.' She fishes in her bag and pulls out the knife.

'Cool,' I say. 'Fags and a knife, perfect health points booster.'

She gives me one of her 'what the fuck, Dan' looks. The old Rhoda's back. Maybe she's right. Maybe we are going to make it through okay.

Her phone beeps. She hands it to me. 'I can't,' she says simply.

*It's warm from her hand, and for a few seconds I avoid looking at it, bracing myself. But fuck it. I know what to expect. They're just bullies. It's just hazing. I thumb the message open.

<r u sure?>

I hand the phone back to her.

'That's it?' she says. 'Fuck.'

'Napumla said to answer honestly.'

'And that's what we're going to do.' But she doesn't make a move to tap in a response. 'So, Dan. This is it. Are you sure?'

Her eyes search my face, and I can sense that there's a part of her, some small part, that wants me to say no. That wants to stay here.

I open my mouth to say what I'm thinking, what I'm really thinking, which is that I'm not sure. That I'm tired of running. I'm tired of being scared. That maybe I should just go back to work.

'Dan?' she says. 'What is it? Yes or no?'

This is it. *Tell the truth.*

'Yes,' I whisper. She blinks and I can't tell if she's relieved or disappointed.

She types in: <yes>

She hits <send>.

The door clicks and swings ajar, a short patch of featureless concrete illuminated beyond. We step through. The door slams behind us with finality. Rhoda pushes against it, but it doesn't budge. There's no going back.

Rhoda flicks her gold Zippo, lengthens the flame. I make out the edges of another door a few paces ahead of us. I try the handle and the door moves. It can't be this easy, can it? *It's not the how, it's the why.*

I pull the door open.

'No fucking way,' Rhoda breathes.

I can't speak. I know exactly where we are, I can feel it in my gut.

We're home.

PART 2 >>

PART 2

chapter 23

RHODA

I hesitate for a second before I go in, double-checking that I can still hear the reassuring drone of the vacuum cleaner in the background. Yep. All clear. I'm not too worried about getting caught. I'd heard Dan's mother ('call me Rose') firing instructions at Florence on her way out this morning, and from past experience she'll be gone for at least an hour. Pushing the Rat Dogs away with my foot so that they don't follow me in, I shut the door behind me and glance around. Rose's bedroom looks exactly as I expected it would: an overabundance of throw cushions, peach satin curtains and a carpet so thick you could hide a corpse in it.

The Rat Dogs whine and scratch outside the door, and I crank it open slightly to let the spoilt little fuckers in. Clarissa, the smaller of the two and some kind of inbred miniature poodle, blinks at me through rheumy eyes before skittering in and struggling onto the bed, immediately infesting the room with her sickly stench. She's way past her sell-by date; covered in lumps that I'm pretty sure are cancerous. The other one – Lulu, a less decrepit version, but just as revolting – hesitates by the door, growling softly.

'Shut the fuck up,' I hiss at her. She whines again and slinks away, pausing at the top of the stairs. I'm tempted to boot her down them, but it's not her fault she's a racist. Bad upbringing.

Now, where to start? I decide on the bedside cabinet. I have to strain to pull open the drawer – it's stiff with lack of use – and it springs out suddenly, almost tipping its contents onto the carpet. There isn't much here. Just a few old receipts, a couple of HRT patches and a neglected Jodi Picoult novel. No cash, no vibrator; not even a bloody diary. Boring.

Next, the chest of drawers. Most of Rose's underwear is of the giant beige figure-control kind, but I unearth one skimpy g-string that still has its price tag attached. Then, bingo! My fingers find the edges of an envelope that's squashed beneath a stack of elasticised girdles. It contains several glossy photos of a paunchy white man with a comb-over. I flick through them. In most of the photos he's sitting on a couch next to a black Labrador, mugging for the camera. Dan's dad? I can't see any family resemblance and, judging by his disastrous jumper, the photo was probably taken some time in the eighties. Neither Rose nor Dan has mentioned any sort of father figure. Must be some kind of embarrassing family scandal. Mementoes of dead relatives usually have pride of place on the mantelpiece; they're not usually stuffed like dirty secrets in underwear drawers.

I move onto the double-door closets. Impressive. Rose clearly doesn't stint on her clothing budget. I pull out a Christian Lacroix jacket that looks like the seventies has thrown up all over it, and an Ann Klein skirt that has to be at least two sizes too small for her. I run my fingers over the skirt's fabric. Nice. Expensive. I hold it up to my body and glance in the mirror, shaking my hair over my face. A few of the extensions are looking a bit frayed, but they'll do for now. Behind the curtain of hair, the scar's hardly visible at all. It's the rest of me that looks like a bag of shite. My green silk dress is in the wash at the mercy of

Florence, and it's surprising how much I'm mourning the feel of its expensive material on my skin. Especially in comparison to what I'm wearing now: a pair of Dan's black sweatpants that hang on me like clown trousers, and a T-shirt that reaches my knees. I'm not too charmed by the *Nightmare Before Christmas* logo on it, either, but beggars can't be choosers.

I decide to take the skirt – Rose probably won't even miss it. Clarissa whines as if she's just read my mind.

'I won't tell if you don't,' I say to her. She cocks her head on one side as if she's considering this, and the gesture makes me hate her less.

The vacuum cleaner drone cuts out. I shove the skirt under my T-shirt and usher Clarissa off the bed and out into the corridor. I shut the door behind me and tip-toe back into Dan's room.

After the diseased dog stink and the cloying perfumed scent of Rose's room, the stale fag smoke that permeates the space is almost a relief. But *Christ* he's a slob. The coffee mug on the window ledge is full of fag butts, and the place is littered with discarded socks, computer game covers and boxer shorts. There's even a graveyard of cigarette ends carelessly stubbed out on a CD next to his side of the bed. He's become a dedicated chain smoker – even managing to out-smoke me. We've nearly finished the carton of fags I brought back with me, and I have to scratch around the room to find a half-empty packet.

I plonk myself down in front of the laptop and quickly scan his Gmail account (there's nothing of interest – not even spam), and then click onto the missing-children page on Facebook that I've been haunting like a stalker ever since we returned three days ago. Nothing new. I'm not sure if I'm relieved or disappointed. For the last three days I've been scouring the news sites and trawling Google, but there's nothing about a missing white kid anywhere on the web. Dan keeps assuring me that there's no way rich white folks wouldn't kick up a media stink if they thought their kid had been abducted. Still, it's a total fucker that I can't remember the kid's name.

Should I try phoning Zinzi again? I finger the phone in my pocket, but can't muster up the energy. I tried her when we first got back, but her phone just beeped and then cut out. The bitch is either blanking me, or letting me know that I'm in serious shit. I know I should just head straight to the flat. But fuck it. Do I really want to deal with a pissed-off Zinzi right now? Do I, *fuck*. What if she gives me a hard time and I crack? I could still be suffering from post-traumatic stress disorder, after all.

But that's bollocks and I know it.

The only thing I'm suffering from is the usual Rhoda insecurity bullshit, and if I'm in the throes of some sort of delayed shock reaction, the symptoms haven't shown themselves. If anything, the overriding emotion I'm feeling is boredom.

In fact, coming back has turned out to be a total fucking anticlimax. Even the first few minutes after we stepped through that door and found ourselves back in the real Highgate Mall were seriously low-key.

You'd think we'd have danced around in glee at our lucky escape, maybe fainted with relief, kissed the travertine tiles and sobbed with joy. That would have been a normal reaction. But we didn't do any of that. In fact, for several minutes after we made it through, we just stood numbly outside a shop selling expensive homeware, ignoring the stares of the shoppers and staff behind the display windows. Finally I nudged Dan and said, 'You think this is another trick?'

'I don't know,' he said.

'You think we're actually *back*?'

He shrugged.

'It doesn't feel... right...' I said, unable to put what I was feeling into words. Because 'real life' looked... different. Not quite how I remembered it. The people seemed to be... greyer, less substantial almost, as if I was looking at them through misted glass. Dull, featureless, everyday. But that was probably just the effects of exhaustion and stress.

'What now?' I said.

'Let's go home.'

'I don't have a home.'

'Yes, you do,' he said.

And then he'd taken my hand and led me towards the exit door.

It was as simple and mundane as that.

Thankfully his car keys were still where he'd dropped them when I'd accosted him in the parking lot forever ago – hidden beneath the front wheel. Wordlessly we climbed in and drove away, as if we'd just spent the afternoon buying a pair of new shoes, or comparing prices at the iMac store.

Of course, things didn't go so smoothly when we arrived at Dan's place.

I wasn't shocked that Dan still lived with his mother – I'd been expecting that. What did throw me was the place itself – a double-storey pseudo-mansion, ringed by razor-wire, electronic gates and a landscaped garden. I'd assumed Dan fell more into the poor-white demographic.

We barely turned off the engine when Rose flew out of the front door, shrieking at the top of her voice, and almost breaking her ankle as she stumbled in her high heels.

'Daniel!' she said, throwing her arms around him. 'Where have you been?' She stood back to assess him. He looked like utter shit, but at least his hair hid the wound on the back of his neck. 'I even called the police but they refused to take it seriously. What have you *done* to yourself?'

'Mom,' he said wearily, 'I'm fine. This is Rhoda.'

Up until that point, Rose only had eyes for her son. There was a short, awkward pause while she took in the full beauty of my smudged make-up, and, of course, the colour of my skin.

'Rhoda will be staying with me for a while,' Dan said.

Face rigid with shock, she opened her mouth to say something, but then the two Rat Dogs let rip, dancing and nipping at my ankles.

'Lulu! Clarissa! Shh!' she snapped. 'I'm sorry. They're not good with strangers.'

I knew what she actually meant: they weren't good with strangers *of colour*, but I smiled benignly. 'It's fine—' I said, but Rose wasn't listening.

She turned to Dan again. 'Where have you been?'

'I'll explain later, Mom.'

'Are you hurt?' she said. She grabbed his arms, but he shrugged her away.

I put on my best posh English accent. 'It's all my fault, Mrs...?'

'Call me Rose,' she snapped automatically. 'What do you mean, it's all your fault?'

I took a deep breath. 'Dan saved my life.'

Rose's mouth dropped open, and even the dogs ceased their hysterics. '*What?*'

'It's a long story,' I said.

'Go on,' she said, holding my gaze.

'Mom!' Dan said, sounding just like a small boy. 'Can't we do this tomorrow? I need to sleep.'

'Dan,' I said pointedly. 'Your mother deserves an explanation.'

Dan looked at me in surprise. He'd never seen this side of me: well-behaved Rhoda. Articulate, charming, and utterly full of shit.

Slightly mollified, Rose ushered us through into the lounge.

Dan and I sank into the couch and Rose sat opposite us, back rigid.

'Well?' she said. Her gaze kept sliding over my body, taking in my bare feet, my dress, the hair extensions. It was pretty clear she didn't know what to make of me.

I knew I'd need all my wits about me to get through this, but exhaustion and disorientation were taking their toll. Fortunately lying is one of the few things I'm very, very good at.

'I came out here on holiday,' I began. 'From the UK. You can probably tell that from my accent.' I smiled at her, but she stared back, impassive. 'Anyway, I'd just popped into the mall where Dan works, and had parked my hire car in the car park. I was climbing out when, out of nowhere, these two men held a knife to my throat.'

'No!' Rose gasped.

'I'm afraid so,' I said, allowing a tremor to enter my voice. Dan was staring at me in frank astonishment.

'They took my bag, my passport and everything.'

Rose's gaze drifted down to the bag at my feet.

'My other bag,' I said. Shit. 'And then Dan appeared. He saw what was happening and jumped in to help.'

Rose let out a little scream and clutched her throat. The Rat Dogs whined in unison. 'Daniel! You could have been stabbed!'

'I owe Dan my life, Rose. It looked like they had... plans for me as well.'

'And this was at the mall? Highgate Mall?' she said, her voice full of horror. 'When? What time?'

'Quite late. Nineish, wasn't it, Dan?'

He was still too gobsmacked to respond.

'Appalling,' Rose said.

I nodded. 'It was terrifying. I don't know what would have happened to me if Dan hadn't come along.' I was beginning to enjoy this.

'But you've been gone for almost two days!' Rose said to Dan.

Dan and I shared a glance. Just two days? How the fuck...

'Daniel! Where have you been all this time?'

'That's the thing, Mom,' Dan said, 'we—'

'After Dan threatened them, they dragged us down to the basement and locked us in a storage garage,' I jumped in, improvising wildly. 'And we've only just managed to get out of there.' I held her gaze. I didn't really give a shit if she believed me or not. 'A security guard let us out.'

'But... two days?'

'Yes,' I said.

'Thank God they didn't...'

'Kill us?' I said. 'All down to Dan. He convinced them not to.'

'Daniel? Is this true?'

I had to give Dan credit. He didn't even hesitate. 'Of course.'

'But you must be starving! Daniel, shall I make you something to eat?'

'We're fine, Mom.' He fumbled in my bag, pulled out a box of smokes and lit up.

'Daniel!' Rose squealed in horror. 'What are you doing?' She stood up. 'I'm calling the police.'

'It's just a cigarette, Mom!'

I couldn't help the snort of laughter. Rose glared at me.

'I won't lie to you, Daniel. I am gravely disappointed to see you... you...' The woman couldn't even say 'smoking'. 'But the police need to know about your... ordeal!'

'Mom,' Dan said, 'it's under control.'

'But this... this is a... Something must be done!'

'It's fine, Rose,' I said. 'We've already spoken to the police.'

'Why didn't you call me, Daniel?' Rose said.

'I didn't want to worry you,' he said. I gave him a small smile of encouragement.

She opened her mouth to speak, but Dan stood up.

'*Enough*, Mom,' he said, and I could tell by the expression on her face that she wasn't used to being spoken to like that, especially not by her son. 'Look. We really need to sleep.'

Realising she was beaten (for now), Rose ran a hand through her highlighted curls. 'I'll get the spare room ready,' she said.

'Don't worry, Mom,' Dan said. 'Rhoda can stay in my room.'

Her skin began to turn puce under the thick coating of her make-up. 'I really don't—'

'I don't want to be any trouble,' I interrupted in the sweetest voice I could muster. She shot me a look of pure suspicion. I realised then that Rose wasn't stupid and I'd have to watch my step with her. But the story was the best I could come up with at short notice. And it wasn't as if we could have told her the truth. That would have led straight to the nuthouse.

'Where are your things?' she said to me. 'Your luggage. Weren't you staying at a hotel?'

Shit. That was the problem with lying. I hadn't really had the time to think things through.

'Come on, Rhoda,' Dan said, taking my hand. 'Let's go.'

Without another word to his mother, Dan led me straight up the stairs and into his bedroom. Although I would have murdered for a shower right then, we both collapsed onto his single bed. And we were both asleep in seconds.

I type another combination of the words brown+mall+alternative+reality into Google, but a quick scroll down the page doesn't reveal any links I haven't seen before. Fuck it. Not even the obscure conspiracy theory sites have any accounts that even approximate what Dan and I have been through.

The smoky fug in the air is starting to get oppressive. Grabbing the box of Turkish fags, I head out.

I pass Florence in the hallway. She's angrily spraying the mirrors with Windowlene, wiping the glass clean with furious strokes.

'All right, Florence?' I say.

'Ja,' she snaps, glaring at me. I smile back at her. I like

Florence. She's a snarly old seething pot of resentment, but at least I know where I stand with her.

I wander out into the back garden, pushing the Rat Dogs back inside with my foot when they try to follow. I light up and sit down on the patio step.

I need to make a plan. I need to decide what the fuck I'm going to do next. I can't stay at Dan's much longer. I have no way of knowing if Zinzi still has my stuff or if she's chucked it out or sold it or whatever. The only good thing I've got going for me is that I have absolutely no desire to try and score any blow. In fact, even the thought of a joint doesn't appeal in the slightest.

I stub out the fag and head back in just as Rose comes bustling through the front door. Shit. If I'd known she was back I would have stayed in Dan's room.

'Oh, it's you, Rhoda,' she says, trying to look pleased to see me. 'How are you this morning?'

'Fine thanks,' I say.

'Have you eaten?'

'Yes thanks,' I lie. My appetite for food has gone the same way as my appetite for drugs.

She hesitates, torn between politeness and her obvious anti-pathy towards me. It's the first time we've been alone together; Dan usually provides the buffer between our mutual dislike.

'Will you join me for a coffee?' she says.

'That would be lovely, thank you.'

She nods curtly. Her foundation is caked on thick, accentuat-ing the creases around her mouth. Still, she knows how to dress.

'Florence!' she calls. 'Please bring a cafetière into the lounge.'

I make myself comfortable on the couch, sitting with my back straight and ankles crossed, à la Princess Di.

'This is such a lovely room,' I say. It isn't. It's as bland and unimaginatively furnished as the lobby of a mid-range business hotel.

'Thank you,' she says, slightly thrown. I let the uncomfortable silence stretch on. We covered the basics on that first awkward morning: where I was from, what my parents did, etc., but she hasn't yet dared stray into more personal areas. I'm looking forward to seeing if she'll do so now.

Florence slinks into the room, face like a smacked arse. Whenever I see her I can't help but stare at her skin – it's as wrinkled and weathered as a raisin's, and has that leathery look to it you see in elderly sun worshippers or alcoholics.

'Here you are, madam,' she says to Rose.

'Thank you, Florence,' Rose says without looking at her. The Rat Dogs pad through, yap at me and then slump at Rose's feet, filling the room with their stench. Florence shoots me a baleful glare and shuffles out.

'So. Daniel's at work,' Rose says, stating the obvious.

'Yes.'

'And have you heard from the police?'

'No.'

'Shame. This whole thing. The… incident. How dreadful for you.' Her sympathy's as phony as Jordan's tits, and she doesn't even attempt to sound genuine. I begin to feel a slight smidgen of respect for her. 'Have you contacted the British Embassy about getting a new passport?'

'Yes,' I lie.

She clucks her tongue. 'I was wondering… How long will you be staying?'

I put my feet up on the coffee table and dunk one of the WeightWatchers biscuits into the coffee. 'I'm not sure. Why, is there a problem?' I gaze up at her innocently. 'You must let me know if it's a problem my being here, and I'll let Dan know immediately.' I blast her with a full-wattage smile and she can't help but respond. That's the thing about being a miserable non-smiling bastard: when you do, it totally disarms people.

'There's no problem,' she says.

'Good.' I nod towards the mantelpiece above the fake fire-place. 'Nice collection of photos.' They are all of Dan: Dan as a baby, chubby and cheerful; Dan in school uniform, uncomfortable in his blazer, but still grinning at the camera; and then Dan as a gangly almost-teen, acne scoring his cheeks, the smile long gone, looking every inch a magnet for bullies.

'Aren't they lovely? He was such a super child.' She pauses. 'Rhoda, may I be frank with you?'

'Of course, Rose. Please.' This is going to be fun.

'I was wondering. What is the... nature of your relationship with Daniel?'

I pretend to look confused. 'The *nature*, Rose?'

'I mean... are you and he...'

I click my fingers and notch up the cut-glass accent. 'Ah! You want to know if we're fucking each other?'

The look on her face is priceless. She's about to speak, but then my phone beeps, making both of us jump. I check the screen; as always, the beep of a phone still has the power to put me on edge. But it's Dan.

'Speak of the devil! Sorry, Rose,' I say sweetly. 'I'll just have to take this.'

She's still trying to regain her composure and just waves a hand in my direction.

'Hi, *Dan*,' I say. 'What's up?'

'Just checking in.' I can hear the hiss of his breath and he draws in a lungful of smoke. He sounds exhausted.

'How's it going?'

'It's not.'

'You get in any shit for missing work?' Rose shakes her head in disgust at the swear word and I wink at her.

'Not really.'

'Where are you?'

'Having a smoke break.'

'Where?'

'Out back. Where everyone goes.'

'Fuck it, Dan!' I say, my voice rising, forgetting about Rose for a second. 'You're in the corridors? Behind the shop?'

He doesn't speak for several seconds. 'It's cool, Rhoda.'

'Dan, it's totally not cool.' I glance at Rose. She's doing her best to pretend she isn't hanging on every word. 'Look, get out of there and we'll talk about this tonight, okay?'

'Sure. You okay?'

'Yeah. You know me.'

He doesn't answer that. 'See you in a couple of hours.'

He hangs up, and I listen to the dial tone for several seconds. I nod, smile and then say, 'Love you too,' just for the hell of it.

Rose flinches, as I knew she would.

I'm outside lighting up the last of the fags when Dan pulls into the driveway.

'Hey,' I say, as he hauls himself out of the car. He looks finished. The dark rings around his eyes are becoming a permanent fixture. 'How was work?'

'Fucking nightmare.'

'So why don't you quit?'

He shakes his head in exasperation as if I've just said something completely insane, and glances towards the front door. The silhouette of Rose's body looms behind the frosted glass.

'I think your mum wants me to leave,' I say.

He plucks the cigarette out of my hand and takes a deep, shuddering drag, blowing the smoke out of his nostrils as if he's been smoking his whole life. 'Don't worry about it.'

He idly scratches at the back of his neck, fingernails digging and poking under his hair and beneath the collar of his shirt. The tips of his fingers come back bloody, and he wipes them on his jeans.

'If you wanted me to leave, you'd let me know, right?' I say. 'I mean, I may be a freak, but I'm not a sponger.'

'I don't want you to leave,' he says, his voice sounding a million years old. 'And stop saying you're a freak. You're not.'

I raise an eyebrow at him. 'You sure about that?'

'Ja,' he says, smiling at me. 'I'm sure. Compared to everyone else we met at that... place, you're actually pretty boring.'

'Thanks, I think.' I try to smile back at him, but the mention of the other mall has unnerved me. It's the first time he's even alluded to it since we escaped.

'I can't stay here for ever, Dan.'

He stares straight at me. 'Why not?'

He chucks the fag-end into the rose bushes and slouches into the house, pushing straight past his mother and heading for the stairs. I follow, giving Rose a rueful shrug as I edge past her.

'Dan,' she calls after him. 'How was work?'

'Fine,' he says, without turning around.

'I'm cooking something special tonight.'

'Great,' he says, without slowing his stride.

When we reach his room he throws his body down on the bed and flings an arm over his eyes.

'Dan?' I say. 'How often do you think about, you know, what we went through?'

He doesn't answer for a couple of seconds. 'All the time,' he says.

'Really? Because I don't.'

'You don't?'

'No. Do you think that's weird?'

'No,' he says. He turns on his side and his breathing changes. Fast asleep.

I rummage in his jacket, retrieve his packet of Winstons, light up and sink back down in front of the computer.

I play a game of spider solitaire, trawl the news sites again, make another sweep of the conspiracy sites, and finally click onto missing.co.za for the third time that day.

I sit up. There's a new face on the front page. A face that looks unnervingly familiar.

It takes me several seconds before I realise that it's mine.

chapter 24

DANIEL

I'm standing in the corridor, propping myself against the smokers' wall with my foot. I pull another cigarette out of the pack and light it with the butt of the last. A few metres away, just past the alcove, Josie's whispering something to Katrien. But fuck them. For once I don't care what they're saying.

That... place... broke something in me. I don't know who I am any more.

Or maybe it fixed me. Maybe I know exactly who I am now. I finger Rhoda's knife where it sits in my jeans pocket. I found it when I was digging through her bag for some cigarettes and I pocketed it, almost without thinking. I like having something of hers with me.

Katrien nudges Josie and stubs her cigarette out on the wall behind her. She looks at me as if she's seeing me for the first time, pauses as if she's going to say something, but changes her mind and carts herself back inside.

Josie lingers a little.

'When did you start smoking?' she asks.

Before, I would have sold my soul just to have her speak to me. Now I just feel a spark of irritation. Unbidden, I get a flash of blonde bodies swinging redly in infinite mirrors. I shake it off.

I shrug. 'I dunno. A while.'

'You've been out here ages. Bradley's going to... You can't chain smoke instead of work.' She says it like it's a joke she's sharing with me.

'I give a fuck what Bradley says.'

I know my surliness will offend her, but I like the feel of the scowl on my face, the burn of tar in my lungs. I'm done trying to be nice. I'm done taking their shit. She starts to turn away, but then hesitates. 'Jeez. You're off sick for a couple of days and you come back... all...'

I wait, looking into her eyes without flinching. She is pretty, there's no denying it. She holds my gaze then walks away again. I watch her arse and her legs in her jeans. 'It suits you,' she says without turning around. I'm waiting for that voice inside me to start squealing, *She likes me! Should I ask her out? What will I say?* But that voice is silenced by a thick layer of filth and memory and rage. I light another cigarette with Rhoda's Zippo and stroll back the long way, through the service corridor and to the front of the shop. I take a few puffs in the doorway and grind the butt out against the display window.

Bradley skitters up to me. 'Come on, Daniel,' he whinges. 'That's just not acceptable. You're late for your counter shift.'

I just look at him. It's only in these last few days that I've realised I'm taller than him.

'In fact, take your dinner break now and put a new shirt on. You stink of smoke. And I'm going to dock you an hour.'

Did he sound so high-pitched before? He's like a mosquito.

'Ja. I'm here now.' Katrien and Josie are staring at me, caught in mid-transaction. The bejewelled customer they're dealing with also watches with interest.

Bradley's face drops. 'I – I. Listen here. You can't... In fact, I'm giving you a written warning. It's really unacceptable.'

Did I seriously put up with this before? I'd rather have a whiskey and a cigarette than stand here, and if there's one thing I've learned lately it's that life's too short to waste your time on shit you don't want to be doing. Especially when you know what you'd rather be doing.

'Ag, stick it up your arse, Bradley.' I walk out of the shop, imagining their faces. Josie, Katrien, the customers, Bradley.

So, ten thirty on a Tuesday morning, I'm sitting in the bar at JB's, drinking my second double and smoking another fag. I stick my finger into the hole under my ear and dig around a bit. It's become a habit since we came back. I want to see what I saw when I did it first; I want to feel what I felt. But there's no magical light show; all it does is throb. I wipe the film of bloody mucus on my jeans and take another slow drag.

I don't want to go home. I don't want to deal with Mom's neediness, her constant nagging and watch Rhoda put on her middle-class private-schoolgirl act. The strung-out druggie freak who beat the shit out of me and held me at knifepoint just six days ago seems to be some distant dream. But rather that dream than this nightmare.

Do I mean that? Would I rather be caked in shit, running for my life, or here, at home, doing the same old crap I've always done?

These fucking Johannesburg suburbs: they suck you in. They want you to get comfortable and complacent and enslaved just like the rest of the rats in this city. Working to pay for shit we don't need so that we can feel happy we've got a job. Putting up with prats like Bradley. Or even worse, ending up like my mom, selling herself for a big, ugly house and a car.

I down my whiskey and call for another. I stare at the face reflected in the mirror behind the bar. I'm not the same person. None of this bothered me last week. Nothing bothered me last week except whether Josie liked me.

And what about Rhoda? Is she still playing the game, or is it over for her?

I don't want to go home; I'm scared to find out.

I down another double, wait for the alcohol to hit. It doesn't. I can't even get fucking drunk. But I keep trying till the end of my shift, till my money's run out.

When I get home, Rhoda is lying on a sun lounger by the pool. She's wearing a pair of my board shorts and a vest and has my music in her ears; the dogs are lying in the sun next to her. At least she's not wearing my mom's bikini. The dogs jump up and sniff my legs as I cross the lawn, then look up at me, bemused. They can't seem to find a trace of me either under this smoke and booze sweat. I lean down to fluff Clarrie's head but she flinches away.

Rhoda looks over at me and takes out the earphones. She shifts to semi-sitting and crosses one foot over the other. Her legs are glistening with sun cream. I try not to look at her small breasts inside my top, but fail.

'Dan. I've got to tell you someth—' She stops as my smell reaches her before the rest of me. I sit down heavily on the side of the lounger, almost tipping her over. 'Christ, you don't look too good. You smell like a fucking ashtray a wino pissed in.'

'I just quit.'

'Smoking?'

'My job.'

'What? Why? What happened?' There's something about her tone. It's almost as if she's going to launch into a Rose-like nag. *You give up too easily, darling. Daniel, you really should apply yourself more. You have such promise, but you waste it idling and staring at the ceiling. Opportunity won't knock on the ceiling, my boy.*

'Oh, never mind. What did you want to say?'

Rhoda puts her hand on my arm. 'I'm worried about you. You haven't been... yourself for days now.'

Myself? *Myself? What the fuck do you know about who I am? This is me. Right here. You taught me that. Until you changed. You changed. Not me. You, sitting like a fucking suburban princess on my mother's fucking sun lounger.*

'I'm just tired,' I say.

'Listen, Dan. I say I need to go, I know your mother doesn't want me here, and you tell me to stay. What are we doing? Where do we go from here? What do you want to do?'

I want you to tell me what to do. The only time I ever did anything interesting with my life, I was following you. I need you to tell me what to do.

'I don't know. I need to... I don't know,' I say.

Rhoda starts winding the iPod's cord, looks away from me. 'I'm going to go. It was fun. But I've got stuff to sort out, and the sooner I start the better.' She gets up.

'Wait, Rhoda. I don't want...'

She stands, arms folded, waiting, challenging me to say what I mean. Then when she sees I'm not going to say any more she shakes her head, and I see a flush of anger settling in her face, and I recognise the knife-fighter I met those lifetimes ago. 'What happened to you?' she says.

'You know what happened to me,' I tell her. 'It happened to you too.'

'No, I mean since we got back. At least you could string a fucking sentence together in that place.'

'Rhoda, it's not the same any more.' I slump over and lean my chin on my hand.

But I feel her arm around my shoulder. She's sitting next to me. 'I know...' And now she's smelling the skin around my neck, breathing in the smoke and the whiskey sweat like a memory, and her face is pushing against my skin and it feels warm, and then we're kissing and her mouth tastes different from anything I've tasted before. So much realler than I ever would have believed. Her hands are moving over my clothes and under my shirt and my fingers are on her face, feeling the scars, pressing them into my palms, and I want to fuck her right here, on my mother's sun lounger, and my hands are pulling up the vest, nudging over more scar tissue, and the dogs are milling about, squealing, not knowing who to protect, and then they bolt away, yapping with glee and the garage door is shearing open.

My mother is home from bridge.

'You need to move out,' Rhoda licks into my ear.

By the time Mom's rattled out of the car and through the house onto the patio, Rhoda and I are straightened up and sitting half a metre apart, looking innocent. I make a show of lighting up a fag for Rhoda and then myself as Mom picks off her heels and tiptoes across to us, the dogs trotting at her feet, tattling tales in Pomeranian. I know how much the smoking bothers her and sometimes I ask myself why I want to hurt her, but no answer comes. I just like smoking. It distinguishes me.

'Daniel, I wish you wouldn't. It's so... unhealthy.'

I blow out a stream of smoke in her direction and she flinches, then shoots a disapproving look at Rhoda. To my surprise, Rhoda grinds out her cigarette on the edge of the pool. 'Sorry, Rose. I am trying to cut down.'

'It's okay, Rhoda. It's not you I worry about. It's Daniel. I told you about Alvin... and I just wouldn't... want—'

I stop listening. She *what*? She told Rhoda about Dad? No fucking way. I glare at Rhoda. Her eyes shift, her gaze landing anywhere but my face. 'I've got to go.' I get up and stalk inside and grab my keys from the kitchen counter, but now Mom's parked behind me. I can't very well go outside and ask her to move her fucking car before I make my grand exit, can I? I go upstairs and slam my door, making sure they can hear it down in the garden.

I slump on the bed, which Florence has made neatly. She's picked up Rhoda's clothes and shaped them into sharp little passive-aggressive squares stacked on the chest of drawers.

There's a perfunctory knock on the door, and Rhoda barges in, ready to argue, Clarissa at her heels as backup. 'Dan, don't blame your mother fo—' But she stops when she sees I'm laughing.

'I'm too old for this shit, Rhoda.'

'Yes, you are.' She sits down on the bed next to me. Some of the electricity from earlier is still coursing and I touch her hand. She laces her fingers through mine.

'I would have told you about Dad, you know. It's not some big secret.'

Rhoda doesn't say anything, but there's an expression of pity on her face. I don't want to be pitied.

'Did she tell you about Frank?' I ask.

'Uh, a bit. Just that she was seeing a married man.' She takes the cigarette from my mouth, taps the ash worm into the saucer by the bed, takes a long drag.

'Ja. The slimy fucking bastard.' I pause, wondering how much I want to tell Rhoda. All of that was before. This is now. 'Do you know how she's able to shop and play bridge all day, and live in this house and drive a Merc?'

Rhoda takes a last suck and grinds the butt out. 'I can guess,' she breathes out with her smoke. Clarissa curls onto the rug in the sun and starts licking herself.

'Ja. And meantime Rank Frank is sitting at the head of his company, appearing in public with his happy family, probably fucking another five women until they get too old for him. Then he pays them all off for their silence, a fraction of the income from his dodgy business deals.'

'I'm sorry, Dan.'

'Thanks.' I miss my father. He smoked till he died of lung cancer. I light up another one, then scratch at my neck-hole.

Rhoda slaps my hand away, just this side of friendly. 'Stop it. Please.'

I hear my mother chatting to Florence downstairs in the kitchen as she chops up something for lunch. I can't remember what it was like before. Was Mom always this long-suffering? I basically tell her to fuck off, and fuck your dead husband too, and she goes into the kitchen to make me some lunch. Have I always been such a bastard to her? She should have thrown me out a long time ago.

'What happened at work?'

'Ag, just that prat, Bradley. He's such a fucking toady. He shat on me in front of everyone for smoking. I was just making up for all the smoke breaks I didn't take.'

Rhoda doesn't smile. 'You weren't smoking in the corridor again, were you? I thought you'd promised.'

'Jesus, what's the big deal? Everyone smokes there all the time. None of them get eaten by fucking monsters. It's never going to happen again. It never happened. Down the end of that corridor is the fucking Woolworths receiving bay, not some monster-infested never-neverland. It never happened. We're in the real world, forever and ever and ever. This is it. It's over.'

Rhoda stands up, angry. She jabs at the hole behind my ear. 'This happened, fuckwit. This happened!'

'Ouch!'

'Sorry.' She sits down again and stares out of the window for a while. 'It doesn't feel over.'

'What, you want a text message to tell us what to do next? Check your phone.' I say. We both pause. I know she's wishing, just like me, that something will happen. But there are no message beeps; there's just the sound of a dog barking next door, traffic on the road, someone mowing a lawn a few houses away.

'This is it, Rhoda. Game over.' You don't even get three options here.

Rhoda swings her legs up on the bed and lies flat on her back. I shift down from my slump to lie next to her.

'I don't know what to do next,' she says. 'If I was trying to score some coke or weed, I'd know exactly what was next.'

'You tempted?'

'Not at all. Fuck, whatever happened down there – whatever didn't happen – was the world's greatest rehab programme.'

'But they don't tell you what to do next.'

'They don't tell you what to do next.'

It's quiet for a while. I listen to the food blender downstairs, to the sound of Florence knocking about with her broom, Clarissa scrolfing on the rug. The mowing down the road has been replaced with hammering or hacking. Rhoda's breathing slows and deepens. I look over to see if she's sleeping.

'I wanted to tell you,' she says without opening her eyes. 'I'm on a missing persons website.'

'Jeez. Seriously?'

'Yeah. Looks like my parents are trying to track me down.'

'But we weren't gone that long.'

She finally opens her eyes and looks into mine. 'Dan. I haven't spoken to them for over four years.'

chapter 25

RHODA

For fuck's sake. I know she's in there. I can hear the tinny sound of the *Bold and the Beautiful* intro behind the door.

I jam the buzzer again, holding it down with my thumb. 'Zinzi!'

Finally I hear the clump of footsteps. 'Who the fuck is that?'

'It's me!' I call.

I hear her fumbling with the deadbolt, and the door creaks open. 'Yeah?' She stares at me through the security gate, no sign of recognition on her face. Her eyes are bleary, ringed red, and a waft of dope smoke floats out of the flat to greet me. We've been cousins for fuck knows how many years. Nice to know some things don't change.

'It's me.'

She does a ridiculous double take. 'Woah! Rhoda?'

'The one and only.'

'Fuuuuck! Check out the hair! What you done to yourself, girl?'

'Like it?'

'You kidding? You look hot, man. Seriously.'

She unlocks the gate, and stumbling slightly on her heels, waves me in.

Bloody hell, has she been smoking herself stupid all morning?

Whorls of smoke drift in the air, creating a smog cloud just beneath the ceiling. But I'm relieved. She's talking to me, at any rate. I grab the TV remote and kill the sound.

'Where the fuck have you been, Rhoda? You have any idea the world of shit you're in?'

'I've been trying to call you for days, Zinzi.'

She looks at me blankly. 'Oh yeah. My phone.' She giggles. 'I lost it. Or someone nicked it, I dunno.'

'When?'

'Ages ago. I don't know. Last week some time.'

'So why didn't you call *me*?'

'I lost your number, didn't I? Was on my phone. And that's fucking gone, so...' She loses her train of thought.

The flat is in an even worse state than usual, dope pips scattered over the floor, an avalanche of Rizlas, overflowing ashtrays and dirty glasses on every surface. After staying at Dan's pseudo-mansion, Zinzi's place is truly decrepit in comparison; basically one step above the Handsworth squat I used to stay in. Bass from next door thumps through the partition walls, and the smoke's beginning to make my eyes swim. I pull open the curtains and crank open a window. The day is hot and still, so it doesn't really help.

'You look cool, though, girl. Wherever you been, it suits you.' Zinzi slumps down on the couch and starts rolling another joint. 'So. What's his name?'

'What you on about, Zinzi?'

'The man you been with, Rho. I mean look at you. Must be a man.' She licks the edge of the joint and fishes around for her lighter. 'But I've been worried. I tell you, I was saying to Thabo, maybe she's been kidnapped, taken by sex slavers or something. But he was like, "Rhoda? That girl? No ways. She can look after herself." Should have called, though, Rho. Least you could have done.'

'Zinzi, I *did* try and get hold of you, you're the one without the fucking phone, not me, remember?' I hope she doesn't think to ask why I haven't been around before now. But thankfully this jump of logic looks to be beyond her.

She shrugs. 'Whatever.' Then her face lights up. 'Shit, Rhoda. You've got to hear this. Last night, we were like totally wired and then Thabo said we should head into—'

'Yeah, yeah, Zinzi,' I cut her off, not wanting to hear about her fucked-up night of snorting lines off dirty toilet seats or whatever she got up to. 'Look, I need to know what happened, after I, you know… didn't come back that night.'

'Happened?'

'With the kid.'

'Oh yeah. Well, you tell me, girl. You're the one that disappeared into thin fucking air.' I glare at her and she sighs. 'Fuck. First thing I knew was when Carlos phoned from Highgate Mall, and I was like—'

'Hang on. Who's Carlos?'

She rolls her eyes and giggles again. She's really beginning to piss me off. 'The kid, retard.'

'Hang on. He phoned you? From the mall? The night I disappeared?'

'Yeah.'

'You mean he's safe?'

'Yeah, course. Some security guard found him wandering around.'

'Fuck.' I'm almost faint with relief. I have to lean forwards and take deep calming breaths.

'Hey,' Zinzi says, 'you okay?'

'Yeah. You've no idea how I've been freaking out worrying about him.'

She giggles again. 'Chill, Rhoda. See, that night, I got back to the house, and was like, where the fuck is Rhoda? And then

Carlos phoned from the mall saying that he was lost. So like me and Thabo went and got him. I tell you, Rhoda, the security guards were pissed off at you. Crazy pissed off. So was I at first. But I know you, see. I knew you must have got yourself into some fucked-up situation.'

She's saying something else, but I tune her out. Because fuck me.

The kid was never in the corridors at all.

It was all for nothing.

For *fuck* all. Everything that Dan and I had been through. It was all a wild goose chase with nothing to show for it but a screwed-up mind and a hank of fake hair.

'Hey! Rhoda!' Zinzi clicks her fingers in front of my face. 'Wakey, wakey! You want a hit?'

She hands me the joint, but it's the last thing I feel like. I take a drag anyway, letting the smoke roll over my tongue, but not inhaling.

'So the kid's really okay?'

'How many more times? Christ. He thought I was going to be pissed at him. He said you told him to wait in some store for you.'

'Yeah. I did. He ran off.'

'Little fucker. Knew that was what had happened. Hey, why'd you take him there in the first place?'

'Had to meet Jacob.'

She nods as if this is perfectly understandable. As if it's cool to take a kid to a mall to score some blow. Has she always been like this? Compared to me, I'd always thought of her as the responsible one. The one with the flat, the job, the car, the boyfriend. Weird how everything is shifting, how after those two little days of craziness the whole world seems different. Warped. Fucked-up.

'Fuck, though, Rhoda. I was pissed off about the Honda.'

'Yeah. Sorry,' I say.

'You know I got your back, girl, but sheesh.' I can tell Zinzi is now completely stoned out of her gourd; she always puts on her b-girl American accent when she's smoked too much. 'You're lucky I stashed a spare key. But you owe me a hundred bucks – lost ticket fine.'

'I'll pay you back. You still got my stuff?'

'Course. In the bedroom.'

'But what about the kid's parents? Didn't they freak out?'

'Nah. Never knew. Only got back at two. They probably wouldn't have given a shit anyway. That reminds me. What the fuck's the time?'

'Eleven.'

'Shit. Got to be at work just now.' But she makes no move to get up.

'So you didn't call the cops or anything?'

She snorts. 'Course not, Rho. I mean, the security guard fucker wanted to. Said you assaulted him. Don't blame you, though. He was a cunt.'

'But you said I was in serious shit?'

'Oh that. See, Ma phoned me.'

'Thought you said you lost your phone?'

'Yeah. She phoned me at work.'

'And?'

'Your folks. They're fucking freaking out, man. Going crazy with worry.'

'But why? I haven't spoken to them in years. For all they know I could be banged up in a South American prison.'

'Yeah. But they've been kind of keeping tabs on you, haven't they?' Zinzi looks sheepish. 'Look, when Ma phoned I kind of let slip that you'd disappeared, and she let your mum know.'

'Fuck, Zinzi!'

'Hey! What was I going to say? Oh it's cool cos Rhoda does

this all the time, specially when she's on a coke binge? And by coke, Ma, I don't mean the fizzy stuff that you—'

'Okay, okay. But you could have at least covered for me.'

'You were gone for days. I couldn't lie to them. I mean, what if something had happened? How was I to know you were off getting a fucking makeover or whatever the fuck you been doing?'

'Christ.'

'So, Rho? When do I get to meet the new man? What's his name?'

'Daniel,' I say without thinking.

'Daniel? What kind of a name is that?' Her eyes skate over my body, lingering on the green silky dress. 'Where the fuck you get that dress? He buy you that? He's got taste, I'll give him that.'

'Nah,' I say. 'I got it at the mall.'

'Can I borrow it some time?'

As if it would fit. But I keep my mouth shut, stub the joint out in the ashtray and head to the bedroom to fetch my bag.

I stomp into the hallway, slamming the door behind me.

'Dan!' I shout up the stairs. I can't wait to tell him about the kid. I've been phoning non-stop since I left Zinzi's but all I've been getting is voicemail. 'Dan?'

He's probably slumped on his bed or playing endless stupid computer games again. But he needs to hear this.

'That you, Rhoda?' Rose calls from the back of the house.

I wander into the kitchen. She's sitting at the breakfast counter, a bottle of Tanqueray, a six-pack of tonic waters and a jaggedly sliced lemon in front of her. I've never seen her drink before. Not even a sherry.

'What's going on, Rose? Where's Dan?'

'He's gone out. We had a bit of a... fight.' She's speaking with the exaggerated care of someone trying not to slur their words.

'I see,' I say.

'And I felt like a drink. You ever just feel like a drink?'

I sit down on the stool across from her. 'What sort of fight?'

'I was just asking him what his plans were. Now that he's quit his job, I was just asking about his future plans, and he just...'

'Freaked out?' I finish for her.

'Yes.' She plops one of the lemon circles into her drink and we both watch in silence for several seconds as the tonic fizzes around it.

'What's got into him, Rhoda? He never used to be like this. Cold, distant. Just...' She catches my expression and speaks hurriedly. 'I know it's not you, Rhoda.' She leans forward and blasts me with gin breath. 'You're good for him. I can see that.'

Woah. Maybe Rose has been at the valium or something. 'You think I'm *good* for him?'

She nods. 'I do.'

'Why?' I'm honestly curious.

'Since he met you he's become more... confident. More... aware of himself.' Jesus. 'It's towards me that his attitude's changed.'

'Look, Rose,' I say. 'I think he's still dealing with what we went through.'

'Probably,' she says, taking a large sip of her gin and tonic. 'You think I'm a bad mother, Rhoda?'

'Of course not!' The old Rhoda would probably have said 'damn straight you're a bad mother' just to get a reaction. Just to watch her crumple. Dan's not the only one who's changed.

'Never managed to find a good father figure for him.'

'Is there such a thing as a good father figure?' I say.

She shrugs. 'Who can say? Not in my universe there's not. Why don't you join me?' She shakes her glass in front of my face, and a dribble of gin splashes onto the counter. 'Whoopsie!' Her face suddenly clouds over. 'Come on, Rhoda. Have one with me. There's nothing sadder than an old woman drinking alone.'

Why the fuck not? I need to celebrate the fact that the kid – Carlos – is safe. 'Actually, I'd love a drink, Rose.'

She sloshes at least three fingers of gin into a glass and hands it to me. I do my best to dilute it with tonic, but there's not much space left.

'Jolly wolly good,' she says. 'I had a lover who used to say that. Jolly wolly good, he'd say.'

'Is that why you dumped him?'

'No,' she says. 'Other way round. He dumped me. But you think that would have been a good enough reason to sling him out?'

'Definitely.'

She throws her head back and hoots with laughter. She leans forward again. 'He was boring as shit. Enormous cock, though.'

I almost spit out my drink. She's way drunker than I thought. I fish around for something to say, settling on: 'Where are the dogs?'

'At the parlour.' She grabs the knife and stabs it into the lemon. 'I keep killing them off!'

'The dogs?'

'No! Men. I'm the kiss of death. The black widow of Bryanston.'

'That's not true.'

'Either that or I chase them away.'

'But what happened to Alvin wasn't your fault, Rose. You didn't give him lung cancer.'

She waves her hand in the air. 'Yes, yes. I'm talking about *before* that.'

I sit back and wait for her to speak again. May as well let the old bag get it off her chest.

'He had an affair. With his tart of a secretary. That old cliché. Went off with her to some fetid love nest.'

'Dan never said!'

'Dan never knew. Alvin was only gone a week. Came back to me, tail between his legs. Three months later, he was dead.'

Tears are beginning to glisten in her eyes.

'How many have you had, Rose?'

'Men?'

'No, drinks.'

'Just one for the road. A very large one!' This time her giggle is hollow.

'Well,' I say, draining my glass and struggling not to gag as the barely diluted gin hits my throat. 'I'd better go and—'

She clamps a veined hand on my arm. 'Rhoda? Can I ask you something? Something personal?'

'Sure, Rose.' I owe her that, at least.

'How did you get the scar on your face?'

I flinch. I assumed she was going to grill me about Dan again. But of course she's noticed the matt of scar tissue. She'd just been too polite to mention it before.

'You really want to know?' I say.

'Yes. I really do.'

I decide to tell her the truth. 'I tell everyone it's a burn scar, but it's not.'

'Why do you do that?'

'Shuts them up. Means that I don't have to go into the actual story.'

'Why didn't you get it fixed?' she says.

'Because I'm a bitch,' I say.

She smiles at me. 'I'm all ears.'

Should I?

Fuck it. She pours me another drink, and I find myself telling her the whole fucked-up story. How Mum and Dad were driving home after they'd dragged me along to one of their literary parties. How they'd both been drinking, in high spirits, Dad celebrating his new position at Brighton University. How the car had come out of nowhere, spun towards us in slow motion.

How they were both fine, not even a scratch, not even whiplash. How I was anything but fine. Flung through the windscreen. Should have been dead. Shattered hip, dislocated shoulder, and not forgetting the jagged tears in my back, and, of course, my face.

'When did this happen?' Rose says, suddenly sounding way more sober.

'Five years ago. I was about to start university.'

'You were? What were you going to study?'

'English. At East Anglia.'

'So why didn't you go?'

'Good question. I was angry. Still am. And... well, look at me. I was in hospital for ages.'

'Skin grafts?'

'Yeah.'

'How awful for you. But surely they offered you plastic surgery?'

'I was sick of operations by then. And anyway, I guess I wanted them to remember what they'd done every time they looked at my face. What a bitch, huh?'

'Makes two of us, Rhoda,' she says. 'It's understandable.'

'Is it?' I look up at her in surprise.

She waves her drink again. 'Sure. Never underestimate a person's propensity for revenge. But, Rhoda, no parent can live with the thought that they've hurt their child. It's unbearable.'

We sit in silence for several minutes, both of us lost in our own thoughts.

'Rose,' I say, draining my drink. It goes down easier this time. 'Can I use your phone?'

She's waiting for me in the lounge, the half-empty gin bottle and a fresh can of tonic on the coffee table.

'How did it go?' she says, although she's now so pissed the words sound more like: 'Hozs shiir go?'

I smile at her. 'Really well.' I wipe my face again. Shit. My cheeks are still damp.

'Oh, don't worry about that, Rhoda,' Rose slurs. 'I'm a veteran of crying jags.' She takes another slurp. 'What did your parents say?'

'They want to help me out. They're sending me some cash.'

'Good.'

'They want me to go back to the UK.'

'And what do you want to do?'

'Can't stay here for ever, can I?'

She hands me a drink. 'Well, I think it was brave of you to call. Cheers!'

She clanks her glass against mine. My head's beginning to swim, but I take another sip. Pure gin. I down it anyway.

'Jolly wolly good,' Rose says. 'Shall we have another?'

'Yeah,' I say. The alcohol is really going to my head now. 'Why the fuck not?'

Rose starts laughing and I find myself joining in.

'Why the fuck not indeed?' she says.

So when Dan comes home, he finds me and his mother in the lounge dancing to 'Copacabana', the overturned bottle of Tanqueray dribbling the last of its contents into the carpet.

chapter 26
DANIEL

For fuck's sake.

I barge past Rhoda and Mom doing their fucked-up woman bonding whatever it is, take the stairs two at a time and slam my bedroom door shut. I'm hungry, but now I can't very well go downstairs to raid the fridge. I take a cigarette out of Rhoda's pack and light it. I stand by my window and look out over the walls and gardens. The old couple next door are sunbathing by their splash pool. They're crinkly and red and I can just about hear the cancer munching at their age-spotted skin.

I fiddle with Rhoda's knife in my pocket. What's happened to her? Or is this who she really is? Were the street-smarts and anger just a façade to cover up her boring middle-class self? I watch the leather corpses turn themselves over to roast their backs. Clarrie pisses against a bush in our yard. This is it. This is the rest of my life. I stub out the cigarette on the window sill.

I grab my wallet and my old phone – the dead gelphone on the night stand now looks like a deflated grey balloon – and head downstairs again.

'I'm going out.'

'But you just came in.' Mom tries not to slur. Rhoda stands

watching, unsure. 'Have something to eat.'

I walk up to Mom, brushing past Rhoda without acknowl-edging her – I can't deal with her and Mom at the same time; they shouldn't be occupying the same space.

'Mom. I love you. Thank you for taking care of me.' Where did that come from? I was planning on saying something else entirely, but that just seemed the right thing to say. I leave before she can say anything in response.

I stride along the pavement, not really knowing where I'm heading. I see Florence ahead of me, on her way to the Sloane Street taxi rank. I check my phone: it's five fifteen already. 'Hello, Mister Daniel,' she says as I catch up to her. Now that she's out of her lavender polyester housecoat she's different, more relaxed, and she gives me a slight smile. The fact that I'm walking along the pavement – something only workers do in Bryanston – seems to put us on common ground, and for a moment we inhabit the same world. I wonder what she thinks of Rhoda, whether she feels more connected to her because she's black, or whether Rhoda's outlandish clothes, her English accent, just make her another one of us.

'Have a good evening, Florence,' I say, realising as I say it that I've never imagined what Florence's home is like. I know she's got two grown-up kids and a grandchild living with her. But what does she do when she goes home? Who cooks, who cleans, how many rooms does her house have, does she have a TV? Do her kids work? Who gets up for the baby? Is she the same bleak and silent woman at home, or does she sing songs to the baby? Does she tell stories? I can't imagine her sitting around a table with her family and laughing. Florence starts existing at eight in the morning and blinks out of being at five. And as I pass her, she leaves my mind just as quickly.

The sun is sinking into the dust and car fumes on the horizon are turning the sky and its cloud scraps pink and orange; the remnants of blue are luminous. I stop walking. I watch the colours mixing, the rays shifting and the clouds moving. I want to save that light, take it with me. I stand on the pavement, staring, ignoring the rush of luxury cars, taxis and bakkies grinding past; they are just a hissing soundtrack to the light show above.

When I snap out of my trance I realise that I've fiddled Rhoda's flick-knife open and nicked my index finger. While I walk, I suck on it to stop it bleeding, and the taste of blood in my mouth reminds me of kissing Rhoda yesterday. I remember the feel of the scars on her back. I want to believe that she is still dangerous, that she's not a suburban princess who lives to buy clothes and get drunk with old women.

At Sloane Square I wander into a pool bar. It's still quiet this early, just a group of boys playing at the table nearest the bar, a rock band warming up in the room upstairs. I buy a beer and sit at the bar. I look at the bar-top slot machine blinking away and the strips of biltong packets hanging on a rusty nail gouged into the bar's strut. Is this me in twenty years, escaping the repetitive duties of my home and my family and coming to drink and waste my pocket money on a pathetic corner-pub gamble? The idea horrifies me. Have I forgotten how to be happy? If I allow myself to admit it, that's all I want: to be happy. It's not very hardcore, but it's true.

I flick out Rhoda's knife and gouge my name – Dan, not Daniel – into the wood of the bar top. The barman is unpacking crates of beer and doesn't notice my vandalism. Out of the window across the bar, the sun has set and a deep, dusty blue replaces the psychedelic stain. I'm leaving a memorial, proof that I was here. I test the knife point against my finger, and then stash the blade back in my pocket. Suck the blood again, think of Rhoda.

'Dan.'

It's Rhoda. Of course it's Rhoda.

'How did you find me?'

'Followed you, didn't I?' She's wearing a pair of jeans, one of my black T-shirts and her shitty Converse. Much better than that fucking dress. As she steps up to the bar stool the denim tautens around her hips and arse. I signal for two more beers. The band upstairs lets out a squeal of feedback. A cymbal crashes.

'What's the matter with you?' she asks.

The old Dan would whine: What's the matter with you? You're the one who's betrayed me. Blah blah blah. But I don't feel like it. She doesn't owe me anything. She never promised me anything.

I shrug.

'You're pissed off because I'm getting on with your mum?'

'As long as you're not like her,' I mumble.

'What's that supposed to mean?'

'You seem very comfortable in Bryanston. For a crack-whore.' I try to stuff the word back into my mouth, but it's too late. She winds up and gives me the biggest smack across the jaw I've ever had. Bigger than any of the punches she dished out in the mall. I reel off the bar stool and crash into two others, cracking the back of my head and my spine on my way down. I land square on my shoulder. Rhoda is up and over me, ready to pile in and smack the shit out of me but the barman restrains her.

'Cool it,' he shouts, but I can see he's enjoying the spectacle of a guy being beaten up by a girl for a change. The pool players gawk across at us.

Even as the pain adds up to an excruciating seethe around my back and neck and head I'm looking at Rhoda and thinking, That's more like it. I lie there and look at her struggling in the barman's arms. I would smile if it weren't so sore.

'I'm sorry,' I groan. 'I deserved that. Evens?'

She stops writhing and the barman gradually lets her go. 'No more bullshit, okay, or you're out of here,' he warns as he goes back around the bar.

Rhoda helps me up, the cords in her arms tightening, the dark skin over them stretching satiny. We take our beers across to the far end of the bar where it's unlit and empty and sit down in a skanky black leatherette booth. The band is belting out a bad metal cover and the lead singer is screaming to mask his awful voice. Rhoda still hasn't said anything, and I wonder if I really hurt her feelings.

'Sorry. Really. I didn't mean it. I was just...'

She still says nothing, smiles vaguely as if she's not listening.

'I was just feeling... you know,' I try.

She looks like she's about to say something, but doesn't. Instead, she takes a gulp of beer, looks out the window.

'You know you're not...' I say, digging myself deeper into the hole. 'And anyway, you've never cared about what I called you before. We had plenty of fights in... there. We're still friends, hey?'

Nothing. She just fiddles with the beer bottle.

'I hurt your feelings, huh?'

She takes a large gulp and puts the bottle down, and suddenly she's alive again. 'Wanker. You couldn't hurt a fucking fly's feelings. You've got to try harder than that. I've been called plenty worse before. By people who meant it.'

I smile, relieved. 'You look nice tonight. More...'

'More myself?'

'Ja.'

'How's your head?'

'Sore, thanks.' I rub my hand over the back of my head, and my fingers brush the scab under my ear. It's healing quite well. 'What happened today? Are you okay?'

'What do you mean?'

'You look sad.'

'No, actually. I'm... You know I told you I haven't spoken to my parents for ages?'

'Ja?'

'I called them today.'

'Oh, well done. Was it okay?'

'Yeah, it was. I...' She takes another slug of beer.

'That's good. I'm happy for you,' I say when I realise she's not going to say anything more.

'You working tonight?'

'Nah. Day off.'

'Great. Let's have some fun tonight,' she says, and she puts her hand on my leg. Then she turns and kisses me, smooths her hand along my thigh, getting closer and closer to my crotch, just stopping short each time. For a bit, I'm worried that she'll feel the knife in my pocket and ask me where I got it. But just for a bit. Her mouth tastes of cigarettes and beer and gin. And I can taste that her life was hard, I can taste that her life was rough, I can taste blood from her gums, I can taste her pain: this is who she is, not some mallrat, poolside lapdog; not some suburban bridge-playing mother.

I move one hand to her back, under the shirt, feeling those scarred ridges as her hand finally reaches my dick. I pop open her fly and she bites my tongue and undoes mine. We're working each other and trying to suck the life out of each other, and my head is throbbing like it's going to shatter and every nerve is screaming and alive, and I'm kneading my hand over those scars, mixing the scar tissue with her living tissue, merging it and her and me, and I'm fingering her and she's pumping me and I come all over her hand, over my hand, up onto her shirt. And she slumps over my shoulder, her neck slick against mine, the scar on her face rubbing against my stubble. It's heavy, it's sore, it's real; it's who we are.

'I thought you'd... become... that you'd changed. That you'd become... like them,' I say.

She blows some breath into my ear, still holding me. 'You

don't listen, do you?' She takes another breath in as if she's about to say something, but doesn't. Instead, she wipes her sticky hand on my T-shirt, buttons up her jeans and climbs over me and heads to the toilets. My head is pounding now, my shoulder already stiffening into a spasm. My tongue is bleeding and my cock has been grazed against my zip.

That's more like it.

When she comes back, we sit drinking, not talking much as the bar fills up with students and embryo salarymen, as the music gets louder, as the band starts playing, as the pool balls clack and the beer bottles crash. We don't talk much, except about the next beer, or to swap comments on the chick with the whale tail or the guy with the mullet. We don't say much, but I'm planning the future. I can see it for the first time. I wonder if she can too.

Despite the stale smoke in my mouth, stale sweat in the sheets; despite the amount we drank last night, I wake up clear-headed. Not a trace of a hangover and only a dull ache from the bar fight. It's half past six – we've only slept for five hours, but my mind is racing, and I know that there's no way it's going to shut up and let me go back to sleep.

I lift Rhoda's arm off my stomach and get up. As I do she stirs in half sleep and smiles at me. I'm kind of surprised that she doesn't wake up screaming and run out of the door.

I walk over to the window and open it. The dogs have just run out and are sniffing the dewy grass. I breathe in the fresh air. It's moist and green. I hear the morning songs of bulbuls and thrushes; hadedas probe into the damp ground for worms and crickets. Rhoda and I could rent a flat. We wouldn't need much. A crappy car, a crappy TV, a pile of books; we'd live on bread and lentils and fuck all day. We could do it. Mom would help me, and maybe Rhoda's parents could send her some cash.

I hear the crumple of Rhoda shifting up against the headboard, the flick of her lighter. I turn to her. She's wearing the T-shirt from last night and nothing else. Her long, brown legs chart the length of the white duvet, crossing at the ankles. She's stretching and yawning, rubbing her hands over her head and face, the cigarette clutched between two fingers. When she notices me watching she points her cigarette at me, offering me one.

I nod and she lights another. 'Dan, come here. I've got to tell you something.'

'What?'

'Come here.' I don't like her tone. She's going to fuck up my mood.

'Rhoda, I was thinking,' I say, to stop her from saying what she was going to say. 'What do you think about us getting a flat together?'

She says nothing, turns away. Takes a long time stubbing out her cigarette in the saucer on my side of the table. Swings her legs over the side of the bed, her back facing me. Just sits. Fumbles behind her for another cigarette. Lights it. Still turned away.

'How would we pay for it?' she says at last.

'We'll find jobs.'

'I don't even have a fucking work permit, Dan. Soon I'm going to be here illegally.'

Why's she sounding so pissy? 'My mom would lend us some cash.'

'Christ, I'm not sucking another day's charity out of that poor woman. You just take her for granted, you know that?'

'Jesus, Rhoda, chill. I was just thinking, okay? Thinking aloud. Forget it. It doesn't fucking matter.'

She says nothing.

'What did you want to say?' I ask.

She shifts across the bed and sits on the side closer to me and the window. She takes a long drag.

'Dan, you're a sweet... a great guy.'

Oh shit. Here it comes. *Fuck!* How did I manage to fuck this up?

'Uh-uh. Don't say it.' I rush to put on my jeans and T-shirt, grab my shoes and am out of the door. Behind me Rhoda's saying, Wait, wait, but I'm not listening.

I've forgotten to grab my car keys, so I'm going to have to walk, and the closest place to get cigarettes and alcohol is the Highgate Mall. As I walk, my mind starts striking bargains with my life. I can't believe that last night meant nothing; I've never had a stronger feeling about anything in my life; for once in my life I've had a feeling strong enough to believe. It can't be a lie. *It can't.*

I cross Main Road on autopilot, barely aware of the black Merc turning in front of me and the rattling taxi that misses me by centimetres. I don't even know what Rhoda wanted to say. I should have let her speak. So I should just turn back home and say, Sorry, what did you want to say? But I keep walking to the mall. I'll come home to her with a proper apology... and a proper plan. I check my pockets. My phone and my wallet are still there from last night, Rhoda's knife too. I'm going to draw all my money from the bank. I'm going to get my back pay – whatever tiny pittance it amounts to – from those cunts at the bookshop. I'm going to show it to her in my hand. I'm going to say, Rhoda, we *can* do it, we *can* make it together. I'm going to buy her some flowers; I'm *not* going to take her for granted.

chapter 27

RHODA

The sunlight dances over the chlorinated water, and I stretch out my legs and take another slurp of coffee. The Rat Dogs lie under my sun lounger, snoozing and chasing dream rabbits.

The hangover isn't as bad as I thought it would be. Just a slight headache and the occasional lurch of nausea. Nothing I can't handle.

The patio doors open and Rose stumbles through. She looks awful, her eyes hidden behind huge Jackie O sunglasses. I watch her with interest, curious to see how she'll treat me after our afternoon of booze-fuelled shared secrets.

'Morning, Rose,' I say.

She grimaces slightly and lowers herself onto the chair next to me. 'Good morning.'

'How are you feeling?'

'Terrible.' She runs her fingers through her unwashed hair. 'I will never drink gin again.' She attempts a smile. 'Was I awful?'

'No worse than me.'

'I apologise if I embarrassed you,' she says slightly stiffly.

'You didn't.'

'You are a good liar, Rhoda.'

She's got that right.

She fidgets with her sunglasses. She's clearly got something on her mind. 'Rhoda. Have you told Dan yet?'

'Told him what?' But I know exactly what she's talking about.

'That you spoke to your parents. That you'll be leaving shortly.'

I squirm in my chair. God knows I'd meant to tell him I was leaving. Wasn't my fault he'd upped and left in one of his Dan emo sulks. Wasn't my fault he'd blocked his ears and buggered off.

'Don't leave it too long,' she says. I watch her carefully, wondering if she heard us after we got back from the bar. It wasn't as if we'd even attempted to keep the noise down. Who knew Dan had *that* in him?

'I won't, Rose.'

'Where's he gone? I heard him leaving this morning.'

I shrug. 'I don't know.'

I decide not to tell her about his hissy fit. It won't take him long to realise how insane his little happy family daydream is. He must be off his fucking head to want to settle down with me.

Florence comes out with a bowl of muesli for Rose, and a banana for me.

'Thanks, Florence,' I say.

'You're welcome, madam,' she says, and I almost drop my coffee mug.

Rose pulls her sunglasses down onto her nose and stares at her in astonishment. We both watch her slouch back into the house.

'I never thought I'd crack the nod from Florence,' I say.

She smiles at me, but it doesn't reach her eyes. She pushes the glasses back into place. 'Wonders will never cease.'

I lie back, thinking about last night, thinking again about what Dan had said before he left this morning. Talk about unrealistic expectations. I try and picture it. Me and the Emo Kid hooking up, settling down, renting a flat, getting jobs at the mall, popping out a couple of kids for Rose to spoil on weekends.

As if.

Time to get this show on the road.

I swing my legs off the sun lounger.

'I'm off, Rose,' I say to her.

'Where are you going?'

'I need to book a flight.'

I can't read her expression behind the enormous glasses, but she must be relieved at the thought of having Dan all to herself again, despite what she said yesterday about me being a good influence on him. And I guess I know too much about her for her ever to be really comfortable around me. 'Why not do it over the internet?' she says.

'I thought I'd go to a travel agency. See if I can get a last minute deal. My folks can transfer the cash straight into their account.'

'You know where to go?'

'There's bound to be one in the mall, isn't there?' Just saying the word 'mall' makes my stomach twist, but fuck it. I have to get it done.

'You want to take the car?'

'It's not far.'

'But walking alone – it's not safe, Rhoda.'

'S'cool,' I say. 'I can look after myself.'

Yeah right, the voice says.

I was wondering when it would return.

You can do this.

My palms are sweating, and I'm not sure if the nausea is a result of last night's drinking or from being back here – back where it all started. My pulse is galloping and my chest feels tight, constricted. The mall's artificial light seems too bright, the tiles too hard under my feet, and saliva floods into my mouth.

Relax. Nothing's going to happen.

Early-morning shoppers ramble past me and my stomach lurches again. I can't get my head around how normal they all look. But what was I expecting? Seeping sores, bandaged stumps and outrageous plastic surgery?

Get your act together, for fuck's sake.

I automatically start walking, shaking my hands to try and erase the panic-attack tingle in my fingers, part of me keeping an eye out for a travel agency, the other part thinking about how my life is about to change. Thinking about Mum sobbing over the phone, whispering, 'We're so sorry Rhoda,' over and over again. Thinking about heading back to the UK, going to university, carrying on where I left off, as if the last five years never happened. As if what Dan and I went through is an easily erasable glitch in my life.

I hesitate. I'm right in front of the computer store – the one I'd raced to that night when I'd frantically searched for the missing kid. The Lara Croft cut-out is gone, replaced with a Wii Fit display. I can't resist glancing up at the signage, almost expecting to see one of those crazy literal signs we'd seen in the other mall.

A trio of teenage girls push past me, knocking against my shoulder. They don't stop to apologise, and one of them – a pug-faced girl with ratty hair – even turns to glare at me as if our collision is my fault.

The old Rhoda would have grabbed the back of her top, made her apologise. But the old Rhoda wouldn't be on her way to buy a plane ticket. She'd be plotting the next score, coming up with other inventive ways to fuck up her life.

Don't be so sure the old Rhoda has gone anywhere.

I climb onto the escalator and cruise down, checking out the shops below, looking for the South African version of a Thomas

Cook. A bunch of people are heading up on the opposite escalator. Among them I catch a glimpse of a familiar khaki uniform.

Oh fuck.

It's Yellow Eyes. I'd know that paunch anywhere. He's barking something into his walkie-talkie, and for a second our eyes lock. He seems to look right through me, but I'm not going to take any chances.

Trying not to make it too obvious, I skip down the remaining steps, and, keeping my head down, I walk briskly into the nearest store – one of those high-end designer boutiques – and start flicking through a rack of dresses, keeping half an eye on the door.

A saleswoman drifts over. 'Can I help you?'

'I'm just browsing,' I say.

She tries to smile politely, but it's not convincing. Her gaze skates over my tatty Levis and the oversize Marilyn Manson T-shirt I'd pulled out of Dan's drawer after he'd left. I stare back at her, and she nods and wanders away.

A fat man's shape drifts past the window. Yellow Eyes? Fuck. I can't tell. I grab a dress at random and head towards the changing rooms.

'Madam?' The shop assistant calls after me.

'I want to try this on.'

She looks from me to the dress, the fake smile losing its wattage. 'But it's a size forty.'

'So?'

Now the smile disappears entirely. 'I think it might be slightly too big for you. You can't be more than a twenty-six.'

She's right of course, but I hold my ground. 'I still want to try it.'

'Madam, you do know the price of it?' She glances at her fellow assistant, a thin woman who's pretending to fold a cardigan next to the till.

'No,' I snap.

'It's 1,700 rands.'

I try not to flinch. 'So?'

'I thought you might like to know,' she says.

'Forget it,' I say. I look her in the eye and let the hanger drop, the dress crumpling into a heap on the floor. I stalk out, cheeks blazing with humiliation.

For a second, I feel a pang of regret. That would never have happened back there. Back when I was a Shopper and not just a scruffy nobody.

Don't think like that.

But I can't help it. I fumble automatically for my phone, and scroll down to Dan's number. Some part of me needs to speak to him, maybe to put things in perspective; maybe just to hear a friendly voice.

It goes straight to voicemail.

I lean over the railing and look down into the floor below. I can make out the familiar blue signage of Only Books, which, bizarrely, makes me feel slightly better, more grounded. And there's a Flight Centre a few doors down on the opposite side of the aisle.

Fuck it. It'll only take a few minutes to book a ticket and then I can get the hell out of here. Maybe meet Dan for lunch, have a few beers, tell him about the stupid cow in the dress shop, have a laugh. Maybe while away the afternoon by the pool.

I jog down the escalator, keeping a lookout for Yellow Eyes. I think about popping into Only Books for old times' sake, but the glass doors look firmly shut. Stupid idea anyway. I haven't forgotten that blonde bitch who treated me like shit when I was looking for the kid.

There are two heavily made-up women sitting behind the travel agency's counter, both speaking rapidly into microphones attached to their faces, vicious red fingernails skittering over their keyboards. They could be sisters, right down to their straightened hair and identical blue blouses, except that one is skinny to the point of emaciation, the other as comfortably padded as an old sofa. I hesitate, and the plump one waves me vaguely towards a couch set back against the wall. I sit down next to an elderly man who's clearly also waiting for their attention. He nods at me, and carries on flicking through a brochure for the Cayman Islands. He smells faintly of soup and doesn't look like he can even afford a weekend away in Margate.

The plump agent smiles at him and he gets to his feet. I try and attract the anorexic one's attention, but she's suddenly found something fascinating on her computer screen. I watch the five clocks on the wall ticking my morning away. Tokyo, New York, London, New Delhi, Johannesburg. The minute hand flicks over to 10:17.

A tall bleach-blonde woman clatters into the shop, talking on her cellphone. Her eyes scan the room and she immediately sits down in front of Skinny, who smiles at her and instantly stops what she's doing.

No fucking way.

'Excuse me,' I say loudly.

Plump looks up. 'I'll be with you in a minute, ma'am,' she says.

'It's not you I was speaking to,' I say, nodding in Skinny's direction. The blonde turns around to look at me curiously, and I point at her. 'I was here before she was.'

'I won't be long,' the blonde says. 'I have a very important meeting—'

'Like I care less,' I say. 'I've been waiting. You pushed in.'

The blonde and Skinny share a look. I glance at the elderly guy for backup, but he drops his eyes. Bastard.

'I'll be with you in a moment, ma'am,' Plump repeats. 'Please, just be patient.'

'Why should I be patient? I have been patient. That bitch just pushed in!'

The agents gasp, and the blonde purses her collagened lips and immediately starts texting someone.

Am I overreacting? But fuck it. I'm not putting up with this shit twice in one morning. Plump runs a hand over her hair and does her best to smile at me. 'Ma'am, please calm down. There's no need to—'

'Who are you telling to calm down?' I say, getting to my feet. 'What, you think because I haven't shelled out for fake tits and botox that I'm just going to let myself be treated like this?'

Plump's chins wobble slightly. 'Ma'am? If you don't calm down then I'll have to call security.'

The elderly man starts to mumble in disapproval. Skinny's fingers reach for the phone.

'Oh fuck you,' I say. 'Fuck all of you. You wouldn't last five fucking minutes in...'

In where?

I have to get out of here. I have to get out of here right now.

My heart is speeding up again, and my fingers are beginning to stiffen up again. If I don't get out of here immediately I'll be right in the throes of a full-force panic attack.

I leave at a run, barging past a cleaner pushing a trolley, not looking in which direction I'm heading.

'Lady?' a familiar voice says behind me.

It's Yellow Eyes. Oh *fuuuuck*. I shake the hair over my face, making sure the scar is hidden, and turn around. I tense myself to make a run for it, but there's still no trace of recognition in his eyes.

Now what?

But I suddenly know exactly what to do.

I stand up straighter, look him up and down as if he's a piece of dog shit, and blast out waves of Shopper superiority. It feels good. It feels *right*. And it's working, he seems to shrink into his uniform, and he nods deferentially at me.

'Is everything all right, ma'am?' he says.

'No, everything is *not* all right. I've just been robbed.'

'Robbed?'

'My wallet was taken. Pick-pocketed.'

I point back to the travel agency. 'I saw him run in there.'

Yellow Eyes hesitates. He's such a fucking useless bastard. How many scarred black women with British accents has he come across lately?

It's not just your appearance that's changed, Rhoda.

'Well?' I say. 'What are you going to do about it? I'm on holiday here. Is this how you treat tourists?'

He fingers his walkie-talkie. The mention of the word tourist seems to jog something in his memory. But I hold my ground.

'Wait here, please, ma'am,' he says. 'I'll be right back.'

Now's your chance.

My phone beeps. I grab it out of my pocket, thumb through to the message.

Oh *fuck*.

chapter 28
DANIEL

There's so little money in my account, I can draw it all at the ATM. No longer in the mood for getting wasted, I buy a soft drink at the supermarket and start heading towards Only Books. I check my phone to see if Rhoda has left a message. Fuck, one missed call. Rhoda. I check the time – 10:17. I'll call her back when I'm done. Just thinking about facing that fuckwit Bradley makes my heart thunder. But I need to keep calm. I've just come for my back pay, I'm not looking for a confrontation.

The bookshop's doors are closed. What the hell? I check the time again. Then I see Bradley through the window wandering around with his iPod on and a checklist on a clipboard and I realise he's doing the monthly stock reconciliation. Taking his time about it too. The recon only involves a spot check of thirty titles and running a routine on the computer. It should take half an hour at the most. Fucking hypocrite. He would be all over me if I took this long. I rattle on the door and wave my arms but he's bopping away to his Barry Manilow or Britney Spears or whatever the fuck pricks like him are into, and it's only when he turns around that he eventually sees me. He startles, goes red then white then red again, then puts on his boss face, removes the earphones and comes to the door.

He opens it a crack like I'm some sort of mugger, and says, 'What do you want?'

'I've come for my back pay.'

'Huh?'

'My money. I want my money.' The waitresses at the coffee shop next door are watching. 'Come on, let me in, man.'

Grudgingly he opens the door a little, just wide enough for me to squeeze in. Then he slams the door behind me as if he's afraid he'll be inundated by a flood of insatiable customers who don't realise that the shop is closed for his Very Important and Highly Skilled Stock Reconciliation. *It's Thursday morning, dickweed, there's nobody here.*

'If you think you're getting your job back, you've got another thing coming,' he says. He's in his early thirties yet he talks like an old man.

'I just want my back pay. I worked seven shifts this month.'

'You – let's put it politely – resigned.' He grins to himself. 'What makes you think that you're entitled to anything?'

'The law,' I say, trying to sound convincing. I have no idea whether I'm legally entitled to anything or not. I just need to get my fucking pay and go. Every minute I spend in here is a minute too many. He makes a show of checking his list and moves across to poetry. Ja, right. Stock thieves are going to steal poetry.

'You want to do it the legal way, buddy?' says Bradley. 'Fine. Let's do the whole grievance procedure, a disciplinary enquiry. Let's see after six months of that how much back pay you're entitled to. We'll have you on malicious damage to property, we'll have you on gross insubordination, we'll—'

I've had enough. 'Just shut the fuck up.'

'What?' Bradley's eyes widen. Then I realise: he's scared of me. He thinks I'm going to beat him up or something.

Jesus, I wish I could do something like that. But instead I

store up my rage inside me. After how many shifts did I walk home, screaming inside because of this petty cunt, because of the aggressive, loaded, 4x4-driving bitches who take out the pain of their dry vaginas and their failed marriages and their failed affairs and their failed facelifts on us automatons behind the counter? I made myself worthless, all for three peanuts an hour.

'You heard me. I'm fucking sick of this place.' I'm trying hard not to start whining, or worse, crying. This place makes me into someone I'm not, into someone I don't want to be. I just want to leave here for ever. 'Just give me my money and you never have to see me again.'

He's back to his old smug self, that wary look gone from his eyes. Fuck, I've let myself down, shown him my weakness. 'There's no way I'm going to help you now, Daniel. File your paperwork with head office and I'll see you at the hearing. I'm done with you.' He turns to walk away.

The hole beneath my ear starts throbbing with a buzzing, electric pulse. I grab him by his shoulder as he goes.

'Don't walk away. I swear I'm going to—'

He swats at my hand. 'I'll have you for assault! I told you I—'

I feel a surge of power, the rush of a lifetime's rage flooding through me, the pressure centred at that hole in my skull. My muscles seem to swell. I feel a slickness oozing down my neck, into my collar. Then all the pressure snaps, every molecule pushing towards a single, overwhelming movement. I shove Bradley into the side of the bookshelf.

He squeaks and then his face spasms, his head kicks back.

'If you just give me my money...' I say, but he's not listening. He's got this strange expression on his face. I can't tell if he's laughing or what. But then his arms start juddering and his knees slacken. Fuck, is he having some sort of fit?

'Bradley?' I say. His head lolls to the side, but he stays upright, his heel's knocking spasmodically into the side of the bookshelf behind. Thump, thump, thump, thump, thump.

Oh fuck.

From the side I can see the two slatwall hooks that spear deep into Bradley's back.

For a second, his rolling eyes find mine but his stare is empty. Then there's a rattling gurgle like a cough full of phlegm and Bradley sinks inwards like a deflated toy.

I shuffle in reverse to the back office, my eyes stuck on him until he's lost behind another bay of shelves. I tap in the office access code automatically and slump down on the stock receiver's chair. What the fuck just happened? Remember, think. It's important that you remember every detail. *What did you just do?*

All I wanted was to get my money.

Oh shit.

Oh shit.

Oh fuck.

Fuck.

What the fuck have I just done?

This is it. This is the end. It's over.

No flowers. No happily ever after.

Christ, I've fucked it up.

And Rhoda is the only person I can ask for help.

My phone's display reads: <10:27>. Just ten minutes since I got here. In just ten minutes you can break your entire life.

I key in a message. <rhoda, im in shit. I'm at the bookshop and ive fucked it up>

I immediately regret pressing send. I shouldn't involve Rhoda in this. But I can't unsend the message, can I? I pray for a failure message back, but there's nothing, then a little green tick next to her name. Shit, man. I need her.

My stain just keeps spreading.

I fiddle with Rhoda's knife in my pocket.

I pace over to the office's small window, feeling sunlight on my face. A Woolworths delivery truck reverses into a delivery bay below me. That's the bay Rhoda and I went in all that time ago. It seems like a different life. If that hadn't happened, I wouldn't be standing here, trapped. I wouldn't have met Rhoda either.

The trees in the high-end cluster development across the road are bright green this morning, and the cars that drive by are a palette of shiny tones. A swirl of pied crows is catching a thermal above the clusters, rolling and flickering black and bright white, black and white, black and white, rolling and lolling like they've got all day. I close my eyes, and I hear singing. I watch the crows flickering, black and bright white, elegant outcasts, black and white like lights, like beacons in the sky, calling, soaring like they own the sky. The sky is a perfect, washed blue. 'You almost ready to open, sweetie?'

The voice snaps me out of my trance. I wheel around.

'Oh, it's you, Daniel,' says Josie. She's wearing jeans and a pert white sweatshirt and carrying two cups of coffee. 'What are you doing here?'

'Uh…' Then it hits me. I'm such an idiot. There I was with a primary-school crush on Josie, while all along she and Bradley were behaving – and fucking – like adults. I didn't understand what that meant until I met Rhoda. And what surprises me most is that I don't even care.

'Brad was really pissed off with you,' she says with a laugh. 'He's never going to give you your job back. Did you speak to him already?'

'Um, no.'

'I'll never tell Brad, of course, but Katrien and I thought it was great. Everyone fantasises about telling their boss to fuck off. We had a drink for you after work.'

'Oh.'

'So? Are you going to ask him for your job back, or what?'

'No. I just want my back pay. He told me to wait here till he's done.'

Josie sits at Bradley's desk and hands me one of the coffees. 'I got this for Brad, but you can have it. Two sugars okay?'

'Uh, thanks.' I sit down next to her. I can't fool myself that this is a game this time, but if I *were* playing a game, I'd want to keep Josie sitting here for as long as possible. Anything but let her go out onto the shop floor and discover Bradley.

'So, uh, are you and Bradley... together?'

'Yes,' she says. 'But not exclusively or anything.' She smiles at me over the lip of her cup. What the fuck? Suddenly I'm emitting Josie-attracting pheromones? The truth is I'd rather never see Josie again in my life. She's everything that was wrong with me. I'm trying to convince myself that I've changed, but this shop, having to deal with these people, just drags me down into the past. But the longer Josie sits here, the more time I have to make a plan.

'I guess I acted a bit stupid around you. You're very pretty. You know that.'

I'm not asking, I'm saying, but she answers, 'Weeelll. No, I'm not.'

'You are.'

'Thanks. You're not so bad yourself. You know Katrien totally has the hots for you?'

'No way.'

'Ja. I couldn't see it myself. But now I think I know what she means.'

Fuck. My brain is whirring. All this time... Katrien?

'Here's the part where you ask me out for a drink,' she says, nibbling at the edge of the cup.

Something snaps. 'No thanks,' I say. 'Not interested.'

'What?'

'I've met someone. Someone real.' Josie looks at me, tilting her head like a poodle thinking, and then starts to blush. I can see her trying to fight it, but the harder she does, the more red and blotchy her face becomes. A couple of beads of sweat prickle out around the fluff on her lip. 'And now I realise the difference between a crush and real…'

'Fuck you,' she says.

'Not today, Josie. Not any day.'

Insulting her isn't the best way to keep her here, but somehow I can't stop myself. I've smelled blood. Anyway, very soon someone's going to see Bradley through the window. I've got a minute or two at the most to *find this fucking plan.*

'You're a loser, Daniel,' Josie snaps. I nick my finger on the knife point again. 'I don't know why you think I was…'

I zone her out. Maybe I've found my plan. What's the other way of keeping her here? I take the knife out of my pocket.

chapter 29

RHODA

'You're pathetic, Dan,' the blonde bitch is saying. 'Face it. A loser.'

She doesn't hear me entering the office; she's way too busy enjoying herself. She's even added a pseudo-bored drawl to her voice, as if dissing Dan is, like, *soooo* beneath her.

She flicks her hair, cocks a hip. 'What did you think you were going to do with that knife? Cut me? That's a joke. Wait till I tell Bradley. He'll call the cops, then you'll be screwed.'

I let the door slam behind me. She jumps and whirls around to face me.

'Hi, bitch,' I say, feeling a spurt of adrenaline coursing through my body. I immediately feel energised, powerful, like I've got total control over what happens next. I glance over to where Dan is standing against the far wall, head down. His hair hangs to one side, and I can clearly see the scabbed-over wound on his neck. He's holding my knife loosely in his hand.

'Rhoda?' he says woozily, looking up at me.

The blonde glares at me, tosses her hair back. 'You!' she says, 'Don't I know you from somewhere?'

'You tell me,' I say, taking a step forward. 'Do you?'

'Customers aren't allowed back here,' she says, but now there's a wobble in her voice and she starts to back up. She's not a complete idiot; she can read the expression on my face. 'Tell her, Dan,' she says, looking to him for help. Dan doesn't move.

'Apologise to him,' I say. My voice is oddly calm, I sound reasonable, polite even.

'What?'

'I heard what you were saying. It's a bunch of shit. I think you should take it back.'

'What's it to you? He came at me with a knife!'

'I didn't,' Dan says, his voice still zoned out. 'I wanted to, but...'

I'm moving closer to her now, and she's forced to scramble away, her back almost touching the metal shelves slotted against the wall.

'Dan!' she says. 'Dan!'

I'm now so close to her that I can smell her cheap body spray and see where her foundation has clogged in her pores.

'So?' I say, almost conversationally. 'Are you going to apologise?'

She can't help it. Her face morphs into that sneer I remember from when I'd asked her about the kid, and it's the same sneer I saw on Yellow Eyes' lips the first time I encountered him; the same sneer on the faces of that bitch in the dress shop this morning; the cunts in the travel agency. I don't even think twice.

I clench my fist, draw my bent arm tightly into my body and slam my elbow upwards and under her jaw. A bolt of bright, intense pain shoots through my arm, but I ignore it. Her breath whooshes out, she falls backwards, and her head knocks with a solid clunk on the corner of the shelf behind her. Blood pours out of her mouth; she must have bitten through her lip or (I hope) her tongue. She reaches out, touches her mouth as if she can't believe what is happening, and slowly, without any grace whatsoever, crumples to the floor. As she lands, her head thunks on a pile of hardcover arty-farty coffee-table books.

I don't move for several seconds. I concentrate on stilling my heart, listening to the far distant rumblings of the mall beyond the room.

My elbow aches like it's been dipped in fire – that knocking-your-funny-bone pain that you can almost feel in your teeth – and I straighten my arm experimentally, checking that nothing is broken. It's fucking sore, but I'll live.

'Dan!' I say.

His eyes are glassy. I have to step over the blonde's body to get to him. I take his hands, pocketing the knife in the process.

'What the fuck happened out there, Dan? What did you do?'

He doesn't even glance at the bitch's body. He swallows noisily. 'He was saying, stuff, Rhoda, and I... I... fuck it. Something came over me.'

I nod. *Something came over me.* He just picked up a full-grown man and impaled him. Jesus.

'Is he dead?' he says.

From what I could see when I barged into the shop he certainly looked pretty fucking dead, but I didn't actually look that close. 'I don't know,' I say.

'It was so fucked up. I got this jolt. Like electricity. Like I was plugged in to something. I was so fucking strong.' For a second, a triumphant glint I've never seen before flicks into his eyes. I don't like it. There's something cold and hard about it, but then it dies. Did I imagine it? 'I couldn't help myself. I guess I just snapped.'

'I know what you mean,' I say. I reach behind me and prod the blonde's body with my index finger. Her chest rises and falls shallowly, but she's out cold, her mouth slack and bloody. I'm not sure if I'm relieved that's she's breathing, or disappointed. Her skirt has ridden right up her thighs, but I'm fucked if I'm going to give her any dignity. 'I felt exactly the same. No one should fuck with us, right?'

He looks up at me in surprise. 'Yeah,' he says, deadpan. 'We're the revenge twins.'

There's a pause while we both replay what he just said, and then we're laughing. Great raucous waves of laughter, tears rolling down our cheeks, both of us losing our balance and clutching each other with the force of it.

'We're, like, totally hardcore,' he sputters, when he can breathe.

'The hardest mutherfuckers in Joburg,' I say.

'Like, gangsta-syle,' Dan says, forking his fingers and waving them in the air, and we're off again.

Then, as if by silent agreement, our laughter snaps off. My legs are shaky, probably from the after-effects of the adrenaline.

He stares down at the bitch's body, a strange vacant expression on his face. 'Fuck, Rhoda,' he says. 'We're fucked.'

'No shit,' I say.

He wipes his hand over his face, a familiar gesture. Then, absently, his hand moves behind his head and under his hair. 'We're dead,' he says.

'Not necessarily,' I say.

'Huh?'

'Think about it. How will they know it's us?' I say. 'Did anyone see you... do that to the guy outside?'

He shrugs. 'No.'

'So if he dies – and let me tell you, Dan, he didn't look like he'd be playing a round of golf anytime soon – then we have no witnesses. Could have been a robbery gone wrong.'

He looks down at the girl. 'She's not dead.'

There's a lump in my throat. 'Not yet,' I say.

Our eyes lock.

'You mean... ki... Finish her off?' Dan says, watching me carefully, making it clear that this is my call.

I try and look nonchalant as if I'm a hit man in a Tarantino movie, used to killing and death, always wisecracking and talking shit while I blow someone's head off. Could I do it? I didn't have any problem almost breaking her jaw.

But this is different. This would be final. Do you really want to deal with that?

'I'm not going to kill her,' I say.

He looks relieved.

'So let's think about this logically. Will there be other staff coming in soon?'

He nods. 'Yeah. The store should have been open already.'

'So sooner or later – probably sooner – someone's going to come in and find that bloke you whacked.'

'Yeah.'

'Then we'd better get the fuck out of here.'

'Where to?'

'Fuck it, Dan, do I look like I've got all the answers?' A picture of Yellow Eyes jumps into my brain. 'We can't go out through the front...'

'No shit, Sherlock.'

'Okay... We can get out through the delivery entrance, can't we?'

'Yeah, Rhoda, but then what?'

'You can come home with me.' I blurt it out without thinking.

'Home with you? But you don't have anywhere to stay.'

'I mean... to the UK.'

'The UK?'

'Yeah. Why not? I mean...' But my voice trails away. Stupid. There are small hurdles to consider, like the fact that Dan has just killed someone, I've probably just broken someone's jaw and the British authorities aren't that keen on letting wanted criminals through immigration these days.

'But I'll need a visa for the UK,' Dan says, as if this is our only problem.

Could Zinzi help us get away? As if. Scoring dope is about the height of her powers.

Dan pulls his cigarettes out of his pocket, lights one, hands it to me, lights another. We stand in silence, smoking over the blonde's body.

'So,' he says.

'So,' I say.

'If we're caught we'll go to prison.'

'They'll throw away the key.'

'You know what will happen to me in prison,' Dan says.

'Yeah,' I say. 'I don't think it will be a picnic for me, either.'

'But you could leave,' Dan says. 'You could chance it – get to the UK.'

'I'm not leaving you, Dan,' I say. And I mean it. 'We're in this together.'

'So what can we do? Go all *Natural Born Killers* and run off into the platteland?'

'The where?'

'Never mind.'

We finish our cigarettes in silence. Dan stubs his out on the carpet and I do the same.

Neither of us wants to be the first one to say it.

'We could go back,' he says in a small voice.

'Back where?' I say. The saliva has dried up in my mouth.

'You know where, Rhoda.'

A scream cuts through the air. Then someone – a woman – shrieks: 'Oh my God! Brad! Help! Someone! Help!'

We have to make the decision now.

'Let's go,' I say.

'Where to?' Dan says, holding my gaze.

'You know where, Dan.'

And the weird thing is, now we've made the decision, my heart suddenly feels lighter. I almost feel relieved.

I lean against the wall and catch my breath. The corridor we're in doesn't look at all familiar; the walls are smooth polished concrete instead of the rough brick I remember from before. The door ahead looks bland and forgettable, like the others we've pushed through so far. And where are all those numbered doors? They can't have just disappeared.

Why not? Stranger things have happened.

'Are we going the right way?'

'How would I know?' Dan snaps. He's also out of breath.

'Fuck it, Dan, some help would be nice.'

'I'm doing my best!'

Talk about fucking déjà vu. We're bickering like we did on our first trip into the bowels of the mall.

'I seriously don't remember this,' I say.

'Ja. Well, it's not really surprising,' he says.

'What the hell are you talking about?'

'We were being chased by some sort of monster thing,' Dan says.

'It wasn't a monster, it was a hobo.'

'Whatever.'

'You think they'll follow us down here?'

I shrug. 'They won't know to look, will they? That blonde bitch—'

'Josie,' he says, sounding almost peevish. 'Her name's Josie.'

I glance at him in irritation. 'Whatever, Dan, Josie the Blonde Bitch is out cold and so... hang on.'

I push through the door, and the temperature immediately seems to drop several degrees. This corridor does look familiar – it's ill-lit, slightly damp and there are doors cut into the brickwork. I try the handles one after the other, until finally one gives.

'Thank fuck!'

'What?' Dan says, catching up and peering past me.

I point towards the rusted can of Vim and the dried-up maggot that I'd picked from Dan's hair all those aeons ago.

'Okay,' I say. 'We're on the right track.'

'We are?'

'Don't you remember?'

In unspoken consent we both enter the room, and sit down, backs against the wall. I'm hit with a feeling of weird but not entirely unwelcome nostalgia, almost as if I'm revisiting a place from my childhood.

Dan hands me a cigarette.

'You told me you had asthma last time we were here,' I say, watching as he takes a deep pull of his cigarette. 'You freaked out when I lit a cigarette. How things change.'

He shrugs, and we smoke in silence for a few seconds.

'We're really going to do this?' I say to him. 'Go back?'

'We don't have any choice, Rhoda,' he says.

But that's not true, and he knows it. We could go on the run. We could plead temporary insanity. We could do lots of things. But I don't argue with him. Oddly enough, my mouth is starting to water – all I can think about is the bubbly and canapés at the champagne bar. And I find myself wondering if there's new stock in You Got Sole. Should I go there first? Or maybe...

'Hello? Rhoda?' Dan's looking at me as if he's been trying to get my attention.

'Yeah?'

'You were daydreaming.'

'Sorry. You were saying?'

'We could hide out there. In the other mall... come back when the coast is clear. It doesn't have to be forever.'

'Sure,' I say, playing along. 'Do you think we should at least let your mother know? I mean, if we go to the other mall—'

'When we go,' he says, fingers toying with the wound at the back of his head again.

'Okay. When we go, then.'

'She'll cope.' He drops his eyes. End of conversation.

I dump the fag butt and get to my feet. Dan follows me out into the corridor.

'Okay,' I say, trying to convince myself. 'Around this corner we're going to see those freaky mannequins. Remember them?'

Dan grins at me. 'How could I forget? Let's go.'

We both start jogging around the corner, increasing our pace as if we can't wait to get to our destination.

'Race you!' Dan says.

We hare around the corner, and both immediately stop dead.

'Fuck,' Dan says, sounding almost disappointed. 'They're gone.'

'Way to state the obvious, Dan.'

I walk towards the exit sign at the end of the now empty corridor, pausing to pick up something lying underneath the light. It's one of those horrible false fingernails, this one painted a bright putrid pink. I drop it and wipe my hand on my legs.

'Okay,' I shrug. 'No big deal. Someone's obviously moved them.'

'Who, though?'

'How the fuck would I know? Management works in mysterious ways.' I grin at him, and he gives me a watery smile back.

We're about to head down into the stairwell when my phone beeps. Both of us tense up.

'Here we go,' I say to Dan.

My hand shakes as I pull it out of my pocket. Dan watches me carefully as I click through to the message.

'Fuck!'

'What?'

'It's Zinzi. She wants to know if she can borrow my fucking dress.'

'Oh.'

Despite the shit those phone messages put us through last time, I can't help the stab of disappointment.

'Let's go,' I say, holding the door open for him.

'You think this time we should go straight for the market?'

'Sure. It might be a shortcut.'

'I'm not looking forward to seeing that horrible old rat-eating bitch again.'

'Chill out,' I say. 'We know how to deal with her.'

I start heading down the steps, taking them two at a time. I realise that my ears are straining for any sign that something might be following us – something like that crazy old rabid hobo. But all I can hear are Dan's footsteps and the sound of our breathing.

'Does this look different to you?' I say.

'How?'

'I dunno.' But the stairwell doesn't just look different, it feels different. The stairs smell like concrete stairwells always smell – like piss and damp – but last time they stank of something fishy and dead. And the light isn't fading as we head deeper.

'Okaaaay,' I say. 'You think we've taken a wrong turn?'

The stairs don't finish in mid-air. They go all the way down to the ground, and instead of a black tunnel crawling with rats, there's a bland grey door in front of us.

'I don't know,' he says. 'Maybe they've completed the stairs since we last came here?'

'Maybe.'

But the door's battered and scruffy; the paint peeling and scratched. There's even rust on the hinges.

And there's something else.

'Last time, I'm sure we went much deeper,' I say. 'It was as if the steps went on for ever. Remember?'

'We were scared shitless last time.'

'You're not scared now?'

He shrugs. 'Ja. But at least this time we know what we're letting ourselves in for.'

'Do we?' I pull open the door and walk through.

'What the fuck?'

The bundles of rags are gone. So is the rusted old car. So are the drums and their stinking smoke. And there's certainly no sign of the old woman. There don't seem to be any rats, either. And the place hums with electricity; the strip lighting stuck onto the low ceiling has the look of emergency lighting about it, but it's way brighter than I remember it being.

'Is this the right place?'

'It must be,' Dan says. He gestures around him. 'I mean, the structure looks the same.' He pauses. 'I think it does, anyway.' He wanders into one of the abandoned shops, stepping over a half-empty bag of cement. 'Isn't this where we were going to eat that shitty food?'

'I think so,' I say.

The place looks exactly like what it is – a half-constructed mall food court. But the dust and dirt and filth and ash are gone. The concrete floor looks newly swept. It's the same place without the… trappings. It feels empty, abandoned. Spookily so. The closest things to any sign of life are the conduit wires snaking out of the walls.

Dan's phone beeps. Now it's his turn to scramble in his pocket.

'It must be them!' he says, glancing at me, excitement in his eyes.

His look of disappointment is almost comical. He waves his phone. 'It's Mom.'

'What's she want?'

'Wants to know what time we're coming home for supper.'

We glance at each other, and I swallow the giggle that's

burbling up. Dan's looking stricken. I don't want him to lose his nerve now.

'Fuck it, Dan,' I say. 'We must have taken a wrong turn.'

'Impossible,' he says. His eyes skate around the cavernous space, and he starts heading toward one of the pillars.

'Where you going?'

'Check,' he says, bending down and picking something up. He holds it aloft. 'Recognise this?'

It's a watch. 'Fuck. Is that your watch? The one that old bitch took?'

'Ja,' he says. 'Look, Rhoda. Someone probably came down here, did a major clean-up. It has to be the same place.'

'Yeah,' I say. But there's more than just a niggling feeling of doubt. 'So if this is the place where we saw that horrible old woman, then the market must be this way.' I start heading to-wards the large, open-plan area to our left.

'Wait!' he says.

It's strange walking through it in the light. 'Last time we were here it felt way bigger,' I say.

'Ja, but we had to feel our way in the dark, remember?' Dan says.

Something occurs to me. 'But what happened to that door?'

'What door?'

'You remember. There was a door that led to nowhere – it was bricked up.'

Both of us scan the space. The wall alongside us is smooth, the plaster unbroken. None of it looks newly applied.

'You know, Rhoda,' he says, 'we were really freaked out. We were traumatised. And you were...'

'I was what?'

'On drugs,' he mumbles.

'I'd had a bit of coke, Dan. That heightens perceptions, it doesn't warp them.'

'Whatever. Look, just now we'll come to that ramp down-wards and that fucked-up sign...' Dan's voice trails away.

'Looks like we've found it,' I finish for him.

We both jog towards the slope that leans down to the next level.

Dan gets there before me. 'Hmm.'

'Well?'

'See for yourself.'

The sign is way smaller than the first one, and reads: 'Con-struction workers only. Trespassers will be prosecuted.'

Dan's already heading down the slope to the next level. I have no choice but to follow. There's a white door straight in front of us.

Now that does look exactly as I remember it, thank fuck.

As I sprint to catch up with him, I almost trip over something in my path.

It's the lamp – the one we'd cadged from the old hag.

'Look!' I shout to Dan.

'See?' Dan says, sounding triumphant. 'I told you we were going the right way! It's just the different light playing tricks on us.'

'Yeah,' I say. 'You're right.'

He lights another cigarette and we bounce it between us. Now we're here, neither of us is in any great hurry to go through the door.

I stub the fag out under my heel, and reach over and touch Dan's cheek. 'Okay, Dan,' I say. 'Deep breath. At the top of this stairwell we're going to enter that mirror room. You sure you'll cope with that?'

'Yeah,' he says. But his smile is forced.

'Okay.'

I reach behind me and he takes my hand. I pull the door open and we head up the stairs. I try to ignore the fact that the once-gleaming white tiles are grubby and covered in mildew (that can happen in a week or so, right?), and in no time we're facing the door at the top.

Neither of us mentions that the sign is gone.

'Ready?' I say.

'Yeah. Let's do this.'

I half close my eyes in case we're about to be hit with that blinding light, and push open the door.

chapter 30

DANIEL

It would have been a relief to find the mirror room, to be chased by that slavering monster. To run along corridors populated with zombies and dead mannequins, to get threatened by the malicious Management. We would have known we were on our way back there.

But as one door after another just opened out onto another concrete corridor leading back to the half-built food court and the deserted parking lot, we started coming back down to earth. Like waking up from an exhilarating dream, desperately trying to cling to its frays before they all drift away in the cold morning breeze. I could see it in Rhoda's face: first a forced optimism, then as the reality hit home – that we were going nowhere, that there was nowhere but here – she couldn't mask her disappointment. Those bubbly dreams of champagne and high fashion, of being in demand, of being pampered like she deserves melted out of her face. Some of the joy drained out too. I realised for the first time that running made her happy.

I tried to convince myself that we had imagined it all, my weak mind always ready to make a compromise, but I knew in reality we had simply lost our chance. When we ran away from that other mall, we became uninvited: we had had our chance at belonging to their world and we had rejected it.

The ninth day of waiting.

We've still got a choice. There's always a choice. We can either go back home, face our punishment, or stay here, hoping against hope that Management will call us again. I won't manage a brief, vicious life in prison hell. So we wait. If we wait just here, if they change their minds, all it will take is a step through the door.

We've built a decent-enough nest for ourselves out of cardboard boxes, newspapers, drop cloths and plastic sheeting left behind by the builders. We've found a safe route to the trash compressor. There are more than enough half-burgers and chips, boxes of leftover popcorn and jumbo soft drinks to survive on. But there's no soap or toothpaste, very little fresh water, and I feel the food eating me from the inside.

Rhoda looks like she's done this before, nestling into the plastic bed with a contented sigh when she sleeps. I hate to think of how she's lived. She opens her eyes and sees me watching her and tells me to fuck off with a smile. I go to our piss-hole in the never-was restaurant we've dubbed The Seashore. We sit there sometimes, looking out over the parking lot, listening to the subterranean thrum of the traffic locked away outside.

'Watch out, Dan, that seagull's going to shit on your head,' Rhoda warns.

'Yeah, well, this dolphin's just bitten your leg off, so there.'

'Dolphins don't bite people, fuckwit,' she complains.

'This one does. It's a starving, mutant, underground dolphin. All it eats is the burger boxes we throw away and it has developed acid saliva that can shear your flesh off with one lick.'

'Okaaaay...' she drawls, and we don't laugh. The Guardian is always ranging the corridors in our minds.

We sat at this table when the grey woman came to speak to us. I remember banging my head on the ground as I tripped over. Right there. I'm sure I do.

Time folds into itself here. Our phones still tell us the time when we switch them on occasionally, always hoping in vain for some message, some invitation, but when you're just waiting, time and dates are just meaningless numbers. The neon strip lights always burn. Rhoda and I have walled our flatlet with thick black plastic sheeting, so we get some darkness when we need it. We measure our rhythms by the muffled growl of the traffic outside – the outside that we never see down here. The building sighs and ticks and shifts like a body, alarms its gurgling stomach, the rumble of delivery gates its gaseous exchange.

It's my turn to do groceries today. I come back from the garbage enclosure with a bagful of half-burgers, some warm blue milkshake and half a bottle of flat sparkling water. I've also found some outdated flowers – carnations, but still – and a cluster of melted-together tea-lights. I set them up on a table in the food court while Rhoda dozes. She's been sleeping a lot lately, finding comfort in dreams, passing the time while we wait.

My shuffling about wakes her; she smiles to see the little galaxy I've made in the food court and comes over to join me, stretching groggily and rubbing her hands over her head. She digs in, putting aside some of the unused tomato sauce sachets. A suck of ketchup makes a good pick-me-up.

I sometimes think of Bradley, stuck on that bookshelf, gasping, his legs kicking. I didn't mean it. He shouldn't have been so important in my life. He should have been nobody to me; but there it is, he became my fate; he took my life for his own.

'You look sad,' Rhoda says.

'No. I'm fine.'

'You want to leave, don't you?'

I've thought of the options so often, and I know this is the best one. 'No.'

'We'll get back. I'm sure of it.' But I've never heard her speak with less conviction.

'We weren't just dreaming?' I say.

'No.'

I say nothing.

'Thanks for the flowers. You're the nicest boyfriend I've ever had. Even introduced me to your mum.' She stops talking like she's said something wrong.

'It's okay,' I say. I'm worried about my mother, but what would hurt her more? Me here, missing as far as she's concerned, or me in jail being raped, getting Aids. I've stopped listening to the voicemails she leaves on the phone. I can't listen to her pleas, the tears in her voice, the slur of her words when she's been drinking, the promises to 'get me the best lawyer in Joburg'. To her trying to convince herself that the police must have made a mistake, that her son, her Daniel, couldn't possibly have done anything wrong.

At the same time I'm thinking of the poison inside me. How long do we wait here? How long must we eat rubbish? It should be the least of my worries, I suppose, but ever since my dad died, I've felt cancer hiding in my bones, a time bomb in my blood. I'm in terror of being poisoned by my own body, and I'm terrified of feeding the fire inside with all this filthy crap.

'We'll get out of here, won't we?'

'We will, Dan. It won't be long. Or we'll make another plan.'

That night when we switch on our phones I have a message. Rhoda hears the beep-beep and hurries across from the brazier where she's starting a fire. 'I told you, Dan. Game on! We're in.'

I don't know how to disappoint her. It's another text from Mom, but Rhoda reads the news on my face and slouches back to the fire. This time I thumb the message open. <Daniel, love. Please. Just one word. Just let me know you're okay. Please. Love, Mom>

I wish I wasn't hurting her so much. I want to phone her, or maybe a message would be better. <I'm fine, Mom. I'm sorry. I love you, D> But the airtime on both our phones has expired.

'You could go into the mall and call her?' suggests Rhoda.

'I suppose.' But that doesn't change the fact that I would hurt her even worse by going home. Rhoda seems to know what I'm thinking. She goes back to the fire and pokes at it with a length of steel bar. I get up and join her, staring into the flames.

'What about your parents?' I ask her.

'What about them?' Rhoda sounds snappish and brittle.

'Don't you worry that they think you're dead? In some sort of trouble?'

She pokes around at the plank-wood coals for a stretch. 'Sometimes,' she says. 'But probably not as often as I should.' I don't get what she's saying but I take her hand. She responds by grabbing me around the waist and then drawing herself to me. She's warm, and I kiss her cheeks. 'We're going to be fine, right?' she says.

'Ja,' I say, and kiss her again.

'If we're just waiting,' says Rhoda later, 'let's not go out of our fucking minds while we do. Listen. Here's the game. I make the first run. Get something valuable. Then it's your turn. We're scored on time, on the value of the item we get, and the danger of the mission.' She's talking like a gamer. In another world we would have met at the online gaming centre at BlastCon. We would have hit it off and bought each other graphics accelerators for Valentine's Day. We would have lain next to each other in bed with our laptops burning fast bandwidth, slaying monsters and warriors from all corners of the world. We would have made a good team.

We hear the traffic dying down, wait a while, finish our dinner, stoke the fire. Then Rhoda sets off. 'Wish me luck!' There's some spirit back in her, something that's been lost these last few days.

Fourteen minutes and thirty-seven seconds later, she batters back through the food-court doors with a thumping, rattling, trundling, yellow and grey thing.

'Holy fuck, Rhoda, that's brilliant!' She's got us a cleaner's trolley, complete with two square yellow buckets of water, a mop, a broom, a dustpan and brush, assorted cleaning rags and a spray bottle.

'And check it out.' She bends and pulls two bottles of liquid soap and a pack of single-ply toilet paper out of the yellow vinyl trash-bag section.

'You're my hero!'

'But, Christ, I almost got nicked. That fat bastard Yellow Eyes was just stepping out of the pisser as I got out into the mall. I just managed to duck behind a pot plant as he came by. I had to wait for ages till the coast was clear. Would have been five minutes faster if it wasn't for that.'

'But you get double danger points. You have earned ten million four hundred and ninety thousand five hundred and seventy-three points for that round.'

'Oh, did I mention the man-eating dolphin?'

We strip off our clothes and wash with delight, keeping one of the water buckets aside for drinking. I watch her as she lathers, feeling human for the first time since we came down here.

When we turn on our phones that night, Rhoda has a message. She reads it then deletes it.

'What was it?' I ask, stung that she didn't show it to me.

'Oh, nothing. Just Zinzi.'

I almost make an issue of her not sharing the message with me as we've always done, but she looks sad, so I shelve it.

I know we're just playing, but somehow it seems like a matter of life and death. I want to beat her. I want to get something equally useful, even better. I stay awake the whole night thinking of phone chargers, airtime, but who would we phone? And where would we plug them in? I think of stealing a generator and a microwave oven from Game, and while I'm about it how about a fridge and some chairs and a table and a bed and some silky sheets and plush cushions and toilet doilies and some fucking gold bars? Either I'd need to smash my way in at night with a forklift or saunter in – and out – by day. Not half drawing attention to the fucking murderer on the run.

That's it!

I'm so keen to get going that I wake her up. 'Time me,' I say, handing her my watch, and I'm off.

I head to the middle food-court door, and up the stairs to the portal that once led to the other market and up again and the long way to the roof parking on the opposite side of the mall. If they get me on camera inside the mall, I don't want them seeing where I came from. I duck into the nearest entrance, the old, quiet dry-cleaners-and-tattoo-parlours wing. As I guessed, it's deserted. A repaired watch in the dry-cleaner's reads: <02:45>. I hope the chief security guard is soundly asleep in his office and that Simon and the fingerless guy are patrolling somewhere else or, more probably, smoking at the main entrance.

Oh well, it shouldn't take long anyhow. I jog through the familiar arcades, stopping short when I get to the doors of Only Books.

I cup my hand over my eyes and peer into the darkened store. There's a laminated photo hanging on the end of the shelf, a small, drooping floral wreath pinned up next to it. So that's it; he's really dead. I knew he was. It all comes back in a disembodied rush, like I'm watching a movie in fast-forward. It doesn't seem like it really happened. But I do remember Bradley's unearthly gasping, the kicking of his heels. It looks like they've replaced a patch of carpet by the poetry shelf, the new corporate blue darker than the old material.

Don't hang around, fuckwit, you're on camera. Christ, that will give them something to think about. The murderer returning to the scene. They'll know it's me. Who else would it be at three in the morning?

I came out here for a reason and I'm not going back until I've got what I came for. I'm going to get Rhoda some flowers. Some fresh flowers. Roses, tulips, irises, those long, flowery ones, not expired, rat-shat, scent-sprayed carnations. Plus a trolley of non-perishable groceries to boot. And a can opener. All courtesy of Woolworths.

I guess I'm on about eight minutes now. Maybe I'll be late but I'll earn a shitload of utility points. Maybe invaluable brownie points too.

I duck into the corridor behind Only Books, run past my old alcove without a glance. That *was* my alcove, my safe place. Now I've got another one. Down to the end, to Woolworths' cold-delivery door. I type in the code. 1-2-3-4.

Beeeeeeeep.

Huh? 1-2-3-4. Slowly, carefully, this time.

Beeeeeeeep.

Fuck! They've changed the fucking code. I try again, for luck. 1-2-3-4.

Beeeeeeeep.

So much for that. The longer I'm out here, the better the chances that one of the security guards has checked the monitors, so I can't waste any more time now. I'll have to come back empty-handed. Big hunter, me. Big provider.

Oh well, it's just a game.

I head back the way I came, and in a box outside the back of

Only Books I spot a stack of discarded proof copies. I scoop up as many as I can carry, resisting the temptation to browse through the box and make a good selection, and run back past the dry-cleaner's and over the roof, sticking to the dark shadow of the wall all the way. I duck back through the deserted wing's door and lock it behind me with the deadbolt.

I stop to catch my breath, sit on the stairs and browse through the books I've collected. I've lost the game already – this round anyway – so may as well take some extra time to make sure I'm not bringing any Danielle Steel or James Patterson back to Rhoda. I haven't heard of any of these, but they look okay.

As I bundle the books in my arms and stand, the lights go off. The building's electric hum winds down with a whine and a shudder. Then I hear it. It starts in low, with a moist gasping sound, like wet sand sucking on a beach. Then it gets louder, and I feel something dripping on my neck, hot breath ruffling my hair.

I spin around in the dark, my feet almost skidding down a stair. 'Who are you?' I say. I struggle to keep my breath under control. I feel another drip in my hair, the phlegm breath reverberating through the narrow stairwell.

'Where are you?' I say

Rhoda said it was just a hobo. Rhoda said it was just a hobo, I chant to myself, like a protective charm.

Then the screaming starts up, at first like a klaxon deep underground, then it cycles up, louder and louder like a hundred beaten children, up and up, like the scream of a thousand dying soldiers, the suffering of a million electrocuted animals, hell's choir in this tiny, stifling space, too loud, the noise alone is going to deafen me, crush the breath and the life out of me. I feel the slick saliva spattering on my head. I'm trying to get down the stairs, but my feet won't find them. I can't find up or down.

It's going to end this time. I stop. I deserve it this time. I'm ready.

Lights on. I shield my eyes. The noise thunks and then winds down gradually, whirring as it slows. *It's a backup generator.* A fucking backup generator. In need of maintenance and some oil, but a *goddamn fucking backup generator.* The vent above me gradually stops dripping. Air-con condensation. Seriously.

'Hey, Rhoda!' I'm calling down the stairs before I'm out the door. 'Rhoda! You'll never guess...'

She's rushing across to me. 'Jesus, Dan. I was scared. You took so long.'

'I'm sorry, I...'

'What did you get?'

'Oh, nothing. I wanted to get something else –' saving my big surprise for the next round '– but all I managed was these.' I show her the books.

'That's fucking brilliant, Dan!' She's so excited about the books that she grabs me and gives me a big kiss.

'Jesus, they're just some throwaway—'

'Holy shit, Dan... What better to do while you're sitting around waiting? Ten billion points for you, boy. No wonder you were excited.'

'No, it was... I wanted to tell you about the monster.'

'The monster?'

'It was nothing all along. It was just a fucking—'

'You saw him? Dan, you know what this means?' She's racing ahead now, I can't get a word in. 'He, the monster thing – whatever the fuck it was – came from the other side. Not here. It means we're in. You got us in.'

'No, wait. I'm trying to tell you. It was just the noise of a generator. We were just fucked up, freaked out. We made a monster out of nothing.'

'Hang on, you've got something...' She reaches over and picks something off my head and holds it wiggling between her fingers. A fat, white maggot.

We spend the next couple of days waiting for a sign, for something to happen. For a message, an invitation; even for Security to burst in and arrest us, but nothing. Slowly we deflate again, overeager, overreaching balloons, gradually realising that of course I didn't get us in again, gradually realising that all I did was get a maggot in my hair.

Rhoda's been sleeping a lot again. I've been too restless to sleep. I read a bit, but can't concentrate. I wander around the deserted wing, trying to find something we've missed. I stare up at the ceiling, and into the round hole we've looked at a thousand times, but inside it I see a shadow of something I've never seen before. I take a brand from the brazier and poke it as high as I can reach, and there, just illuminated by the furthest edge of the flame's light, is the shape I thought I saw. It's a square rung in the wall of the tunnel.

Without waking Rhoda, I wheel the cleaning trolley underneath it, and use it as a makeshift scaffold, just high enough for me to reach in. I haul myself up. It's a manhole shaft, going straight up. I remember the endless shaft we went down on our way to the other side. Surely this one can't go anywhere very far, but still I hope.

I can't see more than about eight rungs above me. Each is spaced a good arm's span away from the other and climbing up is exhausting, a series of pull-ups. I count the rungs as I go. As I climb, the circle of light below me gets smaller and smaller, until it's no bigger than a coin. I'm gripping onto rung number forty-nine when I hit the cover. It's a concrete manhole cover, and heavy, so I shift myself into a backwards position and shove upwards with my shoulders and back until it budges. One more shove and there's a small gap to work with, and after that it's easy enough to move the cover and clamber out.

A breeze hits me, the air fresher than anything I've ever

breathed. I fill my lungs, breathing out the recycled poison from inside. I'm on a narrow ledge in the middle of the sheer external wall of the Highgate Mall. The ledge is about a metre deep and a few across, no way off here except down. Thirty metres or more. Gigantic neon signs advertising flagship stores flicker above me. Edgars, Only Books, Woolworths, all boasting to the traffic jam far below.

I sit against the wall and look at distances I haven't seen for weeks. It's an autumn dusk, a smoky Joburg sunset; I can see the far horizon stained luminous orange. I can see the plumes of various veld fires around the north of the city, the haze of cooking fires, the gasses from the cars idling furiously on the main road below. The black shapes of returning birds stencil the sky, and street lights and security lights all around the suburbs flicker behind leaves that twitch in the breeze.

I breathe in again, trying to replace every molecule of the stale oxygen in my blood and my marrow with fresh air. I think of Rhoda lying there, forty-nine steps below me, huddled in her pile of dusty grey drop cloths. I bet she's dreaming of quartz lights bounding off marble floors, of cognac sales, of polished brass and crystal façades. We're the same, she and I; we created a fantasy world for ourselves inside there, but this is the real world, outside, down below. The traffic jams, the flashing, seductive neon. That other place never existed; we can never escape. This is where we are.

I take another few deep breaths, watch the sky move from orange to red to purple. Watch the last birds go home. Then I go back down the shaft, rung by rung.

When I get back down to the parking garage, Rhoda is toasting mould off some buns over the fire. She looks over her shoulder and smiles at me. I muster my strength and my will and go round the back of her and clasp her waist.

'Find anything interesting?' she asks.

'Nah, just a dead end.'

'Hm,' she says, and turns back to the flames.

I go back to our room and lie back on my pile of cardboard. It was a mistake to go up there. I know it will take time before I can delude myself again. But I've got to try. For Rhoda.

I shuffle through my plastic bag of personal stuff, looking for the book I was reading. It's about a guy who can walk through doors into the future, but can't always find the door back to the past. My phone's lying on top of it and out of habit I take it out. Despite myself, I hope. I thumb it on. The battery indicator is flashing red. A minute later, I hear the beeps. I've got a message.

Drawn by the beep, Rhoda rushes over to me, eyes alive with that eternal hope.

'This is it, Dan,' she says. 'I can feel it in my gut.'

I'm suddenly reluctant to read it.

'Well?' she says. 'Go on!'

Hands trembling, I thumb the message open and read it.

<Members Only. Buy any three books from the Only For You selection and get one free. Stand the chance to win R10,000 in Only Books vouchers. Enter now!>

'Fuck.' Rhoda turns away in disgust.

I'm fucking worthless. That's all she'll ever get from me: disappointment. I drop the phone on the concrete floor and the - battery skitters out under the brazier. Let it burn. I don't care anymore.

It's Rhoda who picks up the pieces and huddles in the corner of our den; she doesn't look at me. She fiddles with the phone, sighing under her breath, pissed off with me for breaking it. I turn my back to her and settle in with my book. It's going to be another long night.

A minute's silence. Then

Beep beep. Beep beep.

'Dan.'

I turn to her. 'Huh?'

She looks at me from across the room, fire dancing in her eyes.

'Game on,' she says.

ACKNOWLEDGEMENTS

S.L. Grey thanks Lauren Beukes, book.co.za, Nic Cheetham, Isobel Dixon, Rina Gill, Adam Greenberg, Sam Greenberg, Bronwyn Harris, Lily Herne, Savannah Lotz, Charlie Martins, Toby Mundy, Oliver Munson, Laura Palmer, Alan Walters, Carol Walters, Pagan Wicks, Ben Williams and Sam Wilson.